RUSH TO
FREEDOM

A Novel

BRENT G. BARKER

Rush to Freedom: A Novel
Copyright © 2024 Brent G. Barker

Palo Alto House

ISBN 979-8-9908699-0-5

Printed in the United States of America

What Readers Are Saying...

"*Rush to Freedom* it certainly is, but it is also a rush toward gold, a new beginning, a new state. Two runaway half-sisters are pursued by slavers bent on seizing their own kind of treasure. Freedom is in the arms of a family that begins in deception and ends in affection. A family being born. *Rush to Freedom* is visceral and suspenseful from start to finish."

ROB SWIGART
author of *Mixed Harvest: Stories from the Human Past*;
Stone Mirror: Novel of the Neolithic; and *The Delphi Agenda*

"In this evocative debut, Barker brings two independent, strong-willed characters together in a simmering love story as they flee across a wild and emotionally charged landscape to freedom. Lush and gorgeously written."

LUCY SANNA
award-winning author of *The Cherry Harvest, A Novel*

"*Rush to Freedom* offers the reader more than a dazzling adventure tale. It's the compelling account of a man and a woman who find love and family while overcoming danger and heartbreak on their way to a new world."

ROBERT C. YEAGER
author of *The Romanov Stone*; winner of IndieReader's
Discovery Award for General Fiction; and winner of an
Independent Publisher's "ippy" award for suspense/thrillers

"*Rush to Freedom* was a book I couldn't put down and didn't want to get to the end of. Besides thrilling me with romance and adventure, it deepened my understanding of history—of wagon trains, the Gold Rush, and most significantly, slavery fighting for a foothold in the new freedom-loving west. The book touched my heart and taught me what it really means to be a family."

SHERRIL JAFFE
prize-winning author of *Scars Make Your Body More Interesting*;
Expiration Date; and *You Are Not Alone and Other Stories*

"Brent Barker has written a powerful historical novel. He doesn't just evoke the horrors of slavery and the dangers and excitement of traveling by wagon train through the wilderness to California. I was transported back in time, feeling the past as though I were living it. His fascinating characters—Ezra, Beth, Camille and Maddie—suffer complex relationships that demand hard-won intimacy that must be tested and earned. Reading about them I gained insight into the human heart. Barker's book is utterly engrossing."

JANE SWIGART
author of *The Myth of the Bad Mother:*
The Emotional Realities of Mothering

"*Rush to Freedom* turns the traditional family saga on its ear. Compelling, quirky characters pull you in and keep you there. You'll catch your breath often, laugh a lot, but may also shed a tear or two. For certain, you won't want to put it down."

ANTOINETTE MAY
author of *The Determined Heart; The Sacred Well;*
Pilate's Wife; and Haunted Houses of California

*Dedicated to Jane, my wife
and our beloved daughters
Kat and Julia*

⇒ 1 ⇐

BETH

St. Louis, February 1849

They called it the Blue Spot, Beth's Board, Pilot's Inn, Long Porch, or House of the Red Queen. River pilots would try to catch a quick glimpse of the sapphire blue building as they eased their massive steamboats the last half-mile to the levee. It was always good luck to catch the blue spot, they said. To the bullyboys in the saloon next door, it was Beth's, the queen they vowed to protect from the roustabouts and drunks who stumbled in and out of their tavern doors. Not that she needed protection. She could snap the head off a dragon, they said. To the merchants and tradesmen who rumbled up and down the muddy street in their wagons bouncing barrels of beer and sausages, it was the generous porch that held their eye—the one that wrapped the long blue front with an apron of white posts, deep shade, and rocking chairs. To Elsbeth McCorry, it was her entire world.

RELAXING AFTER THE BREAKFAST RUSH, BETH LOOKED OUT AT THE Mississippi, sitting on her elevated porch with morning coffee, talking with Eb, one of sixteen river pilots that called the Blue Spot home when in St. Louis. "Where to this time?" she asked. "Back to New Orleans? When should I expect you back?"

"Couple weeks. No, heading west up the Missouri River to Independence and other trailheads, which means the steamboat deck filled with them sleeping, drunken gold miners and the river filled with them half-submerged trees swept downriver in the flooding winter rains. Keeps me alert, on my game, dodging and weaving around root balls the size of rooms and broken branches like lances wanting to pierce my boat."

"Better stay off the whiskey."

"Got that right. Need ma wits about me." He turned, leaning toward her. "What about you, Beth? Ever urge to travel? Go someplace different? See you working hard, same things, same place every day, year in year out. Happy to give you a ride sometime. See the sights." He looked her up and down more overtly than usual. *What a clod. Not the least subtle or appealing.* Beth's stomach turned, the hair on her arms bristled. She waved his invitation aside but without a bruising rebuff.

"Got too much work right here," she said. A bit portly but not unhandsome when he was cleaned up like this, she thought. But he made her nervous and not for the first time. She pulled her shawl closer. *Stay calm. I know these men. Know how to ward them off. Keep them in line. How to be tough, even harsh when called for. Fortunately, Eb will be leaving before I have to insult him.*

His observation bothered her, though. She did wonder what was out there beyond her small world. *Truth, I've never been north of here, never west, only a tad south, and can't fathom what it's like for Ezra, who works the wilds most of the year.*

He said he would come by later today if he had time . . . But, by God. She looked up, sat forward, then stood up. *Isn't that him coming up the road? Yes. But riding in Old Bill's supply wagon with his horse tied behind? Very strange and he's early.*

Her mind was scrambling to make sense. *Why? Is something wrong? More bad news? He rattled me yesterday with his cavalier talk of leaving for California. Forever wasn't clear. But implied. Out of my life for good? I was afraid to ask. Bastard. Sometimes, too unaware to ask what I might think about his leaving. What I feel. Must think I have an unbreakable heart.*

She moved to the front of the porch, adjusted her bonnet so that some of the red curls poked out. *He likes them; always has.*

Bill brought the wagon up to the fence in front and let the horses nose into the grass.

She said goodbye briskly to Eb, standing there in pressed uniform, sea bag hanging from one hand. He swung the bag over his shoulder, nodded at Beth, then heavy-footed his way down the steps onto the gravel path between two front gardens, dead with winter. After closing the gate, Eb frowned at the two men—strangers to him—sitting in the buckseat, then cast an inquiring look back at Beth. She waved him on. He glared at Ezra, a tall, lean muscular man, in a menacing, jealous manner, Beth noticed as he glanced back at her. Before ambling down the road.

Ezra climbed down, reopened the gate, and walked up the pathway, eyes locked on hers at first, then his eyes shifted sideways, upward as if distracted by some thought. *Is something wrong?* She wanted his full attention. He was usually as attentive as a hawk. To get his attention, his interest, she slid her bonnet off and put it on the railing. Then pulled out the comb holding her tight bun in place, shook her head and let the dark red hair tumble down and curl about her shoulders.

To anyone who knew her as long as Ezra, she looked ten years younger this way, not the svelte beauty she once was but at thirty-seven something richer, a more mature face with a strong nose, intelligent, penetrating green eyes, a more womanly body that she knew Ezra liked. Came up to about Ezra's shoulder without her boots. Just the right size in her mind.

She ran her hand through her hair, turned her torso just a tad to accentuate her figure. But it didn't catch his eye. *Look at me, you son of a bitch.*

He seemed too nervous to notice. Off-kilter, somehow. Even his stride, usually so strong, so upright, putting his chest forward with confidence, was today different. More cautious perhaps, not wobbly, but a touch hesitant, tentative. *He's got some secret he doesn't think I can read. He has me frightened. Hasn't told me what's wrong. Yet. But I feel it, fear it. He's leaving me for good.*

MADDIE'S VOICE RANG OUT FROM BELOW THE BURLAP. "BILL, WHERE did Ezra go?" I'm trying to peek, but I can't see him. Doesn't he want us anymore? You probably know. Your Ezra's pa, aren't you?"

"Shh, Maddie, don't be so nosy," said Camille.

"I like being nosy. So are ya? Ezra's pa?"

"You two make me laugh," said Bill. "Remind me of my grand-daughters up in Crow Country. Too lame to get up there anymore. No, not his pa. I was a friend of Ezra's father and used to run supplies—that was their family business—out to the wilderness.

"I knew Ezra as a boy, even met his friend Daisy, your look-alike. Oh, she was a pistol. And when he was a young man, I helped Ezra escape from sorrow after his wife and child died."

"How'd she die?" asked Camille.

"See. You're nosy too."

"Childbirth. Awful. Day after the funeral, Ezra ran. His world exploded and he ran to the wilds. Stumbled about in the mountains, real greenhorn, looking for me, he said. But it were me finally tracked him down. Took him under my wing, taught him a new world. How to trust his instincts, use his senses to survive out there. Adapt to every change in land and sky. To mountain snow and burning deserts. Befriend tribes, wild creatures, honor customs, learn medicine. Find shelter, food, water in uncomfortable places. Of course, I had to teach him how to hunt all over again. Walk a forest floor in total silence."

"You sound like a good teacher," said Maddie. "That's what Camille was for me. Did he like learning?"

"A natural. Picked up skills almost immediately. Became as gifted in the wild as any man I ever met. Those early years we became close as kin, like you two. When I wandered into old age and lame legs, he returned the favor. Taught me how to survive in this rough and mon-strous world, this jangle of St. Louis."

"Bill, you talk so different," said Maddie. "You make pictures in my mind. I like it."

"I think Maddie means you speak about the wilds in poetic terms," said Camille, "not plain and rough like we'd expect from a woodsman."

"Poetic? Ha. I suppose something rubbed off on me from my two miserable years in college."

EZRA TOOK OFF HIS FLOP HAT AND STRODE UP ONTO THE LONG porch, now smiling in that easy way she liked. But she knew by the third step up the stairs something *was* wrong. She crossed her arms, braced herself. Maybe guilt over abandoning her. *That's what this is about, isn't it? Bring me the bad news early, will ya? Think ya can just come waltzing in for pancakes and sadness?*

She was going to miss him, this time possibly for good, and fought the emptiness before it engulfed her. It was only yesterday, casually discussing his new life in California, opening a new supply business, she realized how drawn to him she had become over the years as he grew more mature, complex, mysterious. At forty-seven, he was almost a wonderful thing, a wild thing.

She didn't think she could live without him, even though he was never there. Well, gone a year or two at a time. *But still he keeps coming back for me. That's something isn't it?*

She stood firm. "Wasn't expecting you so early," she said. "Something up?"

"Need a favor," He looked her straight in the eye, then wavered, hesitated. Turned his head, swatted his hat against dirty buckskin.

"Ask, then. You don't have to dance about with me." She paused, trying to read him. "Anything. Within reason, of course. Or, maybe you actually did come to dance." He'd have none of her humor. In fact, he looked sick.

"I have two runaways—"

"What? No! Damn it, Ezra." She pushed her palm straight toward his face. Shook her head. "No. I'm through with that. I thought we agreed it was too dangerous. I'm under suspicion of running a way-station. Being an abolitionist sympathizer. I can't see their spies, but sometimes I sense them watching from that thick patch of woods over there."

She glanced up and down the muddy street out of habit.

"Two girls," he said. "They're not slaves, not exactly. I thought I might put them down in the hole until I have time to get them on their way. Tomorrow or the next, or the day after that."

"Girls? Two, three days? Down in the hole? What are you talking about?" Beth looked out at dear old, gray-haired Bill, who waved at her.

"Beth, you OK?"

"Yes, watching Bill. What do you know about these girls? You're hiding them in Bill's wagon, aren't you? I can't see them but reckon they're the reason that tarp keeps jiggling. Or is that burlap?"

"One's young, Black, says she has a freedom paper. The other's white, older, her mistress, suppose. I pulled them off the levee, fighting off two slavers trying to snatch'm. I cracked one's skull, threatened to kill the other."

"Snatching runaways and sex slaves happens every day down on the levee. Why these two?" *He's again avoiding my eyes. There's some deeper secret he's dodging.* "Ezra, you better tell me straight out if you want my help."

"Yes, OK, but . . . well, it's hard to explain. The Black girl looks just like Daisy."

"You're seeing ghosts, Ezra."

"No. It's as if she walked right back into my life."

"She's long gone. Probably dead. You know that."

"Dead?" He took a step back as if she'd stabbed him. "OK, yes. Suppose you're right, of course, after thirty-eight years. But, Beth, the looks, the gestures, the voice. Same size, the way she moves, cat-like, quick, even same age when she disappeared. Nine years old."

"She didn't disappear. She was sold by your father to keep you two apart. Forbidden love, your mother called it."

Ezra reached for Beth but pulled his hand back. "Will you help? I've no right to ask, but—"

"They being hunted?"

"They say not, but probably. Rich family, and these girls are not very good liars. There could be a bounty on their heads. If so, it's probably not the law after'm. Family, more likely."

She closed her eyes to collect her thoughts. Could she take the risk? If he really believed this young girl might be the reincarnation of Daisy, he was completely thrown. She was shocked at how the confusion and agony of this look-alike girl was twisting his face. His usual steadfast composure, his normal equilibrium shattered.

When she opened her eyes, he was still there, looking even more desperate. "Okay. Take the wagon around back and make sure those girls stay down, under cover. When you're absolutely certain no one is watching, get'm quickly up the fire escape. I'll meet you at the top. I'm not putting them down in that terrible hole, Ezra." Breathing deeply, she shook her head. "You know, I shouldn't do this for anyone, not even you."

Ezra nodded gratefully and walked to the wagon.

Calm down, get a grip. Her mind was racing, trying to focus, scheming. Since one is white, well-born, and traveling with her slave maid, they're not really runaways. Keeping them upstairs—away from the hiding hole—will help cement the lie should the patrols come looking.

Beth stood sentry on the porch, gripping the pistol deep in her pocket, as they drove off. Another wagon passing fast in front of her house hit a rut hard, and cabbages flew over the side. They rolled like green cannonballs along the ground, with crows swooping in, hopping on top of them, flapping.

He's putting me at risk, but he has a right to ask me, of course. For years we've helped each other. Thanks to some of my river pilots, I've smuggled runaways onto the steamboats north to Chicago and west to Independence, where Ezra leads them into the western wilderness to freedom. But things are different now, riskier—fiercer politics, bigger money in the hunt, slave patrols, vicious bounty hunters, even detectives. She shivered, remembering that terrifying moment a few months ago, when she barely stopped in time, before being caught and hanged.

Beth waited a few minutes after the wagon turned the corner to see if anyone followed or took interest. If so, she thought, *I can quickly cut through the yard to the back and wave them off.*

It was the thought of putting two girls in the hole that was making her stomach churn, her neck sweat. She had sheltered men, boys sometimes, strong women, but never girls down in the muddy cavern beneath her cookhouse floor. Smoke and hot grease seeping through the boards, spiders and rats crawling about, while the runaway slaves waited day after day for the Railroad to move them along by steamboat or wagon.

But the Underground Railroad had stopped running in her direction the day her two conductors were lynched. *I remember the terror I felt seeing their necks cracked, their dead weight hanging from that chestnut tree down by the courthouse. Thank God those conductors never divulged my secret waystation, and those slave patrols never found the hole. My blessed protectors, the bullyboys, had steered them off on a goose chase down by the river that day. The day God washed the bullyboys' sins for all time, in my mind. Bless them, dear God, for doing your work.*

Beth slipped inside and up the center stairs of the boarding house to her large apartment on the third floor. She stood in the hallway landing, listening for the movement of tenants below. No one stirred or called out. Once inside her apartment, she bolted and barred her front door, then walked down the hall into the large, dimly-lit parlor at the back. Her heart was pounding. *Stay calm. You can do this.*

The window looked onto the fire escape. Ezra stood juggling a rifle loosely in one hand, watching over the backyard and alleyway. The girls were huddled down on the landing against the house to avoid being seen from below. Beth saw a small brown leg resting beside a thin white arm. She wondered about them. Her own hands were trembling. Goosebumps marched up her arms. *For better or worse, I'm committed now.*

She unbarred and opened the door. "All clear?"

Ezra stepped aside to let the girls pass by. "Go on in. It's okay. Beth, this is Camille and this is Dai—"

"Maddie," the Black girl corrected. She glanced wide-eyed at Beth before following Camille into the house.

Beth stared at Ezra. *Don't ignore me. I'm doing this for you.* She extended her hand. "Ezra, you come in too. Five minutes."

Ezra waved down at Bill, put up five fingers, ducked his head, and stepped through the door. They entered Beth's spacious parlor, dim and cool with heavy draperies nearly closed. The air was scented with lamp oil and rose water, spiced with cinnamon bread. Plush chairs and sofas covered in muted red and green brocade sat atop a carpeted meadow of pale roses.

The girls circled about the cushioned expanse, running their hands over the rose-petal skin of polished wood, looking in the mirrors, grimacing at their filthy faces.

"Girls, sit over there." Beth pointed to a sofa in the center of the room.

She closed the door partway to shield herself from the morning light streaming in. Ezra stood awkwardly. She was glad of it. She wanted him obligated. This moment was fraught, not just with danger but her fears of farewell. Did he feel the same? She could only infer, never ask.

"I'll take them for the night, maybe more, because I know you have your brother's party. Is this a farewell party for you and your nephew Homer?"

"It is. As well as an opportunity to bring possible investors into the enterprise. I'm tonight's showman to assure them this gold rush is real and will last."

"I want to hear all about it. To be clear, Ezra, I'm going to keep these girls up here in my rooms. *Not* down in that filthy hole."

"Thank you. They won't be so terrified up here in all your gracious comfort. I'm grateful, Beth. Truly. I know it's not fair, but you're the only person I trust with runaways besides Jacques."

"By now you'd think I'd have learned to expect surprises from you," she said, her eyes narrowing.

She twirled her hair back up in one quick move and put in the comb. Ezra reached for the loose tresses that spilled out, then pulled his hand back. *Has he ever touched my hair?*

She changed the subject. "I do want to hear about you settling in California, though. Especially if tomorrow or the day after's the last time I'm ever going to see you . . . You bastard. You think I'm not upset about this? Think I should just be quiet and complacent? And now bringing these girls last minute shows you are in fact a sentimental son of a bitch. Not for me, mind you, but for them. Do you understand how that hurts? Do you?"

Watching him, Beth was pleased to see the conflict roiling in his eyes, his face. She hadn't known until yesterday that he planned to start over in California, not thinking of her, not asking her. Of course, it was none of her business, but never again? It opened a hole inside her that had no bottom.

COME AND GO AS HE MIGHT—SOMETIMES A YEAR OR MORE between—he still stirs my interest. Ten years ago, maybe more, I was running on cobbles, hit a loose one and went down and my ankle screamed in pain. Or maybe that was me. It was dinner time no one around. I tried to crawl to find a crutch of some sort. Then a shadow of a horse, voice of a man.

"Don't move," he said. "If it's broke, I'll get you to a doc, if there's one around here."

He didn't ask permission, he just took off my boot, felt my ankle, probing with gentle fingers, then down to the bones in my foot, up to my calf.

"Nothing broken. I'll bind it, get you home."

He pulled bandaging as if by magic from his saddlebag. Then got me to my feet. I tried to hobble a few steps, but the pain was sharp.

"How far?" he asked. Shook his head when I told him blocks away. "I can carry you or put you up on my horse."

He didn't wait for an answer. He lifted me up into the saddle and guided the horse slowly, holding my ankle steady. At the boarding house, no one around to help, I pointed to the stairs. Third floor.

"I can carry you in my arms like a child, but I'd be off balance on these steep steps. Okay, over my shoulder, then," he said, "like a sack of wheat."

I winced. "Please not wheat."

He laughed, such a wonderful laugh. "Okay, a bag of soft, fresh flour then, you'll smell like biscuits, Sunday morning." He leaned down and I draped myself over his shoulder.

We climbed slowly. The bouncing brought out his smell—sweat, musk, leather and some other natural scent as transporting as his voice. He held my ankle so it didn't bounce. Took me in, set me down, made some tea. Then whiskey, to ease the pain. We talked half the night.

"Your name is Elsbeth? Sounds like a fairy tale name. How about Elsbi? Okay then, just Beth. You're quite pretty, you know." So direct it startled me. I edged closer to his voice, his scent. I wanted him to stay but he had business. Odd business. Woodsman, wilderness trader, trail guide kind of business. Gone most of the year. A widower. A lonesome man.

"Me?" I said. "No, I'm single, determined to stay that way, just so we're clear."

He laughed again. "Clear. No traps. Hope to see you next time I'm in town. Heading to Oregon in two days. I won't be coy. I like you, Beth of Elsbeth. Everything about you. Don't want to scare you none but with so little time, I want to say you're more than just beautiful, you're a bit wonderful." I thought the response that came to life in me had died, but I was wrong.

He left and didn't return for two years. I was busy but never forgot his face, his voice, his words. That delicate touch on my leg. I wondered over the years, what if I were to love him? What kind of life would I have with a wild man? I have a business to run. I can't be chasing wolves in the forest. We were an impossible pair. Yes. And yet I loved him like no other. And was surprised by that. Thank God, he didn't like shackles any more than I did.

"Beth, what are you thinking? You went silent, drifted off for a few minutes."

"Sorry. Now, before you go, what else do you know about these two?"

He shrugged. "Not much. From Louisiana. Camille's seventeen, appears high-born. Maddie's got more grit than what's safe for a nine-year-old slave. She says she's not—claims to have a freedom paper—but neither one is a very good liar. No city ways, but they fought those slavers hard" He shook his head in wonder. "They were a sight to see, Beth. An amazing surge of power and courage you wouldn't believe now looking at their tired little bodies slumping on your sofa. Oh, and hungry. Been living in the streets for three weeks."

"Food I have. And if you want to come back here directly from the party—I know it will be late, but you'd be welcome. I can fix you up a bed downstairs." *One of my empty rooms*, she thought. Clean sheets, dust and tidy up, air it out. Wood in the fireplace. Kindling ready to flare. *I'd like to do that for you*, she thought. *Create a little nest. Care for you in some small way in these last days.*

Ezra took her hand in both of his, holding it a moment longer, more tenderly than she expected—those strong hands of his—stepping close enough to kiss her. He was tempted, she could see it, but as usual he didn't reach for her. *Nor I for him.* Slowly, he disengaged, put his filthy hat back on, tipped it graciously. Then he headed down the back stairway.

She was dripping with sweat. Her heart skipping. Her head being squeezed in a vice of conflict. *This is going to be harder than I imagined. Dear God, you got any ideas?*

I have my world, he has his, and now he's going to create a new one. Without me. No room for me. Didn't even ask me. Why?

Because he knows I won't budge.

BETH STOOD TEN FEET AWAY STUDYING THE GIRLS SITTING ALERT and fearful on her sofa, their wary eyes asking for mercy, she thought. Camille sat upright with perfect posture, her legs tucked one behind the other, hands folded, as if she were in mannered company. Even filthy, she had that keen French air, that penetrating look, intelligent nose. Maddie's feet stuck out, too short to find the floor. Her arms fell protectively over a tan package in her lap, tied with blue twine. Camille had one hidden behind her like a pillow.

To see better, Beth walked across the parlor to open the curtain. The mid-morning light flooded in. Then she pulled up a hassock to get closer. To look them over. *Such an oddity*, Beth thought. She had no experience with children. In all her years in this house she had never had girls sitting in her parlor. Beth's hair and arms tingled with curiosity. Camille's disheveled state. That weariness, fatigue from days on the run, scrounging for food, sleeping in alleys had taken a familiar toll. It took Beth back to her own journey, when she first arrived destitute and desperate at age fifteen from Kentucky. *Was it really twenty-two years ago?*

Camille seemed Beth's opposite, from a home of wealth and privilege. But to become powerless in a cruel new place, at the mercy of the streets, they were not so different.

And Maddie—well, it was nice to finally see the face that haunted Ezra. But it was so much more alive, playful, and earnest than she had imagined Daisy. Beth tried to envision Ezra at age nine smitten with this girl. Not so far-fetched. But the filth, the smell of them was overwhelming.

"You two look like you been sleeping in those clothes for weeks. Swear, you're dirtier than ticks. Are you banged up?" She reached out and took Maddie's face in her hands and turned it slowly side to side. "Did you get jumped? Hurt?" *Beautiful face*, she thought. "Good. No cuts, no deep bruises."

Maddie smiled. Beth turned, but Camille saw her coming, set her jaw and braced herself against Beth's impending touch. There was a deep purple bruise running down her neck to her shoulder. Another behind her ear. Beth folded her hands. "See, no touch. Where are you from?"

"Louisiana." Camille blinked rapidly, then teared. "Sorry. My father owns a sugar plantation. He betrayed us.

⇒ 2 ⇐

JENNY

Louisiana, Four weeks earlier, January 1849

hat would Camille do if Jenny died? Her mind was racing, searching for elusive answers as she crept down the back stairs.

The library door was ajar. She slowly pushed it to avoid being seen. Smelled the sweet smoke and brandy and saw shadows on the wall of three or four men. They were on their feet, talking about the new harsh slave laws. A chill ran up her spine, but she had no time to listen.

Opening the back door, the cold air shocked her and stopped her breathing for a moment. She slipped on her shoes and threw a dark cloak over her head and shoulders and pulled it tight. She ran down the broad hill studded with moon shadows of oaks and magnolias toward the slave shanties. Even in damp winter, the scent of sugarcane clung to the trees.

She hesitated at the door to Jenny's cabin, which had been left partly open from the foot traffic of well-wishers and caretakers. People were inside. She could hear their soft voices and a hymn off in the distance, with slow cadence and a sad, suffering tone. *Was it for Jenny?*

She stared at the door. It was missing a few boards and had been patched and re-patched for the winter with old papers and pieces of tarp. Gathering her nerve, she stepped inside. There were four women crowding around Jenny. When they saw Camille, they pulled away. One squeezed Jenny's arm and brushed her face and then hurried out, the others behind, smiling at Camille to thank her for coming.

Camille stood stricken at the change. Tears flooded her eyes. Dear God. Jenny was soaked, limp, shaking with fever but still bright-eyed. Only a few days ago, she had been chasing after the chickens. The terror of death immobilized Camille as she remembered her own mother dying. Mother's long agony. Her father in pieces, consumed in grief and anger. She herself lost, wandering alone about the great house like a ghost, blaming herself. It all came back in a single flash.

Jenny's fingers tugged her forward. "Come here, child," she said. "Don't be afraid. Sit with me. Maddie stay in your room like I said?"

"Yes, lying by the fire, eating. She's so scared, Jenny. Why did you want me to come alone?"

Gathering herself to offer comfort, Camille sat down on the stool next to Jenny, caressed her wet cheek, refreshed and refolded the cloth on her forehead. Searched her face. This was the woman who had taken her in her arms when her own mama died, when she was only seven, two years younger than Maddie. Jenny was so reassuring, so full of hope. *She saved me. In time, saved father too. Brought him back from a dark place.*

She took the cloth from Jenny's forehead and freshened it in the pail of water next to the bed. She wiped Jenny's face, then her neck.

"Child, I'm going to die tonight. Now, shh, that's the way it is going to be. I've had a talk with God, and he said I won't be a slave no more."

Imminent death sent Camille plunging into darkness, while tremors shot like lightning from her toes up through her face and scalp, escaping into the room. The candle on the table flickered, bringing Jenny's face in and out of darkness. "No Jenny, you can't die, not now, not tonight."

"Shush. Now, don't interrupt, Camille. I got some wind left. Let me talk. Your mama asked me before she died to watch over you every day. To take best care of you. And be a mama to you. She said she trusted me, and no one else." She coughed, deep and hoarse, then paused, wiped her mouth, panting for breath.

After a few moments, "You've been more than good to me," said Camille.

"So, I need you to grow up. This very night. Into a woman," said Jenny. "I need you to take care of my Maddie, in the same way I took care of you." Jenny coughed, gasped for breath again. "Camille, there's no one else. I've been praying, asking God to find someone to care for her. He chose you."

Camille stared at Jenny, her throat thick with dread. Then took her hand, weak, damp with sweat. "We'll take good care of her."

Slowly, Jenny reached up and took Camille's collar, pulled her face close. "No, Camille, not 'we,' *you*. She's a small, scared thing that loves you. I need you be her *mère* until she's eighteen."

"What?" *Please don't ask this of me. I'm not ready.*

"Promise me, in front of God, right here, right now that you'll look after her like she was your own."

"But . . ." Jenny's dark eyes pleaded with her. Camille began to shake. *Could I do that? Raise her like my own?*

Jenny's eyes flared, then softened. "This be a wicked world, and the only thing God ever gave me worth having was the two of you."

"But, Jenny, I can't . . ."

"Please Camille. I need you to promise me before I can go. Promise me."

Camille fought to catch her breath, conflicting thoughts coursing through, tearing her mind apart. *But she's in such pain. I can't deny her.*

Finally, Camille nodded. "I'll take care of her. Promise."

"Something you don't know, Camille. When your mama died, your father was as lost in grief as any man I ever saw. Sometimes I would just rock beside him on the porch." Jenny jerked forward, coughed and spit dark yellow phlegm into a rag. Then fought for breath. "There, better, gotta breathe, calm myself. Sometimes on the porch, like I said. Sometimes in the rocker beside your mama's bed. Sometimes I let his sorrow fill me. Sometimes I would love him with my body the way your mama did. Not like man and wife behind closed doors. Still master and slave. But I pretended otherwise, to care for you, help him recover, and God knows, protect myself . . ." She jerked up, wheezing, panting for breath. Finally, sank back down. "And then one day I was with child."

Camille stood and stumbled backward. "You mean . . ." She paused, her eyes widening, heart racing. "My father . . . is Maddie's?"

Jenny put her hand out gently. "I think you've always known."

Had she? Her throat tightened. They had played together in Camille's room since Maddie was a toddler. She had helped raise Maddie, read to her, taught her everything, and loved her like a little sister. *Was I blind not to see it?* Father had none of the same rules for Jenny and Maddie when Jenny lived in the *grande maison* as a special maid.

Camille walked over to the fireplace and threw in some more kindling. The fire leapt. She stared into the flames, feeling the heat on her face, wondering why she hadn't seen it. *I was happy for the first time since mother passed—happy beside Maddie, Jenny, and father recovering,* she remembered. *Blind to anything that would break the spell.*

She gave Jenny a ladle of water, then freshened the cloth and gently sponged her face. Jenny was still coherent but sweating more profusely and shivering harder. The ticking that covered her straw-and-shuck mattress was drenched with sweat.

"Let me put something dry underneath you." Camille looked around at the worn clothing and rags hanging on wall pegs.

"Stop fussing, child."

Camille's eyes were tearing. "Why did you keep this from me?"

"You were a child and might have let something slip. Had to protect my Maddie. You understand how dangerous that can be? She could have been taken away."

Jenny coughed, sat forward, put up her hand to pause and gasp for breath. Finally, settling back, Jenny reached under her heavy, wet pillow and pulled out a piece of folded parchment.

"This paper is from your daddy. I don't read, but had it read. It says that Maddie is free. Free-born, and by your daddy. People thinks she's slave, 'cause I'm slave. That's the law. But she ain't. It says so right clear on this paper." She handed it to Camille, then rolled on her right side and coughed, spitting in the bucket.

Camille unfolded the parchment. Although it was mottled and worn on the outside, inside it was crisp and clean, the blue ink bright and the handwriting bold and elegant, her father's distinctive style. The clarity of intention and the certainty of his love for Maddie. It surprised her and cheered her. "This is so wonderful," she said.

"Now you hide that paper, *chère*. And you swear to me, before God almighty who is standing beside my shoulder that you will keep her free."

"I promise. I'll take care of her."

"And keep her *free*," said Jenny. "Free! Understand? Not a slave. Never, ever a slave. Promise?"

"Yes. Free."

Camille pulled the blanket higher and reached across Jenny to grab an old winter coat off a peg. She put it on top of her, then laid a fresh cloth on Jenny's forehead. The fever was raging.

"Tonight you have to get stronger." Jenny stared at Camille, eyes wide. "Now, shh. God is giving me some last wind, saving it for you. I've been praying God will make you strong. To grow you up while you sleep. This very night. 'Cause there are things you still don't understand."

Camille gripped the blanket, bracing herself. *How could there be more?*

"Your new stepmother, Priscilla. She has plans. She walked into *la grande maison* the day after she wed your father, two years now. She took one look at me and at Maddie's eyes—same hazel brown as yours, same upward tilt at the corner—and she knew everything. She threw us out. She got designs. Nasty woman, she got designs. Now she wants to marry you off to that Dufort boy, to get her hands on their land, to grow the plantation holdings."

Camille shuddered at the thought. She detested Pierre.

"She's a wicked woman. And she wants to sell my Maddie downriver. Someplace they work field slaves 'til they die."

"No, Father won't let her. I can reason with him."

"Your daddy won't help you. That Priscilla knows how to turn a man's shame against him."

"You're wrong. He promised Maddie to me, my personal maid. We'll bring Maddie in the house with me, just like it was before Priscilla arrived." She blew on Jenny's neck to cool her off.

Jenny stroked Camille's cheek lightly. "Camille, you have to trust me. It's not safe here for you or Maddie." She stopped. Her face twisted.

"Need some breath'n." *Not safe for either of us.* The words echoed in Camille's head.

Jenny's face relaxed; her panting slowed. She took a couple of rattling breaths.

"You're in God's hands now. Get some sleep. And let God work on you 'til the morning And send Maddie back to me. So I can tell her after I leave here tonight, you'll take care of her. And love her like a mama. And take her to freedom."

"I don't know if—"

"Of course you can. God's already working on you. When you wake, you'll be strong enough to leave this plantation for good. Your daddy's a powerful man. You'll have to make a run for it. You can flee upriver to the free lands."

Camille wiped the sweat from Jenny's neck.

"It's time, Camille. You be brave. You always been brave; just raised not to believe it."

With a frail hand, Jenny stroked Camille's hair in the familiar way Camille loved. "Just keep that freedom paper hidden. Because they're going to come in here after I die to find it and burn it."

Camille took the paper and held it up to the firelight again, reading the words written in her father's hand. There was no doubt of his intention to free Maddie. Camille folded it carefully and slipped it in her undergarment.

"Now, go, child. Get my baby, while I can still breathe. Tell her to come sit by my side."

THE FUNERAL WAS THE NEXT DAY IN THE SLAVE CEMETERY. Camille's father, Antoine Bonnaire, fourth generation on this land, said a few words at the gravesite in a gray, patrician manner. Camille's throat was too constricted to get out her prayers. Maddie had slumped to her knees and couldn't stand up, weak from crying through the night beside her mother.

Camille reached down and pulled Maddie up by her shoulders, wrapped her arms around her, and began to bundle her back to her cabin.

"Camille, I want you to come back up to the house after you put Maddie to bed," said her father. "Maddie needs to sleep, and I need to talk to you. In the library, right away."

Some of the slave women understood his meaning. They gathered around Maddie and lifted her up in their arms, carrying her away. Camille turned and walked silently back to the house, one step behind her father. They made their way to the library, where he closed the door.

"Camille, I need to discuss with you Maddie's future. And your own."

There was an ominous undercurrent in his voice that should have made her cringe with fear. But she didn't. She was stubborn and took to heart Jenny's words.

She knew, as soon as she walked into the library and took one look at Father's determined face, she knew she'd run. *You're not going to sell me and my little sister off.*

"As I said, I'm thinking of your future, trying to ensure—"

"Of course, Father. If you don't mind, to ease things, I'd like to take Maddie for one last time together on a trip to New Orleans. It would ease her anxiety. We could stay with Aunt Genevieve. As you know, I need to go anyway to begin shopping for my trousseau. After all, if I'm to be married . . . it takes time to prepare for a big wedding, as you know."

His face melted into a smile. *He obviously expected a battle or a torrent of tears.*

"Splendid," he said. "You've become such a responsible young lady. I can arrange passage to New Orleans tomorrow. I'm sure Priscilla will agree."

"The new fashions from Paris will be arriving any day, but please don't encourage her to tag along. She doesn't like Maddie and will only make our trip uncomfortable."

"Understood. You have my support."

3

GETTING ACQUAINTED

Back in Beth's parlor

R emind me again," said Beth. "Who was Jenny? And what was
your father's plans for you two?"

"Jenny was Maddie's *mère*," said Camille. "And my
mammie for the last ten years. He was going to let Priscilla, my new
stepmother, sell Maddie off into field slavery. And sell me blind into an
arranged marriage to a man I despise. All to expand our holdings. Jenny
warned me on her death bed. She made me promise to keep Maddie free.
And told us we had to run. To freedom. To find a place that would allow
us to live together openly as half-sisters. I don't know where that is."

"Well, it's certainly not St. Louis," said Beth. "Maybe north or west,
but, well . . . So, you didn't just *leave*? You *ran*. Is that right? Very brave
of you. Tell me how you did it. Couldn't have been easy . . . Wait, I'm
getting ahead of myself."

Turning to Maddie, Beth pulled on the twine. "What's in the
package?"

"It's mine!" Maddie pulled the bundle to her chest with both arms.
She looked at Camille, then relaxed her grip. "A dress. Camille got one
too, but she's embarrassed."

"I'm not going to take it from you, dear. Just curious," said Beth.

"It's blue," said Maddie.

Beth pulled at the material on her own skirt. "Like the one I have on?"

"No," Maddie said slowly, looking quickly at Camille, then back to Beth. "Mine's brand new. Bitty white flowers. Yours is old. Is that okay to say, Camille?"

"Fine with me," said Beth, laughing. "I appreciate an honest girl. You can show it to me after you take a bath. There's a tub of water down that hallway." She pointed. "Right down there. Still warm. Clean. Was going to use it myself. You're welcome to it."

Maddie turned, peered down the long interior hallway where Beth pointed. "Do you own all this?" she asked. "This whole big room? And more rooms, even a washroom down that long hallway."

"Yes, this is my apartment, and I own this entire building. In case Ezra didn't tell you, this is a boarding house, three stories, but I reserve the entire third floor for my own privacy. I don't want my tenants knocking on my door. Out that front door, down that short hallway behind you," she pointed, "is the landing with stairs that go down to the second floor, which has ten bedrooms. All my tenants are river pilots, who board here when they are not guiding their steamboats. Another flight of stairs takes you to the first floor, where I have six more bedrooms, a dining room, entry parlor, and indoor kitchen. I also have an outdoor kitchen to prevent fires.

Now come with me, you two, I'll show you the layout of the place, and where you'll be sleeping tonight."

She led them into the long inside hallway, designed by Hannah to branch off the big parlor and run parallel to the main hallway. To their immediate right, she pointed to cabinets, pots and pans, counter, sink. "This is my small indoor kitchen." She grabbed ahold of the pump handle. "This takes some work, but I can actually pump water up here from a cistern, thanks to Ezra. He's very handy and generous. Next is my office. Stacks of notebooks and paper because I run a business." She kept walking. "And just beyond on the right is the washroom. See?" The door was open. She stepped in and they followed. "That big copper tub is filled with warm water for you two to soak in and wash off the grime. Go ahead, feel the water." Maddie put her fingers in.

Stepping out, she said, "Across the hall, that door is to the smallest of my four bedrooms. No need to show you. The door next to it is a storage room for supplies and food stores."

Beth walked another five paces down the hall and stopped at two large closed doors facing each other across the hallway. "Ready for a surprise?" She opened the one to the left. "This is the big guest bedroom where you'll sleep tonight."

Maddie squealed and ran for the big poster bed with lace canopy, fluffy comforter, and a pile of rose-colored pillows, but stopped short just before she jumped. She looked at her hands and grimy dress.

"Thank you, Maddie. After your bath, you'll be clean enough to run and jump on the bed. And put your face in those soft pillows." Maddie's face brightened and she touched her cheeks.

Camille pointed to the door across the hall. "That must be your room."

"Indeed. I'm right across from you in case you get scared." Beth opened the door to a richly furnished bedroom. The girls sucked in their breath. Maddie's eyes wandered the walls decorated floor to ceiling like a tapestry. It had a large comfortable bed, a plush couch facing the window, an elegantly crafted vanity with mirror and banks of both large and tiny drawers. Beth tapped it. "From France after their revolution," said Beth.

Maddie continued to stare at the walls. "Camille, look at the beautiful birds and flowers and waterfalls and ponds. A garden, here. Lakes and trees over there," she said. "I love it." The walls were papered, Beth explained, in a Chinese garden print, a special export from Canton.

"I love it too. Makes the room truly magical," said Camille.

"It's my place of rest and withdrawal after a long, busy day. See that big stuffed chair by the window? That's where I curl up, read, generally at night when all is quiet." She put her hand on the large side table next to the chair stacked with books, scrolls, a candelabra, and a teapot platform with a warming candle.

"All right, you two, back to the parlor."

Maddie ran back, sat down and hugged her package to her chest. "Maddie, I have an idea," said Beth. "Why don't you bring that wonderful new dress with you and I'll walk you back to the wash room and get you set up for a long leisurely bath. That warm water is all yours. Don't want it to get cold. Then after you bathe, maybe something to eat. Would you like that?"

"Can we eat first?" Maddie asked. Springing forward, her package fell to the ground.

"No, dear, after. I need to talk to Camille right now. Come with me, bring your dress."

She walked Maddie back to the wash room, where the large tub was filled with enough warm water to pass Maddie's waist. "Put your whole hand in, feel it."

"I never had a warm bath with this much water," said Maddie, swishing her hand around. "Usually just a basin. Can I really get all the way in it?"

"Of course, and let yourself lean back, soak for a while, relax. I know you're scared. You don't know me. But Ezra brought you here because you're special to him and he wants me to protect you. You're safe here. Here's some soap and a soft washing cloth. Now be sure to wash your hair. But be careful soaking. Don't fall asleep in the tub. Hear me, Maddie? That can be dangerous when you're this tired. I'm putting a towel and some clean undergarments on the stool, a bit big for you but will feel comfortable. I'll leave the door ajar so we can hear you and you can hear us in the parlor. We won't eat until you're done."

Walking out, she shook her head. *This is ridiculous,* she thought. *Where does this sudden mothering impulse come from? I don't know any mothers. Not personally. My tenants have wives and children, but the impulse is not from them. My own mother? That was so long ago. I had moments when I felt her tenderness, but home was cramped, angry, desperate, hardscrabble. Well, at least Ma fought to protect me when I left.*

No, more of this mothering came from Hannah, bless her soul, who took me off the streets right here, gave me a home, tutored me, and taught me by example about mothering. Didn't fully realize that until just now. She lifted her eyes, whispered, "Love you, Hannah. Thank you for all you taught me and the life you gave me."

Back in the parlor, Beth sat close to Camille on the sofa. "Now tell me how you got up the courage to run. You were stuck on what I would imagine to be an isolated plantation in the Louisiana wetlands. How did you get away? The details are important." *Don't want to scare them*, she thought, *but better find out if they're being chased.*

"A good friend of my father has a barque with a captain and a small crew. He was visiting Father, and the day after Jenny's funeral was sailing back to New Orleans. I suggested to Father that I accompany him, stay with *Tante* Genevieve, and do some shopping for my trousseau."

"That was a brave thing to do. Almost trapping yourself."

"It worked. Father was so taken aback, so delighted I had accepted my fate, he agreed to let me go. And since my remaining time with Maddie would be so short, he'd let me take her with me. And promised he wouldn't let Priscilla interfere."

Beth laughed. "So you *are* a good liar. Ezra said not, but I'm hearing a clever girl."

"Maybe clever, but dear God, I was so scared of what I had started. I had just committed myself to marrying that horrid Pierre. You're right, I set my own trap. But as Jenny said, 'Now it's time for you to reach down and pull up your brave.'"

"You certainly have it in you."

"My first thought was *Tante* Genevieve would take Maddie into her household and keep Priscilla away, and I could visit often. Then, when she was old enough, we would bring out the freedom paper and Father would be forced to recognize her as free-born."

"But wouldn't you have to marry that awful Pierre for that to work?"

"Yes, but I was still too afraid to run. I knew I had to run but where could I possibly go? At least Maddie would be protected. But things got bad fast. After dinner, *ma tante* and *Cousine* Elise were talking about how slave laws had become more severe in Louisiana. *Harsher* was the term they used. I asked *ma tante* if a grant of freedom would hold in a court of law if the owner changed his mind after signing the paper. She said probably not.

"It was shattering. My mind reeled with panic. I choked. My eyes teared and I excused myself to go to the toilet closet. I had Maddie's freedom paper tucked in my bosom. I touched it and it suddenly felt fragile. Now, I better understood why Jenny begged me to take Maddie and run.

"The worst part," Camille added, "was when *ma tante* went upstairs to bed. *Cousine* Elise slid close, took my arm in confidence, and told me she could see how beautiful Maddie would become, and that by age sixteen or seventeen would command a good price at the Quadroon Ball."

"'The what? What do you mean?' I asked.

"'Oh, quite the annual event,' said Elise. She went on to explain that beautiful mixed-race girls were brought to the ball in fine dresses, often by their mothers, and sold to wealthy men to be kept in style as a *plaçage*, in what they call a 'left-handed' marriage. Often, Elise emphasized with her eyes growing brighter, if the girl was very lucky, she'd be kept with her own fine house and carriage along Rue Rampart. Sometimes even given slaves of her own."

"Dear God," said Beth. "And their wives put up with this?"

"Yes. I was astonished too. And horrified when Elise offered up Maddie as some wonderful prize. My little sister, a *placée?* It turned my stomach to think of someone like Pierre putting Maddie in a gilded cage, his hands all over her. And at the same time possibly married to *me*. I was sick, woozy. I stood up fast, knocked over my glass of wine. I was enraged but the danger facing Maddie and me cleared my head. Elise and I cleaned up, gossiped, made arrangements for the next day, then I went to bed."

"So you decided to run?"

"Right then and there. God yanked me hard on the spot. He told me to 'wake up!' And gave me the strength, just as Jenny said he would, to take Maddie and go. I was terrified, furious, but also set in motion. Determined. I didn't sleep that night, planning our escape."

"How, tell me," said Beth.

"I arranged to have *ma tante's* driver drop us off at 8:00am to window shop before Elise arrived at the store when it opened at 11:00am. We left everything in our rooms as if we were returning that evening. We had three hours to walk away from the shops, quickly hire a carriage to the wharf, and buy tickets on the first steamboat north. We covered our faces with dark veils.

"As a precaution before I left the plantation, I had taken all my money, a few pieces of my mother's jewelry sewn in my dress, her wedding ring, and a few essentials."

"And you still think you got away clean. With no one in pursuit?" asked Beth.

"I think so. The steamboat left promptly at 10:30am bound for St. Louis. I purchased a small stateroom. Most people on board were sleeping on the deck. Gold miners heading for California. But with my mother's wedding ring on my finger, they left me alone when I went for food."

"That took real cunning and courage to set out on a voyage like that into the unknown," said Beth. "It must have been quite a shock when you got off. This is a hard city. I suppose those thieves took your mother's ring?"

"Everything. Ripped open the hem of my dress to get the jewelry."

"What do you imagine your aunt did when you didn't show up? And your father?"

"I don't know. Panic. I presume they contacted the day police or night watchmen or hired a detective to search for us. They may have assumed we were kidnapped. 'Girls disappear all the time down there,' my father told me as a word of caution before we left."

"If kidnapped, they'd expect a ransom note within a few days, would they not?" said Beth. "It didn't come, so your father's likely in New Orleans right now managing a frantic search for you. Do you have brothers and sisters in line to inherit if you were to die or disappear?"

"I had two older brothers, and both died, one at age eight, the other at twenty-two."

"That makes you his sole heir. I imagine your father, obsessed with name, standing, and heritage, will turn the earth upside down to bring you back. Would he not? Ezra said those slavers that grabbed you on the levee mentioned a reward. Did you hear that too? Any word of a bounty?"

Camille shook her head. "I was too terrified to hear much."

"I'd like to check the newspapers today," said Beth. "There's a section on runaways. You imagine you got away clean, but . . ."

"I'm clean but what?" said Maddie, waltzing in and twirling in her new dress, hair wet, face shiny, barefoot. "My boots aren't going to look good with this dress, but I don't care."

"Be right back." Beth disappeared into the kitchen.

"She's getting us food," said Camille. "Beth was asking me about how we got away. First from the plantation. Then from *Tante* Genevieve. Then away on the steamboat."

"And got off and robbed and hurt," said Maddie. "You still have big bruises right there." She touched the side of Camille's neck. "You're going to like the bath. Wonderful warm water all over your body. Never felt anything like it before."

Beth returned and set down two bowls of warm leftover stew and a large tray with bread, butter, jam, honey, and cheese. "Wait! Lift your hands, Maddie. Thatta girl." She draped a large towel over the front of Maddie's dress as a giant bib.

Beth pulled a chair up close and poured some tea. They grabbed food with both hands and ate like ravenous wolves.

"Go ahead, stuff yourself. Don't be polite," said Beth. Without asking, Beth picked up their empty bowls and went for seconds. She set them down and watched them dive in, less frantically this time but faster than polite. "After you're done, Camille, you can have that bath to yourself. I put another bucket on the fire to heat it up. Then you can try on your new dress, and if it doesn't fit, I have another. Where in the world did you get those dresses? I forgot to ask."

Camille swallowed hard, cleared her throat. "Ezra bought them. Said we'd do better with you if we had clean clothes."

"Ezra?" *No one in my whole life has ever given me a gift so personal as a dress. Certainly not Ezra. And I wouldn't have it if he tried.*

"Are you married to him?" asked Maddie. "Bill said . . . well I'm not allowed to say."

"No! I'm not married to nobody! You know what happens when you marry?" She was surprised at the sharp edge to her voice.

Maddie shook her head, looking puzzled as she chewed on a wedge of cheese.

"Everything around you, everything you see, everything you think you own"—she gestured—"this furniture, this house, the dress on my back, this very dress would belong to him." She tugged at her collar. "I couldn't own a business, sign a contract, borrow money. I couldn't own a boarding house. I couldn't do what I do best. What I love. Do you understand?"

Maddie shook her head. "No, I own my dress. Ezra said if I wasn't a slave, I shouldn't dress like a slave. So now I'm not a slave. Just washed it off."

Beth rocked back, chagrined. "You did indeed, child. You cheer me."

"I'm sorry Ezra didn't buy you a dress as well," said Camille.

"Thank you for the thought, dear, but I have plenty of dresses. Ezra knows that."

"Bill said we reminded him of his granddaughters in the land of Crows," said Maddie. "'Too lame to get back there,' he said. "He sounded sad. He talks different, Beth. Said it must have rubbed off on him in a place he hated. Do you know where that is? Why did he go there?"

"Maddie, please, that was private," said Camille.

"Not that part wasn't."

"Quite all right," said Beth. "I'll tell you the little I know about Bill. His family lived in a small town along the Missouri River, and Bill, youngest of four boys, was a wild kid. Truly wild. Ran away time and again, trying to find those big mountains out west he heard and read about. First at age ten, spunky kid jumped on a steamboat, went as far as Independence, where the trails across the prairie begin, before his older brother dragged him home."

"He bought a ticket like we did when he was only ten?" Maddie asked.

"No, the steamboats sometimes made stops at his town, and he snuck aboard and hid. Did it again two years later. He got farther up-river, closer to the mountains, before he was arrested as a stowaway and sent home with a stern warning. He promised his parents to stay away from the wharf."

"But he didn't, right?"

"Right. He tried for a couple of years, but he talked every chance he got with men who had been to those mountains, and the temptation became too great."

"He's like us, Camille, a runaway."

"The last time, Bill, now nearly sixteen, was put in chains in the hold of a steamboat heading back down river. His father had to pay the steamboat fare and a hefty fine.

"Finally, Bill's mother said, '*Enough*.' She sent him off to Boston to live with a wealthy aunt who promised to turn him into a gentleman. She had him tutored day and night for a year, under guard, mind you, then sent him to Harvard. That's a fine old university, Maddie. He hated it. Only thing he liked was poetry, geography, and botany, as I understand it. He stayed there for two years. As a reformed young man, spiffed up, he returned home to visit his parents during summer break. He dazzled them; they felt proud."

"And then at the end of summer he went back to Boston?" Camille asked.

"No, two weeks after he came home, he ran off to the mountains, this time for good. His mother gave up. He was eighteen and had picked his own life journey in the wilderness. The man loves tall tales, poetry and loves to blab as you know. Did he really go to Harvard? Some say not but I think he did."

"Does he write poetry?" Camille asked. "I'd like to read some."

"In his mind he does," said Beth. "When I pressed him years ago, he said, 'Don't see any reason to write them down, then fix and polish them over and over. Fretting gets in the way of new poems want'n to bloom in my mind. Time writing them down and fuss'n be like plugging up a good stream.'"

⇒ 4 ⇐

Jacques and the
Freedom Paper

That afternoon

By noon, the girls were asleep in the large canopied bedroom, when Beth slipped in and whispered to Camille. "Follow me. Don't wake Maddie." She walked the stumbling girl down the hall into the parlor space, then turned the corner into the shorter hall to the front door. Beth tried to hide her twitching hands; this was going to be difficult.

"Sorry, I know you're groggy, disoriented. You're still half asleep but can you focus for a moment?"

Camille leaned on the coat rack to keep her balance and nodded.

"I have something important to do," said Beth. "I'll be back in a few hours. After I leave, I want you to lock this front door and then the door to your bedroom. She tapped the front door. This is the only way into the apartment, so you'll be safe. Don't let anyone in. Anyone. Do you hear me?" Camille nodded again, rubbing her eyes.

"Then listen. First, I'm going to look in today's newspaper to find out if anyone has placed an ad searching for you. Second, I'll be meeting a dear friend who can help you. If you trust me enough with Maddie's freedom paper—and I know we just met so this will be hard for you—I will ask him to make copies and notarize them. He'll return the original along with multiple copies in a day or two. These can help protect Maddie. I'd trust him with my life."

"I don't understand," said Camille.

Beth watched the panic wash over the girl. Camille's sleepy eyes suddenly turned alert . . . No, Beth. I can't. Please don't ask. It's the only proof we have."

"That's the point, Camille. Some man, sometime, somewhere will stop you and demand to see her freedom paper if you say she's not a slave. You show it to him and the man either tears it up or puts it in his pocket."

"No! Don't say that!"

"Sooner or later it will happen, and Maddie will then belong to him. I can see the terror in your eyes. Please understand me. You're at great risk with a single piece of paper, the original grant of freedom. You'll need multiple copies, legally notarized, to disarm a thief, to protect her. One copy filed with a lawyer or a court of law ahead of time. One copy for you to show when asked. Another hidden on your person. One hidden on Maddie. And several more copies with people you trust and will vouch for you before the law. The original in some very safe place."

Beth watched Camille's face twist in confusion. "I just don't know."

"Of course not. You're very careful. I'm sorry to frighten you, dear, but you will need this defense when you are out on your own. Do you grasp what I'm saying? I know it's unfair to pull you out of bed to make such a decision. But I need to move fast, right now, today. Do you trust me enough to have copies made?"

Camille reluctantly pulled out the mottled, folded paper. "I understand your point about duplicates but letting this out of my own hands terrifies me. Please be careful with it. This paper's all we have.."

"I understand. It's sacred. My friend will keep your trust. He's a lawyer, very savvy, works secretly for the Under-ground Railroad. Now lock up and go back to bed. Lock your bedroom door as well. Don't tell Maddie, please. It will only scare her. Let's get the copies made and the original back in your hands before we explain it to her . . . probably tomorrow or the next day."

"God be with you, Beth."

OUTSIDE, PULLING THE WOOLEN SHAWL OVER HER HEAD, BETH TOOK a deep breath to settle herself, and stepped off the porch into the early after-noon drizzle. She felt her chest tighten. *What have I got myself into?*

She walked briskly on the raised side of the street, careful not to slide into the muddy wagon ruts. Reaching the cobblestones that led into the city center, she doubled her nervous pace, her boots echoing off the cold paving.

Merchants crowded the narrow, covered walkways with their goods and displays, forcing Beth to stay in the street to make time. Startled, she lost her footing the moment a shop door opened, ringing a small bell that sounded oddly crisp and cheery in the damp gray air. She was on edge. Even that tiny bell set her off.

She stuffed her hands into her coat pockets to calm herself, nearly stumbled over a drunk in the gutter next to Keimler's tavern, and moved on. She was now stepping into something strange. Something slowing her gait as she walked, but not the sensation of sticky mud underfoot. More overhead, a garish noise wafting in the wind, trying to penetrate her mind, surrounding her. Head down, she clenched her fists and moved faster, trying to outrun it. It followed her, growing louder.

The roar of the chaos on the levee assailed Beth's ears from two blocks away. The compression of voices shouting, laughing, screaming, arguing; the squeal of wagons, and high-pitched trembling whinny of frightened horses. Thousands of miners trying to talk over the noise, loud enough to be heard by the man next to him.

She'd managed to avoid this place for weeks, ever since the gold miners began flowing in, and now coming in surges. There was no other place for the horde of miners to collect and entwine like this. St. Louis was the final transfer point for steamboats heading west up the Missouri River, the mouth of which was just a few miles north of here. She stopped, bent over and put her hands on her knees to take a deep breath to brace herself. Her face twitched at the tangy smell of river water, the pungent grip of sweating, unwashed men, mixed with rancid cooking oil, fresh manure, charcoal, and the mingling rot of discarded bits of food and vomit.

Why did I agree to do this? If there's a bounty—and I'm about to find out—these girls may not have a chance. That's why I'm wading in. That's why, Ezra, you better not dump and run. You hear me? I know you won't, I know your integrity, but you're scaring me.

Turning the last corner, the stew of foul air and monstrous congestion took her breath away. She flattened herself against a brick wall, to orient herself, and scout a path through the maze. As far as her eye could see, the massive steamboats were nudged in tight, the no-nonsense stern-wheelers alongside the floating filigreed palaces. Spreading out across the broad levee she saw a frenzy of traffic, miners, wagons, drays, and teams of horses hauling in and hauling out, bumping, shouting, a melee with all the agitation of a boiling pot. Supplies everywhere. Piles of cotton, tobacco, machinery, and lumber. Sacks of coffee and spices, flour, racks of canned sardines. All being unloaded and reloaded by bustling roustabouts.

Her eye found an opening. *This is it.* Taking a deep breath, she plunged in. She held her nose and jimmied her way through the crowd, twisting and dodging arguments and fist fights with more politeness than she felt. "I'm sorry . . . excuse me . . . please let me through, thank you . . . hands off, mister." She gritted her teeth as if biting through leather, determined to reach the small feeder streets on the far side.

Men drawn to her, surrounded her, egging for attention, conversation, arguments, intimacy. She swatted them away with a quip or a gesture but could snarl effectively when she had to back someone off. She knew how to slap with sound and word.

To her right, scores of tired, half-drunk miners shuffled to stay on their feet and keep their place in line. They kicked their heavy packs along the ground, careful not to jab the sharp pick-points into their shins.

Even in line, the rambunctious miners celebrated, bantered, whooped with excitement of the open road, of the freedom from social constraints. They growled, spit, cursed each other, cursed the noise, the congestion. Sang in small clusters: hymns, jigs, bright tunes of the day, obscene sea shanties.

Suddenly, leather cracked, and Beth jumped back with a sharp stab of fear in her gut. To her left, someone high on a horse shouted, "Clear the way!" Beth inched through several people in front of her who had stopped in their tracks. She watched in horror as a string of Black men in iron collars and chained ankles shuffle-stepped toward her. When they were directly in front, her mouth fell open and she heard a high-pitched keening sound coming from her throat. Her dismay turned to anger, turned to fury. Her stomach clenched. Her mind storming in conflict. *Do I let it pass or try to stop this outrage?* Her sanity pulled her up short. *Don't do something stupid, Beth. You're on mission. Get to Jacques with the precious paper.*

She wrapped her aching arms around herself as her feet danced nervously side to side watching these Black men prodded forward like creatures bent for hell by a slaver on a horse with a broad-brimmed hat that hid his eyes, knife and whip at the ready. She stood frozen with anger, temptation. Knife, whip, pistols, sheathed rifles, all weapons announcing the man's intent to kill should anyone, Beth included, step out to protest, interfere.

Her heart softened as she watched three fearless Quaker ladies in prim black disregarding the man's threats, trailing beside the captured men, singing a hymn and stuffing cornbread into their welcoming mouths. Without open hands, they wolfed at the bread. Beth's tears ran down her face watching the crumbs and sweat fall onto their torn bare feet. The slaver, perhaps overcome by the Quaker's fearless tender touch in the grace of God, let them feed his flock without a word.

In a few minutes, the slaves disappeared, swallowed into the sea of miners and wagons. The distant refrain, "Clear the way," and another crack of that awful whip, made her cover her ears. *This is why I do this,* she reminded herself and pushed her way through.

Beth made her way to where the crowd thinned, and the narrow streets branched off before she stopped and breathed deeply. Damp with sweat, she stretched her back, rolled her shoulders, her neck to release some of the tension. Then grabbed a paper from the first newsboy in her path, a short lad working the outside perimeter, who was shouting, "New gold strike on the Yuba River! Read all about it! Join the Rush!"

With the *Daily Union* firmly under her arm, Beth went down an ancient, quiet side street, Rue du Commerce, and turned the corner, heading toward Schneider's Goose, a tavern and coffee house that served deckmen and roustabouts, merchants, and businessmen.

She began to breathe more easily after the chaos. *Thank God, Ezra pulled Maddie and Camille out of this madhouse.* Why on earth did those girls wander down here in the first place? Hunger? Probably. She remembered their feverish faces as they ate this morning before Maddie collapsed on the sofa, Camille climbed into the warm bath, then both staggered off to bed.

Thirty yards from the Goose, Beth bent down and dipped the tip of her finger in mud, then covered her hand with the paper. At the door, she wiped her boots on the mat. Glanced in all directions, and once clear touched her muddy finger to the fourth nail indentation on the right side of the doorframe. Barely visible, it was a signal to Jacques Quellet indicating her need for help.

Jacques had secretly worked with the Underground Railroad for years. Beth knew little about his daily routine but knew his reputation. In public circles he was an accomplished, respected lawyer, with a slightly tarnished reputation for showing sympathy to free Blacks and slaves. She imagined he lived in perpetual fear. *Man remains under suspicion, but Ezra says he has friends in high circles that act to protect him.*

Before she walked in, she paused to catch her breath, settle her scrambled thoughts. *Focus, Beth*, she told herself. She went over Jacques's rules one more time. If he was already inside dealing with a client, Jacques would be seated close to the front, and she could signal him with the tilt of her shawl as she headed toward the back tables. If he had not yet arrived, he would see her mark on his way in and find her.

Entering through the long, narrow front tavern, Beth glanced at the workmen seated to her left on stools at the polished bar. To her right, she checked the fashionable couples and businessmen clustered around small round tables. The noise was high, reflecting off the low ceiling, the light dim and yellow, flickering from candles on the tables and whale oil lamps along the walls. No Jacques.

She walked past the bar casually, shawl covering her red hair, hoping not to be recognized. A second rule: If he were in the broad open dining area in the back, and if his top hat extended over the edge of the table, it meant get out, fast.

The hair on the nape of her neck tingled. Beth assumed a serene countenance and a posture of confidence as she walked into the back-dining area, spacious enough to seat a dozen square tables. Surveying the room casually, her eyes did not rest on anyone. No Jacques. Her eyes drooped. Her throat clutched with disappointment. Maybe too early. Maybe out of town. Maybe this, maybe that. *Stop it, Beth. Stop fretting. One task at a time. Sit down.*

Searching for an advantageous place to sit, she was drawn to the roaring fireplace at the rear, which cast a warm glow over the room. Half the gouged walnut tables in that area were empty and comfortably spaced for privacy should he come. She raised her finger for coffee and took a solitary table near the fire where she could spread out her newspaper. The air was warm, comforting, thick with the aroma of tobacco and roasting coffee beans. The warmth wicked the dampness from her shawl and shoulders, eased the chill in her bones.

I hope he's still keeping to his routine of dining at 2:30, she thought. *I may be early.*

The waiter placed a steaming cup of coffee in front of her. After he left, she raced through the shipping news, solicitations and promotions, want ads, slave auctions, missing people, and finally, runaways.

She stopped breathing. Her heart pounded in her ears. *Dear God, there it is.* She pressed her palms flat down on the paper to keep them from shaking. That son-of-a-bitch father.

$1500 IN GOLD. WANTED, INFORMATION ON THE WHERE-ABOUTS OF TWO RUNAWAYS FROM LOUISIANA, A SLAVE GIRL, AGE NINE, ANSWERING TO THE NAME OF MADDIE, SHORT, SLIGHT, WITH COPPER SKIN; AND A YOUNG WHITE WOMAN, AGE 17, ANSWERS TO THE NAME OF CAMILLE, FAIR SKIN, BROWN EYES AND DARK HAIR, MEDIUM HEIGHT. CONTACT THE FAMILY'S AGENT IN ST. LOUIS, MR. LEROY JENKINS OF THE JENKINS DETECTIVE AGENCY. ATTENTION

BOUNTY HUNTERS: IF EITHER IS HARMED, IN ANY MANNER
WHATSOEVER, THE REWARD IS FORFEIT. BONUS FOR EARLY
DELIVERY OF RUNAWAYS TO SAID AGENT.

Her stomach cramped, her body on fire. She could feel her face flare.
She tried to cover her distress with her hand, then turned to stare
directly into the fireplace. *I can blame the flush on the fire.* She fought
tears. But they poured out and wouldn't stop. She took out a handkerchief and dabbed her eyes while her mind raced, again fighting for
control.

$1500 dollars? Jenkins? The Jenkins Agency was the most ruthless
in the city, a law unto itself. She knew of women hauled into their
warehouse for interrogation on the smallest offense, threatened with
torture and rape. Louise Pennyworth, in for a debtor's quarrel, said she
could still hear the screams in her head.

That ad was an act of *treachery*, nothing less. Maddie's own father,
proud author of her freedom paper, now condemning her as a slave in a
public forum. It would give license to every slaver's and bounty hunter's
most sadistic practices. "No harm Whatsoever," the ad said. *Ha. Jenkins
will brutalize these girls—torture them, if necessary—to raise the ransom.*
Anyone willing to pay $1500 will surely pay $2500, and Jenkins will
blackmail the father. That's his game. Maybe the father is too dumb to
know the kind of depraved man he hired.

Beth stole a furtive look about the room. No one was paying the
slightest attention. She carefully turned her back on the patrons and
tore the advertisement from the paper. Then she picked up a pile of
newspapers lying near the fireplace. Arranging them chronologically,
she began to thumb through. The ad had been placed yesterday as well
as today, but not the day before, or the day before that.

So, the hunt had just begun in St. Louis, probably preceded by other
cities coming north up the Mississippi. She was certain a reward this
big would put many desperate people in St. Louis on the lookout. $1500,
fast, easy money, equal to three years' pay for a workman. Word would
spread, gangs would scout. *Ezra, damnit, do you know about this?*

One odd thought crept into her mind that lifted a welcome smile.
She put the coffee cup down, thinking of Camille's father, imagining his

rage when he discovered he'd been deceived by his daughter. *Man has no idea of Camille's strength or cunning. No idea who he's dealing with.*

"Waiting for someone?" said a quiet voice above her.

Startled, Beth spun around, covering the ad as best she could with her forearm. Jacques was smiling down at her, hat in hand, his broad face with his protruding ears a welcome sight. It had been more than a year. He had new gray around his temples but still had that look of vigor. She closed the papers awkwardly.

He raised his voice with an air of formality to clue the room. "May I join you? Miss McCorry, isn't it? My memory is not as sharp as it used to be, but I seldom forget a face. Jacques Quellet. We met at the minister's house after service, I believe. I don't mean to be forward, but can I buy you another cup of coffee?"

She, in turn, extended her gloved hand, feigning surprise and delight for the curious diners. "I'd be honored. So nice to see you again."

He pulled up a chair and sat down in such a way as to shield their conversation from others. "It looks quite safe in here today," he said. "You didn't see me, but after I came in, I searched the room for a good five minutes before I dared come over. What is it? I thought you were out of the Railroad business."

In a lowered voice, she said, "I *am* out of the business, but Ezra brought me two girls he rescued; they're now in my care. I have a freedom paper that I would like you to witness, copy, and notarize. Perhaps three, four, five copies. And I would like you to consider keeping one in your safe . . . I say *consider*, because there is a complication that could pose some danger for you."

He didn't flinch. Beth had always held a powerful sense of trust in Jacques. She had worked with him off and on, but almost never face to face. She watched him once defend a free Black woman petitioning for her children being held as slaves. A most brilliant display that, when the woman won her children, shocked St. Louis. Beth knew only fragments of his secret work for the Underground. He was careful, known publicly to be a sympathizer, but not considered a traitor by the powerful forces in the city.

"Give me the particulars," he said, in a calm, measured voice.

"It's a nine-year-old girl."

Jacques blinked and sat back. She unfolded the ad and put it in front of him. He read it quickly, folded it, and pushed it back. "Hide this. Do you have her paper on you?"

Beth slid it across the table. He put his hand on top of it and raised his voice to talk in pleasantries until she was able to scan the room for listening ears. When all seemed preoccupied, she nodded.

He unfolded and skimmed the paper quickly. "Good. It's dated, signed, sealed with his imprint, and unambiguous in its intent. It will hold up—at least in the courts I can steer the case to." He refolded it, tucked it in his breast pocket, and studied her face. "I'll help you," he said.

"You would do this for me?"

"For you and this girl—if you promise to protect me. You will mention my name to *no one*, not to her, not to friends, relatives. No one, except Ezra. Agreed? Once I begin, I'm in as much danger as you from Jenkins and his brutal mob, and they'd destroy me. They've been itching for an excuse. If I have your word on this, I'll help her."

"Of course." She patted his hand and smiled for the second time that day.

"If you're hiding this girl, keep her whereabouts quiet. Don't trust anyone. I will make multiples—maybe five or six—so you can disperse the copies. Keep them close, but the original not on your person. When the time is right, and you tell me she is safely settled, I'll file one in a friendly jurisdiction. That'll help bring the court to her defense when we need it. I'll leave the copies in the usual place. Tomorrow, early afternoon."

Jacques paused, as if debating whether to finish his thought. He leaned forward and lowered his voice. "But I warn you, Beth. Don't ever let this girl be taken back to Louisiana. Their laws are vindictive. She would be enslaved, freedom paper or not."

"God bless you, Jacques."

"I'll need it," he said. He stood and strode out without looking back.

It was late afternoon when Beth skirted the crowded levee on her way back to the boarding house. The clouds had darkened and the gray mist drew the world in close around her. Her thoughts slid from Jacques to Ezra to the girls, wondering if she should take the time to find him.

What was she going to tell the girls about the bounty on their heads? Perhaps she wouldn't say anything; the vengeance in Camille's family would overwhelm them. Just get them out of town quickly. Secret them onto a boat to Chicago. It would have to be Wednesday, Patterson's boat.

The mist had turned to drizzle that soaked through her shawl and bonnet. She stopped to rearrange her shawl and look around, an old habit. A man fifty yards behind her glanced away when she turned toward him. While others scurried to get out of the rain, he stood idle. The blue cap was familiar. Where had she seen him? Near the Goose? Was he following her?

No matter, she'd give him the slip. Beth went around a corner and hurried down to Tavern Row, into Arnold's Saloon, and out the back door. She trotted through the alleys for a few blocks, then walked back to the streets.

The sky opened up and the rain came harder, turning the world around her from slate to black. It pelted the streets, taunting Beth to get inside. She put one of the old newspapers over her soaked bonnet and shawl. Visibility was near zero when she reached her gate, trying to keep her footing in the slick mud and manure. A bolt of lightning lit the darkness. She lifted her head. Trapped! Two men in her face. Startled, she spun around to run. Blocked. She turned back.

Three tall men in broad hats and long coats, cinched with pistol belts, surrounded her. Each held a rifle. They pressed in closer. They ripped the paper off her head. Fear rose thick and sour in her throat. Her mind scrambled in defense. *Who are these men? Why did they jump me?* Panicked, her knees wobbled. *Don't fall, damnit Beth. You're strong. Fight them.*

Suddenly, the three bent over her, their brims funneling rain onto her head, face, shoulders.

"Stop it!" She screamed loud enough to startle the two in front of her. "Back off! You and you," she said, jabbing her finger at each of them. "Back up, so I can see your faces," she snarled, finding her commanding voice. She sensed the man behind her standing firm, but the two in front took a half step back. She glanced sideways at the street and saw a fourth man, shooing people away.

Beth stared angrily at the one who appeared to be the leader. "What do you think you're doing? Surrounding me. Surprising me. Threatening me. What do you want?" She had seen this man before, knew him by reputation, remembered his evil eyes. She'd watched him scalp a man for interfering with one of his captives. He had done it with horrifying efficiency, a couple of swipes, then tossed the bloody patch at the foot of a woman gaping at him. What would he do if he captured the girls? Torture? Rape? Her mind careened from one terrible thought to another. At least the freedom paper was safe with Jacques. Confidence, she told herself. *Bluff these bastards.*

She sharpened her edge. "I said what do you boys *want?* See that sign! No vacancy! Go on now. Git about your business. And you . . ." She spun around and pushed the man who had been pressing her from behind, then turned quickly back to the leader, slipping her hand into the large pocket in her skirt to find her pistol. She kept it hidden, uncocked, ready if things got out of control.

"You know why we're here," the leader said with a scowl, opening the gate. "We hunt runaway slaves and you got two. We're the law."

"Hogshit. You're just a nasty slave patrol. Work'n outside the law. We got no runaways. Now get off my land!"

"You got two this morning, Little Black one. And a bigger one, older, white enough to pass as a real person. My men saw them go in, never come out. We're here to take them away. They're ours!"

She jumped in front to block his path. "They're long gone. Moved them onto a steamboat north around noon."

"Liar. Saw them go in and my spies been watching. Never come out."

"You think I don't have ways to get people out without being seen. Ever heard of tunnels? How many you think I've got?"

"I'll find out what you got in there. Move!" He slapped her hard. "Lying bitch!" He grabbed her by the throat with one massive hand, lifted her up onto her toes, shook her like a wet blanket, then froze when he heard a pistol cock. On her. He stared at her, saw her skirt pocket bulging. He put her down gently. "Better aim that somewhere else or you're dead," he snarled.

"Or you're dead," she said. Her pistol was aimed to the side but she eased the hammer down silently. "Like I say, nothing here for you. I run a respectable boarding house. Inside you'll find a dozen tough, armed river pilots who don't like to be disturbed. Men who will take your head off if you storm in there, start opening doors. Now get off my land. You have no rights here."

A splash of light as the side door of Cassidy's Tavern opened. Collins, the barkeep, tossed out a bucket of filthy water and looked over at the armed men at Beth's gate. A flush of relief coursed through Beth's veins. An opportunity, she thought.

"Beth? You all right?" Collins shouted. "These men arguing with you . . . Your tenants? Friends of yours? They bothering you?"

"Stay out of this," said the leader in a gruff tone.

"Help!" Beth shouted.

Collins turned, shouted into the tavern "Beth's in trouble!"

"Shut up," said one of the slavers as he jumped to cover Beth's mouth with his hand. She yanked her head away and pushed the barrel of his rifle to the ground. It fired. Collins and the two men behind him peering out ducked.

Beth saw the leader, still tightly holding her arm, flinch at the gunshot. Then as he stared at the bright tavern doorway, she watched his eyes widen, his mouth open, then looking dumbfounded as four men with guns burst out of the saloon. They raised their rifles, staring down the slave patrol. Two more appeared in the doorway. Others pushed from behind. Within seconds there were nine men spreading out. Some advanced cautiously like hunters. Others lifted their rifles from where they stood into firing position. Beth's heart soared. *Bless these men.* Her rapid breathing, the trembling in her hands and eye muscles continued but the tightness gripping her heart eased.

Glancing in all directions, the leader recognized a hopeless situation. He and his men were fully exposed and outgunned. If it came to sudden open fire, they wouldn't last a minute. He put up his hand. "Stand down," he shouted. His two men lowered their weapons, edged away backwards, eyes on those men pointing their rifles.

Halfway across the street, with the tavern rifles still pointed at him, the leader stopped and turned to face Beth. He casually pulled out a cigar. She stared him down. Arms folded, legs spread, head back, cheeks stinging, neck sore from his choke hold, she defied him. She was breathing fast, her throat raw, but her mind was clear. *You're not going to walk in here and terrify me.*

The leader made a slow dramatic display of lighting his cigar, puffing it to get the burn started. Then slowly extended his arm, moving the long, lit match stick toward her fifty feet away. He held it out, pointing it at her face for a good five seconds, then dropped it to the ground and smiled until the mud put it out. *Is he threatening me?*

She knew in her heart it was not over. Not with these men. Not with Jenkins. Not with the bounty this large and likely to grow. They'd be back. *Ezra, you're unaware but I'm waiting to tell you the battle we never expected has been joined. I need you by my side.*

BETH WALKED INTO CASSIDY'S TAVERN WITH AN APPEARANCE OF confidence, thanked the men for helping, and searched the room for people she might hire to guard her place. She'd need help. Thinking of that man's arm reaching toward her, pointing a lit match. Holding it there to intimidate. *He's threatening me with fire*, she realized. *I'm not imagining it.* She felt a hollowness inside without Ezra to help and prayed he would return before the big party at his brother's house. Even if for just an hour. In her mind, she kept seeing those menacing faces jumping out at her in a bolt of lightning.

"Who were those men?" asked Collins, wiping the bar clean. "Nasty bunch. Glad we could drive them off."

"Yes, I can't thank you enough. Just some low-lifes who mixed me up. Collins, I need to hire a few of the men in here for day guard and night watch. Just to make sure that gang doesn't return. Maybe three, four. Good pay, and a quart of your best Irish whiskey, *after* they serve their time. There will be no drinking on the job." Every ear was listening. She turned to the room. "Any takers?"

Three men jumped to their feet. Two looked limber, sober, and physically imposing. She knew these men, but not well. The third stumbled and fell over his chair.

"You two follow me," she said. "Bring your weapons, extras if you have them. And ammunition. I'll set you up. Mike, Pete, isn't it?" They nodded.

She helped the drunken man steady himself enough to sit back in his chair. "You can guard this table."

She looked around the saloon. "Anyone else? Easy work, good pay, gentlemen. Thank you again. And God bless you."

She saw a couple of dozen men at tables scattered about playing cards, gossiping, joking. It was still early. They waved her off. "Maybe later," one said. "Yeah, later," another shouted.

The barkeep called out. "Beth, Seamus will be back in about an hour. I know he'll be interested. I'll send him over."

"Thanks."

She was soaked with rain and sweat, shivering as she walked out. Her heart wouldn't settle. Her mind was racing to plan this out. She would station Mike or Pete in the shadows of the porch in front, the other under the fire escape behind the house, and ask Seamus to circulate in the outer shadows, taking cover in that clutch of woods to the side. He was a hunter, stealthy, and a crack shot. Maybe others would show up later. She'd spend the night standing guard just inside the door to her apartment, knowing the girls were safe inside, waiting for Ezra to show up.

She felt some relief, but her attention was now focused on Camille and Maddie. She had been gone for hours. Hopefully they were still asleep. Catching up after weeks of interrupted sleep in the streets. She remembered that feeling, the dread of someone grabbing her while she slept.

BETH CLIMBED TO THE THIRD FLOOR, OPENED THE DOOR TO HER apartment and tiptoed in. All quiet, dark. She walked straight down the hall into the grand parlor and found Maddie and Camille curled up on the sofa, looking anxious. She could see they'd been crying, at least Maddie. Fortunately, they had comforted themselves with food. Spread out, they had helped themselves to bread and jam and cheese and managed to make coffee from chicory and used grounds.

"Good, you got more to eat," she said. "Have you been awake awhile? Did you hear commotion? I'll try to explain—"

"Beth, my freedom paper?" said Maddie, tearfully. "Camille said you took it. Did you bring it back?"

"Did Camille explain why I took it, to have copies made? I gave it to a good friend to make legal, notarized copies. You'll get it back tomorrow, dear. I'm sorry to frighten you. You'll be much safer out there in the world showing a copy, keeping the original hidden."

"But when? I'm scared without it."

"Tomorrow, Maddie, with four or five copies. Copies will make you safer."

Leaning forward, Camille said, "Beth, by the look on your face . . . you're soaking wet. Neck bruised. Did someone hurt you? Are we in trouble?"

Beth paused, nodded. "Maybe. We don't know yet. I don't want you to leave this apartment, or go downstairs, or talk to anyone. And when you go to bed tonight, I want you to put the bar across that bedroom door."

"What's happening? Tell us."

"Just a precaution. I've hired some strong men with guns to guard the house. I want to be prepared. Ezra will be here later tonight. So, you can sleep soundly."

"I don't think I can sleep anymore," said Maddie. "I'm wearing my lucky dress to protect me."

Beth's mind flashed to the torn ad she had tucked inside her underwear. She could not possibly tell these girls their own father had unleashed a world of bounty hunters. *No harm whatsoever, the ad says. Ha. Just a siren call for the likes of Jenkins.*

She knew Jenkins on sight. Tall, muscular, powerful face with a bull neck, scars, missing a ring finger, slight limp. He wasn't one of the three men who tried to storm her house, come after the girls. But she had no doubt Jenkins was behind this. His men, she realized, had been watching her come out of the Goose, and had probably tailed Ezra from the start. Maybe she should go back to Cassidy's in an hour or two and hire more men. Maybe get these girls out of here. But wouldn't they be expecting that, hoping for that? Of course. Much easier, catching the girls out in the open on the run? *Dear God, I'm at war,* she realized.

She could feel the tears flooding into her eyes, so she got up quickly and excused herself. "Right back," she said, choking on her words. She walked down the inside hall to her bedroom, directly across from that pretty bedroom where the girls had been sleeping. She lay down and took a deep breath to release the knotted up tensions of the day—the crush of the levee, Jacques, being jumped in the dark at her gate, the slavers trying to storm her house, the standoff with the slavers and the men from Cassidy's Tavern, and that dreaded burning match. Her insides tumbled out of fear of these men so determined to get the girls.

She sat up, took a deep breath. *This won't do, Beth. You're stronger than this. You know how to handle fear. How to handle men. Even dangerous men. More importantly, these girls need your strength. Right now, you're all they have.*

She walked back to the parlor, wondering what to make for dinner. It would be nice having their company. Maybe she could put them at ease. Make them a good, hearty soup for a cold, wet evening. Lots of bread, butter, cheese, sautéed apples, some of that homemade jam one of her river pilots' wives sent. *What else? I'll ask them. Just so we don't have to go out.*

Three of us snug in our castle. That's how she thought about her boarding house. Her tenants had the first two floors. She, queen of the castle, had the entire third floor, giving her privacy and security. Dominion. One door into her apartment, and thanks to Hannah's design, a spacious apartment that opened up like a branching tree.

"Girls, what should we make for dinner?" she said, walking into the parlor. Hannah had taken down a wall between two rooms to make this a grand space. "Would you like to help make a soup? Beef or pork? Lots of vegetables to throw in. And how about biscuits? Sautéed apples for dessert? Or cookies? Come out here into the kitchen and take a look. Anything that strikes your fancy."

⇒ 5 ⇐

FAREWELL PARTY

That evening, at the home of Thomas and Martha

T he rain had stopped, and the smothering clouds finally broke, brightening the night sky. Ezra strolled across the moonlit lawn of the family home, then stopped to stare up into the barren arms of the sprawling elm he and Daisy climbed as children. The lower branches, same twists, thicker than ever.

He was nervous, head sweating, his breathing racing along with his quickening heart, and the discomfort of formal dress didn't help. *Stop. Relax*, he told himself, *calm down.* He'd need all his charm and courage to get through this party. Do his duty for Thomas. In this old house filled with fading memories of joy and anger and unbearable pain.

He walked more slowly. Another few minutes and he'd be up onto the broad veranda of his brother's house, a large two-story that had been the family home for four generations. From the yard, the sight jarred him. The house was lit up like a lantern. He pulled at the stiff collar and stretched the back of the long, confining black coat he purchased and had fitted that afternoon.

Strange juxtaposition, returning to the house of sorrow for a festive night. He'd need a few whiskeys to settle into the evening. *Relax*, he reminded himself, *your brother needs you. Martha is waiting.* The guests, he imagined, buzzing like mosquitoes.

He paused before reaching for the door, sensing more people on the other side than he expected, certainly more than he wanted to meet. A few steps to his left, he stared through the parlor window at the large portrait above the fireplace. Stared at his wife, Abigail, Abi. Smiling, young, timeless, standing arm-in-arm with her sister, Martha. Abi's eyes caught the lamplight as if she were still alive, waiting for him to come home. Calling him in. Damn awful.

Everything had happened so fast in this house when he was a young man: courtship, passion, marriage, hope, happiness, childbirth and death. He remembered the helplessness of that last day, his dead infant son bundled at his side, tears falling on Abi, his beloved—unresponsive to his pleading. Her horrible agony.

Twenty-five years ago. But there in oil, she never changed. *If you could see me now, Abi, you wouldn't recognize me.* He wondered if her presence in the house would haunt him tonight.

Walking a few steps to the other side of the door, Ezra peered in at the expansive dining room, teeming with dinner preparations. Two long tables pushed end to end being set by servants in crisp gray uniforms, overseen by women in bright, broad dresses pinched at the waist, tight v-line bodice and low shoulders, latest fashions. They fussed with the condiments, candelabras, silver, napkins, and stemmed glasses up and down the long table. Martha had gone all out.

Glimpsing a young face with a mop of brown curls approaching the window, Ezra's heart softened. He slid into the shadows, his back to the wall, smiling for the first time tonight. His niece of ten, Megan, peered out with both hands cupped to the glass. He eased along the wall up to the edge of the window, then reached over and tapped the glass with one finger in front of her nose. She jumped back, mouth wide, eyes wild. Then her face broke out in laughter. "He's here! Uncle Ezra is here!"

The door flew open and Ezra's older brother, Thomas, large and silhouetted by the light, pulled him in and leaned into his ear.

"Sorry Ezra, I promised you only a few, but when word spread that we were planning a farewell dinner for you and Homer, off to the gold fields, well, there was no stopping the requests, pleas, and outright blackmail to attend. I bowed out of the fracas and Martha managed to hold the barricades at thirty, perhaps thirty-two." His laughter as usual was deep, hearty, then he slapped Ezra on the back. So Thomas.

A manservant took Ezra's rifle, pistol belt, and top hat, while a crowd hovered waiting for introductions. "Who are all these people?" Ezra asked Thomas in a low confidential tone.

"Old friends, family you wouldn't recognize, business acquaintances, and a few skeptics waiting to pounce on you, have your scalp. They think this gold is pure humbug, and our new business venture wicked folly. A trick, they say, on the part of the contemptuous renegade brother to bankrupt the family. It's delicious." He laughed again. Clearly enjoying Ezra's discomfort.

Shaking hands, exchanging greetings with a dozen strangers, Ezra finally saw a familiar face walking up. He kissed his niece Phoebe and met her new husband, Harold. A handsome pair, glowing with love. "I'm sorry you were away at the time," she said. "The wedding was in the backyard last June. Blue sky, a white dress among white blossoms." Ezra was struck by her oval face and lustrous hair. The resemblance to Abigail was stronger than ever.

"Where's Martha? I want to pay my respects," he said to Thomas.

Thomas clapped his hands overhead to clear a path, and steered Ezra through the guests into the dining area, a spacious, bustling room that glowed like sunset from the chandelier. "Where'd she go?" Thomas asked aloud, looking about. Mixed aromas of curry, mint, rosemary, and a hint of roasted lamb filled the air, a covered tureen on a side table added the earthy scent of squash.

Martha emerged from the kitchen with a server carrying a plate of crayfish. When Ezra smiled and caught her eye, her face flushed into radiance. So much like her younger sister, Abi. She fluffed the back of her hair while weaving her way among daughters, nieces, neighbors, and women he didn't recognize.

She embraced him heartily, kissed him. "This is all for you, Ezra, you and our precious Homer. So that you two might take our love with you to California. He by ship with the grace of God, and you by steamboat, wagon train and grit. You leave Friday?"

"Saturday. I found a spacious cabin on the *Andrew Jackson*, thanks to one of Beth's tenants, all the way up the Missouri River to our trailhead at the mouth of the Platte River."

"I truly hoped you were home to settle, Ezra. Setting up this business venture with Thomas and Homer is a fine thing, but it's not enough. You know that, as well as I. You must start again, establish your own family and rejoin ours. Perhaps after you make your fortune you'll return to St. Louis and live close by. Or better yet, here in the house again as you and Abi once did, may God rest her soul."

"Couldn't even if I tried."

"Ezra, there are two available women here that I want you to meet . . . I know, I know, I shouldn't meddle. Promise me one thing— no fighting tonight with Thomas. Just let it lie. Promise?"

He hadn't thought to bring up slavery tonight, but a few whiskeys and a few barbs and his temper might take over. "Agreed. And for your part, let's not dwell on marriage."

Thomas pulled Ezra's arm. "Come, brother, I want you to meet our guests. You and Martha can catch up later. I'm sure she's still trying to marry you off. First to her younger sister, and now to anybody else that will have you. A diminishing bevy I assure you, given your prospects and weathered appearance." Martha swatted his shoulder and swore in his ear.

Steering Ezra into the parlor, over to a corner, Thomas turned serious. "Ezra, two things. First, we have at least five potential investors here tonight: Dubois, Hennessy, Johannson, Toussaint, who I think you know, and Wagner. Speak to them if you can.

"Second, Homer. He hasn't slept in days. He's never been to sea before, and the danger is weighing on him. Talk to him. Calm him, if you can. I'd appreciate it. He trusts you. He lost two good friends last year. They disappeared in a Caribbean storm. He fears the same."

A tall, young, handsome man with coal black hair, dark eyes, and angular features waved at Ezra from across the room, then worked his way over. Ezra had always regarded Homer, even as a boy, as a confident, fast-talking, shrewd lad, but judging by his expression he seemed off his stride tonight.

"I don't know if father told you," said Homer, "but I must get to New Orleans fast to renegotiate. I leave tomorrow. The ship owners now claim our supplies will take up more space than we contracted for, over half the entire ship."

There was an unusual hesitancy about Homer. It wasn't clear whether it was the voyage or the negotiations. "You'll do well, I have no doubt. You have a head for business and trading," said Ezra. "The owners just want to squeeze a few hundred dollars more if they can. Give it to them in exchange for more secure stowage. Make sure the captain lashes everything down tight and keeps the crew from selling our goods off in every port."

"Good point," said Homer, then looked away.

Ezra put his hand on his nephew's shoulder. He was almost as tall as Ezra, equally slender, but his hands were soft, not yet hardened by arduous work.

"And don't worry about the voyage. In two weeks, you'll learn to ride the swells, hold your own on the rigging. You'll relax, grow to respect the power of the sea, become as superstitious as the rest. And enjoy the blur of evening rum."

Homer nodded with a blank face. "I can never tell when you're joking."

Ezra threw in the sweetener. "The only thing you'll really have to worry about are the women. Brazil, Argentina, Chile, and Panama, each more wonderful than the last."

Homer's face brightened.

"If you have anything left in you by the time you get to San Francisco, you'll be able to concentrate firmly on business. There are no women in San Francisco."

"None?" Homer's face fell.

"I'm toying with you. Your father tells me you've become a real ladies' man. Is that true? You have the looks and presence."

"But no women?"

"A small minority. Can be a hard place for women. Some in hiding from aggressive men in the street, others walk around in disguise. A few travel with protectors. But of course, always the brazen women of the night, most working out of the gambling houses, but be careful."

Homer stared at Ezra with new gravity. He no longer seemed at a party. "My father knows so very little about me. I want to strike out on my own. Out from under his yoke. This idea of yours, Uncle Ezra, to supply gold miners half a continent away from Father has been a Godsend for me. Truly. I want to thank you."

He patted Homer on the shoulder. "No need. I'll be glad to have your partnership out there. We'll meet again in San Francisco in six months, eight months."

Poor Homer, he's got that look of money about him, Ezra thought. *If he gets off the boat in San Francisco and is not careful, he'll be fleeced within two days.*

"One bit of advice, lad. When you arrive, get off the ship in workman's clothing if you can. Dress down. There are bandits lurking at the wharf looking for a wealthy mark."

Homer smiled, nodded, pulled his tailored lapel. "Not like this getup, huh?"

"Or mine," said Ezra, laughing. "So uncomfortable."

Martha dinged a musical chime and summoned everyone for dinner. Megan ran and grabbed Ezra's arm. He escorted her into the dining room.

The place card had Ezra seated in the middle of the long table, between the oldest and the youngest. Megan to his right and Great Aunt Ester, eighty-nine, the family matriarch, to his left. She had come to St. Louis when it was a small French trading center. Everyone in the family knew she understood more than she let on, and she ran things without anyone knowing exactly how.

Ezra had been fond of Aunt Ester since childhood, especially after she raked Ezra's parents over the coals for selling Daisy, his best friend, the girl he loved, that in fact everyone in the household loved, into field slavery. "For no good reason," Aunt Ester screamed at his parents. "Because the boy loved her? Shame on you two."

Ester found Ezra hiding in the barn that day, shivering like a wounded dog, crying, and held him. "You did nothing wrong. You loved her. Pure as snow. Your parents were fearful, and fearful people do evil things. When you're older, go find Daisy. I'll give you the money to buy her free."

This memory came over Ezra in a flash the moment Aunt Ester took his hand at the table. "That woman, Beth, the one you hide from the family, maybe you should open your heart to her before you leave. I like her. I know more about her than you think I do."

He didn't want to ask her what she knew, not here at the table. Could she possibly know about Beth's work on the Underground? If so, she was keeping it secret.

In his mind, he saw Beth in her parlor talking to Camille and Maddie in a reassuring way. But suddenly he felt a sharp foreboding like the jab of a thorn. He had a premonition of something dark, threatening but without form. He pushed the fear away as nonsense. He needed to concentrate.

Clearing his throat, Thomas, at the head of table, stood and raised his glass to silence the room. He was a man of above average height, heavyset with graying hair and sparkling eyes that contrasted with his pasty complexion, the result of years in dim shops and warehouses.

"Please make yourselves comfortable. I want to toast my dear son, Homer, and my prodigal brother. As you know, Ezra has rejoined the family business after a quarter century in the wild. Tomorrow, we begin. We send Homer with a shipload of supplies around the horn to San Francisco—shirts, pants, boots, picks, shovels, and tents—everything an enterprising miner needs. Ezra takes his last overland trip with a wagon train of families—that's right *families*—then meets up with Homer in California, completing the link in our new trade route. I fill the supply lines from here. Homer oversees warehousing in San Francisco. And Ezra moves the goods directly into the gold fields for sale. So, please, raise your glasses. To Homer and Ezra. Godspeed in your journey. May you enjoy health and good fortune in California."

Thomas sat and the soup was served up and down the table. Squash with carrots and a diced root Ezra didn't recognize, ginger, and something biting, perhaps lime. The food here is becoming more complex, he realized, with so many new ingredients coming upriver from the international markets in New Orleans.

After the soup bowls were picked up, servants brought out rich platters of vegetables, duck, lamb, and crayfish, followed by steamed sweet potatoes, pickled beets, minted curry, cranberry sauce, and thin slices of veal soaked in Bordeaux sauce. Large platters of mixed food were place in the middle within easy reach. Wine glasses were refilled. The table turned alive with laughter, light, cordial discussion of the food, fashion, family, politics, business, and the gold strike

They ate their fill in the soft candlelight and finally slowed down, sitting back, resting their utensils. Martha was congratulated for the superb meal. She smiled, passed the praise to the staff, then as the eating faded, invited the chef and the entire kitchen staff to come out and be acknowledged. The entire table applauded them while their faces beamed.

Catching Ezra's eye, Thomas indicated that it was time to start. He stood, tinked his glass to quiet the table. "As you know, there is no conversation in St. Louis these days without Gold-the-Almighty creeping in. And here we are tonight celebrating the start of a new venture to gold country. Yet skepticism lingers about California. I've heard the talk. There was gold in Los Angeles six, seven years ago, and it came to nothing. President Polk recently announced that the gold strike in California was real. But what does he know? He'll be out of office in a few weeks.

"Everyone wants to believe these tales of a bonanza, but we've seen these stampedes before. Humbugs created by land speculators and their newspaper allies. So, I've asked my brother who has been there to say a few words. Ezra, please tell these good people what you've seen with your own eyes. Is this gold strike real? And most importantly, can it last beyond the season?"

Ezra searched their expectant faces. For the moment, they stopped whispering and were staring at him, some smiling, some leaning forward, a few frowning. The servants walked up and down the table refilling wine glasses. Ezra tugged at his tight collar. He didn't want to be selling these people a dream of easy riches. In fact, it's damn hard work panning for gold. He didn't have to lie, he knew, just spin the fantasy up a bit. A bit of plain old huckstering so Thomas can line up a few more investors. *Damn it, it was your idea, Ezra, to take the supplies directly to the miners,* he thought, *so play your part tonight: pitchman.*

He took a deep breath. "I won't stand if you don't mind. What I tell you is from my own personal experience. I've been in California eight times in the last twenty years." He saw a few gasps. His niece Phoebe, directly across the table put her hand to her mouth in dismay.

"I knew the place once as a sleepy backwater of Mexico. A year ago, that world was shattered, overtaken. Right now, there is a gold fever in California that would put our own industrious St. Louis to shame. It's business, business, everywhere, all the time. Soldiers are abandoning their forts. Merchants are closing their shops. Everyone running from towns for the gold fields. The word of a gold strike was first carried down the western trace of South America by ship, and experienced miners started coming up from Peru, Ecuador, Chile. Then word spread to the east coast of our country and Europe. Now the novice miners are coming from everywhere. And the rush, to tell you the truth, has just begun.

"If you want to get a taste of this, go down to the levee one morning and take a ten-minute walk through the chaos as men line up for the steamboats to take them to the trailheads.

"San Francisco, two years ago a town of eight hundred now has tens of thousands and the ships unload more every day. There are no rules. No police force. Laws are up in the air, confused, not exactly Mexican, not federal, not state—there is no state and there is no territorial recognition yet. Nothing's fixed. Everyone's new, starting over." He saw some eyes widening, some leaning forward.

"What do you mean by starting over?" asked one elegantly tailored woman sitting near Martha.

Ezra paused. Took a sip of wine.

"I mean step into anything that interests you. Gamblers become dentists by putting out a sign, and dentists become gamblers by putting on a coat. No questions asked. Ground lots in San Francisco are sold and resold in a day, sometimes hours. The place thrives on a mania of gold dust and gambling, afraid it will all end in a single bad bet.

"So will it?" asked Mark Wagner. How long can it possibly last? I have my doubts."

"Good question, Mark, but my guess is you'll be asking the same question in five years. The gold fields are bigger than your imagination, spread out over hundreds of miles, in every river and stream flowing down out of the Sierra mountains. And in dry beds that used to be streams.

"My partner and I have been filling our saddlebags with gold for years from the river banks. Just enough for expenses, not enough to start a run. We've kept our mouths shut. We knew word would come out sooner or later, and the rush would begin. But we preferred later. Liked our own little secret gold streams up in the foothills.

"So, you're saying this gold rush is real? And will last?" asked Svet Johannson

"Yes. Very real. And will it last? Yes, most certainly." He saw two people shake their heads and brush his comment away. "Why do I say that? Because there is more gold there, Svet, than you can grasp. I've explored these rivers and streams and I can tell you how I think it works. The gold washes down in tiny flakes we call *dust*, pulled from the granite and quartz formations in the high mountains. It comes fast and then where the crashing water suddenly slows down and spreads out in the foothills, the heavy gold flakes have a chance to settle. Down into the streambeds. Down into the gravel. Down between the rocks, under the boulders, burrowing like gophers."

Ezra paused, took a sip of wine, and others did as well.

"Keep going," one man said.

"Excuse me, Mr. Adams, please give me a realistic sense of scale," said Victor Toussaint, lighting a cigar. "How big are these fields? In total if you can?"

"We don't know yet how extensive the fields are. Miners are still spreading out, discovering new loads. But the band of foothills where the gold is abundant is perhaps twenty to thirty miles wide and runs north-south for a few hundred miles. Eventually, maybe three hundred miles. So, for scale, think of this. Imagine a thirty-mile-wide ribbon of gold-bearing lands that would stretch from here, St. Louis, to Chicago."

A simultaneous gasp. "What! From here to Chicago? Amazing . . . Hard to take in." They shouted their excitement side-to-side and across the table.

"No, just fairy tales. All lies," shouted one man.

"Oh my God," said Homer. "Uncle, I had no idea."

"Okay. Calm down, everyone. I'm not exaggerating. That's why," said Ezra, "even with the tens of thousands of miners already there, and likely another hundred thousand miners on their way as we speak by ship and wagon train, the gold will last beyond this summer. And the next summer and the summer after that. On and on. How long can it last with such feverish activity? We don't know."

Ezra put up his hand to get their attention. "But, but . . . remember one thing," he said, pausing, looking up and down the table. "Something you don't hear about. Yet. All this is still *surface mining*, stuff you pan from streambeds or dig from shallow banks. Soon the truly experienced miners will start digging tunnels and shafts into the high mountains looking for the gold veins embedded in the rocks." He saw a couple of doubtful faces that he then spoke to directly.

"So, I put it to you, how long can it last? I'm convinced the gold will last long enough for people to settle—remember the climate out there is mild—start farming, building towns and cities, putting their fortune to work. Before we know it, create laws, then probably petition Congress to become a state."

Several people laughed out loud and wagged their hands to dismiss the thought.

"Bah. That's a bit too far," said Toussaint. "What kind of state would that be? A gold state?"

"I'll stop here and answer your questions as best I can," said Ezra. The table sat quietly for a moment, stunned. Ezra could see them trying to absorb all they had heard, whispering to each other. Did they believe him? Enough heads were nodding to make him think they did, but a few scowled.

A woman opened her mouth to speak but she was cut off by Reynolds, a second cousin—a tall, thin man with a gray beard—who cleared his throat loudly at the far end of the table. Everyone turned. "Thomas, I speak for many when I advise you to be careful. You may well be sending your eldest son on a fool's errand and putting your business and the welfare of your family at great risk on the word of this fancy-free, savage brother of yours. Sorry, children, Aunt Ester, but I must speak my mind. Where has this errant brother been for twenty-five years? Panning gold? Oh, please! Don't be taken in by this scheming, this horseshit of his. He's not panning gold, he's panning our pockets." Ezra smiled at the mixed laughter and jabs.

Martha flushed and Thomas rose again to respond, but Aunt Ester would have none of it. She put her hand out to make Thomas sit, then lifted it high in the air, paused for effect, than smacked it hard on the table like a tyrant, loud enough to rattle the plates. Ezra saw several women gasp.

Ester leaned forward, staring at the man, her eyes burning. "Now listen to me, Reynolds. Our family, your family, came here when this was nothing but a trading post. If we had your spirit of adventure, we would still be in Philadelphia or rotting in debtors' prison in Liverpool. So none of your nanny pants. If these boys have the gumption to start a business venture in gold country, let them. My blessings abound to them." She leaned back and patted Ezra's hand and said to the table, "I like my savage man."

The floodgates opened. The guests regaled each other with the latest stories and rumors—fairies that eat gold then turn into dust. A Mexican plot to take back the land. Gold-laden ships so heavy they sink two miles out to sea. Then repeated the fables up and down the long table. They pitched the wildest ones to Ezra to verify or deny.

Ezra stayed out of the arguments but reached into his coat pocket and pulled out a large deerskin pouch tied carefully at the top.

"This is gold dust," he said.

Conversation stopped dead. He lifted a small line of gold flakes with his fingers and let them cascade sparkling in the light back into the pouch. "From the American River. I'm going to pass the pouch around, and I want each of you to take a pinch or two and put it next to your plate. You can eat the dust; some believe it cures gout. Or just stir it around. In California, this pinch will buy you a whiskey, maybe an apple or two, a potato. Take the pinch home with you."

Every eye followed the bag of gold as it made its way around the table. Most took two pinches and deposited the gold in a small conical pile on the tablecloth beside their plate. They stared at it, then pinched it back up, rubbed it between their fingers, and watched it fall, glittering in the candlelight. It spread out and had to be swept carefully with a finger back into a pile high enough to pinch up again. Conversation dissolved into small knots of side-by-side delight.

Ezra had reckoned nothing would convince them more than the touch and feel of gold itself. The bag went around a second time.

He sat back and looked about at the elaborate dress, the warm and painted faces. Like an exotic tribe, but a tribe rigidly bound, feasting at a square table in a square room in a square house on a square street. Someone in the Ioway tribe, or maybe it was Mandan, had stumped him once when he asked Ezra at the fire circle why the white tribes worshipped squares instead of circles. The tribe laughed and the men and women arranged themselves into a square, laughed even louder, and moved back into the social comfort of their circle.

People continued to nibble and talk and idly play with their gold piles. Careful to wipe their hands before pinching. The pouch made a third round. Reynolds's wife told him to eat some gold to sweeten his sour mood. She pressed it to his lips and tongue, and it glittered on his teeth.

The dinner plates were removed, then dessert brought in: a compote of canned peaches and plums, and sweet cake with whipped cream and cranberry sauce.

It was time for the *coup de grâce*. Ezra reached into his pocket and pulled out a polished gold nugget the size of a goose egg. He held it aloft between his fingers and turned it to catch the light. The room gasped. Elsa Johannson whooped. "Gold is a soft metal that likes to clump like this," said Ezra.

He handed the nugget across the table to his niece Phoebe. "This is your wedding present, darling. Sorry I wasn't there." Her face brightened. Damned if she didn't have Abi's smile.

Phoebe cupped the heavy nugget in both hands while her husband, Harold, supported her hands and stroked it. She walked down to the end of the table to show her mother, and then to the other end to show her father, who started passing it around. One by one the guests studied its knobbed surface. Felt it. Stroked it. Bounced the heavy weight in their hands. Following the nugget, Phoebe walked behind the guests, enjoying their sighs when they first held it, looking up at her with their eyes shining. They fingered the surface knobs and dips before they passed it on. Carefully, hand to hand, as if it were a precious egg that might break and spill its golden yolk.

Thomas rose from his chair, clinked his glass, and waved a piece of paper. "I have in my hand further testament to the abundance of gold and life in the camps. A simple letter, written by a young soldier to the family of a runaway boy now working for me in our warehouse. This tall gangling thirteen-year-old named James is looking for a wagon train to California to find his brother, this soldier. Ezra, I think you should consider hiring the boy for your journey. Strong, hardworking, smart. And real talent working with animals. Be a valuable teamster."

"No thank you, Thomas. I'll have enough problems guiding eighteen families across the continent."

Thomas unfolded the soiled piece of paper and began.

Dear Ma, Pa, Grandma, William, Evan, James and Jess,

July 3, 1848. My hands are near frozen and cut with gravel from the days digging at Sutter's Creek, a camp of eight of us here on the western slope of the Sierra Nevada, so I can barely hold a pen no more. I can't sleep. Pulled near a thousand dollars in gold from a deep hole under a boulder that we pushed out of its socket this afternoon. We'll go back for the rest tomorrow. We are too excited to sleep, and too tired to get up. Everyone's deserting the army, navy, ships, and towns and finding their way up here. There seems to be gold in every stream, and even in the dry diggings where the water used to run. The Indians look at us like we're crazy and we are. I was with the army until everyone just took off for the gold, and I up and quit too. I'm sorry Ma, I been sinning as much as most, mostly swearing, and I drink every night to take off the chill and give my body some peace. I ache from picking and shoveling and panning from sunup to sundown, except on the Sabbath when we sing the Praises and hear the Word, before we start gambling. I like to gamble but I lose and I know it's a sin. I've seen too many men lose everything and who don't care cause there is always more gold. My clothes are falling apart. This is not what I intended to write, but it's my only piece of paper and I can't start over, and the post is going out at sunrise. Pa, I hope you will come out and join me. There's a fortune here. Not any place anyone would want to live. We all just want to go home. Tomorrow is the Fourth of July, and we are going to raise the roof. Shoot out the stars. I figure this letter might get to you by Christmas. May God watch over all of you. Keep you in Health and on the path to Providence. I hope to see one or two of you on the American river come this time next year. Just ask for the richest man in California.

Your son, Joshua Turner

Thomas pointed at Ezra. "Did this soldier, this Joshua Turner, capture it?"

"He did. Tough life in the riverbeds panning for gold. Feet freezing, hands raw and bloody, bedroll on the rocks. Awful food. Night and day a fever-driven madness for gold."

Thomas waved the letter overhead. "Did you hear what the soldier said? *'My clothes are falling apart!'* Just as sure, his leather boots must be rotting in the streambeds. Gloves worn through at the finger tips. Pick handle ready to break. Pan rusting away! This man needs supplies. *All* these miners need supplies, and they pay in gold. And I say, 'Hold on boys, we're on our way!'" A cheer went up around the table. Even Reynolds cheered.

Thomas, the ever-affable salesman, Ezra thought. He shook his head in wonder at his brother. That letter was a bit of genius to bring the hard-knock realities of the gold camps into the minds of this comfortable, cushioned crowd. All to open their wallets and take a gamble on the trade business. *Hell, maybe he and I aren't so different after all,* Ezra thought. *It was me that brought out the gold dust. Held up the grand nugget for a carnival display.*

Glad Beth isn't here to see this. Me showboating. Yet here I am, Beth, amid all this tomfoolery and I can't stop thinking about you. My dearest friend. I'm astounded at this one thought that pounds in my head—I can't bear to leave you. I want you beside me, Beth. Right now, here. Close enough to smell and touch and yet I never do take that step, do I?

The party grew louder with dessert, wine, and brandy.

He knew he should stop drinking. He was becoming a sentimental old fool like the rest of this maudlin crowd. Now on their feet, hugging and patting and cheek pecking and dripping laughter all over each other like honey.

With Aunt Ester and Megan gone, Ezra, still at the table, stretched out his elbows, took off his coat. His face flushed. The rich food and good alcohol were turning his thoughts warm and fluid. He missed this feeling of family. Imagined what life would have been like with Abi and children. A completely different life, one totally unaware of the life he did have. Isn't that the strangest thing? This life and death and death afresh come life anew.

Okay, no more alcohol for you, he thought.

His warm floating thoughts turned again to Beth in her parlor with Camille and Maddie. He hoped they were getting on well, but something else was beginning to crowd his thoughts. Was it guilt or fear or both? The rescue had been such a hasty decision, actually no decision, just compulsion on his part and then in panic the rush to Beth. The imposition, the burden he placed on her shoulders. Did he leave her in danger tonight? If there was a large bounty, he realized, he may well have. Preparing for tonight, he'd been careless. Hadn't taken the time to check the newspaper section on runaways.

Bounty? First it was a thought, then a jangle of discordant thoughts, flashes of Beth, then a prickle of fear at the back of his neck.

That premonition again. It quickly spread through his body like fever. Sweating, he yanked off his stiff collar. Tried to push the foreboding away. But it persisted, something shapeless stalking her. He drank water to swallow, loosen his throat, counter the alcohol. Then downed two more glasses of water. The sweat dripping from his forehead drew attention.

In his mind, he reverted to his familiar world. Trust your senses, Old Bill had taught him in the wild. Stay alert to your instincts, all of them no matter how subtle, trivial they seem, wherever you are, or you'll die. Bill could close his eyes, smell and pick the breath of a stalking cat out of a passing breeze. His instincts had saved Ezra several times.

Something was wrong. The premonition grew stronger. *Stop it, Ezra, you know they're fine, comfortable, protected. Just enjoy yourself.*

"*No, they're not fine!*" he said aloud. Two women turned, stared.

Panic ran up his back. His hands, arms were now trembling, heart pounding. He had to clear his head. He grabbed nearby glasses of water off the table and chugged. *I have to leave. Now! Faster, damnit. Go.*

Ezra gave hurried apologies to Martha and Thomas, Homer, Phoebe, trying to suppress his fears. But his words came out rushed, garbled and his family seemed to read him but held back. Only Martha reached up and took his face in her hands, trying to steady him. "Are you ill? Something you ate?"

"No. Thank you for tonight." He shook off people gathering around, wanting to ask questions. Gave them an incomplete goodbye, then picked up his rifle and pistol belt and raced out the front door without his top hat.

He ran through the yard into the street and kept going. Running off the alcohol. Running with fear, stoking a furnace of anger at the dark force, at whatever, whomever was threatening them. *Help me, God. Fly me there. Sober me. Give me strength.*

⯈ 6 ⯇

ARSON ATTACK

That night at Beth's place

The boarding house was dark, the neighborhood asleep. Mike tugged his coat against the chill. He had been guarding Beth's place for hours, concealed in the deep shadows of the porch, sitting on a hardback chair, his rifle propped against his knees. His friend, Pete, was guarding the back of the house, and Seamus, the hunter, was circling the wooded area like a cat, undetectable even to Mike's trained ear. Silence hung over the deserted streets except for a few barking dogs.

Sudden light bloomed when the front doors to Cassidy's Tavern swung open, and out poured a clutch of drunks at closing time. Loud and morose, the men shouted goodnight and stumbled down the road.

Mike couldn't see them through the trees but listened as their voices faded.

Among the last to leave were two men carrying a bottle of whiskey and some shot glasses. Joad, leader of the arson squad, and Finn, one of his henchmen with the gift of gab, had spent the last three hours in the saloon, learning names and getting the lay of the land—the basic floor-plan of Beth's boarding house, the exits, her location, and how it was being guarded tonight, and by whom.

Joad and Finn retrieved their weapons stashed in the bushes and signaled to a third, Jethro, who came out of hiding and crossed the street. They whispered, pointed, and Jethro, a hired killer who preferred a long knife to guns, slipped into the woods in the side yard to find Seamus.

Mike was on his feet, watching from the shadows, as Joad and Finn, feigning drunkenness, approached the boarding house. They opened the front gate, slurred a few drunken bars of an Irish ballad, staggered in, and stopped short of the front porch, swinging the bottle overhead. "Hey, Mike, brought you a whiskey." Silence. They laughed it up. "O'Donnell and Claiborne sent us with this bottle," said Joad, slurring his words. *"Jus fa youz and Pete and Seamus."* Finn fell to his knees on the ground laughing and snorting in pretend stupor.

Mike emerged from the shadows and walked down the steps, rifle in hand, smiling. Joad handed him a glass of whiskey. As Mike downed the first glass, Finn rose, clubbed him hard from behind. They bound and gagged Mike and dragged him into the tall weeds to the side of the front yard. Still breathing.

Joad and Finn moved to the back, lured Pete out with the same refrain—drunken laughter, familiar names from the tavern, and amber whiskey that glowed in the torchlight. They cracked his skull, bound and gagged him, and threw him into the brush, bleeding. Not dead but out cold.

Out of the wooded shadows, startling the two attackers, Jethro emerged with a bloody knife. "Got'm. Could feel him coming. Took him from behind. Quick and clean. Seamus never heard me, never saw me."

"Here's your money," said Joad. "You can go or stay if you want to make some more money helping us smoke them out."

"Not me. You got enough men and I hate fire," said Jethro.

FOUR MORE SLAVERS BROUGHT A WAGON UP THE ALLEY BEHIND Beth's. The men quickly unloaded buckets of camphene, whale oil, rags, and wet combustibles to generate smoke.

At Joad's command, they sealed off Beth's back door and side exit with chains and placed buckets of accelerants on both sides of the house.

"We'll start right there," said Joad, pointing to the large window of the first-floor dining room at the back of the house. "Nice and slow, boys, lots of smoke to start a stampede. Left them only two ways out where we'll be await'n."

They broke open the window and tossed a pile of greasy rags soaked with camphene into the spacious room. Then slowly lowered their fire-bomb to the dining room floor and pushed it toward the far wall with a long pole, while carefully holding on to the long fuse. "Don't drop it," said Joad, "and don't light that fuse until I give the word. Now ease in that whale oil and give it time to spread." They poured in five gallons of whale oil and watched it run across the floorboards.

"We'll smoke'm out before we torch the house. Get ready. Tenants will start flying out. In all the confusion just make sure you grab both girls, the older near-grown white one and the small, younger Black one. I want'm bound and gagged, but not hurt. Hear me? *Not hurt!* Them's Jenkins's orders if you want to get paid." Joad stopped and looked them in the eye. "Jenkins wants them for sale. Then we'd be free to kill the red bitch. But leave her for me. I want to do it. Understood?" The men nodded, put on their strange orange bandanas to be recognized in the smoke, and went to work.

The fire started softly, with flames running along the floorboards, chasing the whale oil. The rags smoldered and their smoke billowed along the ceiling. The muffled explosion of the firebomb coated the room in burning hog-fat and ethyl alcohol. For an instant, the dining room flared like a beacon into the back alley. Then the fire settled down and went to work eating the house from the inside. Smoke curled and climbed the walls, staircase, and vents like serpents. The slavers positioned themselves, two at the front door, two at the fire escape in the back, and two roaming the sides.

A SHOUT STARTLED BETH AWAKE. SHE SAT BOLT UPRIGHT IN HER chair and felt the rifle slip from her lap onto the floor. She heard crashing sounds and yelling from the second floor. Someone screamed, "Fire!"

She picked up her rifle and went to the front door of her apartment, listening, pressing her palm against the wood to feel for heat. Heard no sound on the landing. *Are we under attack?* she wondered. The door was still cool, but wisps of smoke curled under the bottom, burning her eyes. She slid the oak bar aside, ducked down low to avoid getting shot, then undid the latch and swung the door open, rifle up. She stared into the dark. Nobody.

She stepped out onto the landing. Down below, through the smoke, an orange glow pulsed from the far end of the second-floor hallway. She took a few steps down the stairs, covering her nose with her bandana. A tenant ran out onto the second-floor landing with an armful of possessions.

She fired her rifle into the ceiling. "Everybody out!" she yelled. "Take someone with you!" Plaster rained down, dust mixing with the smoke.

The girls. Instant fear jolted her heart and set her in motion. She slammed her door shut, barred it, picked up her lantern, and started down the inner hall toward their bedroom through a thick haze lit by a shimmer off the window in the back. She pounded on the bedroom door with the butt of her rifle. It was barred from the inside as she had directed. "Wake up!" she screamed. "Camille! Maddie! Now! Wake up!"

Nothing. Smoke seeped up through the cracks in the floor and slid like fog under the bedroom door. *Unconscious?* The thought terrified her. How could she get them out? Her chest tightened, her hands shook as she pounded again with the butt of her rifle and kicked and hollered. The door shuddered but held.

She heard shouting from down below, doors slamming, feet moving fast along the hallway, and furniture being roughhoused aside. But not a sound from inside the room. She screamed, pounded, waited. Then ran for the fire axe in the closet.

Just before she plunged the axe into the door, she heard loud coughing and a raspy voice. "Are the slavers out there?"

Thank God. "No, open up," she shouted.

Camille swung open the door. She had pulled the front of her dress over her nose and mouth, eyes red and running, blinking in pain. "What's burning?"

"The slavers are trying to burn us out." Beth yanked the bedsheet, took out her knife and cut it into wide strips. "Wet two of these in the basin, tie them around your mouth and nose. Here, let me help you, Maddie. That's it, good and tight. Then get your boots on." Fortunately, she had told them to go to bed with their clothes on.

"Are they going to capture us?" Maddie asked.

"No. We're smarter than they are. Now take these extra strips, wet them in the copper tub or basins in the kitchen and parlor. We'll need them to breathe. Camille, bring that pistol I gave you. Yours too, Maddie."

Camille was frantically searching the side table, bed, dresser, her pockets. "The freedom paper," she cried.

"You gave it to me, remember? To be copied. It's safe. Now, come with me and wait for me in my parlor, but stay away from that window that looks out onto the fire escape. I'm going to go check to see if it's safe for us to go down, or whether it's now a trap."

She glanced out the window at the third-floor fire escape landing and what she could see of the stairs. Good. No one had climbed up. Nothing but smoke. She unbarred and opened the back door and edged out onto the landing. The escape itself was intact, felt solid under her feet. No sign of anyone. But down below, a strange yellow-orange light flared from the first-floor dining room and smoke billowed up the exterior wall. She stepped cautiously, testing. No heat rising. She bounced. It felt sturdy so it must still be solid down below.

The stairs leading down to the second-floor landing of the fire escape were obscured in smoke, but not yet touched by fire. Good, she thought. She and the girls might still be able to get down two flights and jump to the ground if needed.

"Pete, you there?" she called from the third-floor landing. The fire was making hearing difficult. There was no response. She lifted her head and shouted to the neighborhood. "Wake up! Fire!" It was mostly dark everywhere she looked. She bent over coughing. Smoke was billowing up the side of the house near the escape.

Suddenly, a man wearing an orange bandana stepped into the dim light on the ground, moving backward, trying to get a better angle to see her. "Beth, that you?" He swung his arm, motioning for her to come down. He held a rifle loosely at his side.

"Pete? Seamus? Who's that?"

"Come on while you can. Hurry. Yeah, Seamus."

That didn't sound right but she moved cautiously to the top of the stairs, trying to see her way clear. She put both hands on her rifle in case she needed to aim. "Move back where I can see you," she shouted.

She heard the girls behind her, suddenly step onto the landing. She swatted at them to stay inside the parlor, but they froze.

The man walked backwards, further into the yard for a better vantage. "Don't worry. We caught'm what did this to ya! Shot three. Chased off the rest. I can't see you. Bring those girls. Hurry up."

A shot of adrenaline shot up her spine. How did he know she had girls? He couldn't see them from that angle, and she hadn't told Mike or Pete or Seamus. She took a few tentative steps down the stairs toward the second landing. Another man came into view, startling her. "Who's that?" she yelled.

"Seamus—Pete. No time, Beth. Bring everyone out," the man yelled. Strangely, he was also wearing an orange bandana. Something was off.

She reached the second story landing. The stairs to the ground were completely obscured in smoke, but not on fire. One of men was standing on the stairs, a faint outline. He moved; the boards squeaked. "Come on, damnit. Let me help you," he shouted.

She eased back and glanced up to see the girls walking down toward her. She waved them back frantically. They stopped, then instinctively squatted down, Camille in front, Maddie behind.

The man on the ground yelled, "Come on, staircase is burning. Bring them two with you. That's right." A lie, the staircase was too dark to be burning. She pulled back, lowered herself.

The man on the stairs had taken a few more cautious steps, then stopped, and now was moving more slowly upward. She sensed he was in a crouch, hunting. She dropped to her knees, twisted around, and pushed the air with her hand toward the girls. *Go back*, she mouthed the words.

The first thing that appeared over the edge of the landing was the tip of a rifle, straight up but starting to drop down toward her. Then the top of a hat. She flattened herself, lying prone on the landing, waiting. "Can't see you," he said. "Ain't no good you get'n burned to biscuit."

He sprang like a panther onto the landing with his rifle aimed for her heart, but she wasn't there. Startled, confused, the man looked down just as she fired up into his chest. He fell backwards down the stairs. She screamed for the girls to run and heard their feet pounding up the steps. She stayed in place and pulled out her pistol. The man below fired at her, yelled for other men.

As she waited, listening for the girls to make it back inside, pistol ready, she heard metal cans banging underneath the staircase and smelled and heard fuel being sloshed around. She sprinted up the stairs, dove through the doorway, slammed the door shut, and barred it just in case.

She grabbed the carafe of water from the sideboard and held it towards the girls. "Wet your rags again and wrap them around your face. Tie them tight. We have to go down the front."

An explosion of light, bright as dawn, filled the room as the fire escape and landing burst into flame. Beth pulled them to the floor. "Stay low."

Beth raced into her bedroom at the end of the inner hall and opened the window. "Mike, Pete, Seamus, where are you? *Ezra, please God, bring Ezra now.*" Lights here and there appeared around the neighbor-hood. A fire bell clanged. She heard boots running hard outside, shouts for a bucket brigade. It sounded like a crowd was gathering in front; she couldn't see it but heard dozens of voices yelling at the same time. *A crowd! Thank God.* It was their best hope of escaping the slavers. She could feel the fire moving against the floor boards and slammed the window shut.

Now heading for the front staircase, she moved quickly through the parlor, out the front door of her apartment and onto the third-floor landing, with the girls following. Beth crept down the stairs, her rifle reloaded, the girls ten steps behind her crouched low. Camille carried a second rifle, with a pistol tucked in her pocket, as did Maddie. All wearing wet bandanas, dripping and steaming in the heat. Were there slavers inside the house? The interior was not yet engulfed in flames, so it was possible. Smoke rose up through the stairwell like a chimney.

Now down on the second floor, flames framed some of the ten doorways. Every door was open but one. Beth kicked it and jumped back. Flames shot out of the empty room, then as if breathing, drew back. Beth yanked the door shut.

She turned to the staircase, then took three, four cautious steps toward the first floor. Her entire body tense, alert. Startling her, a tenant, Potter, yelled and charged down the steps behind her, bumped her, and frantically continued down to the front door, carrying a satchel. A man near the door with one of those orange bandanas stopped Potter, held him by the shirt collar, and pointed up, asking about girls.

"What girls? Crazy bastard, let go!" Potter yanked himself free, ran, and jumped off the porch.

Beth backpedaled up to the second-floor landing. Her mind was racing, fighting for control. They were trapped. Couldn't go back, couldn't go forward. She checked Camille's rifle and pistol, showed Maddie how to cock hers. "Use the pistol up close."

Maddie's eyes froze as a shadow moved. A strong arm suddenly grabbed Beth around the waist from behind and yanked her to him, knocking her rifle to the floor. He had a pistol at her head. Maddie screamed.

FROM BLOCKS AWAY, EZRA SAW THE GLOW OF FIRE RISING FROM THE middle of a dark city and its light reflecting off low, gray clouds. The air carried the scent of pine, oak, burning cedar, and more—hints of burning paint, scalded metal, and the cloying smell of turpentine and lamp alcohol. This was no woodshed or cookhouse fire. It was bigger, the smells more complex—a home, a hotel, a business.

Hearing the fire bell, he ran harder. Turning the final corner, he saw the boarding house ablaze. The entire back a sheet of flame. The first floor, where the dining room once stood, an inferno. The one side he could see was smoking, not yet engulfed, but from his limited view the front appeared unscathed. As he raced toward it, the side facing him flashed. Fire was climbing the wall but not in sheets, in ropes. Then another tendril of flame out of nowhere splashed up the side, and another, as if someone were throwing accelerant up the walls.

He tore off his coat and fought his way through the jostling crowd in front of the house. Controlling his fear, coiling his rage, he was stone sober and prepared to strike. No sign of Beth and no one had seen her, nor any girls. He leapt over the railing, onto the porch to find a man with an orange bandana barring the door.

"No," the man shouted, blocking Ezra with his rifle. "Getting everyone out."

"Where's Beth? Who's left in there?" Ezra demanded.

"Nobody," the man said. "Get back."

"Then why are you here?" Ezra elbowed the man to one side of the doorframe, then lifted his rifle over his head, pretending to squeeze by. "Who's in there?" he shouted.

"A couple of runaway girls. Nothing to worry about. Stay back."

Ezra brought the butt of his rifle straight down on the slaver's head. The man dropped like a stone, out cold. He ripped off the man's mask. Someone he'd never seen before. He pulled the man away from the doorframe, wrapped the strange orange bandana around his own face, took the man's rifle, and started up the stairs through the smoke, shouting. "Beth, are you—"

"Schmidt?" A man stepped out from behind a wall on the second story landing, took two steps down, his rifle pointing at Ezra. He was wearing the same bandana. "Get back down. Go tell Joad I got'm . . . tied and ready."

Ezra's heart leapt. *Careful, careful,* he told himself. His mind was reeling. *Hurt her and I'll kill you,* he thought, but the man had the jump on him. *Bluff him.* He was waving his rifle at Ezra, directing him. "Go on . . . git Joad up here, now."

Ezra took a step backward down the stairs. "Yeah, sure. I'll tell him."

"Tell him I got the bitch up here, ready to bleed. Joad said he wants to cut her himself. Somewhere away from the crowd."

I'll kill you, Ezra thought, his mind exploding with rage, his muscles tightening. *Careful, careful.* He needed control, focus. He had the momentary advantage of confusion, bluff and smoke, he thought, but the man was looking at him suspiciously, waving his rifle impatiently. Ezra eased down one more step.

"Hurry up. I got her. Go tell . . ."

Ezra flicked his eyes up to the right toward the landing. "Yeah. That her? Redhead Joad wants?"

The man took his eyes off Ezra for an instant, just a quick glance over his shoulder, but enough time for Ezra to drop flat to the stairs. Realizing he'd been duped, the man wheeled and fired wildly before Ezra shot him through the head.

The man tumbled down the stairs and Ezra lifted and propped the body as a shield. Waiting for the next slaver to appear on the landing. No one. A few more seconds, still holding the body. "Hey up there, Joad sent me," he shouted. "Joad wants you." He waited for a squeaking board, any sound of movement. Nothing. "Joad gave me this message for you." Nothing.

He dropped the body and charged up to the landing. "Beth?" No answer.

Turning the corner, he found a rifle barrel pressed to his face, directly into his orange bandana, pushing him back. He saw Camille's terrified eyes, holding the rifle, trying to make sense of him.

"Stop!" Beth screamed.

Camille, panting, trembling, her feet still tied, cautiously lowered the muzzle. Ezra pulled down his bandana.

"Thank God," he said. "It's clear down there." He cut their ropes. The three now on their feet, smiling at Ezra, whispering. Suddenly, Beth pushed Camille and Maddie at him. "Girls, go with Ezra. Now. No questions. There's something I forgot."

"Wait, what are you doing?" Ezra shouted. "Hey, Beth, what the hell?"

She turned and raced up the stairs into the smoke.

"Don't!" he yelled. "Please!" She didn't turn back.

"Okay, follow me." Ezra walked down the stairs carefully with his rifle pointed straight ahead, the girls creeping five steps behind, their weapons still in play.

Beth dashed into her apartment, down the short murky hallway, directly into the parlor. Some light from the flaming fire escape but everything distorted by heavy smoke. There were no edges to be seen, just blurs of furniture in the diffuse pulsing light. She coughed, bent over to slow her heart. Then systematically eased her way along the wall guided by her hands to the carved Italian cabinet. She felt for it, down to the second drawer and rifled through the contents for her deed, money, and Hannah's treasured brooch. She kissed the brooch, then stuffed everything deep into her pocket. Then from the bottom drawer picked up more ammunition and two extra pistols, both loaded for emergencies.

She could now feel the tremors of the fire moving through her feet. Not just waves of heat, but quick vibrations. She felt the floor shuddering and heard the sound of groaning joists as the house tried to move away from the viscous flames. The room throbbed with firelight from a few burning rafters overhead, from the engulfed back landing, and through cracks now opening in the floor. She could hear the flames licking their way up the outside wall near her bedroom, a low roaring sound of fire-wind eating the paint.

She took a number of fast, stumbling steps to her left and peered into her bedroom. She could see the fire now framing the window, moaning with hunger to seize the walls, chewing to get inside and devour the innards. The flames outside rose up and stared at her directly through the bedroom window. Taunting her, it seemed. It put its tongue against the window and licked it. Hearing it crack, Beth put up her hands and turned away just as the glass exploded. Shatters flew across the room and onto the floor like tinkling daggers cutting at her boots, shredding the quilt. She shook her head, took off her bonnet and used it to swat the shiny slivers from her coat.

The air was stifling. Becoming harder to breathe. As if the fire was eating the air right out from under her. Flames raced in around her feet.

And the falling plaster dust was coating her sweaty face and neck, getting into her throat.

She leapt from the room and staggered out of her apartment onto the hallway landing. Then started down the staircase, coughing, her stomach churning, sick with smoke she'd swallowed, retching. The second story below was now a bright haze with whips of flame darting out of the doorways.

She heard someone charging up the stairway bellowing, screaming for her. Then saw Ezra's eyes above his bandana. "Thank God," he said. "Scared me half to death. Follow me."

"Where are the girls?"

"Safe with Alex and Douglas."

"Something you don't know, Ezra. There's a fifteen-hundred-dollar bounty."

He clenched his fist. *No wonder they're so savage.* "Let's go. We're the last."

The last. After twenty-two years, these would be her last steps, her last look. Ezra led her down to the first floor. She could hardly see the walls as she slid her hand along the old wallpaper, groping her way toward the first floor, breathing hard. Tears were battling the smoke in her eyes. She felt Hannah slipping away, and with her, the security and comfort Beth had known since she was fifteen, when Hannah rescued her from those rapists and brought her here into a new life. Now in the stairwell, her beloved home was dissolving before her eyes, the woodwork cracking in the heat, the varnish bubbling on the handrail.

"Forgive me, Hannah," she murmured.

A few cheers went up as Beth and Ezra staggered through the door onto the smoking porch. They waved, bent over, coughing, trying to finally breathe deeply and clear their lungs.

When Beth raised her head, she saw Alex, Doug, Fritz, Camille and Maddie in a bucket line passing water from person to person, still trying to save her boarding house.

Alex nodded, suggesting the girls were safe. But she didn't trust the situation. A few slavers were still likely out here, stalking without their orange masks through the crowd, looking for an opportunity to snatch the girls. She'd ask Ezra to whisk them away, perhaps to his brother's house. But where'd he go? *Damn it, Ezra.*

The rest of the neighborhood had branched out, trying to save itself, rushing water and barrels of beer from the tavern to the sides of nearby buildings. She saw men climbing the neighboring roofs, kicking the flying embers, swatting at any bright cinder that fell. She searched the crowd for orange bandanas. Of course they would have taken them off at this point. Must be fifty, a hundred people out here fighting the fire.

Ezra searched the crowd and then the shadows, trusting his instincts to recognize the slavers when he saw them, even without their bandanas. Dangerous as it was, he wore his, hoping to draw them out without getting shot. They were still here; he could feel them evading him, trying to find a last, desperate way to steal the girls.

Suddenly a moan in the tall weeds. Ezra waded in carefully to find Mike bound and gagged, blood covering his head and face. Ezra untied him and helped him to his feet, swearing.

"I'm OK, bitch of a headache. But look at this fire. I wanta gut these bastards."

"You know what they look like?" asked Ezra.

"Two of 'em. Give me a gun. Where's Pete? Seamus?"

"Don't know. They disappeared."

Beth moved through the crowd, searching for Ezra, and for her tenants. She had to be sure they were all out. She worked her way left and right, circling back, counting tenants. If she saw the slavers who did this—three she knew on sight—she wouldn't hesitate. Some of her tenants were working the bucket lines, others chasing down embers and airborne shards of flaming wood.

There! "Wait, Ezra," she shouted. Beth raced after him and Mike, who looked like they were hunting on the edge of the crowd. "Ezra, hold up. The girls—"

"I know what you're going to ask, Beth. We have a plan to get the girls out of here. We just killed a slaver trying to get close to them, after he yelled to one of his pals. So they're clearly not safe. Mike, Alex and I will make them disappear, poof, and then I'll move the girls to

Thomas's house without being followed. Mike's idea, but too difficult to explain right now."

"Try me."

"We'll take them through Cassidy's Tavern to a secret door he knows. It'll work."

"Thank God. You sure? I don't want you to get trapped, killed."

"Nor you. Mike and Alex will protect you after I leave. Please stay close to them. You're a target too."

Beth continued to search for her tenants, while she tried to watch Ezra out of the corner of her eye. She saw Ezra and the two men approach the girls, quickly take their hands and whisk them fast through the crowd straight toward Cassidy's Tavern. Then all five jumped quickly over the debris through the frame of the missing side door and disappeared into the dark. Saw no flames inside. A few minutes later, Mike and Alex jumped back out through the same doorway and took up guard behind a tall pile of firewood. It wasn't clear how much, if any, of the building was on fire or how Ezra and the girls were to escape. But clearly Mike and Alex knew the secrets of Cassidy. Ezra mentioned a secret door. Door to what? To the alley on the far side? The stable? A tunnel? *God be with them.*

Finally convinced the tavern was not on fire, the girls were on the road to safety, and all her tenants were out of the house, Beth turned back to her home. She was halfway across the yard when the flames exploded with volcanic fury, shearing the night sky. She put up her arms to protect herself, then quickly checked to see if there were embers on her clothing.

The fire had stopped whispering its intentions, stopped toying with the crowd, and now roared with the satisfaction of a beast clawing its way toward the heart of the building. The street in front became bright as day, with a throbbing, pulsing sun at its center.

The crowd pulled back and shielded themselves from the new blast of heat. The bucket lines moved back but refused to quit. They fought on for every building.

Unable to stay away, Beth returned to the fire, as close as she could get, her chest seized in anger, her heart torn with terror and grief. Her beloved home groaned in agony; she heard it clear and reached out her hand as if to talk to it, help it get up and magically walk away from its pain. Now her pain. Her business, her world, her life was collapsing in on itself. The tall vertical timbers cracked and leaned inward, sinking but still fighting to hold on.

In her mind, Hannah's house called to her. She held herself rigid, trying to contain her fury, tears rolling down her face, helpless to stop the total loss of everything she was, owned, wanted to be.

Finally, as the timbers collapsed, Beth broke. She threw her head back and screamed in blind rage. Loud enough to startle the fire fighters and bring help.

She slumped to her knees and bent forward. Sparks and tiny pops of embers landed on her shoulders and bonnet. Mike and Alex raced up, swatted and brushed the sparks away. Then carried Beth off before the fire consumed her.

≫ 7 ≪

ASHES AND BREAKFAST

Next morning

Beth circled the smoldering ruins throughout the night and into the pale glare of dawn. With stooped shoulders, ash clinging to her sweating face, neck, arms, she stared dumbfounded at charred beams and three partially collapsed chimneys that stood sentry in upright silence. Where once a beautiful house stood, a black crust covered a seething bed of orange coals that pulsed, still shooting embers into the grey morning.

As much as her legs ached and her lungs and stomach were filled with smoke, she could not walk away. She tried but was drawn back to grieve and search for remnants. A table leg, a brass candleholder, a burnt shoe.

When she closed her eyes, she could make the house reappear, every room and hallway, the smell of the kitchen, the shouts of her tenants, the busy days and comfortable quarters, easy afternoons rocking in the shade on her porch, her snug reading chair by the window to the woods. When she opened her eyes, it was black as death. Worse, she was back where she had started twenty-two years earlier—alone, empty-handed, destitute.

She stretched her stiff back, then walked up the street to survey the damage. Cassidy's Tavern had lost part of a wall to a falling timber.

Other buildings had holes burned through their roofs and walls. Windows smashed open with water dripping from the sills. Thanks to the water brigades, most of the neighborhood was standing.

She passed men, grim-faced and blackened with soot, who continued to stalk the perimeter, chasing sparks and flaming splinters tossed like propellers into the wind.

Back at her ruins, the fire captain brought Beth part of a broken jug he'd found in the back. "Arson, for sure. Smell this." He put it in front of her nose. "Whale oil." He pulled it away and lifted some pieces of charred rag from a broken bucket. "And this, camphene, lamp oil. I also found a chain wrapped around the backdoor handle. Any idea who'd want to burn you out? Why?"

"No, no idea."

"Well, I'll keep looking," he said. "Reckon somebody knows who did this. When we find'm, we'll hang'm."

A merchant across the way lured her over, holding up a milk ladle. She took a drink. Sweet, thick, coating her mouth with butter, washing away the bitter ash. She took a second. He offered food—a fry cake, cold bacon—but she refused, having no appetite. She had swallowed too much smoke, now felt dizzy and nauseous. At his insistence, she put an apple in her pocket. Her fingertips caressed the folded deed and searched through the gold coins and spare pistol balls to find the brooch. She wiped her hand on her skirt before she unwrapped it.

Still intact, her finger traced over the intricately carved ivory cameo. Hannah had given it to her the day she died. She had been wearing it the day she rescued Beth from the streets. Said it always brought her good fortune. Beth kissed it, whispered a prayer to St. Hannah. She returned it carefully to her pocket, then took out the deed, opened it, and grimaced. She stuffed it back in.

Someone touched her shoulder, startling her. Beth spun with fists raised and saw the weariness and pain in Ezra's eyes. Lines etched his face. He looked older. Never had she seen him in such agony. It matched her own. *Good*, she thought. *You brought this on.*

"You're covered with charcoal." He ran one finger lightly along her cheek.

She pushed his hand away. It was too intimate, and she was too angry.

"Come here." He borrowed a pail of water, soap, and a clean cloth from the merchant to wash her face and wipe her sweaty hair while she stood, eyes closed, trembling, hating him. "The girls are safe with Martha. I made sure we weren't followed when we left." He paused, touched her arm. "Did you hear me?"

"They're safe?" She moved his hand. Turning about, she stopped when she saw the smoking rubble across the street. She closed her eyes again and murdered him with a knife. He didn't cry out, just bled, until he was a puddle at her feet. "Dear God." She jerked her head. "What's wrong with me?" she said, half in tears.

"You're in shock," said Ezra. "Let's go someplace warm and get you some coffee and breakfast. This smoke is making you sick."

She was glad to hear his voice and feel his presence. Something was left.

He took her gently by the arm. "May I?" No answer. He led her away, or so she imagined. She found herself floating, as if she had no legs, down the street, around a corner. Nothing registered as real. These buildings weren't charred, burnt, broken.

She heard him talking, more like echoes somewhere in the distance. Too hard to listen to words, but his tone was deep and consoling, like warm water. She remembered her love of a warm bath; all the trouble it took to heat the water on her small stove, lug it bucket after bucket to the washroom. And then the sheer wonder and pleasure sinking up to her neck. A good place to drown; she had never thought of it that way before.

"In here," he said. Ducking under a low doorway, he pulled her by the hand. His hand felt solid, like the beams holding up the room.

The smell of coffee and bacon stirred her senses and opened her nose. It began to run. Ezra handed her a handkerchief, and when she blew, the mucus was black. "Keep it," he said, but she didn't want it in her pocket, soiling the brooch or the apple. She tucked it in her boot.

Steering her to a small table in the corner, Ezra pulled out a wooden chair that shone from years of wear. She stood shivering and realized she had been shivering ever since she left the fire. It wasn't the cold so much as the horror of watching her house die.

He made a move toward her and she took a step back. But when he pulled off his coat and wrapped it around her shoulders, she didn't resist. Wanted to but couldn't. It smelled like him and held her snug; it was warm and soothing, like the bath she wanted.

Finally, she sat and watched as he took his seat. It was just like him to try to hide his anguish, but it was all over his face. His hand trembled until he pressed it flat on the table. His fingernails clawed at the wood.

NEVER HAD HE SEEN BETH THIS NUMB, LOST, HER MAJESTIC spirit smothered. There was no animation left in her face. Her hair hung, still filled with soot, and she smelled of charcoal. He had ruined her life, crushed the one person he admired most in the world, out of an impulse to chase a ghost. He didn't know where to begin. Her eyes were everywhere but on his; it was the most awful kind of stare.

He ordered coffee, cakes and gravy, bacon, greens and fruit, whatever they had. He didn't know what she wanted, and she didn't respond when asked. She looked to be in another world. After he ordered, they sat staring into the space just over each other's shoulder.

The coffee came first, thick and dark. Beth took a deep sip, then another. Her eyes blinked with satisfaction, he thought. Brightened a bit.

"Look at this," she said. She handed him a piece of paper. He opened it and stared at an invoice for supplies, then at her face in pain. "I thought it was my deed. That's one of the things I raced back for." Her head dropped and she considered sobbing, just once. Then fought to gain control.

Ezra reached for her hand "I should not have left those girls with you. I . . ."

"Don't."

"I promise you, I'll . . ."

"Just stop."

She wasn't going to let him explain or try to patch things up. That's the way she was. No excuses.

All night he had been tossing, thinking, planning how to fix things. How to get Beth to safety. Rebuild her boarding house. A house just as nice, better perhaps, somewhere new. She was as good as dead in this town.

The planning was not only out of compassion, he realized. It was a way to ease his unbearable guilt. The guilt was as bad as when Daisy was dragged away to be sold after he was stupid enough at age nine to tell his mother he wanted to marry her someday. As bad as when the light in Abigail's eyes went out, and tiny gasping Aaron stopped breathing.

"My fault," he said. He had dumped disaster on Beth's doorstep and rushed off to a party. A party, for God's sake.

"That's not the point," she said. "Those girls are not safe, Ezra. Anywhere. Not with that kind of bounty."

"It's not just them."

"Leave me out of this," she said.

"No, I won't. You're not safe here. You've been exposed."

BETH GLARED AT HIM. SHE KNEW HE WAS RIGHT; SHE WAS A marked woman. The slavers would track her, find her, and burn her out wherever she settled. Perhaps kill her cold. She studied the pleading in Ezra's eyes. He was planning to take her away. That's what this was all about.

"I'll secret the girls to one of the border towns on the edge of Native Territory," he said, "beyond the reach of the slavers. And you—"

"I'm staying here," she snapped. "Go into hiding, join an abolitionist gang."

"What? No!"

It was comforting, not just this moment of frightening Ezra, but to think of throwing her lot into the destruction of slavers. To exact revenge for burning her out. For those thousands of terrorized runaway slaves who had made it to St. Louis—the gateway to freedom—only to have it snatched away.

"You're not joining a gang," he said. "You're not a killer. Those radical abolitionists can be as evil as the slavers they hunt down. Torture them, slaughter their families, burn their farms. You're coming with me."

"Don't tell me what I'm doing." *Does he really think he can bully me after this?*

Breakfast arrived. Ezra clanked a spoonful of beans onto his plate and swirled them around with a piece of fry cake. He put a piece of cheese on Beth's plate, some greens, and told her to eat. She stared at the plate.

"I've incurred a debt to you," he said, "and I intend to pay it." He didn't wait for her response. Put his head down and ate with determination.

She shook her head and served herself some steamed spinach and a few slices of melon that had begun to turn. Then took a bite of a sugar roll and reached for the bacon. She found her mind clearing.

"You have to start over," he said.

She raised her eyebrows. "That's for people like you. I want what was."

"I'm going to rebuild. That's my promise to you."

She put down her fork and leaned forward. "Ezra, you have no money to rebuild. A vagabond with no credit. Everything you have is tied up in that shipload of supplies to California. Besides, you're leaving in three days."

"Two. You'll have to take my word. This is all my fault."

"Not entirely," she said. "I make my own decisions. And I took the risk."

He should know this about me, she thought. *Risk is something I've done for years on the Underground, and something I don't need to explain to him.* She watched the conflict storming about in Ezra's eyes, pleased she could elicit such strong emotions. She had wanted to kill him an hour ago but now was prepared to share responsibility.

I could have hired ten guards, not three, she thought. *I could have sent a courier to his brother's house to retrieve him but didn't want to disturb him. I could have moved the girls to a safer house or snuck them onto Patterson's boat. But I didn't. And now, here I am, no better off than the runaway slaves we pass hand to hand, farm to farm, house to house. And for that matter, no less lost than those two girls.*

"I want you to come with me, Beth."

She waved the words away and sat back. "Go with you? On a wagon train? Ha."

He began talking now, gibberish, explaining things as he always did when he was nervous, but she was able to block him out, retreat into her fantasy. *I'm in my four-poster bed with the morning light in my eyes. Men downstairs stirring, the cookhouse staff sizzling the sausages out back, flipping the griddle cakes. Time to get moving, the best part of my day. Wash my face, clothes on, hair up, then bustling down the stairs.*

But when she blinked, there was Ezra scratching his unshaven beard, his shoulders back, tense, looking puzzled. "Are you all right?" he asked. "I said—"

"I heard what you said," she snapped. She hadn't, of course.

They stared at each other.

"Just give it some thought," he said.

"You want me to come with you on your wagon train?"

"I should have waited until tomorrow to explain but hear me out. Please. You can start over just as easy in California as you can here. Easier. I'll get money fast once there, and with that and my bare hands build you a boarding house in one of the gold camps. Or San Francisco, or anywhere you want. You'll get rich. I'll be able to see you. It'll be perfect."

"Perfect?" she snorted. "Nobody but crazed miners and trappers go out there."

"Ambitious, not all crazed. Farmers, solid workmen, soldiers. And they'll pay a fortune for room and board. I've seen it. Half the gold they dig will flow to you. And then, when you've made money and it's safe back here, you can return to St. Louis. Anyway, I want you to think about it."

"You haven't answered my question. On your wagon train?"

He shrugged. "I'd be able to look after you."

"Better than this, I hope." The thought of being dependent on Ezra in the wilderness, in a world she didn't know and couldn't control, was more than unnerving, it was maddening.

"Or, if you prefer," he said, a bit too smugly, "I can book you passage on a sailing ship." He paused for reaction, but she wasn't biting. "No dust or filthy oxen. Five leisurely months of rolling sea and storms, boredom, seasickness, hanging onto ropes as the swells grow, bouncing around in the hold below. Listening to the banshees scream the foresail as you round the Horn." He paused again to check her eyes. "The wagon train would be much more comfortable. Steady ground, two miles an hour."

"No rain and mud, violent storms, hail, flooding rivers, mountains, bears, snakes?" she asked.

"Well, yeah, there's that."

Beth leaned forward. "You're being serious, aren't you? I wasn't sure. Ezra, only families are allowed on your last wagon train. Didn't you tell me that? Are you proposing we travel as a family, you and me?"

He nodded. "I admit that's a problem. We'd have to lie. Families only, it's in the company charter. But I'm one of the guides, no questions asked."

"Me as your wife? A pretend wife, you're saying?" She didn't know whether to laugh or cry. He knew she never wanted to get married. Ever.

"I'm afraid so. Sorry. I know how bad this sounds to you."

"Do you really?" She paused and drank some coffee, glanced around the room. Their voices had been rising.

EZRA'S STOMACH TURNED AS HE WATCHED THE ANGER ROIL HER face. Any small ray of hope brought on by breakfast had drained away. The pain and weariness crept back in.

He was doing it again, he realized, trying to solve a fiasco with another bad idea. "I'm sorry. You're right, I don't know how bad it sounds to you."

Her voice was stern. "Let me be clear. Let's not joke about this," she said. "I don't want to get married, never have."

"I know, always known that. Fine with me. I was suggesting pretense, not reality. But why? What do you think happens to you when you get married?"

"I'd be out of business, simple as that. That's the law."

"Beth, I'm proposing we escape together to California. That's all. We're not getting married. Lying to others, not to ourselves. Four or five months in the wagons. Then we get you settled in California, build you a new place, and go our separate ways if you want. You get rich, and I clear my debt. It's a simple business proposition."

He could see the wariness in her eyes. As if he were setting a trap for her. They had ten years of trust built up, and he'd burned it down in one tragic night. Sure, she took her share of the responsibility, but that's how she always was, strong and principled. But this was not some principle; this was unknown territory. This was an emotional wilderness, in every imaginable way, for the two of them.

She put her hands flat on the table. "Ezra, just so we understand each other. If I were to do this—and I'm not sure, uncertain that I'd even consider it—there would be no conjugal rights to go with the fake marriage. Second, in California, I own the boarding house you build, not you. And third, when I decide to return to St. Louis, I sell out and leave without your permission at any time."

He nodded. "We're clear," he said.

They finished eating slowly, without talking. Her eyes were beginning to droop. She stared at him like an exhausted boxer in her corner, too weary to slug him.

Maybe after we cool off, and she gets some sleep, he thought, *we can talk this through. Maybe find another solution. Perhaps she should go to Chicago, where she has Underground contacts, or New York. I could arrange to send her money in a year or so. Might be better all around. She could be an awful companion on a wagon train.*

She suddenly stopped eating and pushed her plate away, then laid her head down on folded arms. "I don't know, Ezra. I'm tired, confused. I don't know what I'll do. I just can't imagine going into the wilderness with you."

"I understand. You don't need to." He stroked her hair, and she didn't protest. "Come with me now. Martha's got a cozy bed waiting for you. A bath, clean clothes."

"A bath?" She lifted her head.

≫ 8 ≪

FINDING JACQUES

Next day, late February 1849

zra entered the cool, dark interior, and stood at the back, letting his eyes adjust to the glow of chandeliers high above the nave, surrounded by a crown of morning light through the clerestory. Blue and red stained glass added elegance and mystery along the walls. And wafting in the air of the vaulted interior, a pungent alchemy of smells—from candlewax and incense, perfumes, mold, damp wool, aging communion wine, old wood, and body odor. He scanned the cathedral looking for Father DeSalle. Decorations of Holy Christmas filled every niche. Early mass was over. Preparations for the afternoon mass were quietly underway, trying not to disturb those in prayer.

Ezra found the setting serene, helping to calm his anxiety, yet visually disconcerting, pulling his eye every which-way, from the ornate altar to the slit windows, to the banks of candles surrounding a parade of saintly niches to the grand crucifixion and tall pulpit, to dozens of parishioners scattered about the pews, praying on their knees.

He wandered down the side aisle to the two confessionals, the first occupied, the door to the second open. He saw no priest, so he sat in a nearby pew to bide his time less conspicuously. He was of no mind to pray, but the impulse was there after the disastrous fire and a morning consoling Beth and two terrified girls. "Dear God," he mumbled, "you know our plight. We ask for your grace and guidance through this thicket of evil."

Beth's face haunted him: her pain and explosive anger after they arrived at Thomas's house when he insisted on going alone this morning to fetch the freedom paper and copies. She had not yet slept or bathed. It wasn't safe for her to go. The fire, the destruction, the savage hunt for the girls had her in its grip. Couldn't think straight. With no ability to sense her surroundings, she might easily blunder into a trap. And if recognized and followed by Jenkins's gang, she could easily compromise Jacques and his intermediary, or lead them to Thomas's house.

She finally relented. And couldn't resist Martha tugging her toward that warm bath, a soft bed, and clean clothes. The girls were asleep and safe. Martha's home was a welcome refuge where Beth could relax and get some needed sleep. Ezra said he would be back before she awakened.

She had given Ezra clear instructions: "Approach Father DeSalle in the second confessional, not the first." She didn't say why, but she had been quite insistent. "And do not linger. If DeSalle isn't available, kneel and pray, then promptly leave."

A woman with a scarf over her head emerged from the first confessional, arms folded, her eyes avoiding Ezra's. She walked briskly down the aisle and disappeared into the gloom. A tall priest with a salted beard came out. Ezra stood up. "Father DeSalle? Are you free?" *Free* was the code word Beth had told him to use.

DeSalle smiled faintly and nodded. "Would you like to make your confession?"

Ezra pointed to the second confessional. "Could we use that one?" He stepped in, sat on the cramped bench, and shut the small door. The wooden panel on the small window separating him from the priest slid open, and he faced Father DeSalle through a screen that obscured facial features.

"I'm here to retrieve," said Ezra, unsure if he had used the proper ambiguous phrasing. He squirmed, impatient, feeling claustrophobic.

"Have you something to confess, my son?"

Ezra thought about pushing out the walls of this small black box to give himself elbow room. He tugged at his collar. "That's not why I've come. I'm a courier. On behalf of Beth McCorry. She sent me to fetch—"

"Who?" There was a long pause. "You mean Elsbeth?" The priest looked away, then leaned closer to the screen. "I have nothing for you."

"But I was sent . . . I asked if you were free, did I not?"

The priest cut him off sharply. "You'd better go."

Something had gone terribly wrong. Perhaps he had he come too early. Perhaps the copies had been delayed. Or perhaps this priest thought Ezra was a pretender, a pro-slaver in disguise.

Ezra leaned closer to the screen and whispered. "Should I come back later?"

The priest slammed the panel shut.

Ezra stepped out of the confessional as did the priest.

Father DeSalle glared at him. "I want to remember your face. Who are you?"

"No one." Ezra turned away and left quickly. Halfway down the aisle, he glanced back to look over his shoulder. Father DeSalle was standing in front of the confessional, ushering in an elderly woman, but staring directly at Ezra. His head was slightly cocked, posture tense. Ezra, rattled and angry, picked up his rifle where he'd left it in a niche near the front door.

Outside, Ezra glanced in both directions. What happened? Had Jacques not been able to make copies? Or had he delivered them to the priest as promised, but told him explicitly they were for Beth and no one else? That's possible. If so, DeSalle had the copies but would not hand them over to a complete stranger who could be a spy.

He had to find Jacques. Either go to his office or find a way to get a message to him immediately for a rendezvous. Ezra and the girls—and hopefully Beth—were leaving tomorrow at dawn on the steamboat, and they needed the papers. If not the copies, at least the original. Without her freedom paper, Maddie was fair game in this town. Slave or free, no Black could walk the streets of St. Louis without a paper. And it was much the same everywhere else. Even on the steamboat, he imagined.

JACQUES'S OFFICE WAS ON CHESTNUT STREET. AS EZRA approached, he switched over to the far side of the street for a better view of the bay window on the second floor. If Jacques were at his desk, Ezra might be able to see at least his head or some movement about the room. It had been years since he'd sat in Jacques's office, back when the Underground was not such a dangerous business. He remembered the time Jacques shouted and slammed his fist on the desk after reading the farewell words of a man and wife—clinging to each other and crying, the newspaper said, after they were sold separately at auction. "This is all going to end in war, mark my words!" Jacques had shouted.

Looking up at Jacques's office from the street, Ezra could see no sign of activity. In fact, no activity in the whole building. The curtains were half closed, no sign of candlelight or gaslight in any of the gloomy offices. He walked past the building, then turned and came back, this time more slowly. Still no sign of life. Late morning. His heart was racing. *Calm down.* Jacques was probably out visiting a client for Christmas greetings, he thought. If so, he might have left a note for Beth on the corkboard just outside his second-floor office, indicating time of return.

Ezra stepped through the front door into a wide vestibule with a pale etching on the wall and a coat rack. Ahead was a long, dark hallway; to the right, a vacant office; and to the left a stairway. For a bustling office building on a working day, it was strangely silent. He listened carefully to the shadowy gloom. Something was off. No voices, no footsteps, no doors opening and closing. There was a chill in the air as if the fireplaces had gone out. All at the same time?

He climbed the stairs to the landing and turned toward Jacques's office. The door was ajar, sunlight on the floorboards. But no lamp light. Corkboard empty. Pins scattered on the floor as if someone had ripped off all the notices.

He knocked, quietly called Jacques's name, and pushed open the door. Files were scattered everywhere, ribbon-tied bundles of papers and briefs ransacked. Striped ledgers and thick law books ripped apart.

The massive mahogany desk was flipped on its back, the drawers pulled out, the contents spewed across the floor. The desk bottom was torn apart in an effort to find concealed compartments.

The leaded glass cabinets had been smashed and the interior compartments jimmied open. The black silhouette profiles of Jacques's parents, wife, and two young daughters hanging on the wall had been slashed with a knife. A frontier map of early St. Louis was destroyed, along with native masks and ornaments.

Ezra could envision three, four, five men ransacking the place. Clearly looking for something—files, papers, briefs. But there was an assertive vengeance behind this destruction.

He looked for signs of a struggle and focused on one corner of the room where papers had been mangled and stomped, covered with a flurry of dirty boot marks. Jacques fighting from a defensive position, Ezra thought. Chairs overturned, objects and ceramics shattered, a silver tea set crushed. This was no robbery. This silver was worth too much money to leave here. Moving debris out of the way, he found splattered blood. Not a lot. Not a lethal blow, a wound more likely.

He left the office and raced from room to room on the second and third floors, calling out. No one. He felt the coals in their fireplaces; some still warm. It was as if everyone had left in a hurry. A few hours ago, he reckoned.

Ezra bounded down the stairs and out into the fresh air, then rushed from one side of the street to the other, asking every merchant he saw— men whose business it was to keep their eyes on the street for potential clients—if they had seen someone dragged off. They said no, but there was a momentary reticence in their answers, and they turned away a bit too quickly.

Finally, an old vendor selling turnips from a street cart said, "No," as loud as any, but then flicked his eyes, pointing Ezra toward the river-front.

Ezra hurried down Chestnut. When he reached Third, he began to trot, weaving in and out of the crowds that grew thicker as he neared the levee. Looking down First Street, he saw people moving fast, converging, shouting, pointing. Ezra couldn't understand the words, but they were clearly chasing some excitement. He reached the back of a swarming crowd as they turned the corner onto Market Street.

Halfway down the block, men and women and dozens of children stood, staring up at a new building, a three-story under construction. The pulley system used to hoist building materials was anchored to a wooden beam that extended horizontally from the roof out a good ten feet over the sidewalk, dangling a bag of construction material. Plenty of room to lift and swing a few hods of bricks to the top of the building without banging the wall. Ezra saw men scrambling up ladders and leaning out the open windows of the new building. Police stood at the base shouting up, pushing people back.

Ezra stopped. It wasn't a bag of building materials dangling. It was a man ensnared in a tangle of thick ropes hanging from the protruding beam. Ezra worked his way in closer, squeezing through. The man was swinging by his neck, his head canted at an unnatural angle, the tips of his boots pointing to the ground. His arms were tied behind his back. When the workmen reached out with hooks trying to pull him in, the body twisted by the neck so that Ezra could see him straight on.

Ezra's chest seized and he heard himself moaning, "No, dear God, no." He stumbled backwards, losing his balance. He bent over gagging.

A man pushed Ezra upright and slapped him on the back. "Man hanging up there had it coming to him. Traitor."

Hanging twenty feet in the air, Jacques's face was bloody, bruised, swollen, right side purple. He had been beaten and judging by the blood spreading on his shirt near the waist, stabbed before he was hung. There was a scrawled sign pinned to his chest. "Sign says he's 'a dirty abolitionist,'" said a young boy next to him with a gleeful tone.

"Damn fool boy." Ezra swatted the back of the boy's head, then yelled, "Cut him down!" But his voice was lost in the vengeful taunts and cries of grief all around him. His mind flew to Beth, the girls. His breathing grew short and shallow. Feeling faint, he leaned over and took some deep breaths. He had to get to them. *Keep your wits*, he told himself. *Their lives depend on this, your every move.*

He couldn't stay to ease Jacques to the ground, see him carried to his family, to a proper burial. He had never met Jacques's wife and daughters. Did they have any idea what he was involved in all these years? Probably not, he thought. It would have put them in too much danger.

His heart suddenly leapt and his mind flashed with clarity. Those killers were likely on the lookout, Ezra realized, possibly right here prowling in the crowd, searching for Jacques's allies. Not sure they'd recognize him, but he'd have to melt away, fade into the crowd with no sudden moves to call attention. Circle down through the chaos of the levee to lose anyone who might be following. Be careful on his way back to Thomas's house. Don't lead them there.

Beth and the girls were in far greater danger than he had reckoned. These men were killers. One more day, that's all he needed. They'd be gone. He'd take the girls to Independence. Maybe Beth too, but she was the tough one. He couldn't imagine . . . wouldn't be able to find the words to tell her about Jacques. His murder would send her over the waterfall. She wouldn't leave. Not now. She'd join the abolitionists' war.

But one thing at a time. Keep your wits. Don't try to plan everything out right here, without her, without knowing what she'll want to do. Just get the hell out of here. Carefully. He eased back, yanked down the brim of his hat.

And what was he going to do about Maddie's freedom paper? His chest tightened. The slavers' trap was slowly closing around them. It was clear to him. *Tomorrow's escape is our only option.*

Ezra floated backwards slowly, pulling his bandana up over his nose and mouth, until he reached the perimeter of the dense crowd, then stood watching. All eyes were on the gruesome scene. No one was moving toward him, but his instincts said watch out. They may be coming, circling, tracking. He turned and trotted past the new arrivals, who were pointing and racing toward the swinging man. Around the corner, he suddenly bolted for the crowds at the levee where he knew how to disappear.

He remembered from childhood the back alleys, hidden passages, and concealing woods to get to the family home—now Thomas's and Martha's house—undetected. Circuitous yes, but he must return unseen to protect them. Would those savages dare to burn them out of Thomas's house as well? Thomas was a well-known, pro-slaver sympathizer so they might hesitate, but this particular gang might not care. The thought of the historic family home going up in flames was just too awful. He knew Thomas and Martha had privately discussed the danger last night once they accepted sheltering the girls. But when they learned of Jacques's lynching their fear would balloon. Arson, murder. These men were ruthless, relentless.

From the levee, Ezra took the old hidden byways. After half an hour of weaving and sprinting, he walked into the house, expecting Maddie to race up to get her freedom paper. Others to jump out. But the house was surprisingly quiet.

"They're all asleep," said Martha as she walked in from the kitchen, wiping her hands, to greet him. "We're you successful?"

He shook his head just as Thomas walked in. "Please both of you sit down," said Ezra. "The news is not good."

Martha's eyes widened. Thomas closed his and leaned back in his chair, shaking his head.

"Do you know Jacques Quillet, the lawyer?" asked Ezra.

"I've met him socially," said Thomas. "Very likeable chap. Extremely talented lawyer. From what Beth told us, he's the one making copies of Maddie's freedom paper. And you were to pick them up this morning from some intermediary. Well?"

"That intermediary, I won't say who, chased me off. I went to Jacques's office, found it ransacked, completely torn apart and everyone in the building gone. I sensed he had been dragged away, so I searched the neighborhood. Found him lynched, hanging high in the air from a construction boom over the street, his face beaten badly, maybe a stab would in the stomach. A sign pinned to him calling him a traitor."

"Dear God. This treachery has gone too far," said Thomas. "All for a freedom paper, all for the bounty of one young girl."

"A wonderful girl," said Martha. "Poor child. She'll be so distraught. And terrified. And in so much danger without it. And not just her, Camille as well. Both targets."

"Ezra, you and I will have to do something about this," said Thomas. "We can't let these girls get swept away by these killers."

"And Beth, I'm truly worried about her," said Ezra. "When she finds out. She was very close to Jacques. Worked with him, as you probably know, for years.

"On the Underground," said Thomas. "I now finally understand you two. Not that I approve. But neither do I approve of murdering a man like Jacques for his belief. Or yours. Or Beth's. We'll need to get you four out of town immediately.

"We leave at dawn tomorrow," said Ezra. "I have a stateroom reserved on a steamboat. But we'll need a carriage to get from here to the levee undetected."

"You can use mine," said Thomas. "I'll make arrangements."

"His what?" said Beth, walking into the room in a clean soft blue dress, face fresh, hair washed. "Like my new dress? Martha gave it to me. Such a lovely, generous woman."

"She is that," said Thomas.

"You clean up well, Beth. Gorgeous hair," said Martha. "Did you sleep?"

"A few hours soundly after my bath. Then fitfully. And when I heard you three talking, I couldn't wait. Well, did you get them, Ezra?"

Martha stood. "We'll let you two talk. Thomas, come, I have something important I want to discuss with you." They left quickly.

"Come over here next to me on the sofa," said Ezra.

The luster in Beth's face faded, grew wary. "Well?" she said, sitting down. "You're scaring me. What is it, Ezra?"

"Jacques was murdered. Lynched this morning by the slavers. I can only guess it has to do with the freedom papers. I found his office torn apart."

Beth looked as if she had been stabbed. Her mouth opened and closed silently as she searched for breath. Then she grabbed the front of Ezra's coat, drove her face hard into his chest and screamed, muffling the sound so as not to wake the girls. Ezra held her tight, tears streaming down her face. Her body shaking like a battered house in a storm, as he rocked her.

"You're all I have left, Ezra. We have to leave," she said, searching his face.

"Tomorrow at dawn," he said.

"Did you tell Martha and Thomas?"

"I did," he said. "They know about the Underground Railroad."

"I told them after you left, before I went to sleep. They weren't surprised and they didn't seem to care," she said. "They care about you and me and the girls, but not our politics. They want us safe. Together."

"How are we going to tell Camille and Maddie?" he asked.

"Do it fast, like you did with me. Then hold them, reassure them. I'll do the same. Follow me into the kitchen. I need some water. My stomach is still upset by the smoke I swallowed."

Soon Thomas and Martha returned with a look of new determination. "I think Maddie and Camille are still asleep," said Martha.

They sat down at the kitchen table. "I want you two to read this first draft. It's a freedom paper foe Maddie," said Thomas. "It was Martha's idea and I think a damn good one. She saw the way I took to Maddie, in part because of her resemblance to Daisy. But also, her infectious spirit. It would help clear my conscience, after our family cast Daisy out. So, if I can help rectify our family's disgrace, keep this young girl free, it would be my honor."

"You, Thomas, the pro-slaver?" said Ezra. "Giving her a phony freedom paper?"

"Makes the paper all the more convincing, don't you think?" He laughed. "Actually, does my heart good to help her."

Beth and Ezra put their heads together and read the draft. "I would put this first and this second," said Beth, "but otherwise if feels genuine and heartfelt."

"It is," said Martha. "Things you don't know about your brother, Ezra. His sympathies, needed for the business community, are not those of this household."

"I'm grateful," said Ezra, patting Thomas's shoulder. "I have a soft spot for this girl. One thing puzzles me, though. In the freedom paper you refer to her as Daisy Adams."

"I can't very well call her Maddie now, can I? Not with every bounty hunter looking for that name? Besides, it's a sentimental gift from our family. It makes me feel like we're finally freeing Daisy after all these years."

"Thirty-eight years to be exact."

"OK brother, we both agree it's the right thing to do. I'll recraft it, dress it up properly and have it notarized today. And ask the notary to make several copies—make it five—and to keep his mouth shut. It should give Maddie some peace of mind."

"BETH, COME WITH ME," SAID MARTHA, HOLDING OUT HER HAND. "I want you to follow me up to the attic." Beth put down her spoon and trailed after Martha.

As they walked to the staircase, Martha elaborated. "I have trunks of old clothes up there, in good condition, that will fit you, and many other pieces we can stitch up to disguise the girls as little old ladies. I know that seething bunch of evil blackguards will be hunting for them on the levy tomorrow. Will do my heart good to deceive them."

After they climbed into the attic, Martha plumped some cushions on an old silk settee. "We can start with this trunk," she said. She opened the lid, pulled back the linen liner and lifted out two dresses neatly folded. "You know, Beth, I've been watching you and Ezra together . . . Oh, this will look good on you." She held it up. Small tawny print on soft cream, slender bodice. "I think this will fit you nicely.

"I can already see the tenderness in him toward you, Beth. Little things. But tenderness I haven't seen in him in for twenty years. He's a wonderful man. I've been trying to marry him off, but today I realize he has been holding out for you all along."

"You think so," said Beth. "He's so unpredictable. Has disappeared on me for years at a time. And two days ago, he told me he was leaving for California. I assumed for good."

"I think he's afraid to love again," said Martha. "He lost Daisy, then Abigail. Both disappeared in the blink of an eye and he's probably afraid if he loves you truly, you'll disappear too. Like some ancient curse. That's my hunch. Up until now you've been an elusive creature so he can keep coming back safely and never have you and never lose you."

"Elusive in the sense I never want to get trapped in marriage. Never have and he knows it. He accepts it. So, I guess I'm safe enough for him."

Beth stopped, holding up a dress. "Oh, look at this one, Martha. Green silk, low shoulders, elbow cut. It's so beautiful. I wouldn't dare wear it."

"Of course you will. We'll put it in your takeaway trunk. Special occasion dress. Maybe on the steamboat. They have nice restaurants. You'll knock him out with this one. I saw that hunger in his eye when you came in wearing that blue dress."

"Do you think?" She smiled. "There are times out of the corner of my eye when I think I see his desire. Shocked me. Thrilled me, if truth be told. But fleeting. I think we are cursed."

"Listen, you're smart, lovely, and from what Ezra tells me hardworking, and dedicated. From my limited knowledge, I'd say just about perfect for him."

"He asked me to go with him on his damn wagon train. I can't imagine anything worse."

"Staying in St. Louis would be worse," said Martha. "I wish it were otherwise. I think if you were here, we could become good friends. I'm sorry he's been hiding you from me all these years. I imagine for fear we would turn you in, jeopardize your work on the Underground. But that life is gone, and you will need someone to help you create a new one. You couldn't find anyone better than Ezra."

"Not sure what I want right now. I've never wanted to get married."

"I can understand why. You'd feel captured, owned. Marriage is a bit like that. The law supports it. But Ezra knows how to love a woman. Not many men do. I saw it up close with my sister, so I know it's true. He has that gift."

"Stop. You're scaring me," said Beth. "I either lose him completely when I get off the steamboat or go with him to some place I can't even imagine."

"You're going to have to trust someone at some point," said Martha. "But right now, we must focus on getting the four of you out of town safely. Undetected, onto that steamboat."

"Agreed."

Martha fingered a few more dresses. "You like these four? And here in this second trunk are some others. A few fancy dresses, but many very practical frocks, day-to-day work dresses and full aprons. I'm going to send you off with two trunks, Beth, one just for you, one for the girls."

"I love you for all your kindness," said Beth. "I'll be sorry to lose your company."

"And I yours. But at least we have today, and I can hopefully help you comfort these terrified girls," said Martha.

⇒ 9 ⇐

ESCAPE BY STEAMBOAT

St. Louis Levee

Reaching the outskirts of the levee, the horses suddenly shied, reared and the coach skidded to an abrupt stop, pitching Beth from her carriage seat onto the girls sitting opposite. Ezra tugged her back onto her seat, opened the door, and jumped out into the early morning mist. Two large steeds snorted, stomped on the cobblestone, and tried to back the coach up, while the driver engaged the brake.

"What happened?" Maddie asked.

Beth listened to Ezra argue with the driver about getting closer. "We have a good three, four hundred yards to the damned steamboat," he shouted. "Barely see it. What is Thomas paying you for?"

"See for yourself, Mr. Adams. Damn well packed too tight for a carriage this size."

"We're stuck," Beth said over her shoulder, looking out the window for a possible path through the morning congestion—a tangle of supply wagons, carts, animals, and heavy drays moving at cross purposes, along with thousands of restless men in knots and long lines, dragging their gold mining gear. She saw scattered barrel fires throwing bright sparks into the gray morning sky, like fireflies in the mist. Men in blankets pressed close to the barrels, their hands extended to the flames.

A steam horn sounded, deep as fog, as the first boat of the day departed.

Hidden in that swarm, Beth knew, bounty hunters, slavers, and detectives with keen eyes were prowling. This was the best time for hunting. First runs of the day, the busiest, the most confusing, a time when runaway slaves and those with a price on their heads were most likely to make a run for it.

She and Ezra had planned for a quick, short dash from the shelter of Thomas's carriage to the boat . . . not this.

She'd have to steel the girls. From years dealing with frightened runaway slaves, she knew the greatest danger was telegraphing panic. The hunted give off quivers, like trembling rabbits ready to bolt, tiny tremors the trained eye can detect.

Maddie tugged on Beth's skirt. "Where are we? Why did we stop? Are we in trouble?"

She reached for Maddie's hands and smiled with authority. "You be brave now. We'll be walking from here. Take a deep breath, Maddie. You too, Camille. Both of you. That's it. Now put your fears on the seat beside you and leave them right here." She patted the seat. "Understand? When we get out, you'll be calm. So calm. And do exactly as you are told, no complaints. Maddie? Camille? Agreed?"

They nodded but looked stunned as she fussed with their clothing, all from Martha's attic, loosely layered. The shoulders were too large for their small frames but had been tucked and quick stitched. The hems stitched to ankle length to avoid stumbling.

"Listen up. You're playacting old ladies. Playing dress up in the attic. When we walk, you're going to take small, slow steps, slightly stooped, like old ladies." Beth lifted the hood on Maddie's heavy cloak over the girl's bonnet, tucked her hair out of sight, then pulled the sides of Maddie's hood forward to shield her face in deep shadow. Camille followed suit with her own cloak.

"I can barely see," said Maddie.

"Means they can't see you. Put on your gloves. Once outside, we'll pull down your veils. I want none of your skin showing."

All three startled, lifted their heads to the noise. The trunks scraped along the top of the carriage as their luggage was removed. Other voices. Beth patted the pistol in her pocket. If the men who'd murdered Jacques and burned her home to the ground so much as showed their faces, she'd . . . *No. No bloodletting. Nothing rash,* she scolded herself. *Control, not vengeance.*

The carriage door flew open. Ezra was tense, angry. He had strapped a holster belt over his coat and pushed an extra pistol in the front. He held his rifle in one hand. "I hired two men and the trunks are already on their way." He helped them out of the carriage, one at a time. "Don't trip on those dresses." His voice was tense.

Out in the cold wet air, with strangers streaming past them from all directions, men who emerged from nowhere in the pale light and shadows, Beth felt the terror of being hunted. She turned, lightheaded, disoriented.

Ezra took her by the shoulders. "Take charge of these girls. They're bewildered. Spooked."

Beth breathed as deeply as possible. "OK. Of course." She pulled the girls' hoods forward and eased the thin, black mourning veils down over their faces.

She smiled, her voice turned warm, steady. "You're going to be all right. Just remain calm. Try not to look all around you, just straight ahead. Don't draw attention. You're an old lady. Now listen to me. Maddie, you grab the belt at the back of Ezra's coat, that's it, right there, and hold it tight. Camille, you hold Maddie's other hand and don't let go. I'll be right behind you." She made sure her red hair was fully hidden under her bonnet and lifted her hood.

"We're ready, Ezra."

They followed him single-file, weaving through the dense, noisy crowd, circling wagons and piles of cargo like a snake through thicket. The girls were out of Ezra's line of sight, so it was up to Beth in the rear; she was the first line of defense. She couldn't help but grin watching the two padded lumps in front of her shuffling along, stooped over, half-blind, like elderly women weighed down with age. It was a wonderful disguise. It had been clever of Martha to suggest it, and generous of her to provide the two trunks of clothing. The elderly shuffle step gave the girls something to focus on other than their fears, and their playacting was convincing.

Ezra had told Martha that if Beth decided to join him on the wagon train, a family train, they would have to pretend to be married. At that, Thomas howled, and Martha gasped, as if it were something important and wonderful. As the two men walked out of the room, she overheard Thomas say to Ezra, "No sex? Hogwash. You'll be up her skirt before you hit the prairie." Beth was more amused than worried. She knew how to handle herself, and Ezra had never and would never force himself on her.

She had had a twinge of jealousy at Martha's circumstances. The woman still had her fine home, her family, her security, and the continuity of her life. Beth was starting over with nothing, heading either to the small dusty town of Independence on the edge of Indian Territory, or traveling toward the raw gold fields walking beside or riding in a dumpy, dirty wagon.

"Not a bad journey. Only four million steps and we'll be there," Ezra told her in the carriage, as if that might cheer her up. Sometimes he could be such an ass.

A coarse-looking man caught Beth's eye and began walking beside her, talking nonsensically, trying to win her favor. He reeked of alcohol and sweat and filth. Beth pointed and told the man her husband was fully armed and jealous, but the drunken pest laughed at her. Finally, the pest jumped directly in front of her, breaking her hand connection with Camille.

Beth stepped firmly onto his right boot, pinning his foot to the ground, then shoved him fast and hard with both hands. He reeled backwards, his arms flailing for balance, and when she lifted her foot, he sprawled onto the cobblestones into the crush of traffic. A man tripped over the drunk and kicked him.

Beth ran to catch up and grabbed Camille's hand. "Right behind you. No, don't look behind you." She scanned the crowd and singled out several men she thought were bounty hunters. Men peering over newspapers, not going anywhere, searching faces. They glanced at Beth and the old ladies shuffling in front of her, and their eyes drifted off.

She surveyed the crowd again, left and right. Then her heart jumped. There, to her right, perhaps fifty paces away, the lead slaver, the one named Joad. He hadn't died in the fire after all. He was looking in the other direction. Hadn't seen them. *Don't jerk*, she told herself. *Don't hurry. Just keep going, flowing easily with the crowd.*

A loaded wagon, then another cut off her sight of the slaver. After the wagons passed, Joad was nowhere to be seen. Beth put her hand on her pistol and her faith in their disguise. If he had seen her, he and his gang would be coming at her from behind. But she couldn't look.

As the four approached the loading area, the muscles in Beth's neck finally eased, and she saw some of the tension leave Ezra's back and shoulders as well. They entered the passenger gathering area, with a one-inch-thick rope providing a semblance of order and an illusion of security. The four clustered tightly in the gathering area with their heads together to conceal the girls' faces and inched their way toward the boat. Ezra pointed to the boarding ramp. "Right up there, Stateroom Twenty-Seven B, starboard side. Remember it, Twenty-Seven B starboard, in case we get separated. Repeat it to yourself." Beth heard the girls mumble the room number.

Ezra told them several times to drum it into their heads to go straight up onto the main deck, the working deck, then up the broad staircase to the boiler deck— oddly named Beth thought, since it was the deck of gentility with its white-trim railing, wide promenade, staterooms, dining room, card room, and pavilion.

The girls lifted their heads to get a better look. "Heads down," Ezra scolded.

Beth watched the weary roustabouts lounging on the far side of the gathering area, gazing at passengers moving up the ramp. They leaned on piled sacks of coffee beans and slouched against wagons, tossing unkind remarks to each other about the people boarding. Uneasy, tremors running up her back, Beth feared they might be on the lookout for reward money. A man with a sharp eye for the girls could earn a year's wages in an hour.

"You take the girls up the ramp and I'll distract them," said Beth.

Ezra didn't hesitate, simply handed her a ticket.

Beth held back and let a few of the other passengers flow around her. Before the roustabouts' eyes reached Camille and Maddie, she bent over and conspicuously adjusted the hem of her skirt, showing her ankle and an enticing bit of calf. They stared, fixated, jesting to one another, until Ezra and the girls had disappeared onto the boat.

ON BOARD, BETH CLIMBED THE STAIRS AND WALKED THE promenade with a sense of freedom she hadn't felt since before the fire. She decided not to go immediately to the stateroom. It would be too awkward, trying to settle into a tiny space with Ezra, and too draining to deal with the girls' endless questions and worries. Let Ezra take care of them.

Right now, she wanted nothing more than fresh air and privacy for a farewell to her once beloved home. She leaned on the railing, looking out over her city, studying the mass of people on the levee. She had never thought much about them before, indifferent to their comings and goings. Now, she saw them as herself, torn asunder, leaving their familiar worlds behind.

She remained nervous about slavers spotting her if any were aboard and reached up to make sure none of her hair was poking out the bonnet. Pulled the hood of her cloak tighter. With her hair hidden and her face in shadow, it was unlikely any of the slavers would recognize her. Especially on a crowded deck.

In an hour, she realized, all the fond sights and smells of St. Louis would be gone. She looked in the direction of her boarding house. The blue spot had disappeared, erased from the world. Glad at least that the charred timbers were not visible, she let the waves of emptiness and sorrow emanate from her body and spread out like a hymn over the city.

Men, young miners with no place to rest or sleep other than the deck, smiled and eased toward her. Some took off their hats as if to make an introduction. Martha had been right; she would need the protection of a ring. Martha had pulled the semblance of a wedding band from her old jewelry box in the attic and tied a ribbon around it. "In case you need protection," she said.

Beth took it out of her pocket, untied the ribbon and slipped it on. Placed her left hand conspicuously on the railing, and damned if two young men easing toward her didn't fade away.

She stared at the faux ring on her finger and wondered if she truly had the stomach and strength to see this through to Independence, and God forbid as last resort, on a wagon train to California. Imagine that, not just the filth and fatigue, but living a lie day after day with strangers in a caravan.

It was the women, not the men on the wagon train, that concerned her. Men, with their bluster, had become as routine as the cycle of day and night. But women had been rare in her world, and the thought of posturing as an equal among married women was daunting. Overwhelming. *They'd see right through me in a minute. They have secret, intuitive communication.* She tried to imagine these women, but when she brought their faces into her mind, their eyes, their look, their airs, their attitudes were all disapproving. Martha was accepting, even fond of her, but these fantasy women, never. They would scold her with their piercing eyes. They'd know she was a fraud from the get-go. Martha had said, "You're wrong. Put on that ring, and you become legitimate in their eyes." Maybe. Not worth the risk. Just get to Independence. Start fresh there with the girls. That was her plan—not well thought out, but at least something to build on.

She glanced down at the waterline and noticed the gangplank still in place. Good, that gave her perhaps fifteen minutes to get off the boat, go back and make the best of things. She wouldn't—she knew that much about herself—but she dearly wanted to drop the ring in the water and walk away, unmarried, clean. Join the abolitionists to kill satanic slavers. *Oh, stop it. I'm not a killer.*

A newsboy shouted. He was working the deck, selling the latest edition of the *Daily Union* before the departure horn sounded. She waved, handed him two cents, and turned back to the railing to scan the ads for runaways. There! It was worse than yesterday. Shaking her head, she folded the paper and tucked it in her bag.

Her eye was now caught by a young woman parading along the levee below in front of the departing boats, adorned in bright yellow. She turned in merriment, swinging a full yellow skirt wide enough to keep the men at bay while she twisted a yellow parasol to draw them in. Push and pull. A tease if she ever saw one, but at this moment, she admired the woman for her brazenness.

The flirt kissed the palm of her gloved hand and waving at all the young gold miners on board, who clamored to the rail two deep. They pushed in on either side of Beth and waved back at the bright yellow canary. "Goodbye dreamers, goodbye lovers, you long gone and lost forever darlings," she yelled up to the men who threw kisses back.

"I kiss you back. You wonderful chirpy yellow bird," shouted one young miner.

Beth had heard of this woman but had never seen her. She was quite mad, but adored and protected by the roustabouts and merchants, who considered her good luck for the St. Louis steam traffic.

The young men on the boat around here were not much older than boys, with their apple-bright grins. They swapped tall tales of California, bragging about the gold they would find. She watched and listened in amusement.

"Gold that will cuddle our ankles in the streams," one said.

"Nuggets big enough to fill a wheelbarrow," said another.

"Gold that drips from the mountaintops like a honeycomb," said a young Kaintuck. That one broke his comrades into peals of laughter. They slapped him on the back, but he didn't know why. You could practically smell the country corn on the boy's breath. Silly child. Ignorant bastard. His accent brought back memories, some quite fond, of the land and people she had left.

Fled was more like it. The last time she had taken a steamboat into the unknown, she was fifteen and on the run, terrified of her abusive father who wanted to sell her. Overland north through the Kentucky hills to the mighty river, then a stowaway down the Ohio River to the Mississippi, then the short jaunt north to St. Louis.

Now, here she was at age thirty-seven on the river and once again on the run.

She leaned on the railing, savoring the last few minutes as the boat backed its way out of the slip, its fierce horn blowing. It slowly rotated its bow to the north, then reversed wheel and dug its monstrous paddle into the water, clawing its way forward like an animal digging dirt, all to make gain against the swollen spring current running south.

"There you are." She jumped as Ezra squeezed her shoulder from behind. "Sorry to scare you," he said. "Camille and Maddie are resting, probably asleep by now. Exhausted and angry when I told them they couldn't leave the cabin until I was sure the ship was safe. I locked them in. Camille seemed to think we could demand a better room. Need to scrub some of the privilege off that girl."

"What's the stateroom like?"

"Crowded. I was glad to get out of there. Windowless box, with a narrow bed on each side, rickety table in the middle. Small chair and a stool."

Narrow beds? She searched his face. They had not talked about sleeping arrangements; everything had happened so fast. "How narrow?"

"The girls can have one bed, you the other. You'll have room enough to sleep. I'll make do with the floor."

"Thank you. That's considerate."

She reached into her bag and pulled out the newspaper folded to the ads. "The bounty reward just jumped to two thousand dollars this morning."

"What!" He read the ad in its entirety. Beth watched his eyes widen. He looked up at her, then went back to reading, seemingly trying to absorb the details and consider the impact. "Where did you get this?" he asked. "Bastard. Still refers to Maddie as a slave girl."

"Newsboys were working the promenade while you were in the stateroom with the girls. People were grabbing them. There must be fifty copies floating around this boat," she said.

"It's not the miners, it's the professional hunters I'm worried about," he said. "The ones that take this run to Independence all the time, hoping to pick off a prize."

"Thank you for settling them and locking them in."

"Would you like to take a walk?" he asked, pointing toward the bow. "See if we can identify the bounty hunters? They should be easy enough to spot, the way they search the crowds."

She shook her head slowly. "No, I think I'll just stay here."

"It'll cheer you up. You know there's a restaurant here: parlor, lounge, gambling, music. Lots of things to distract you. Come on, I'll escort you around."

"Like the little woman?" she said in a mocking tone.

His brow tightened and she could feel his discomfort. He moved his hand away from hers on the railing. "I'll leave you in peace, if you prefer," he said.

She caught him staring at the ring on her finger. She covered it with her other hand. "I hate it . . . in case you are wondering. It makes me a lie."

"Can I see it?" he asked.

She uncovered the ring, and he lifted her hand and stared at the gold, then twisted the band gently on her finger.

Beth turned her head away, embarrassed, afraid of his thoughts. "Martha found a passable ring in her jewelry box. Said it would help protect me on the steamboat."

The two of them stood silently, side by side, watching the river.

"Do you know what I'm thinking?" she asked.

He leaned on the railing, staring straight ahead. "Not a clue."

"I'm glad. If we have to live this close, side-by-side, day in and day out, I want my privacy. I don't want you reading my thoughts."

"I don't want to read them either," he said. "You can be as private as you want. Let's walk."

They circled the ship twice on the promenade, trying to spot hunters. It became a game. She took his arm, more for show and to hold her footing on the rocking boat than companionship or endearment.

They talked in pretend leisure, never looking at each other, nodding signals to evaluate this pair of men or that pair of eyes. The bounty hunters seemed to travel in twos, one a spotter, the other a snatcher. Spotters were never preoccupied by ordinary things, always skimming over people in close range. Snatchers kept their eyes moving at mid-distance, five people ahead, adjusting position to capture their mark unaware.

The ship seemed fairly safe. One suspected pair proved to be gamblers looking for prey. Another focused on grown Black men, of

which there were perhaps a dozen, all freemen judging by their confident dress and manner and pistol belts.

But Ezra remained cautious. "Some bounty hunters hide away for a
day or two, just waiting for the runaways and escapees to let down their
guard. I told the girls that was my reason to keep them in the stateroom
for a few days."

At the bow, they rested where the crowds had thinned. Watching
the advancing river in silence, Beth held Ezra's arm comfortably at last.
"This is not so bad," she said. As she had in her earlier life, she enjoyed
being at his side at leisure.

Soon, the river water ahead became two swirling, intermingling
strands of brown and green. As the boat moved north, the strands began
to separate at the mouth of the Missouri River. To starboard, the Mississippi water was as clear and green as springwoods. To port, a brown,
silted tea signaled the vast river-road west to the prairies, the Missouri
River.

The river and Ezra's gentle attention, even affection, took some of
the sting out of her heart. She wrapped her hand on top of his and
pressed in close to block the wind from her face. She snuggled him in a
way she never had before. He responded warmly. Took comfort in his
breathing. They had escaped.

A shot rang out. Ezra pulled her hard to the deck and drew his
pistol. Acres of birds, ducks and geese exploded into the air, this way
and that against the blue sky.

False alarm. She stood and saw a large brown goose lay upside
down on the sandbar, his long wings splayed. A few miners, fifty feet
down the promenade, whooped with joy and slapped the shooter on the
back. They offered him a drink.

"Dear God," she said. "Such a reckless world we're entering, Ezra."

⇒ 10 ⇐

JAMES

Four days west

Beth and Maddie stood alone on the bow of the boat, relishing the brisk morning air while Maddie read aloud from her new freedom paper, savoring the sound, the cadence, the many strange words like "hereafter" and "manumission," when suddenly the steamboat swerved sharply to port. Maddie slammed into Beth as fine spray flew in their faces

"Careful, you'll get it wet," Beth said. She grabbed the thick linen paper from Maddie's hand, wiped off the beading mist, and put it back in her bag.

"I want to read it again."

"You already know it by heart. You can recite it if you want to practice. Wait . . ."

Beth glanced around to make sure no one was approaching within earshot. From their perch on the bow of the boiler deck she only had to move her head slightly left and right. No one in sight. Beautiful spot but too much frontal western wind up here to attract people, she thought. And their voices masked by the churn of the steamboat paddle, the blustery wind, the wash and slap of an agitated river.

The ship veered again, this time sharply to starboard, forcing them to grab for the railing to keep their balance. The *Andrew Jackson* had been weaving all morning, dodging massive uprooted trees from the upriver spring storms; some half submerged, the branches and roots entangled with other trees into dangerous knots that could grab a boat. Snag steamers had been working this part of the river ahead of the *Jackson*. With grappling hooks, they cleared the main channels as best they could. Nevertheless, the boat had to weave around those they missed.

"OK, now let me hear it," said Beth. "Say it as if some rough lawman in Independence stops you, grabs your collar and demands to see your paper."

By now, it had become an incantation for Maddie. She recited from memory. *"Let it be known to all who inquire that I, Thomas J. Adams of St. Louis, before the laws of Missouri and the judgment of God do, on this day, March 14, 1849, set this girl, Daisy A. Adams, hereafter and forever free . . . Should anyone doubt or question this manumission . . ."*

"Good. That's good, Maddie. You're in control. Remember, be calm, respectful. Be serious. Don't be scared. You have every right to be where you are. To be free. Understand?"

"Yes, Beth. I'll be serious. This morning just so happy to be outside that stinky box in fresh air with you, it makes me want to do jumping jacks and cartwheels."

"Understand. Just don't draw attention when others are around. Ezra and I think you and Camille are safe today. That's why we're letting you out for a stroll. Now, no more about the freedom paper when we walk the promenade."

Beth closed her eyes, pulled her coat tight and drew the chilled wet air into her nostrils. The tang of reeds and marsh mud had never seemed so real, so vital, and life so fragile. They were all fugitives now. A light breeze chilled her cheeks and puffed her bonnet. "Just smell the fresh freedom, Maddie." She embraced the girl—a new, odd sensation for Beth, holding a child in her arms.

"Now let's stretch those legs. I want to show you parts of the boat you've only heard about. Last chance. Only one day to Independence."

Beth led Maddie around the promenade, from bow to stern and back again, without fears. She and Ezra discovered last night that the slavers and bounty hunters had already offloaded their captives, so it felt safe to bring these stir-crazed girls out for fresh air. One at a time. Ezra had taken Camille.

"Beth, how can I be good if I have to lie all the time?" Maddie asked.

"Not all the time. Sometimes, we're forced to lie to protect ourselves. Ever pretend not to be mad even when you were furious? Tell the overseers on the plantation what they wanted to hear?"

"*Ma mère* did all the time. Sometimes when I was alone, they ask me who I was and what I was up to. And I'd lie. They'd grab my ear and say, 'you're lying,' then fling me aside."

"Did they ever beat you, or whip you?"

"Not when we lived in the *grande maison*. After they threw us out, they did. A lot. They switched my legs someth'n awful. And sometimes my back. For sass'n. For go'n up to Camille's room. For be'n lazy and for laugh'n. And for nothing at all. Maddie pulled her skirt up above her boots. "See."

Beth stepped in front and spread her skirt to block the view from passersby. The scars were faint, lighter than her skin, like spider silk wrapping her calf. Beth glanced around. Nobody was paying the slightest attention. Five miners standing at the rail were pointing to a large oak floating down the river.

"You never told me what you did on the plantation, or your *mère*. Did you work with her?"

"I used to dust and wash and sweep and clean in the *grande maison* when *ma mère* was a house slave. After we was put outside in the shanties by Miss P., I plucked eggs from the nest, fed the chickens and chased 'em down for the chopping block. Slopped the hogs—got to know them, silly Millie, and grumpy Harold Hog—and helped *ma mère* in the big garden. I liked that. Hoe, and pull worms and bugs off the pole beans, collards, corn, cabbages. Saving them in a jar for the special song birds come a calling."

"But you didn't work out in the cane fields?"

"Come sugar time, I pull the seed-cane off the stalks and go plant them in new fields. Scatter the mice and clear the snakes that like to bite me. Sometimes, I run water out to the men."

"Men out in the field?"

"Men cut'n cane. And men in the grinding mills. Men in the mill covered like dusty ghosts, sweat'n streaks down their face like war paint. And those poor dead men—that's *ma mère* calls 'em—cooking up sugar in the boiling house."

"What do you mean?"

"Slaves that cuss the overseer. He whips them raw and puts'm in the boiling house cooking up sugar. Or puts them other side of the field working the indigo pots. Some working there till they die. That's what I night-sweat dream they gonna do to me when they catch me on this boat, or in this new town."

"Nobody's catching you. And nobody's going to put you in a boiling house for coming with us."

Maddie gripped Beth's skirt. "Will you stay with us after we get off the boat?"

"I, well . . . Don't know yet. If not, Camille will take good care of you. Ezra wants me to continue on with him to California, but I don't want to spend four or five months on a wagon train, mostly walking beside the wagon into the wilderness." Beth turned away from Maddie's imploring eyes. They had already talked about this.

"Come on, you wanted to see the boat, remember."

"Tell me *maybe*," said Maddie. "Just say *maybe*."

"I already said maybe, didn't I?" The girl was relentless. Beth would take a look at Independence, a good hard look, before deciding whether she could start her new life there. She was not going to be pushed one way or another. "OK, dear, maybe." Maddie squeezed her hand, smiled.

They circled the entire boat along the broad promenade one more time, then climbed the stairs to the open area on top of the boat, the Texas deck they called it, where the pilothouse sat square and prominent. From the railing up there, they could see the whole of the river: the silent brown curves, the shallow bars, willow trees with their brooding faces leaning over the riverbank to drink. Here on top, Beth noticed, the sway of the boat was more soothing, less annoying. More understandable.

Maddie laid her thin arms on the railing to rest her chin. "Beth, I just keep going up rivers and rivers and more rivers. Farther and farther away, to where I don't know." She grew silent, then pointed to some noisy ducks that descended on a marshy island to starboard, chasing away the egrets. And to a solitary pelican cruising low along the river-bank parallel to the boat.

"Look. There she is! That's her," shouted Maddie. "Same pelly bird. Probably *ma mère* watching over me. You know, I told you, she became a pelly bird when she died. Now she's guide'n us someplace. Keep'n me and Camille safe."

Beth took Maddie's hand. "Come on, stop brooding and dreaming, I'll show you all the rooms you've not been able to see. But first, put your gloves on, shift the bonnet forward and pull your veil down."

Back down to the boiler deck, Beth ushered Maddie through a long, wide corridor with a number of brightly lit rooms to the left and right. They stared into the card room. Men hoarding their cards against sweaty chests, smoking cigars—men who glanced up, men with faces blank as lizards.

Another fifteen paces and they entered the wide, inviting expanse of the dining room with its tall ceiling, fine moldings, and leaded windows. It was alive with chatter and music. Men and women, bright and flirtatious, flushed with alcohol and gorging on breakfast platters of fish, game, puddings. A violinist worked the room. Beth was surprised to see so many prostitutes getting a jump on the day—patting the hands of men, talking with postured heads and seductive tones.

"I see some Black people," Maddie whispered. She pointed and lifted her veil. Beth pushed the veil down and shushed her. They moved slowly as they stared at the table of freemen wearing fashionable coats, their pistols and top hats on the table, drinking port with eggs, greens, and hushpuppies. We must be shedding civilization, Beth thought. No Black man would openly sport a pistol like that in St. Louis.

Beth felt a hip nudge, then Maddie flicked her eyes toward another Black man, pouring a glass of Champagne for a sensuous woman as dark as blue coal, wearing her hair tied up in a flamboyant orange and yellow Caribbean scarf. As the violinist approached her, the woman sang soprano in a Jamaican lilt, waving a delicate silver spoon in the air like a conductor.

"She's so pretty. Is this where you and Ezra eat when you bring us those nice scraps? I'd like to sit at one of these tables and sing while we eat. Can we do that?" Beth shrugged without comment. Her stomach turning sour with the thought of sitting with these girls so exposed.

They returned to the promenade. "What's on the deck down below this one?" Maddie asked.

"Oh, the staging area for moving goods on and off the boat. And the storage holds for supplies, miners' equipment, wagons, animals. We don't need to go down there."

"What kind of animals?

"Mostly work animals. Horses, mules, oxen. Stinks down there."

"Please, can we go down? I love animals," said Maddie, dancing her feet. Beth hesitated, then watching the light in the child's eyes, gave in.

They walked down the stairway and crossed the short staging area of the main deck into the cargo holds. They moved cautiously, letting their eyes adjust to the dusty light. Beth's chest tightened and her arms tingled with nervousness. She could see storage pens ahead, cordoned off with slats and rope. The light dimmed and the smell of ripe manure gagged her as they skirted the animal holds—wooden stalls and leather restraints separating the horses, mules, and the hulking, wide-bellied oxen. Maddie walked in front, so Beth could keep an eye on her and remind her not to race. "Slow and steady, Maddie."

One ox turned toward Maddie as she danced past. Not but a foot away, the ox sprayed spittle on her neck and cheek. Beth jumped back and Maddie spun to complain, but the ox bellowed into her face, long and loud, sending her crashing backwards into a stack of wooden chicken crates. The chickens squawked and flapped, startling her again. But Maddie leapt up off the floor laughing, bruised, thrilled with the adventure.

"Shh. Quiet. You don't want to stir up these animals." Beth stared at the oxen slobbering, chewing cud. Ugly beasts. Could I live with them for four months on a trail, she wondered? Ezra said they become like companions in time. For two thousand miles? Nah. One more reason not to go on a damned wagon train.

Past the stables, they moved into the gloomy silence of the main cargo hold, and walked down a narrow aisle between steamer trunks, sacks of coffee and grain, barrels of whiskey, and stacks and stacks of disassembled wagons and canvas rolls of mining gear, shovel and pick handles sticking out.

Maddie stopped. "I hear somebody." A shadow moved in the back of the hold and a shiver ran up Beth's spine.

"Is there somebody back there?" Beth shouted.

No answer. She pulled Maddie behind the wagon beds. They squatted down and Beth took out her pistol.

They breathed softly, listening. All was quiet. After three or four minutes, Beth put her face down to the floor and peeked around. The shadow was moving again, this time up the center aisle toward them in complete silence. She slid back and put her hand over Maddie's mouth. As the shadow passed by, she saw a boy, rather tall, blond, no more than fourteen years old, she guessed. He was gone, swallowed in shadows in an instant.

"He's hungry," said Maddie. "Slaves walk that way."

Looking around, Beth reconsidered her judgment bringing Maddie down here. This deserted hold was no place to run into trouble. "We better go back up." She took Maddie by the hand and led her quickly down the storage aisle, past the stables and holding pens, past the slobbering, lumbering oxen, and into the light.

A startling flash of movement as the boy jumped out in front of them, his hands in the air. Maddie screamed. Beth immediately put her pistol to his chest, pushed him back against a doorframe, and cocked it.

"Why are you after me?" the boy demanded, near tears. "You're not going to tell on me, are you?"

"What are you talking about? You almost got yourself shot, jumping us like that," Beth shouted. "Who are you?" She fought to control her rage but kept her pistol at his chest.

His voice was tight, fists clenched. Tall, thin, very young face with curling blond hair. "Do you have any food?" was the first thing out of his mouth. Then, as if recognizing how much he'd frightened them, added, "Sorry to scare."

"No food," said Beth. She lowered her gun, eased the hammer down, and stared at his nose: prominent, bruised, possibly broken, slightly off center. He'd been punched. Bruises on his cheek and neck.

Maddie pulled out a green apple. The boy looked startled, then snatched it and ate it fast, core, stem and all, like a starving wolf. "I've been too afraid to break open those boxes of sardines back there and let the smell out. Sometimes at night I sneak up on deck and do it fast. Bite, bite, then swallow them almost whole. Throw the rest overboard. Then find some place to wash my hands cause the stink draws the rats down here, come nibbling my fingers. Lots down here."

"You a stowaway?" Beth asked.

"Hiding for four days . . . trying to find food. Any more apples?"

To Beth's surprise, Maddie pulled out a second apple and two crusts of bread and thrust them forward. He devoured the bread first, his eyes tearing with relief, then the apple, mumbling appreciation to Maddie with his mouth full. *Such an innocent face*, Beth thought.

Boy finally swallowed the last, licked his fingers. "Name's James. Some men stole everything first day. They clubbed me, broke my nose I think, took my ticket, money, food, my grandfather's rifle. They said it was payment to keep quiet. Otherwise, they'd report me. Maybe sell me off, indentured to someone, make themselves some money."

"Are you getting off in Independence?" Maddie asked.

"Don't know where that is. Going west. All the way to California. I'm trying to find Mr. Adams. He's on this boat somewhere. A Mr. Ezra—"

"Ezra?" Maddie jumped. Beth clamped her hand over Maddie's mouth.

"You better start talking, boy! Who are you? Who sent you? You a spotter for bounty hunters?"

"No ma'am."

Maddie yanked away from Beth's grasp. "We know him. Ezra. He's with us."

"Are you Miss Beth?" he asked.

MADDIE RACED INTO THE STATEROOM AND PLOPPED DOWN NEXT TO Camille, bounced on the bed. James stood squirming in the doorway, afraid to enter. Beth remained outside in the fresh air where she could stretch her arms, legs. Her body was knotted with anxiety bringing this boy to their cabin.

"Brought someone looking for you, Ezra," said Maddie. "Knows your name and has a letter for you. Needs some food."

Ezra, sitting on the bed opposite her, stood, puzzled, and looked the tall, skinny kid up and down. "Who are you and who sent you?"

James stood up straight, came to Ezra's chin, and ran his fingers through curly blond hair. He brushed his wrinkled pants, reached in his pocket and pulled out a soiled envelope. "I'm supposed to give this to you before Independence. I was robbed, so I been hiding down in the hold."

The ink had faded but the handwriting was familiar. Ezra opened it. He glanced immediately for the signature. Thomas. *What now?*

My Dearest Ezra,

By the time you read this you will be well underway, and I trust in good spirits when I tell you what I have done. I put this boy, James Turner, onto your steamboat, told him to make contact with you, and give you this letter by way of introduction and petition to join your wagon train. You will most assuredly need a wagon for Beth if she is to travel as your wife, as well as a teamster to lead that wagon and protect her while you are off doing your scouting. I highly recommend James. He is extraordinarily good with animals. Reliable, hardworking, surprisingly strong. Surprisingly kind. He learns fast. A runaway from Michigan, he's is trying to find his older brother in California. If you recall, it was his brother's letter from the gold fields that I read that night at the party. Two investors were swayed by that letter and your clever display of gold. As such, I feel I owe the boy a *chance. You will not regret hiring him. Thank you for taking him off my hands, and Martha sends her love to all of you. She is delighted that you are coming into family ways, Ezra, even under peculiar circumstances. As you can imagine, she hopes the girls remain in your care.*

Affectionately, Thomas

Ezra read the letter a second time. *What's next?* He had been hired as a solitary guide. Well, he and his partner, Brose, as a team. How could he possibly . . .? He glared at James. *Some burden foisted on me by Thomas?*

"He gave this to *you*? My brother? Did he tell you what was in it?"

"No sir. He just said it was time to go if I wanted to hop a wagon train to California. He gave me this letter, some food, a week's wages, and a ticket. Had someone slip me on board this ship before daylight."

Ezra raised his eyebrows. Saw Beth standing in the doorway frame next to the boy. "James, is it?" *Disheveled kid.* He turned his attention to Beth. "Let's step outside. James, you step in and you be careful with these girls, or I'll take your head off."

She followed him out, shut the door, and extended her hand. "Well? Let me read it."

Beth read it through, glancing up at him, bewildered, amused, then read it through again. She started laughing. "What a scoundrel, your brother. Off-loading the boy on you."

It had been such a surprising turn of events. Thomas walking into the kitchen with Martha and a draft of a new freedom paper for Maddie. Thomas, a pro-slaver, at least publicly for business reasons, revealing a sentimental side and a willingness to perjure himself. He had been swayed by assurances that Maddie was free-born. But it was the powerful resemblance to Daisy that truly won him over. "I'm doing this for this wonderful girl and for the real Daisy, equally wonderful," he said. "May God forgive our family for selling her into oblivion." Thomas had five copies made by his private notary, one sealed, now sitting with his lawyer, one for himself, two for the girls, and one for Ezra.

"What Thomas suggests isn't such a crazy idea," said Beth. "James as your drover."

"Be good to have another set of hands. But, this kid? I don't know a damn thing about him."

"Extraordinarily good with animals, your brother said. Strong, capable, kind. But only thirteen. We have some time to decide, at least until we get to Independence."

"You still want to get off there?" he asked. "Don't worry. Won't argue. It's your decision."

⇒ 11 ⇐

INDEPENDENCE

Frontier town

Two quick tugs and a long melancholy pull of the steam horn announced the one-hour mark to Independence. The deep moaning horn reverberated in Camille's chest, quickening her pulse and prickling her entire body with dread. Only one short hour and she and Maddie would step off the boat into the unknown. That was the agreement.

Don't panic, she told herself. *Calm. For God's sake, keep calm.*

She clasped her satchel and helped Maddie and Beth finish packing the second bag with that odd assortment of clothing from Martha's attic. Some nice dresses from her daughter's younger years bundled with an armful of ragtag, selected in haste, some merely for disguise.

"Three perfect dresses for you, Maddie. But these, too big, too old lady, too frivolous for a frontier town," said Beth, holding up each of the dresses. "But good material you can remake into whatever you need." She smiled at Camille as if Camille knew how to cut, sew, make clothing, darn socks, crochet sweaters. She kept her mouth shut, embarrassed, but nodded her false confidence at Maddie, who was even more terrified than she was.

She'd learn, by God. No more servants, slaves, dress makers, fashion shops. That life was over. All the better, Camille thought. That old life had too many strings, obligations, restrictions. This new life had hardship yes, but novelty and adventure, too. No plantation rulebook.

Jenny's departing words kept turning over in her mind. "Get to know your brave. You're strong, smart. Now you be needing that brave your daddy tried to bury in you. Time you reach down, grab it and pull it up."

Adapt, survive. Camille would find the means and adjust to what-ever life threw at her. Ezra knew people in Independence who would help them find temporary lodging, give them a start, a job. The Muellers had a bakery, he said. Marse Cavandesh, a farm just outside of town. Irv Johansen, a stable for pack mules, plenty of work this time of year, he told her. Ezra had written letters of introduction for her and Maddie. Of these, Camille would prefer the bakery. She'd pretend expe-rience, show eagerness. At least she and Maddie were beyond the reach of her father and hopefully now the bounty hunters. And in her fantasy of Independence they'd live a life openly with each other, if not as blood sisters, then close companions. She hadn't asked Ezra but imagined these frontier towns would be less rigid about how people lived and with whom.

She assumed Beth, who had already packed her own bag to get off, could help her get started with the practical things she'd need—cooking, sewing, chopping wood, fixing things, even carpentry. Maddie already knew gardening. In her mind Camille imagined a tranquil life. A small home with a vegetable patch. Cow in a barn. Pen with chickens. Cozy fireplace. Warm stew on the table. Music and friends and laughter.

Ezra, who had been pacing just outside the door, leaned his head in. "Let's go to the bow for some fresh air. Get you out of this stale state-room and all this gloom. Lots of beautiful countryside to see before we arrive. Full hour. It's a prime viewing spot for when we land. Watch the scramble as these boys unload their gear. Plenty of time to enjoy the landscape before all of you get off."

Despite the cheery invitation, Camille heard the tightness in his throat. When she caught his eye, she saw a square-jawed, grim, resolute sadness. "Be a sight," he added brightly.

Liar. He's trying to calm us, she realized, but doing it poorly. And trying to hide his longing for Beth. When he said, "all of you," there was a catch in his throat while looking at Beth and she didn't flinch. Beth stood firm, determined to avoid his secret nudge, Camille could tell. They could be a maddening pair.

AFTER LEAVING THE STATEROOM, THE FOUR ALONG WITH JAMES had the full expanse of the bow promenade to themselves. The boat seemed to move more slowly in the final hour, Camille thought, as she leaned her elbows on the railing. A morning mist, almost like fog, rose from the river. Along the shoreline, they passed only thick stands of trees, marshland, meadows, occasional beached canoes, a campfire here and there. And beyond the shore, rolling hills and open land disappearing into morning fog. No buildings. As yet, no evidence of the quiet frontier village of Independence could be seen.

Along the starboard shore, Maddie pointed to a small campfire and the white covers of three wagons shimmering in the morning light, then another fire. And another. "I see some cooking fires and wagons and people walking about."

Ezra came to the railing and stared at the campfires. "Makes no sense this far from Independence. Hermits maybe, but not this many. Must be seven, eight people there. Maybe hunters. Good game around here."

Their conversation drew Camille. She slid down the railing and the three stared at the shoreline. James had walked in the other direction and was now sitting alone on some crates on the port side. Maddie waved him over, but he declined.

Soon, there were more camp fires scattered along the riverbank. First in twos and threes, then a cluster of five. Then ten with circled wagons, grazing mules, spread out between two stands of dense trees. Maddie pointed to other cook fires inland from the river, just barely visible, pinpricks of light receding into the misty countryside.

Ezra paced the deck, deep in thought, glancing at the shoreline, his face tight with anxiety. Clearly upset, Camille thought. He said a few words to Beth then broke away. His demeanor reminded Camille of her father when the crops were failing or the markets falling. Clearly, the concentration of campfires was growing and disturbing Ezra for some reason.

"Camille, Maddie," said Ezra, "I want you to start counting these fires. Carefully. As far back downriver as you can see. And inland, even the ones so faint you're not quite sure."

"But why?" Camille asked.

"Can you do that? Explain what I'm thinking after my head clears."

Camille glanced over at Beth, who signaled for her to do what he asked. By the look on her face, Beth didn't know, either. Camille hated his tone, being commanded without reason to obey. It wasn't like him. His thoughtful, even gentlemanly manner suddenly gone.

"Just be methodical. It's important," he said. "Every fire, all from way back there"—he swung his arm in a long arc—"to the landing ahead. And just on this side of the river. Don't see many on the south side."

The girls divided the task and stood at the rail, counting quietly.

"I don't understand," said Maddie.

"Shh. Do you still have that chalk in your pocket?"

Camille dropped to her knees and chalked some numbers on the varnished deck, then jumped back up and continued counting. Her finger poked at the sparks of light. Maddie knelt down, added more numbers. Back and forth, up and down. Maybe he's trying to distract us, Camille thought. It seemed to be working; Maddie grew less agitated as she became absorbed in the task.

EZRA HADN'T ANTICIPATED THIS. *I SHOULD HAVE*, HE BERATED himself. He saw them massing in St. Louis. And knew none of these miners could risk leaving for California until the prairie was dry enough to hold the weight of their wagon wheels. Spring rains had been heavy. The land was still soft. And these men tend to overdo, packing a lot of heavy gear. They're stuck here until the prairie dries and the feed-grass surges.

He and Beth drifted to a spot down the railing, away from the girls and their keen ears.

"Ezra, what the hell is this? I don't like this place one bit. And we haven't yet reached the town. Looks like an invading army out there. You said—"

"Keep your voice down!" he said. "I sailed by not four weeks ago, and none of this was here. It was as always. Small, friendly trading center with a scattering of mountain men, merchants, guides, indigenous people and Mexicans. Trail activity was nil."

CAMILLE FELT HIM BREATHING OVER HER SHOULDER. HE SQUATTED down, making her lose count. She'd have to start the column over. She bit her tongue, but his overbearing presence was annoying. *If you give me a task, then let me have at it.* She kept her mouth shut.

"When you are done with the raw count, I want you to calculate," he said. She looked up, puzzled, perturbed, put down her chalk. He went on. "I want you to assume there are five fires unseen for every one you can see. And five men to every fire. And finally, as many fires upriver from the landing as downriver. Then give me a total."

"Are you trying to figure out how many men are out there?"

"Exactly," he said.

"Then just say so," said Camille. "I'll multiply the raw count by fifty. I'm not an idiot."

He smiled. "Wasn't suggesting. And now you'll want to know why you're counting." Her face brightened. "It's because it affects everything going forward."

"What do you mean?"

His eyes signaled he couldn't put it into words just yet. He stood, his face hardened with concern, without answering.

TEN MINUTES LATER, AS INDEPENDENCE CAME INTO VIEW, THE steam horn sounded long and deep. The birds stopped flapping, and cruised, gliding while looking around for food.

Even before they docked, Camille saw the quay was teeming with boisterous, rough men, teams of mules, oxen, roustabouts. Men pushing, fighting to board the incoming boat for the next stops at the more northern trailheads. Some on the wharf shot pistols in the air to welcome the men on board, who shot back. Rotting garbage and the sour smell of marsh mud and unwashed men assaulted them.

The girls slid down the bow for a better view. Camille put her arm around Maddie, who gripped the railing tenaciously, frozen. They stared at their new home. Camille fought tears. She wanted to scream. Maddie buried her face in Camille.

Camille pulled Maddie down to the deck boards to keep her from seizing up with fear. "Easy. We'll be OK. I promise," she said.

EZRA FELT BETH TUGGING HIM BY THE ELBOW. "I DON'T KNOW about Independence. Look at this horde, this confusion. This is no town." She paused, stared at him. "I can't imagine how these girls could survive here. Or me, for that matter."

He wasn't about to tell her the worst. This town, swollen as it was, would surge, then empty out just as fast. And like a receding tidal storm take everything with it. When the great *jumpoff* came—a matter of weeks, he reckoned—all of these men would begin racing for California in one whip-cracking, competitive tumult, fighting for position and space on a network of trails.

There would be an unruly, reckless spirit; he could feel it already and had seen it before. Strong impulses, explosive tempers, bad judgment. Freed from the guardrails of civilization, Camille and Maddie could be swept away, grabbed as cooks, drudge maids, servants or sex slaves and sold off. Passed hand to hand, used, discarded.

"We have to figure this out," he said.

"Are you talking about us? What about these girls? They have a say."

"Of course they do. All of us."

He hushed Beth as Camille and Maddie walked over.

Camille was trembling. "I don't think we should get off here as planned. It looks dangerous and Maddie is terrified. Truth, me too." Maddie was clinging to Camille's skirt, peering around at Ezra.

"I understand. That's a rough world down there," said Ezra. "Not what I expected. What was your final count?"

"Men? Eight thousand or so, maybe more. Some fires were so dim. Didn't see any women. No families. Didn't count the few scattered fires on the port side."

Ezra ran his hands up through his hair, knocking his flop hat to the deck. His eyes wide, "Eight thousand! Right here, right now!" he shouted. He would have guessed three, four, five, tops. There hadn't been five thousand miners in all of California six months earlier. And men would continue pouring in from everywhere. By time of the *jumpoff*, he realized, there could be ten thousand, right here alone. *At one single trailhead!* And likely more waves of men after that.

He picked up his hat and swatted it against the railing. "Unbelievable."

"Is that a lot?" Maddie asked.

His stomach knotted. "Yes. Awful." His mind was racing ahead, anticipating what they might find farther upriver at other trail-heads. Because all the trails eventually converged, if the crowds were anything like this, there could be wagon trains stretching for hundreds of miles on a single trail. Jammed. Slowed down. He'd have to convince his own wagon train—still two hundred miles north at the mouth of the Platte River—that this would become a race, and if you start behind, you stay behind.

Camille broke his train of thought. "Ezra, I don't know where Maddie and I will get off, certainly not here, but before we decide, I want to thank you and Beth for getting us this far."

My God, he thought, is she starting to thank me for dumping them in this morass? In this madhouse? He started to respond, but Beth put out her hand to silence him.

"What's that down there?" Beth asked, pointing. "A funeral? Looks like three or four bodies." She jabbed her finger at a spot a few hundred yards upriver from the landing.

A shallow trench down very close to the river with three bodies side by side, wrapped in blankets and tattered cloth. Men with bandanas across their faces worked feverishly. They shoveled dirt onto the bodies as fast as they could and then walked away, without a marker, or even so much as a nod toward the grave. As they made their way up the riverbank, they pulled their bandanas off with a visible gasp. They stepped aside for another wagon working its way down the bank with a few more wrapped corpses.

It sent a shiver up Ezra's spine. Cholera, by the looks of it. But how could it have jumped this far upriver? This fast? Last he'd heard it had just landed in New Orleans.

He could feel Beth and Camille trying to read him. He avoided their eyes, but Beth's voice chased after him. "You know something, don't you?"

He looked straight ahead, considering the implications. She pulled his arm. He disliked being forced into honesty just because she demanded it.

Stepping around to face him, she spoke firmly. "Please don't hold back on me now. Not now. If you do, I'll get off the boat with Camille and Maddie, right here. In this cesspool of a town you said was so quiet and cordial."

"No. You can't . . . not here!" he said. "Please, not here, not now." He had been alone for a generation, and the thought of continuing on without her, likely losing her forever, was anguishing. And worse, possibly condemning them to death, losing her and the girls to this dreaded scourge. He respected her too much, loved her too much to dodge. He owed her a straight answer.

"Probably cholera," he said.

"Beth gasped, then sucked in her breath and stepped back, her eyes darting about in terror. Camille jumped like she had been burned. Maddie turned and ran down the promenade toward James, with Camille chasing after her.

The horn sounded again as the boat settled against its moorings. Men ran alongside to catch and secure the massive lines. The miners on the main deck hooted and cheered and fired their rifles as if they had already arrived in gold country. The gangplank slammed down and was tied into place. A larger ramp toward the stern was lowered and secured.

THE SOUND OF FOOT TRAFFIC ON THE GANGPLANK BROUGHT THE girls to the railing near James who sat on the crates in a stupor. Peering down, Maddie cried. "Is this it? I don't want . . . Please, Camille, I don't want to go down there. Ever. Don't make me live down there."

"We're not." Camille pulled her into her arms. "We're not getting off here. You heard me tell Ezra we're not, that I don't care what we agreed. He can see what's down there just as well as we can. My job is to keep you safe. We'll keep on running."

Ezra whispered to Beth. "Where'd they go? I can't see them. They wouldn't get off by themselves, would they? Here?"

"Of course not. They're down there by those crates where James is sitting," she said. "They wouldn't dare get off."

He exhaled. "Beth, I'm sorry, I misjudged. I'm not leaving them here. Or you either. For God's sake, please don't get off."

"I won't," she said. "Maybe we can find a safe place a little further north at one of the next stops. St. Joe, maybe? Or Leavenworth?"

"Possibly. But this massing of miners here may well be spreading up there. We see men down there clamoring to get on this boat. What they don't know is that it doesn't matter where they start, which of these trailheads they choose, they all end up at the same place."

"What does that mean?"

"All these trails veer off the Missouri River, angling to take a short cut to the Platte River but all eventually converge into one solitary trail skirting the south shore of the Platte. In contrast, we stay on the boat, or at least I do, all the way to the mouth of the Platte River, where it flows into the Missouri River, some two hundred miles north of here.

Which allows my partner and I to guide our train along the *north* side of the Platte. North trail not the southern trail."

"North, south, is there a difference?" Beth asked.

"Yes, some very important differences. Easier for wagons in many ways, and less crowded. Always fewer wagons and more fresh grass for the animals within easy reach. And quite difficult, even dangerous for those on the south side to try to get their wagons across to the less crowded north side. Wagons hit sideways with a sudden turbulent current can tip over, losing everything, wagon, contents, mules, oxen. Then what do you have? Both trails along the Platte take you west across the plains to the Rocky Mountains, but the north side is a far better choice."

"Sounds like you and your partner worked this all out in advance. What's his name?"

"Brose. Yes, we've been at this for years. We know the land and the rivers pretty well. But rivers can always surprise you, the way they curl, scour, cut channels, flood fast from upriver storms, hit you with rip currents you can't see from shore."

"OK Ezra, enough about trails and currents," said Beth, shivering, her muscles tense with fear. "More important to me, and I know the girls will ask me. Are we in danger of these men bringing the cholera with them as they board?"

"No. Well, probably not. I know a few things about cholera from my own experience. First, people with cholera don't walk. They're far too wicked sick. Almost immediately. So, if you see a man walk up the gangplank, rest assured he doesn't have it. And cholera is not one of those diseases, like influenza, passed face to face. No one really knows how it spreads. Doctors say miasma in the air but I think that's horseshit. It takes some other route. Of that, I'm sure."

Beth shouted down to Camille, Maddie, and James. "Girls, we're not getting off!" Camille smiled broadly and waved. Maddie danced about in her favorite dress, light blue with, as she called them, biddy white flowers. Both girls hugged James spontaneously. The boy had been brooding, still waiting to be invited by Ezra to join the wagon train.

FARTHER NORTH, THE BOAT STOPPED TO LET MEN OFF AT THE other key trailheads—St. Joe, Westport, Leavenworth, and Kearny. Leaning on the promenade railing, Camille and Maddie were aghast at the crowds. They turned to look at Beth and Ezra also staring down at each dismal possibility. Ezra shook his head. Beth, her face squeezed in disgust and feeling nauseous, mouthed the word "No," to the girls who smiled in relief and held each other. Camille rubbed Maddie's back and ran her fingers through Maddie's hair to calm her down.

Finally conferring at the front of the bow, they all agreed these were worse than Independence. Small villages and forts engulfed by sprawling encampments of wagons, animals, tents and fires. Garbage and waste, thousands of restless, impatient men fixing their gear in the mud, or wandering about, drinking, gambling, looking for fights, shooting their guns in the air. Some prostitutes working out of a series of tents.

The girls tried to hold up brave faces for Beth and Ezra but were clearly terrified by the chaos at these landings, the muggy stench of men and oxen, the nerve shattering crack of whips and gunfire. They huddled together, their eyes desperate for protection. They were sailing into a nightmare without end.

Beth and Ezra paced the bow and shook their heads in agreement. The girls would never survive these raw-bone camps. "Nor me," said Beth. "Let's be clear about this." It became an unspoken truth among all of them; they would continue on together.

The Council Bluffs, where Lewis and Clark held council with the Otoe tribe, sat in grandeur overlooking the new river town at the confluence of the Missouri and Platte Rivers. Kanesville was the last stop for this steamboat. It would dock, off load, then take on passengers, freight, mail, possibly prisoners for the return run all the way to St. Louis.

Ezra, Beth, Camille, Maddie, and James prepared to disembark. They packed up and moved to their favorite spot on the bow to look over Kanesville.

They withheld their usual disdain, harsh words, anger, disappointment, tearful eyes, and stood staring with blank faces. Maybe not so bad, but no one said so. Beth saw a yellow building up on the knoll, maybe a church—a hopeful semblance of a village beyond.

End of the line. Beth felt the quickening in her blood and brain, her mind scrambling for answers. The boat was going to return downriver. Could she make a go of it here? It was no longer just her. It was them. All of them now. Thrown together, growing fonder of each other through their travails, melding into an almost familial protective posture of care. Even for Ezra, Beth thought. Now that was strange. To feel protective of this wilderness-hardened, resolute, soft-hearted man who could still run shivers up her spine.

"Well?" he said to Beth, while nervously gripping the railing. "Hard to tell from here."

"Yes. Have to take a look-see." She put her hand on top of his, staring straight ahead at her last hope for a settled life on this side of the continent.

⇒ 12 ⇐

KANESVILLE

Council Bluffs, April 1849

As the five walked off the steamboat, Ezra paid the ticket master for the additional run from Independence for Beth, the girls, and James. Carrying trunks, weapons, and armfuls of gear, they struggled up a muddy hill toward the new, ramshackle village of Kanesville. Half way up they stopped to catch their breath next to a large oak. Dropped everything on the ground and stood dumbfounded by the confusion surrounding them.

"Dear God. Is this it? Kanesville?" Beth asked, with an undertone of dread. The girls looked out over the hillside with fear in their eyes at miners as far as the eye could see gathered in clusters, playing cards, gambling, fixing gear, wrestling, throwing knives, sprawling in their tents. Camille and Maddie instinctively moved closer.

"Sorry to say, Ezra, but it looks worse than it did from the boat," said Beth. He grimaced, turning about to face her, removing his hat and running his fingers through his hair.

"Look, a church," said Maddie with a chirp of brightness, pointing uphill.

She's right, Beth thought. Up there, a sliver of hope, a settlement of sorts, beginning at the crest of the knoll with a large yellow church. But it was the approach that gave her pause. Before her, a muddy path up through a hillside of debris, crowded with unkempt men, campfires, wagons, tools. She glanced about for signs of village life but saw no families, no women, no stores, no merchants. Just men and gear. Her stomach knotted at the realization this might be just another campsite, like the ones they passed two days ago at St. Joe and Kearny, miners overwhelming a village. Temporarily filling it with disheveled, forlorn, and careless men, their passions stirred by gold lust, sending residents into hiding, Beth assumed.

"Ezra, talk to me. You know this place."

"I don't recognize it anymore. I don't see anyone I know, none of the villagers. Maybe they're in hiding or left for the countryside. Can't blame them." He pointed up the hill. "Beth, no sense the five of us carting all our belongings up there into the crowd. Maybe better if we leave the girls and James right here where they have the benefit of this shady tree all to themselves while we explore. They're armed and should be OK for fifteen, twenty minutes. Don't you think? I don't see anyone pressing in on us this side of the path."

Beth tried for a pleasant, reassuring face as she turned to the girls and they stepped closer. She gently grasped Camille's hand and tenderly lifted Maddie's chin with her other hand. "Don't despair. We're not deserting you. While you rest and eat, Ezra and I need to take a quick look at the possibilities for this village up above. See if there is any hope for us. And Ezra needs to learn the whereabouts of his wagon train."

Beth signaled to James. "Come here. Listen to me. I want you stay very close, very alert, and guard these girls with your life. You understand what that means? We'll be back in fifteen minutes."

Pushing his curling hair out of his eyes, he stood up straighter, and came to full attention like a soldier. Holding one of Ezra's rifles in his hand. "Yes, ma'am, Beth. I'll take good care of them."

"And yourself. Don't get into any scrapes. Somebody comes, don't be trigger happy. Don't shoot someone because you're nervous. Let them see you're armed. And let Camille do the talking. OK?" He nodded.

She turned to Camille. "If anyone comes around asking questions or seems overly friendly, you do the talking for the trio. Let them see you're armed but try to be cordial. Bluff them if you have to. We'll be back shortly."

It was too muddy to stroll casually. Every few steps, Beth reached for Ezra's arm to keep her balance. She could see the confusion and disappointment in his eyes as he looked at the horde of miners, but she said nothing. Kept her complaints and the knots in her stomach to herself. She glanced back to see James leaning against his rifle, standing between the girls and the men on the other side of the muddy trail. Camille was sitting, talking to Maddie with a rifle across her lap, while Maddie, who had laid her pistol on the canvas bag next to her, was idly picking up and inspecting rocks. The fact that they were the only two females in sight made Beth's fists clench with anxiety. One never knew with men unmoored from family, home, community.

Reading Beth's discomfort, Ezra said, "Don't worry, they'll be fine. All three armed and alert."

"I wish I felt more comfortable about this place," said Beth. "It's one thing to see these miners living like this from a distance, quite another to walk among them. I'm the only woman around up here and I can feel them stop and turn their eyes on me."

He took her arm. "You're a pleasant distraction for them. They're harmless. You're wearing your ring. They'll respect that."

"I believe you. It's just uncomfortable feeling like prey. Thanks for taking my arm."

"Trying to get my bearings," he said, looking around. "Don't see anyone I know, and half the trees have been cut down for firewood. But at least the Lewis and Clark is still open." He pointed to a large planked building that could be most anything—a saloon, a store, a community hall—given the size of the building and the size of the crowd lingering in front. Then Beth saw the faded sign above the door with a canoe symbol: *L&C Tavern.*

"That's where Brose would have left a message," he said. "Almost certainly."

"Brose is your partner?"

He glanced at her, nodded. "We go way back. You'll meet him shortly."

As they walked quietly, she found herself continually searching for women's faces, for children, for some softening presence. This was their last chance to shelter the girls, or for that matter, to start her own life over. Her hands were trembling as the pressure to decide her future grew stronger. Ezra sensed her nervousness, took one hand in his, and without words, squeezed it for reassurance. She kept looking left and right for signs of ordinary life, but everywhere she looked she saw only bored, impatient men milling about, trying to amuse themselves with footraces along a roped off gauntlet, dice and card games, wrestling and knife throws.

The sights and sounds prickled her nerves, but it was the unwanted attention that rattled her. Some men stared at her brazenly; others nodded or tipped their hats. She avoided their eyes and took comfort in Ezra's arm. Now held it fully, firmly as they walked.

He smiled at her, patting her hand.

"It's just easier this way," she said. "Can you imagine the girls in this place?" The locals were wise to keep their women and children out of sight, she thought. But how could she evaluate the town's livability without seeing, experiencing normality. She tried to imagine Kanesville empty of these miners and their debris, with life rebounding, flowers and berry bushes springing forth, a village ordinary and quiet enough to hear the birds, the rush of the river.

Instead, she heard drunken laughter, shouts, endless profanity thrown in jest and anger like darts. And oddly in the background the continuous ring of a smithy's hammer. A short pause, then a hiss of cold water fleeing a hot surface. The acrid smell of quenched metal wrinkled her nose.

"Ready?" Ezra asked her as they stood in front of the L&C Tavern. She smiled and nodded. *I can do this*, she thought, remembering her tenants, rough men she had learned to manage with firmness and banter.

With Ezra in the lead, they pushed aggressively into the saloon and jostled their way through a noisy, dusty den packed with mud-smeared, sweating, whiskey-fouled men. Standing room only. Ripe as a manure pile. Beth held her nose in disgust as men pointed and laughed at her. Her stomach turned sour as she squeezed through tight quarters, with impatient men pressing and pushing from all sides in all directions.

Fortunately, Ezra was like a battering ram. She grabbed his shoulder. "Slow down. I don't want to get separated or crushed. What are we looking for?"

Ezra pointed across the room in the direction they were heading. Nailed and pegged across an entire wall were notices, letters, and messages, overlapping and askew. Men stood two and three deep with others pressing from behind, pawing through the messages, looking for family, friends, wagon trains. Beth finally realized this was the communications roundhouse for Kanesville, at least during the gold rush. As the crowd got tighter, Ezra wrapped one arm around Beth's shoulder, and used his other arm and broad shoulder to clear a path to the postings.

A burly man smiled at her and shouted to his mates as she squeezed by. "I'm going on *her* train."

"Appreciate your help pulling the wagon," she said. Some laughter.

Near the front, she scanned the postings on the wall. "Lex, Pa died. Jeb." "Going back to Cincinnati. Wagon and mule team for sale." "Nashville Company, where the hell are you?"

Ezra pointed, told her to reach for that patch of blue. In the middle of the sprawl, she saw a blue envelope in fine feminine handwriting that read, "Ezra Adams, California Mining Company." Imposing in its formality, the letter stood by itself. She pulled it carefully off the nail, as every eye watched the curve of her hand, her delicate wrist. She could feel heads turn. *Shouldn't have taken off my gloves,* she realized.

Beth was surprised to see Ezra suddenly press himself against the notices and rip something off the wall that he surreptitiously wadded up in his fist.

"Let's get out of here," he said. The two put their shoulders together again to wedge their way through the crowd toward the door.

"Hey, sweet skirt, come have a drink," someone shouted from the bar.

Another thumped a glass. "Over here, pretty bird."

Beth raised her hand and hollered to part the crowd. "Lads, appreciate the flattery but I'm a married woman. Not some damned bird."

"Beautiful, then!" shouted one. "How's that, little lady?" as he helped clear the way and patted Ezra on the shoulder.

"Better," she said, as they reached the door.

Bursting outside, she took a deep breath of fresh, wet air. "The stench in there. How can they stand it?"

At a dry spot next to a small elm, they sat and stretched their legs. Ezra took the letter and handed her the crumpled newsprint. She smoothed it out. Another ad for the girls, but the bounty had been raised. "Dear God. It never ends."

Ezra paused before pulling the letter out of the blue envelope. "You know, if you decide to come on the wagon train, you can't be easy like that. Joking with the men that way. They might take it wrong."

"Are you serious? I've learned a few things in my twenty years running a boarding house. Men like banter. Makes them feel appreciated, connected among themselves. In my case, it makes them want to protect me, not maul me. You saw their faces. Saw the way they parted to let us pass on the way out. Patted you on the back, heralded me. Won them over did I not?"

"Just don't," he said. It wasn't really concern about the wagon train, he realized, embarrassed. It was a hot spike of jealousy. She wasn't like that with him—easy and clever and fun. *Stop it, Ezra, just stop it,* he chastised himself. *She's not flirting. You know better.*

"I'm sorry, Beth. No call for that. A surge of jealousy, if you want the truth. My apologies."

"Your jealousy pleases me," she said.

HE PULLED THE LETTER OUT OF THE BLUE ENVELOPE. IT WAS carefully folded in half. Beth read over his shoulder

Ezra,

You know I don't write, so I have borrowed the hand of Miriam Winthrop, the Captain's wife, to compose this letter. The wagon train includes 16 families, and we are waiting for two more. They may be lost. We are outfitted with provisions for 40 days. The wagons are too heavily loaded to leave early but the Captain says we'll wait your advice. We are camped across the river in Native Territory, about three miles north-northwest of the Mormon Winter Camp, in a large meadow. I brought your ponies across. They have been mighty crabby in your absence. Roan kicked me good, and for that you owe me a bag of dust or a quart of fireshine. So gather yourself, go talk to Mitchell at the North Ferry. I paid him good to get you across at sun up. If he refuses, shoot him. (Miriam does not condone.) See you on the prairie.

> *Your Sometimes Partner,*
> *Ambrose MacCallister Two Eagles*
> *(By the hand of Miriam Winthrop)*

"Two Eagles?" she asked.

"Brose. Everybody calls him Brose, but he likes his Indian name. Crow braves found him—so he says—hooked by a buffalo, lying on the ground near dead, his horse gone. They dismounted to scalp him but saw two eagles perched on a ghost tree nearby watching them. It was a sign. They carried Brose home, called him Two Eagles, and he stayed a year. He has a way with the ancient people out here. Knows someone who knows someone in every tribe. Kept me alive a dozen times."

"Is he native? You never said."

"A stew. Shoshone and Mexican on his mother's side. Nez Perce and Scotch on his father's. And more, I reckon. Badger in there somewhere, by the looks of him."

They walked into the village, poked their heads into the church and found it crammed with rank-smelling miners and kept going. Past a tumble of wooden shacks and adobe buildings used by merchants closed up, a corral, and some open markets. Every place overrun with miners. Supplies were running out, prices marked up on chalk boards, but battered crates of new goods from the steamboat were being opened in a closed off area in the rear with armed guards. Still no women shopping, no children in sight.

CAMILLE, WEARING A BONNET AND WELL FITTED BLUE FROCK AND apron from Martha's trunk, noticed James's body tense and his hand reach around the trigger mechanism. She glanced up to see two men staring at them, pointing and whispering. She stood quickly, put out her hand toward James to say, "be careful," while gripping her own rifle, muzzle down. A tall gangly man in a torn, soiled coat, the other medium height and barrel-chested, his face wreathed in side-whiskers. The same two that had walked by slowly not five minutes earlier.

The gangly one sauntered toward Maddie, who was still wearing her lucky dress, the one Ezra bought her. "What's your name?"

Maddie startled, jumped to her feet, spilling the rocks in her lap, then reached down for her pistol.

Alarm cleared Camille's mind. "Don't cock it," she said sharply, moving quickly between the man and Maddie. She tilted her head back and lowered her eyelids in the way women of her social circle took control of men. A look with an edge of disdain. "You're quite impertinent, sir. And you have no business with us. You should leave before my father and uncles return, so they don't misinterpret your intentions."

Her formality set the man back momentarily but he ignored her, pointed around her at Maddie. "She got a name? And a paper? And you, what's your name?" He glanced at his whiskered friend, who was squinting at what appeared to be folded newsprint. "You two from Louisiana?" he asked. Clearly, his friend was staring at the ad.

James rushed forward. "This is her paper," he said, pointing the rifle at the gangly man's head. James was breathing erratically, his voice cracking. "Get out of here!"

Without flinching, the gangly man casually pulled a pistol and aimed it at James's heart. "You don't want to get yourself killed, boy. Put it down."

Camille rested her hand on the barrel of James's rifle and eased it toward the ground, then stepped around him. "My brother can be rash. My name is Larissa Bolik. This is Vars. And this is our free girl, Daisy." Maddie flinched. "Now who are you?" she asked the gangly man. "My father will not appreciate your aggressive manners."

"Show me her paper, this little Black urchin of yours. I'm the slave-patrol authority here in Kanesville."

"Are you now? My father has all of the family documents. Please come back in thirty minutes and I'm sure he will . . .? And your badge, sir? Identity? I don't see it," she said. The man balked, squinted at her. "Never mind," she said, resorting to bluff. "The Sheriff, the man over there leaning against the wagon, smoking a cigar"—she pointed—"came by just a few minutes ago to see if we were all right. Perhaps you should confer with him. Show him your badge, state your authority and your inquisition of us." She waved at the cigar-smoking man across the way and shouted, "Sheriff? Over here."

As the unknown man turned and glared at the group, then waved back at Camille, the two bounty hunters backed away. "Yeah, we'll talk with him soon enough," said the gangly bounty hunter. The men disappeared into the crowd.

Maddie, trembling, tucked herself under Camille's arm.

"Nice job, Camille," said James. "I was rattled and jumpy. Ready to shoot. You were so calm and smart. That man's not really a sheriff, is he . . . Larissa?"

"No, Vars." They both laughed. Then looked up the hillside for Ezra and Beth, wishing them back quickly. Those men might ask around and come back soon.

AFTER SCOUTING THE LENGTH AND BREADTH OF THE VILLAGE AND finding a scattering of small homes locked and boarded up, some barricaded, Beth and Ezra sat down on some fresh cut logs next to a pile of kindling. He handed her a canteen and they quietly drank. She shook her head. "Kanesville's not the worst of the lot, but close," she said. "The only one we've actually explored on foot."

He nodded and idly picked a stick off the ground. He was stewing, drawing in the dirt with the broken branch.

"What are we going to do about them?" she asked. "We're fighting it, Ezra, but I think we know the answer already. I can't settle here. And we can't leave these girls here alone, hiding until these men clear out. There will just be another group on the next steamboat. My fear, some bounty hunters will make their way this far north. Unprotected, Camille and Maddie will be kidnapped. Carried off for ransom. Somebody, we don't know who, nailed up that ad in the tavern. Dozens may have read it." Her mind storming, she tried sitting on her shaking hands.

He pulled one of her hands out and rubbed it. "You all right?"

"Feel almost sick, Ezra. Trapped. And you know me, I hate feeling trapped. But there you have it . . . I realize there's only one way out. And that's you."

"You're saying you've decided to come with me? And you want to take the girls with us all the way to California? On a dirty dusty wagon train?"

"Do we have a choice? If this were Daisy, your childhood Daisy, would you leave her here in Kanesville?"

He winced, closed his eyes. "Not for a second," he said. "Never. But it's not our choice entirely, Beth. We'll have to talk to them. Maybe they'll surprise us and want to stay here."

She laughed. "Then you haven't been watching their faces, dear."

"Have you ever called me dear before?"

"Practicing for the wagon train. Ha ha. Truth, I am feeling tender toward you. Taking me and the girls on. Can't be easy for you."

They walked back through the congested markets, past the L&C Tavern, past the church with men sprawled asleep in the pews and on the floor. She took his arm as they made their way carefully down the muddy hill.

CAMILLE JUMPED UP AND STARTED IN, "TWO MEN—" BUT BETH CUT her off. There was an urgency in the way Beth motioned for her to sit down.

Camille sat, shaking, her face growing cloudy. "What's wrong?"

Ezra straightened himself, looking unusually stern, Camille thought. "We're giving you a choice," he said.

Camille braced herself. The choices were obvious—stay here, turn around, or go forward. But the way he said it suggested he and Beth had already decided, or at least he had, and not for the better.

"What kind of choice?" she asked in a tight voice. Maddie, responding to the tension, slid close and took Camille's arm. She had been trembling since those two men demanded her paper.

"We can buy your passage back downriver, so you can get off wherever you think you can make a go of it. Leavenworth, perhaps. Or you can stay right here in Kanesville, out of sight until this mob leaves in a few weeks. Or—"

Camille snapped. "Have you already made up your mind? You should know that two men approached us while you were gone, demanding to see Maddie's freedom paper. I wanted to tell you right away, but you cut me off. The men were staring at a copy of my father's ad. Asked our names and if we were from Louisiana. So, bounty hunters, for sure."

Ezra whipped his head around. "Where are they?" The veins on his neck pulsed. "Point them out."

Maddie pointed at James. "He put his rifle right into the tall man's face and I cocked my pistol."

"What?" Ezra carefully lifted Maddie's pistol and eased the hammer down. "Next time, just point, don't cock. It goes off too easily. Now, let me finish. Your third option," his voice falling from stern into that gentle persuasive, almost fatherly tone Camille liked, "is to join Beth and me on the wagon train."

Finally, Camille thought. *He's backed his way into the only sane conclusion. But does he really want us? Was it simply forced on him by circumstances? Or by Beth?* Camille couldn't tell. But there was a kindness in his voice that she hadn't heard in over a week. All the tension in Ezra she sensed as they passed one bad option after another coming upriver seemed to have faded like river mist. She stared at both of them, trying to read their faces. She didn't answer him just yet. Looked at Maddie, standing wide-eyed.

"This is your choice. But before you say yes," Ezra added, "understand this would mean all the way to California. Once we take the raft across that river into Native Territory to meet the train, there will be no return, no exit, even if you hate it. You'll have to walk beside the wagon almost the whole way. Two thousand miles through some harsh lands."

Camille paused, trying to imagine a trek that long. Walking, stumbling over rocks for months, over two thousand miles. "It sounds awful, Ezra. But better than being hunted like we are now. If you could somehow get us to safety, we'd be forever grateful. Maybe California will be safe."

"Probably. But one major problem," he said, pursing his lips. "I'm not sure how we'll explain you. It's chartered as a family wagon train . . . Only families are—"

Beth jumped in. "Our nieces, Ezra! I've already thought this through. My brother's children from Louisiana. Poor man, a widower, died recently, diphtheria, and we became sole guardians." She smiled at Camille. "That would allow you to talk freely about Louisiana."

"Can I be Maddie? Or do I have to be Daisy the whole way?"

"Good question," said Beth. "I'd want you to keep your name. Don't see why not."

Camille sat silent, trying to absorb the idea of playing this family game on a wagon train full of families, few of whom would likely accept black and white sisters. She wasn't going to deny it. She cherished being Maddie's older sister.

As the girls walked off to discuss what this would mean, Beth looked down the hill toward the landing. She saw four people sitting in the back of an open wagon, looking uncomfortable, awaiting transfer onto the steamboat. She suddenly grabbed Ezra's arm and pointed. "Look! Dear God. That's it! No more dithering." To her horror she realized the two Black men in the wagon were chained at the neck, and two Native women were chained together at the wrist and although she couldn't see, probably their ankles as well. And nobody was interfering in their capture

"These hunters are working all the way up here, Ezra. Damn them to hell."

Beth shouted, "Camille, Maddie, you're coming with us! Like it or not! Not leaving you here to fight these bastards alone. And James, we'll need you to come too. To handle the oxen and protect your new cousins."

James, sidelined for days, frightened of being stranded, not being invited, gasped. "Cousins? All the way to California?" He tried to smile, Beth thought, but he turned away, stared at the river, tears welling in his eyes.

"James, come here," said Beth. "How old are you? Thirteen, right?" He nodded. "I want you to sit down right now and write a letter to your mother and tell her you're safe. Tell her you're traveling with a wagon train of families and a good guide, and you're a drover for a family that cares about you. Add a few special lines to your pa and each of your brothers and sisters so they know you think of them. Tell them this will be the last letter before we get to California. Do it fast so we can post it on that steamer down there back to St. Louis. I have writing paper, ink and quill in my bag."

⇒ 13 ⇐

MEETING THE WAGON TRAIN

Native Territory

Beth first glimpsed her new world from the front seat of an open wagon, wedged between Ezra and their young Mormon driver. Her slumbering eyes sprang alert the moment the wagon broke out of the dense trees into a long, spacious meadow. One that opened wide toward the far end, where cattle and horses grazed beside a haphazard circle of wagons, with people cleaning up from breakfast and young children playing tag around five drowsy oxen lying in the grassy green.

They were too far away for Beth to see faces, which suited her just fine. She was not ready to meet individuals. At least not so many, all at once. The delicate hair on the back of her neck felt tender, even sore with anxiety, and the wind didn't help.

Not a minute later, a lone man came riding fast across the meadow. Bareback, his body one with the animal, his long black and gray hair streaming in the wind. Closer, she could see a broad face, crushed nose, and wide cheekbones.

"Is that Brose?" she asked. She was struck by the man's physical agility, his grace of movement, despite a short, solid build. Ezra waved to his old partner and climbed down from the wagon. The two, Ezra told her, had not worked a train across the continent in a year.

Without stopping, Brose put his hands on the horse's back, shifted weight and slid off the horse in one fluid motion, then hit the ground running. He smacked the horse and it trotted away obediently.

"You're late," Brose shouted. "Had me worried. Captain's been fretting about you backing out of our deal."

Ezra pointed at the young children playing in the meadow. "What's all this? What have you got me into?"

Beth noticed that five or six appeared younger than Maddie.

"Yep, we got a mess on our hands." Brose crossed his arms and looked Beth up and down as he talked. "About sixty-five people, including twenty-six kids, and one old grandma. Not like the old days. And you?" He stared at the three in the back of the wagon. "Looks like you brought some folks with you," he said, smiling at Beth. She noticed his eyes had the deep penetrating countenance of mixed heritage.

Still in the wagon, she stuck her arm out as if to shake. "I'm Beth, Ezra's wife. And these are our nieces . . . wards . . . nephew."

"Didn't know he had himself a wife. Ezra, you old buffler, you did well to get married and raise a family in five weeks."

"I want you to stand with me on this. When people ask, you've known my family for years," said Ezra.

"I'll say whatever damn thing you want. Beth, right pleased. Know you been married a good long time. I was drunk at your wedding as I recall."

"I remember. You ended up dancing with the horses," she said.

"That was a horse?"

Beth laughed. She liked this man. Engaging. "Brose, meet Camille and her sister Maddie, and that's James. Nieces and nephew from afar." Brose gave them a big broad wave, but the three sat quietly, looking apprehensive, intimidated. Brose had a wilderness air about him, almost feral, and a rippling movement in his limbs even as he stood. She sensed he could spring like a cat.

"Did you get me a wagon? My horses?" Ezra asked. "Your note said Roan has been acting up."

"They're both fine, gett'n fat, ready to walk the continent. And I got you a prime wagon—oak and hickory, with tight, seasoned wheels. Scrubbed the stink out of it. And six of the best oxen I could find in

Kanesville, healthy and rested." Brose rubbed his thumb and forefinger together. "You owe me some gold, *amigo.*"

"We'll settle later."

Beth glanced toward the circled wagons and her stomach clutched. A middle-aged couple was walking across the meadow in formal greeting, she assumed. The man, tall, athletic, carried himself with trained deliberation. The woman on his arm came up to his chest, swaying in a blue cotton dress as she walked. Both wearing broad-brimmed hats that shaded their faces.

"Is that them?" Ezra asked.

"Yep. Charles and Miriam. Prefers Captain."

"Anything I should know before we talk?" Ezra said

"Military through and through. Not used to undisciplined civilians. He's been waiting to talk to you about when we can leave. He's getting nervous about the growing crowds in Kanesville. Maybe thousands."

As they got closer, Beth noticed the Captain's Roman nose and intense demeanor. Lifting his hat high in greeting, he then swiped it to his side like a swordsman. *Calvary?* Putting on a show for Ezra, she guessed.

Miriam's eyes, Beth noticed, were fixed on her. She waved her hand overhead loosely like an aspen leaf, then pulled her hat back. Dark hair, ivory skin, sunburned nose and cheeks, and deep, searching blue eyes that reached right through Beth's wariness to her heart. It shocked her. Her chest tightened in fear of immediate exposure. She wouldn't last an hour, Beth thought, pretending to be a wife and a genuine social creature around women who knew such things instinctively. *Buck up,* she scolded herself. She pinched her arm. *Buck up.*

"Encouraged to see you're real, Ezra," said the Captain. "Brose speaks highly, but you're four days late. This is my wife, Miriam."

Miriam stood at a respectful distance, a half step behind her husband, presenting a pleasant countenance, without guile or fanfare. Still staring at Beth

"Pleased, ma'am," said Ezra. "This is my . . . uh, wife, Beth."

His stumble is going to make this worse, she thought.

Miriam left the shadow of her husband and walked straight up to Beth, still sitting in the wagon. "I've come to welcome you to the wagon train. Ezra, I'm delighted you decided to bring your lovely family. I had no idea. Beth, I'm so pleased." Her eyes remained focused on Beth, making her squirm. Miriam seemed to converse even when words were not exchanged. "I know you're nervous, no need."

"It's so surprising to be in the company of other women," said Beth, quite honestly. "I saw only two in Kanesville. The same everywhere, towns without women, all up and down the river."

"No lack of women here," said Miriam. "We've been together for nearly two weeks. Now getting used to each other. Most keep to themselves and their families. Afraid of what's to come, I suppose. But a few are hoping for new friends. I'm one of them." She glanced in the back of the wagon. "Your children? Slave girl?"

"No, Maddie's free-born. My late brother's daughters, Camille and Maddie. Different mothers, of course. And Ezra's sister's boy, James."

Miriam smiled at them. "Black and white sisters. Not so unusual but almost never acknowledged. Good for you." She searched their faces. "I can see the resemblance in the eyes and mouth, especially the eyes. So beautiful. Welcome, girls, to the world of wagons." She laughed.

Maddie stood up in the wagon bed. "Are there any girls to play with?" she asked. "I see young ones down there. I'm nine. Your dress is almost the same blue as my lucky dress."

Miriam smiled. "Makes mine lucky too, I suppose. Yes, dear, you'll find some children your age in the camp. Some will call you names, most won't. Don't let them get to you. Camille, welcome. A few young women your age, but married, and one, possibly two eligible young men if you're interested. James, I don't mean to ignore you. Welcome. A few boys, maybe a little older but a bit mean at times. Give them time to come around." James nodded, lifted his hat.

"You have children with you?" Beth asked.

"No, mine are raised and gone. Three boys, off at sixteen, just like your James will be soon enough, I reckon."

"I'm thirteen, almost fourteen," said James.

"Well, you're very tall for your age. Beth, why don't you jump down, walk with me. I'll introduce you around the camp while Charles confers with Ezra. Believe me, they'll be talking for quite some time.

Perhaps your children can unload the wagon and introduce themselves around."

Miriam held out her hand to help Beth down. Taken aback by the friendliness, Beth stumbled over her response as she took Miriam's hand, surprisingly firm.

Is this to be the norm? Beth wondered. *Are Ezra and I be separated from now on? The world of men and the world of women divided, two worlds contemptuous of each other?* Ezra was the only one she trusted on this train; how could they be separated?

Miriam seemed to read Beth's apprehension. "Not to worry. He's not going anywhere you're not going to be." There was a grace and directness about Miriam that surprised Beth, calmed her. She had never had a woman friend and ally in all her years in St. Louis, other than Hannah who was twenty years her senior. Could this be some wonderful turn of fate? A friend, a confidant? *But can I truly open up while still protecting our marriage secret?*

Beth excused herself from Miriam, walked over to the Captain, and put her hand straight out in the style of a man. "I want to thank you and Miriam for walking out here to welcome us. It means a lot to me, to all of us. Let me know what I can do to help."

Stunned, a slight smile, he took a half step back, and shook her hand gently. "Let Miriam get you settled in with the others. Ezra and I have some urgent business to discuss."

She sensed in his eyes a grudging respect. She was not going to be dismissed as Ezra's little woman and wanted it clear at the outset. Ezra looked as if he were holding his breath, his eyes dancing with mischief. Suppressing some comic remark, she guessed.

"Brose," the Captain snapped. "I want you, Doc, and the Reverend to meet us at the oak in an hour. Give me some time to get to know Ezra." He pointed to the large fallen oak, a good fifty yards from the camp.

Miriam took Beth's arm. "Come. Tell me about yourself and your family. Everything."

"Just one moment, Miriam." She turned to the wagon. "James, you stay close to Maddie and protect her. Camille, I don't need to tell you."

Beth kept her eye on the wagon as the Mormon boy drove the girls and James to the camp. Younger children ran to meet the wagon halfway and jumped aboard. The moment the wagon stopped, the trunks and bags were whisked off, the children chattering away with the newcomers.

"Nice girls," said Miriam. "Be prepared, you'll have some trouble with a few of the families. Race talk and race hate and all that. But it will die down, and Charles won't stand for it. One or two may demand to see Maddie's papers, but don't fall for it and don't show them. Free girl. None of their damned business. You and I, we'll stick together, help each other, and get through it. Charles will support us . . . he's quite the abol . . . Never mind, you didn't hear me say that.

"Tell me about your girls, Beth. Who they are, where they came from?"

"Recently from Louisiana. My poor brother, a widower, got swept away last year—diphtheria. Other relatives took the plantation. We took the girls."

"Did they grow up close? Different mothers but in the same household? True sisters, yes?"

"Yes, very close, same home. Camille's mother died when she was only seven. She was raised by a beloved mammie, who took care of the everyday matters. Her father took charge of her education, tutoring, and social training. But the relationships in the household grew more complicated, as he apparently took the slave mammie to his bed when it pleased him."

"And her? Was she a willing partner?"

"Who knows. Doubtful. As house slave she probably had no choice. Anyway, in time she bore the master his second daughter, Maddie, who by law was a slave. But he surprised the woman by granting Maddie a freedom paper. The very day she was born."

"Right then and there? Quite a gift," said Miriam. "Must have been some affection there, don't you think?"

"I agree. But the catch was her freedom had to be kept a secret while she was a child living on the plantation. Oddly, she and Camille didn't know they were sisters but behaved as if they knew instinctively. They played in Camille's room where she secretly tutored Maddie. All I know."

"My God, what a story, Beth. When did the two find out Maddie was free-born?"

"Not until after my brother died. Maddie's mother died within weeks of him but entrusted the freedom paper to Camille before she passed. My brother's plantation went to the male side. The girls were sent to us by steamboat."

My God, Beth thought, *I feel terrible, disgusted with myself. Compounding my original lies with more lies and some sprinkles of truth. Lying to someone who could become an ally, possibly even a close friend.*

"Very complicated," said Miriam, "but they're lucky they landed with you and Ezra."

"I suppose. Their greatest desire is to find a place where they can live openly as sisters."

"Well, they've come to the right wagon train." said Miriam. "And I'll keep confidential what you just told me. Too many nosy women on this train who would twist that story to their own ends. A few terrible racists. You'll see."

"Will there be any other Blacks on the wagon train?" Beth asked. She hadn't spotted any.

"One Black family did contract with Charles—paid their advance—but we haven't seen them yet. Left them a note at the L&C Tavern. You from the south?"

"St. Louis, a bit of both south and north. Been there for years. Originally from Kentucky. Ezra works everywhere, lives everywhere. A wilderness trader and guide."

"Ah, new to this mothering business. A shock, isn't it?"

Beth wasn't sure what expression to use. She raised her eyebrows, nodding. "Yes, an adjustment and at times, a pleasing challenge, I've found."

"With your Ezra gone all the time—scout, guide, trader—our lives must be similar. I'm an army wife, so I know what's it like to live alone for months, even years at a time. Lonely outposts. Weary life."

"I wasn't so lonely," said Beth. "I ran a busy boarding house for a dozen or more gregarious river pilots who take their massive boats up and down the Mississippi and Missouri Rivers."

"Ran it on your own? Without Ezra being there?"

"Indeed. All by myself after Hannah, the woman who took me in, educated me, and taught me her business passed away. And I continued to run the boarding house after Ezra and I were married."

"And Ezra didn't mind leaving you with a house full of men?"

"Oh, God no. And if he did, well, I'm the last person he would tell."

Miriam's eyes brightened. "Your business then? Your *own* business? You're an independent bird. I knew there was something I liked about you. Could sense it, right off. There's a friend for me, I thought." She patted Beth's arm. "The other women . . ."

"I'm nervous about them, quite honestly."

"We've been here go'n on two weeks now, trying to get used to each other. You'll like them—some of them, maybe—but it takes time. They'll spend the first day or two sizing you up, sneaking around, gossiping, probing, so be patient. Everything we do here is in such tight quarters, with limited privacy. You hear everything, even passion. It requires adjustment. Like love in a fishbowl."

"I never thought about the privacy," Beth said. Intercourse had once seemed so inevitable, even pleasurable. But years had passed, and her childhood scars had only hardened. Beth looked closely at the wagons as they approached the camp. Just farm wagons, really—most about four feet, maybe five feet wide, some with tall sides. Maybe eight feet long, some perhaps ten. A wedding bed? *Ha. No chance of that.*

"These tight quarters make these women wary of anyone new," said Miriam. It may prove easier for you, because your husband is so important to their survival. They'll be careful not to offend you to your face. A few will, of course, because they're on edge, snappy."

"On edge? For what?"

Miriam tilted her head, bemused. "They're scared, Beth. We're about to cross two thousand miles of wilderness. Leaving everything we've ever known behind. Facing every kind of fear you can imagine. You know, valley-of-the-shadow-of-death kind of fear. People die out there with nobody to come visit their graves except wolves and lizards."

THREE WOMEN WERE SHARING A COOKING FIRE WHEN BETH AND Miriam walked up, one plucking a chicken, another chopping vegetables. A third kept a young boy at a distance with her arm while stirring an iron cauldron—a petite woman with dark hair and bright green eyes. The boy looked about four, maybe five.

The young mother nodded at Beth. "So *you're* Ezra's wife? I'm Sarah Sturgis, Tom's wife—he's the Doc on this train. And this is Samuel." Beth nodded at the boy and smiled.

Sarah spoke with a mixture of intensity and nervousness, trying to corral her son with her voice as well as her limbs. He wandered over and picked up a handful of feathers, tossing them in the air.

Sarah put down her long wooden paddle, wiped her hands. "You had us on pins and needles, Beth, wondering where you were. Well, not you, but Ezra. Without people like Ezra who know the trails, the land, the dangers, we'd be lost." Her eyes ran over Beth, from head to toe. "And you! Here we expected a solitary frontier man—and you know how frightening they can be—and he shows up, a kindly man with a family. It's a blessing. Wonderful to have you."

Miriam turned. "Maude, Charlotte, this is Beth." The middle-aged woman, sitting, plucking a chicken in a basket of warm water, feathers plastered to her wet arms, reached up and waved, then laughed at her own unappealing hand and pulled it back.

"Maude's husband, Oliver Simpson, is our wheelwright," said Miriam. "And Charlotte's husband, Harold Gaither, by trade a farmer, who will know edibles along the trail, has proven to be a most skilled carpenter."

"I don't think you're going to be able to keep that slave of yours," said Maude, as she brushed the chicken feathers from her forehead with the back of her hand. Sarah raised a finger in warning. Maude nodded. "I'm just saying, it's against the wagon train charter."

Careful, Beth thought, *don't rile her.* She trimmed her voice to a calm, controlled monotone. "Maddie's not our slave. She's part of our family, a free-born Black, and my niece."

"Saw her come prancing by, talking with the white girls like she was queen of the May, and just as good as . . . well, she's sassy, I'll say that much for her. She ought to know her place," said Maude.

What an outrage, but Beth didn't take the bait. "Her place is with us. Our family. And I would appreciate it if you could learn to treat her with as much kindness as I would treat your daughter. You have a daughter?"

Maude lifted her head. "I do. Her name is Ruth. She's ten, out in the meadow playing tag. She doesn't like Blacks any more than I do."

"She will when she gets to know Maddie."

Maude stopped plucking the chicken and glared.

"I'm sure she will," said Sarah, tugging her Samuel with one arm, protectively.

"OK, Maude. You've had your say," said Miriam, stepping between the women. "Maddie is most welcome on our train. Be gracious about it."

CAMILLE SQUIRMED, FEELING TRAPPED BY A GROUP THAT HAD gathered around her, asking questions about Ezra, her life in Louisiana, what she had seen on their trip up the Missouri River, crowds in Kanesville. Standing close by Camille was a young woman with an angelic face beneath a brown bonnet who had said little. But as the conversation drifted to the uncertain departure date, she stepped aside and gently tugged Camille's arm. "Can I talk with you a minute? Over here, if you don't mind."

The girl pulled Camille out of earshot of the group. "Sorry, Camille, you looked overwhelmed and I wanted to meet you in a more personal way. Are you married? I didn't see a ring. I'm Karen Mitchell, married to the Reverend's son, David. I wanted to welcome you personally."

"I appreciate it. Thank you. No, not married. I'm only seventeen and I suspect It'll be a number of years before—"

"Oh, we're close in age then. I'm eighteen. Married three months ago. Never expected to spend my first year, my honeymoon year, on a wagon train. I'm not usually so forward, but I could use a friend on this long journey. I've been searching the camp for two weeks and my instinct kicked in, listening to you. You seem so kindly, good-natured, intelligent . . . well, I'd love to know you better, personally, if you'd care to." Karen put out her hand.

Camille took Karen's extended hand in both of hers, embracing it. "I'm pleased to meet you too, Karen. Thank you for pulling me away from that group. It was getting bigger and I was stuck. Did you get married in anticipation of going to California? To start a new life out there?"

"Oh no, just the opposite. The Reverend Mitchell, my father-in-law, was called by God to go start a church for lost souls in California. He dragged David and me along. Reluctantly. We had a quiet life planned in Gettysburg, our small town in Pennsylvania. David was training to become a doctor. His father said enough of that, we must come with him and help him build his church. And worse, David must train to become an associate pastor, not a doctor. I wanted children right away, but now I'm not so sure. Sorry, I'm nervous, telling secrets, chatting a mile a minute."

Karen pulled her bonnet back and smiled. Thick chestnut hair, freckles around her nose and sunburned cheekbones. Altogether unpretentious, with large, blue eyes. Camille pulled her own bonnet back. Her brunette hair was twirled up in a tight bun.

"Such luxurious hair," said Karen, "and your skin seems to accept the sun."

"I'm sorry your marriage plans were tossed aside," said Camille. "I know what an overbearing father can be like. Seems so unfair to cut David's medical training short and drag you two away. I heard there's a doctor on the wagon train."

"Oh, there is. Doc Sturgis."

"He'll probably need help with this many people and twenty-six children, maybe your husband could apprentice to him. Keep his training going. Keep his dreams, your dreams, alive."

"David's had exactly the same thought. He's waiting for the right moment to approach Doc."

"By the way," said Camille, "thank you again for pulling me away. There's a young man, large, broad-shouldered, who kept staring at me in a way that made me uncomfortable. I think he's been following me around the campsite."

"Ha. That's Tad McGrath, who's actually quite nice. Shy at first, but charming when he loosens up. And handsome in a homespun kind of way. He was smitten at first sight of you, and asked my husband to introduce him to you. David laughed, told him to go do it himself. If he becomes a pest shoo him away."

Maddie raced up with her new young friend in tow, about her height but quite fair, blond with delicate features. "Camille, this is Caroline Burns. She showed me her rock collection and dolls. Her father showed me the guitar he plays at night. Is it all right if we go play in the meadow? Her parents said OK. Please? I can't find Beth to ask her."

"You'll have to be careful out there. Those oxen are big animals," said Camille. "You want James to come along?"

"No ma'am," said Caroline. "It's safe. We're going to sing to the oxen like I do every day. They like it while they stretch in the grass. Mother gave me an hour free from cutting carrots. Can Maddie please come? She likes to sing too, she says. I'll teach her some Irish songs. Fast toe taps. Lullabies and ballads. And she can teach me Louisiana songs."

"All right, you two, go ahead, but stay close enough where I can see you. Then afterwards, Maddie, you can help Caroline cut carrots." Like it or not, Camille thought, I'm going to ask James to watch her from the edge of the meadow. I don't know what's lurking in these woods. Wolves, panthers, bounty hunters.

Caroline and Maddie raced off hand-in-hand between the wagons into the broad green meadow with clusters of lolling oxen. Camille stopped talking to listen as Maddie began to find the melody.

"My God," said Karen, "Just minutes and they're already in harmony. Their voices are beautiful. Did you know? Of course, you knew. Now tell me about yourself, you and Maddie, your family, about Louisiana. It sounds so mysterious. Do the trees really have magical moss hanging down? I heard your father died recently. I'm so sorry. Like us, you had your whole life planned one way, and then your world turns upside down and you find yourself on a wagon train. I hope Ezra and your Aunt Beth—that's her name, right?—treat you kindly."

THE FALLEN OAK HAD A ROOT BALL THE SIZE OF A SMALL HOUSE, the other end held off the ground by massive broken limbs. Ezra and the Captain paced beside it in the damp grass, circling each other, talking about the composition of the wagon train. As they conversed, Ezra whittled a sharp point on a sturdy stick and shoved it into the soft ground, pushing it down with both gloved hands, first in one place and then another.

"Ground still too soft. Light wagons doable. Heavy ones will bog down," he said, pulling it out and inspecting the stick. "Never led a wagon train with so many children, Captain. A few back in '44 when Brose and I took families to Oregon for farming, but nothing like this. We'll have to be careful."

"First for me too, leading families with all their divided loyalties, rivalries, idiotic spats, lack of discipline," said the Captain. "Glad to have your help, you and Brose, keeping them in line."

They took each other's measure, learning about the most recent turning points in their lives—the Captain retired from the army after twenty years, two bloody battles in Mexico, and after Miriam refused to live that way anymore. Ezra was about to retire from the wilderness after twenty-five years to become a businessman in California.

"This will be my last run," said Ezra. "Beth isn't sure she believes me, but I want something more. Trying to find out what that is. California is turning into a land of searching souls, so I'll be in good company."

The Captain grinned. "I'll be searching as well. I must say, I'm relieved you brought your family. Means you have their lives on the line—not just ours."

Ezra stopped and watched as Brose approached from the edge of the meadow with two men. The first, studious-looking, mid-thirties with a boyish face, spectacles, a keen, almost nervous energy. The second, at least twenty years older, thick, broad-beamed like a sturdy boat, with a deeply etched face and a bemused, superior frown. He gripped a Bible in a massive hand that suggested he had started out at a young age as a woodcutter or smithy.

The Captain stood and faced them. "Doc, Reverend, let me introduce our second guide, Ezra Adams. Hails from St. Louis. Old family. Brose says Ezra knows the mountains and trails to California as well as any man alive."

"I'd hope so." The Reverend clasped Ezra's hand in an iron grip. "Hiram Mitchell. Trust you're a God-fearing man who will get us through."

The younger one had softer hands, thinning blond hair, a casual grip, and a quick facial tic, as if he were winking. "Tom Sturgis. Call me Tom or Doc, I don't care which."

"Let's get down to it," said the Captain. The men sat on logs and flat stones close enough to talk easily. The Captain's eyes moved from man to man. "My mission, and your job"— he pointed deliberately at each one—"is to get these families to California unbroken, healthy. I want all twenty-six children and forty adults alive when we get there. No casualties. No wagon train to my knowledge has ever done that. Usual casualty rate is what, Brose? Ten, twenty percent?"

Brose started to speak, but the Captain cut him off. "Just so we're clear at the outset, Ezra, Brose, Doc, Reverend: you advise, discuss, debate, propose. I take everything into consideration, but I decide. And I take responsibility. On the trail, my word is law.

"I need a clear assessment of our situation, Ezra. I'm worried about sharing a trail with this crowd in Kanesville. It keeps growing. Must be thousands. Every day, I see more wagons slipping across the river to get an early start."

"The massing is even worse downriver," said Ezra.

"The question before us is: when should we leave?" The Captain pointed at Ezra. "We're nearly midway through April. What are the options? What's the condition of the trail?"

Ezra held up the pointed stick, covered with ten inches of dirt stain. "Let me be plain. You can see how soft the ground is. We have to lighten these wagons—Brose told me how loaded they are—and leave immediately. Get every wagon down to fifteen hundred pounds to keep the wheels from sinking."

The Captain leaned in. "Did you say immediately?"

They all start talking at once. Ezra held up his hand. "Let me finish. We need to hold on to our advantages. Our current position, our knowledge, our readiness. We do this by getting out fast—leaving earlier and traveling lighter than others. There will be a battle for forage as we journey, so we need to be advancing into the new grass, the freshest, most vigorous growth. Those in the rear will have to move off the trail to graze, a hundred yards to start, then a half-mile, then a mile. If we start fast, we continue fast. If we start slow, we get slower and slower trying to feed our oxen."

The Captain paced back and forth, hands behind his back. "You said immediately, Ezra. I've been telling these families to expect at least one, probably two more weeks, the first of May. How soon is immediately? Exactly?"

"Day after tomorrow. Three days at most. We can use tomorrow to prepare. We'll need more grain and hay in the wagons to tide us over until the grass can sustain the oxen. Change out any green wagon spokes with seasoned wood. Make sure each wagon can be taken apart and reassembled fast—if not, trade it for one that can. Heavier clothing and three or four pairs of boots and gloves for everyone. Materials for repair. Brose says there's a warehouse in Kanesville being resupplied daily by steamboat."

The Captain stopped, looked up at the sky. "Lightening the wagons will be the hard part," he said. Ezra thought he saw the first sign of distress, a crack in the man's veneer. "We'll be tearing these families from their roots," the Captain continued. "They've already stripped down to their most treasured possessions. Heirlooms—china, fine tables, family portraits—that go back three and four generations. One family brought a harpsichord. My own Miriam, a sea chest carved by her great-grandfather. I warned her."

Devoted to tradition and heritage. That's his weakness. Ezra knew the man's vulnerability would come out.

"There's another compelling reason to move quickly," said Ezra, pausing for attention, staring at Doc. "I saw half a dozen bodies being quickly buried beside the river in Independence. Cholera, I'm quite sure. And it may be coming upriver, fast."

Doc jumped to his feet, hands clenched. "I say to hell with their finery. Let's dump it all and go. This is nothing to fool with."

"Not until after the Sabbath! Five days!" the Reverend bellowed, standing powerfully, shaking his Bible at Doc.

Doc shook his own finger, leaning into the Reverend's face. He seemed to grow in stature, physically more powerful. "I'm not going to jeopardize these children!"

"Back down, you two!" the Captain shouted. "Now, sit! Brose, what counts as extra? You've seen the inside of all our wagons. Ezra has not."

"If they can't use it on the trail, it's extra," said Brose. "I saw mining equipment, anvils, heavy chains, logging equipment, farming equipment—all extra. China, furniture, fancy candlesticks, extra. Just millstones. Replace them with things they need to survive on the trail— light, usable, edible."

Ezra watched the pain washing across the Captain's face. It reminded him of Beth's agony after the fire. *Will the man have the strength of character not to give in to the wailing and pleading? Even that of his own wife, Miriam? If he gives in, he will never hold command on the trail. As a military man, he should know that. But he's never commanded families.*

"If it helps persuade," Ezra added, "all that precious stuff will likely be thrown overboard at some point anyway. Trails through the far western desert, when it becomes life and death, are littered with it. China, silverware, fine furniture, books, lamps, paintings."

"Better recourse," Ezra continued, "would be to crate the valuables in Kanesville and ship them by sea from New Orleans. I'm sure the warehouse can do that."

Quite suddenly, the Captain dismissed them with a wave of his hand. "I've heard enough, gentlemen. Go back to work but say nothing to the families. Nothing. Understand? I don't want them gossiping, arguing. I will make the announcement tonight after dinner."

As they separated, the Captain pulled Ezra aside. "Keep your girl close. Maddie, that her name? A slave patrol rode through here a few days ago looking for runaways escaping onto the gold trains."

Ezra's body clinched in fury. He removed his hat, uncurled his clenched fists and ran his fingers through his hair. *So the pursuit continues*, he realized. "She's free-born, you know. And has a freedom paper."

"Won't matter to these men. Don't let her wander out of your sight until we're well on our way. And keep your weapons handy."

⇒ 14 ⇐

DEPARTURE

Only the essentials

On her feet all day engaged in nonstop introductions, inter-
rogations, food prep, cooking, and cleanup, Beth's legs were
aching, her head pounding. She leaned back against one of
the wagons arrayed in a horseshoe formation to relax, watching the
hustle in the center, as the dining area was transformed for the evening
meeting.

"How's your back? Mine's killing me," said Miriam, joining her
against the wagon bed. She rubbed her back on the wood. "Ahh, better.
I thought you did well today, Beth, holding out such a bright presence
all afternoon. Greeting all those suspicious women. Many seemed to
like you, but you'd never know it from their skeptical tone. You tired?"

"Spent. I want to curl up in big bed and sleep. All this scrutiny,
endless jabber jabber, and being more cheerful than I really am takes a
toll. Explaining over and over who we are and where we came from.
How I could possibly own and run a business independently, while my
husband was out making a living in the wilderness. Almost scandalous.
Then justifying our family."

"How about those questions they shot at us during dinner," said
Miriam. "As if you and I know what the men decided at the old oak. As
if Charles would confide in me."

"Or Ezra in me. Those women were so angry I thought Maude would bite you, accusing you of holding out on them."

Beth turned, glanced over again at Maddie.

"You may be a natural at this mothering business, Beth. You have that ever-watchful awareness of your brood. You know exactly where Maddie is at all times. And James, well now, he's as much soldier as older brother. Look at his stance. See, he doesn't get in the way, pitches in, but is really standing guard. Not so much over Camille, as over Maddie."

Beth watched as Maddie helped the other children arrange three large, semicircular rows of seating planks for the big meeting.

"James's been so vigilant after Maddie took some bullying today," said Beth. "I didn't see it but heard—"

"She looks fragile, bone structure more than anything," said Miriam, "but she knows how to stand her ground. Sarah told me she saw three of those older boys corner Maddie and taunt her about being a slave girl. Told her to go fetch this and that. But she didn't run. Didn't shrink. She calmly told the leader, Karl, tall brooding boy, that he was probably better at fetching than she was. Then asked him to get her a cup of water. Karl exploded with rage, pushed her, called her names, and lifted his fist to her face. But she stood firm. Girl's got gumption, give her that. But then James, get this, according to Sarah, came charging in out of nowhere and pushed Karl backwards hard enough he stumbled and fell. James stood over him, threatening. 'Where I come from, we pistol whip bullies like you,' he said. That shut him up, at least for now, and James's rage scared the other two off. But you better stay alert until these people grow accustomed to her. They will in time. She's so easy to like."

"Thanks, I will." Beth now better understood the source of those spidery marks on Maddie's legs from sassing the bosses on the plantation. You'd think she'd learn to cower and shuffle step and stumble talk like a slave. But no, she came back hard, defiant even.

Beth turned, touched Miriam's arm and smiled. "But did you hear about the one bright spot in all this tension. Maddie made a friend, this young Caroline, you probably know her, blond girl, about yea high, from a musical family. They discovered they both like to sing. And

Caroline was holding Maddie's hand as they walked into the meadow. Now that's something."

"Thank God she found someone," said Miriam. "At that age, it takes just one friend to change the world."

Camille settled in next to Karen on the end of one of the seating planks arrayed three-deep in a semicircle around tonight's speakers. They were early and sat alone. Camille didn't recognize the tall boy approaching them with his hat pulled down. He was imposing, with an athletic gait, coming straight at her with intention.

"Here he comes," said Karen. "On guard, lass."

Tad took off his hat and nodded in a show of courtesy. "I noticed you and . . . well, wanted . . . well, to welcome you. I'm Tad McGrath."

"More than noticed," said Karen, jostling him.

He blushed. "Suppose."

"Thank you for coming over and breaking the ice," said Camille. She extended her hand.

"I wondered the proper way to introduce . . ." he said, stumbling, then stopping. He took her open hand, turned it over, stared at it. She curled her fingers slightly in invitation, and he lifted her hand and kissed the back of it.

"For God's sake, Tad, this is a wagon train, not a cotillion," said Karen.

"Sorry if I made you uncomfortable. I won't stay . . . intrude . . . better go."

"Thank you for stopping by, Tad. Being so cordial," said Camille.

He smiled, took a half step back, put his hat on and tipped it before he turned away.

"We get that a lot of that in Louisiana, hand kissing," said Camille. "He's polite. I like that, and for such a rugged looking boy—man, I suppose—he has a tender way about him. Shy, like you said. Not a Louisiana *roué*."

"One thing you should know about Tad," said Karen. "He's a natural athlete and an acrobat. Said he trained two years for a circus. I thought he was joking. Don't bring it up unless you want to spend some time watching him show off."

BETH STOOD AT THE BACK, STILL LEANING AGAINST ONE OF THE wagons, but now with her arm around Maddie as the meeting began. The Captain walked to the center of the semicircle and stood tall, silent, with military bearing, waiting for the young children to settle in around his feet and for the chattering to fade.

"I want, first, to welcome Ezra Adams, one of our trail guides, and his family. If you haven't met them yet, please introduce yourself. I've asked Ezra to say a few words, right after the Reverend gives us a quick blessing—not a sermon, he promised me. You will have a hundred questions for Ezra, but I ask you to hold them until tomorrow. I have an important announcement to make and it will require your full attention this evening."

"Before we begin . . ." the Captain said, pausing, as the families leaned forward. "I want to clear up a misunderstanding you might have about our journey. That is, that your hatred will be ignored. Or tolerated. Or condoned on this train. It will not. The ugly taunts, the contempt, the sneers about Ezra's family will stop. Tonight. I repeat, tonight. These divisions of ours—north, south; slave, free; Protestant, Catholic; white, Black—will kill us out there."

The audience squirmed. Maddie cringed and grabbed Beth around the waist.

The Captain stared at the travelers, scanning from right to left, left to right. "I've seen disciplined armies defeated this way. Riven with hatred, they turn on themselves." His voice rose. "So, no more of your viciousness. None of it! When we march, we march as one. Your family's life depends upon your neighbor's family. Their family upon yours. We travel as one cohesive unit against the elements, the terrain, the misfortunes, even the terrors we face."

The Captain continued, now slowing his cadence. "I'm giving you a choice and I want you to sleep on it. You leave your hatred right here on the ground or you and your family leave the wagon train in the morning. If you leave, you can have your deposit back. If you continue on and your hatred breaks out while we are in Indigenous Territory, I will regard it as mutiny. First time, I will let you make amends. Second time, I will banish you and your family outright. You'll then fend for yourself in the wilderness."

He paused, letting the thought sink in. "Be careful of each other. Tolerant. We need each other to survive. Once we leave, that's the law, take it or leave it." He looked at the silent faces. His voice softened. "Reverend?"

Beth felt Maddie burrowing in. She ran her fingers through the girl's hair, caressing her scalp, her neck, remembering the comfort when her own mother did the same to her. When was that? She must have been very young. She tried to fill in the memory, but it was blocked. She saw the angry face of her father.

Reverend Mitchell held up his hands until the whispers died down. "Please bow your heads." He paused, letting peace settle over the congregation.

"Lord, we beseech You to walk with these families on their perilous journey into the wilderness. To ease their burden, bind up their wounds, shelter and guide them to the promised land. Please bless our leaders with wisdom and our families with the courage to endure. Remind us at every misstep that we are *all* part of Your kingdom, imbued with Your love. Help us to open our hearts to each other, to persevere as one in the teeth of the storm. Through the misery of fatigue, duress, and tribulation we travel as one people under your guiding light. We ask this in the name of our Blessed Savior, Jesus. Amen."

Ezra stepped into the speaker's spot, surveying the crowd. "Thank you, Reverend, Captain, all of you. My family and I are pleased to join you." He looked assured, Beth thought, lean and tall, broad shouldered, and so easily comfortable with himself standing in front of total strangers. She realized she had never seen him at work. Not like this. Tonight, he looked younger than his years.

"I was as surprised by the Captain's rebuke as you were. But he's right. I grew up in a divided family, as I reckon many of you did. For generations my family has been going at each other. Half pro-slave, half free. I've heard all the arguments. I understand the passions, the convictions. But we must set these conflicts aside for our preservation. We will need each other out there. Most especially because we, all of us, have children to protect. We protect them collectively. Agreed?"

Beth saw a few heads nodding but most sat rapt, silent. He had their attention, but she sensed them trying to size the man up. Their lives would depend upon him.

"Now the journey." Beth heard his voice grow deeper, fuller. "I want to assure you Brose and I know every inch of the trail we're going to take. We know the mistakes others have made trying to find shortcuts. We will stick to the fastest, surest route.

"It's about two thousand miles and gets progressively harder. We'll use the first half to toughen you up for the second half. On a very good day, we'll make thirty miles. Average day, twenty. A bad day, we'll hunker down and hope to survive a storm—rain, hail, wind, sand, flood. Anyone over ten years old will be walking most of the way to spare the oxen."

Hands went up. Ezra waved them off.

"Please, catch me afterwards. Our path follows the rivers, the trails along the shore. Trails originally cut by the buffalo and later the native peoples, the *Ancients* as we call them. We travel upriver, moving against the current, directly west for the first thousand miles. We'll start on the north side of the Platte River—it's faster, easier, and far less crowded than the south side. When we leave the plains, we jump over to the Sweetwater River, which will take us right up to the crest of the Rocky Mountains. That's the halfway point.

"In the Rockies all the rivers turn crosswise—no longer flowing east-west, but north-south, wending their way through the valleys between the mountain ranges." He raised his arms, moved his hands around each other in a weaving pattern. "That's where the trails start going every which way and people get lost with crazy maps." He paused, brought his hands down. "But we know the most efficient way through. We'll zigzag these ranges to Fort Hall, a trading post—not a military fort—in the eastern part of Oregon Territory. Then work our way southwest toward the high deserts, where the rivers once again start flowing east-west.

"You will be strong by then, I promise you. Strong, hardy, tough. Able to do things that would seem impossible for you right now. Don't worry. You'll be able to cross the worst desert you can imagine. Scale the steepest mountains. Including the wall guarding California—3,000 feet of granite that comes right up out of the desert, and then climbs still higher.

"Finally, the Sierra Mountains will ease down into gentle foothills and rivers replete with gold. That'll be the fruited land of California. We'll get you there. And make it before the fall weather kicks in and the massive snows lock up those mountains.

"Once there we'll teach you how to pan for gold. We have a camp all picked out as a place to start. Some will stay in that camp, some of you will move on to other camps, towns, even cities. But for all, the journey will be worth it."

A cheer went up. Clapping. People hugged.

Beth watched Ezra take a breath and a quick drink of water, then glance around at the crowd. She noticed his slight smile when he caught sight of her. It pleased her. Her hand went immediately to her hair. That secret smile of his revived her spirit. She smiled back, at first demure, but then her cheeks lifted spontaneously. They had been separated into their different worlds the entire day.

"One more thing," said Ezra, "before I sit down. The family you protect, the family you love, includes your oxen. Now, don't snicker. You heard me. Oxen may look indestructible, but they're not, and your life depends upon them. Treat them with care. The last six hundred miles are going to be hell. You'll be in a massive desert in the burning August sun, and you will be pulling together, you and your oxen. They do not like heat—even less than you do—and need rest and water to survive. Get to know them. Care for them like a dear child. Make sure your drover knows how to talk to them, tend to them, console them, bed them and feed them."

He looked around. "That's probably enough for introduction. Plenty of time to talk with Brose and myself in the next four or five months. Brose you've already met; he's been here for nearly two weeks. What you may not know, because he's a modest man, is that he's a wonderful guide, knows the land, the creatures, and the tribes of ancient people and will fill you with stories and the wisdom of rivers."

The Captain returned to the front, careful not to step on the young children competing to be closer to the speaker.

"A few things that Ezra did not tell you—because I asked him to leave it to me. There is strong evidence that cholera is now coming up the Mississippi River." The audience gasped. "Cholera!" some screamed. They all turned to talk to their neighbor.

"Second—please pay attention," shouted the Captain. "Sit, be quiet. When that army of wagons we see growing in Kanesville begins to move *en masse*, we with young children could easily get shoved aside, pushed to the back of the line. Understand, these are determined men, fueled with greed, armed with fear, and in hard competition with each other."

The families sat up, waiting for the decision to drop.

"So, my announcement. Please pay attention. We must leave earlier than we expected. And travel lighter and faster in order to get ahead and stay ahead of the horde." He paused. "We leave third sunup from tonight."

A cry went up, gasps, groans, angry shouts, a few cheers.

Families rose to their feet, talking and arguing, some hugging.

"Quiet down! Let me finish!" the Captain shouted.

They sat down.

"Tomorrow, first light, I want everyone to unload your wagons *entirely* and divide your goods into two piles, the essential and the unessential. If you don't need it for the journey itself, it is unessential. I will walk around and tell you what to move from one pile to the other. We will leave the unessential here for the scavengers. Or better yet, take your belongings to Kanesville tomorrow to barter for things to keep us alive on the trip—food stores, feed for the animals, sturdy clothing, extra boots, canvas, rawhide, hickory. And if you have small treasures—heirlooms, paintings, precious furniture, fine dishes—that you cannot part with, we can arrange to have them carefully crated in

Kanesville and shipped back to St. Louis for storage. Once settled you can arrange to have them shipped to you in California.

"Ezra and Brose have reminded me that the last of the western deserts are filled with treasures desperate people have thrown overboard to stay alive. Imagine carrying your treasures all that way—seventeen, eighteen hundred miles—just to discard them in the blistering sun to keep you alive."

A stout woman stood up and shouted, "I will decide what is essential in my life—not you. This is his doing," she said, pointing angrily at Ezra. "He started it. Been problems ever since he and his mongrel family showed up. Black girl trouble and worse." Her husband grabbed her by the arm and pulled her down. A few groaned and hissed. People started talking, arguing.

"Silence!" The Captain waved his arms overhead. "This is not Ezra's doing. This is *my* doing. My decision." He pointed at the woman and his voice turned cold as steel. "Stand up! I warned you! Johnson, you and your wife either stand and apologize to Ezra's family right now or leave the train in the morning. I won't tolerate insubordination, dissension, and hate. What'll it be?"

Todd Johnson stood, took off his hat, and put his hand on his wife's shoulder. "I truly apologize for Willa's outburst. It's not her, it's our family heirlooms. We've had them for generations and been carrying the last of them since we left Virginia. They were entrusted to us. Please understand. I truly apologize to Ezra's family for what she said. They are not to blame."

As Johnson sat down, his wife smacked him. "This is all your fault."

Beth could understand Willa Johnson's torment, even feel it curdling in her own stomach, remembering her home and treasures destroyed in fire. But she detested Willa for turning her ire on Ezra and poor Maddie. Another one to watch out for if they stayed on the train.

Maddie slipped free from Beth's arm and crawled under the wagon. "Watch her like a hawk," Beth said to James. "Let her be, but if she runs, you go after her. Fast as you can. Don't let her get to the woods."

AFTER THE MEETING BROKE UP, CAMILLE WALKED OVER AND TRIED to catch Beth's eyes, but five or six women had flocked to her. Beth squirmed, clearly uncomfortable, the women nearly pinning her to the wagon. And all talking at once. They were nervously cordial, offering assurance that she and her family were most welcome, even Maddie.

Camille assumed the threat of being tossed overboard in the wilderness had been sobering. She broke in. "Beth, sorry, but where is Maddie? I took my eye off her."

Beth pointed under the wagon, then moved away, taking the circle of women with her.

Camille found Maddie who had scooted down one more wagon. She nodded at James, standing back but standing guard. Then crawled under herself. She was grateful for the moment of privacy, just the two of them. Maddie sat cross-legged, turned away from Camille, crying.

"They don't like me. And you were off talking to that fancy girl, laughing with her, when those other girls called me a slave. They said slaves ain't allowed on this wagon train. Told them I was free-born but . . . You left me alone. James was there but it's not the same. He's not you," she said, tears sliding down her cheeks.

"I'm so very sorry," said Camille. "I'm with you now. I know what it's like to be alone and to hear people's spite. That girl I was with is Karen. She's really kind and said she likes you. And she said we were very brave to be sisters so openly. Now turn around and face me."

Maddie turned. Camille lifted her own apron and wiped Maddie's face and nose.

"They're saying ugly things," said Maddie. "Two boys said I couldn't possibly be your sister—t'weren't natural.

"God made us just the way we are and wanted us to be sisters. I believe that. He wanted us to be free. He's proud of us, especially you. And He is watching over us."

"I know, but I still feel so alone. I miss my home, my shanty, *ma mère*. I miss my people and Black faces and kind hands. I miss the way we sing praise and sing sorrow into beauty. I miss the music and dancing around the fire. I'm teaching Caroline some of our songs.

"But it scares me, Camille, to be in a world that gets whiter and whiter as we go west. What if there are no Black people or brown people in California? What if they all disappear from earth like *ma mère*?"

"They won't, I promise you. We'll find people of all colors and types in California. Now, listen to me, carefully. We don't have to like these people. We're just traveling with them. Their job is to protect us until we get to California. Our job is to keep you free. Your *mère* is looking down on us, helping us. You said yourself she had become that pelly bird, the one sitting right out there on a stump when we sat down for dinner. Your *mère* gave us Ezra and Beth to care for us. To give us love and hope. And a wagon train with oxen to escape with. And she gave you a new friend on the very first day. Caroline, who sings and lights up like Christmas when you sing with her. That's good for a first day, don't you think?"

"Suppose. But some of these people hate me. That Willa woman—"

"She's disgusting. Forget her. When the rest of these people get to know you, I promise you, most of them will like you. Not all, but most. Just look at you. You're wonderful, perfect, beautiful. Give them a chance. They're all just as scared as you are. Scared of leaving their homes. Scared of what's out there in the wilderness. Scared of strangers and new places. The great unknown."

Camille rocked her, rubbed her back, as Maddie tucked in next to her. "I miss ma *mère* and her songs every night."

"I know. I miss her too," said Camille.

Maddie hummed one of her *mère*'s bedtime favorites, while Camille whispered the words.

Oh freedom, Oh freedom, Oh freedom over me.
Oh before I'd be a slave,
I'd be buried in my grave.
And go home to my Lord and be free.

AT DAWN, PEOPLE CLIMBED OUT AND STARTED TO UNLOAD THEIR wagons mechanically, with looks of dread and anger. Children cried and were shushed. Families arranged things in two piles, sat down to eat a few bites, got up and moved things from one pile to the other, sat down for a few more bites, got up in pairs and fought, tugging things from each other's arms; all without words, private fights between a man and a woman.

Beth had heard them talking through the night, arguing, crying, making decisions, cursing.

After breakfast, they stood and stared at their piles, moved items as small as a hand mirror from one to the other. Fifteen hundred pounds, no more. They finally broke from their own misery to walk around and study everyone else's misery, making suggestions and admonishing each other.

"Those plates are too heavy, Donna. We can have them crated and shipped to California. You're better off taking that good cloth, those needles and yarn."

"I know they're precious, Jean, but just take one candlestick we can use at night. We'll crate and ship the rest along with the silver and miniature paintings from Kanesville."

"Charlie, you don't really need four identical hammers, and sell that damned thirty-pound anvil. You can buy one out there with all that gold you're going to pan."

CAPTAIN WINTHROP ASKED EZRA AND BROSE TO FIND SOME MEN and yoke three or four wagons for the trek to the Kanesville markets. "There is a merchant there, Edward Winslow, with a warehouse. He fills the steam-boats heading back to St. Louis with this kind of merchandise. And he packs crates for sea travel," said the Captain. "Ezra, get what you can for the heavy replaceable goods, like tools, and buy what we need."

People glared at the Captain, waiting for him to walk over and pass judgment. Beth motioned for the Captain to lower his head so she could whisper. He leaned down, looking away with disinterest and pride.

"After you make your decisions," she said, "I'd ask you to please send a few of these other people along with Ezra and Brose, so they can help bargain and vouch for the fact they weren't cheated. And include at least one woman—one used to farm life—to outfit the women and children. That's not me. Charlotte might be good."

The Captain looked quizzically at Beth, then with the faintest smile, nodded. "Very good ideas. Thank you, Beth. I'll do it."

He straightened himself ceremoniously and prepared to review the grim-faced families pacing back and forth in front of their piles. The Reverend offered to accompany him, but he shook his head. "Better in a military manner. Less complicated."

Beth followed at a distance, unable to stay away from the pain in people's faces as they set aside fine china and heirlooms as tenderly as laying their dead relatives in their graves. The sacrifices reminded her of Hannah's favorite chair curling up in flames as she fled the house. The only difference between her loss and theirs was the agony of choice; they have some, she had none. But in the end, that feeling of loss would be just as complete, she realized. None of them had homes any longer.

At the Kilpatrick's wagon, the Captain stopped and examined a few small things, trying to ignore Grandma Bridget rocking in front of her pile. "My son put me in the essential pile and this chair goes with me," she said, gripping the handrails fiercely. "You can bury the chair with me out there in the wilds, but you can't pry me out of it."

"Nobody dies on my train," said the Captain, moving on.

⇒ 15 ⇐

FLOODING RIVER

Fifty miles west

L ow, dark clouds stretched across the prairie, smothering the land, turning everything gray—earth, grass, water—save for a few specks of yellow at the edge of the world. With growing fear, Beth stared at the twinkles of lightning on the horizon. As tiny and silent as fireflies at dusk. *Dear God, more rain upriver.*

The cold, wet April wind whipped her face and drove the drizzle under her collar as she climbed up into the open wagon next to Camille and Maddie. The cover was off to let in the light for the girls who were scurrying on their knees, sealing the inside floor and sides with grease and pitch just as Beth had done with the planks on the outside. Would it hold? Standing in the open wagon, looking at the flooding waters they were about to cross, Beth had her doubts. She was staring at a swollen ford across the Loup River, a northern tributary to the Platte River. In this broad open world of churning water and mattress sky the wagon appeared little more than a tiny wooden box. *More coffin than vessel,* she thought, shivering. Simply not sturdy enough to cross an angry river.

The train had started across the flooding ford at dawn, wagon by wagon, taking one family at a time. But by midday, the sky had turned a cold twilight, and this portion of the river system—normally a passable tributary according to Ezra—was running wider, deeper, faster, and colder.

Beth marveled at the exertion required. Each wagon needed a double team of oxen, two men in front guiding the beasts. And a man on each of the four wheels to lift and turn the wheels through the swill of silt and sand at the bottom of the river.

Late morning and only half the families had made it across, and the rising river had now cut a second channel on the far side of a newly created sandbar half mile downstream, making the journey all that much more complicated. In the gray pall, Beth could no longer see the far shore.

Beth and the girls lashed the cargo down and folded and tied the wagon cover into a tight canvas cushion to lean against while crossing. As Ezra had directed, they made their nest, a place in the middle of the wagon where they could see in all directions yet not get tangled in ropes and canvas should the wagon suddenly flip mid-river.

Ezra shouted, "Careful." Then their wagon jerked, and Beth dropped to her knees and grabbed the sideboard. She felt Ezra's shoulder brush against her hand as he and James began rolling the wagon toward the staging area. There he was, right beside her. Almost face to face. A weary face, furrowed with fatigue, his eyes focused not on her but straight ahead. Without thinking, she reached over the sideboard to brush the mud and silt from Ezra's hair and neck. She could feel him nuzzle to the touch, to her freezing hands. *Keep calm*, she thought. *Strong.* He and James had already made three arduous round trips with other wagons that morning, each worse than the last, he said, fighting the mad rip-current in the middle of the river.

Her mind flashed to the earlier terror and her heart pounded again. The second wagon of the morning had tipped up on its side, nearly spilling the family. Everyone on shore watched, unable to breathe, as Ezra, James, Brose, and two other men wrestled the wagon back down into the water.

Beth wondered if his strength, his heart, could hold out trip after trip. "Ezra, look at me." She turned his face with both hands, searched his eyes, and saw the simple truth. He had no choice.

"Done?" he said, in a friendly voice. "Love your touch but tend to the girls, not me." He lowered his head and continued pushing.

They stopped at the staging area located on some higher ground to the side of the ford, about five feet above the spot where the muddy trail entered the fast river. The Cramer family had just entered the water. Sturgis would follow, then it would be their turn.

Beth took three deep breaths. Her job was to settle the girls' skittishness, get them prepared. She had learned long ago dealing with runaway slaves that it was impossible to calm them if she let her own fears come out. Even for a second. Fear's very contagious.

Ezra leaned over the sideboard. "Anything to eat in there?"

Camille handed him the food bag. He found some smoked venison and passed the bag on to James. Beth gave him the canteen.

"River is gaining on us," he said. "By nightfall, nigh impossible."

He sounded angry. At himself, she assumed. He and Brose had misjudged the flooding, all in their rush to stay ahead of the horde, to get everyone across in one day. They didn't want to have the party separated on two sides of the river for the better part of a week.

THE STURGIS FAMILY WAS IN POSITION. THEIR HITCH HAD BEEN difficult—one lead oxen balked and had to be coaxed and whipped. Now at the water's edge, Sarah and young Samuel sat settled into the middle of their wagon, men surrounding it, talking rapidly.

Beth wished Brose had not told her about the great snake currents that moved through the flooding spring rivers. "Sometimes a mile long," he told her. "They rise up and arch their backs like serpents, then dive down to gouge channels and chew holes. When wagons and horses cross through the body of the snake, it grabs them, shakes them, and sometimes swallows them whole."

At least Maddie hadn't been around to hear that nonsense. Beth pulled Brose aside and made him promise to keep his mouth shut. "Don't terrify these girls."

"OK, but better to know who's grabbing you."

The Sturgis wagon inched forward. In front, two men walked backward, pulling the lead oxen by the harness and the ears, yelling, "Ya! Look at me! Not the river! Ya!" Sarah looked so calm and tender, holding Samuel tight in her arms. The boy twisted around to see his pa, Doc, working one of the back wheels.

Twenty yards into the water, their wheels lifted off the riverbed and the wagon began to bob free. The men were now swimming beside the oxen, holding their harness, eyeball to eyeball, shouting to comfort the terrified beasts. Beth looked for Doc but the men had shifted positions. Samuel turned in Sarah's arms and wiggled one arm free to wave goodbye. Camille and Maddie waved back.

The swollen river buffeted them, splashing over the side, rocking the wagon, and lifting the upstream side slightly. Sarah pulled her shawl up over her head and wrapped Samuel in tight against the cold wet wind.

In the middle of the river, the wagon swerved sideways as it hit the rip current. It began to buck, seesawing, the back lifting and falling, up down, up down. Sarah hunched over and covered Samuel with her body. A tarp blew away as the cargo shifted.

Beth was up on her toes in the wagon, her arm wrapped around Camille's shoulder, holding her breath. Maddie stood up on the sideboard, holding on to Beth. They clutched as one.

Then, inexplicably, the Sturgis's wagon slid down into what appeared to be a trough in the river, calm and low. Momentarily disappearing from view. Sarah's head popped up, looking around. Beth exhaled.

The snake struck, and the wagon jumped from the water as if bitten. Bucking, jerking in wild spasms. The oxen panicked, fighting the harness and the men clinging to them. Sarah clutched Samuel with both arms.

"Hang on to the wagon! The sideboard. For God's sake, Sarah, hang on!" Beth shouted into the wind.

SARAH FELT THE WAGON LURCH, THEN SOME MONSTROUS FORCE
that rose up underneath the wagon bed, lifted, tilted and slapped the
bottom. She clutched Samuel tight and tried to scoot to the higher side,
but the monster suddenly reared and in a burst of fury pitched the two
of them head over heels into the freezing water. And flung loose boxes
and trunks after them. Fighting to keep Samuel's head above water with
one hand, while paddling with the other and kicking her feet furiously
to stay afloat, she shouted for her husband. "Thomas help us!" Terrified,
Samuel too started screaming, "Daddy, Daddy," his arms wrapped
around Mama's neck.

Sarah felt something strange tugging at her feet, pulling. She tried
to kick it away.

Then in horror, she watched an errant wave lift some wooden boxes
and fling them in her direction. She yanked Samuel to her chest and
turned away but an edge of one flying box careened off Samuel's head.
She heard no crack but her son went silent and his head drooped on her
shoulder. She shrieked for her husband, "Thomas! I can't stay up. Help
us, for God's sake."

Sarah clung to Samuel, the two rising and falling in the water until
the weight of her water-soaked dress dragged them under. She thrashed
under the swirling water, trying to kick her way to the surface but
realized the current had tangled the long, dark woolen dress about her
legs, pinning them together. Panicked, she fought to swim upward with
one arm, the other clutching Samuel, her feet wiggling. Then the rip
current, like a thief in the dark, snatched him.

She rose, slapping the water, gasping and shouting. Doc struggled
to reach his wife as she disappeared under the water again. He lifted her
to the surface. She was flailing about, spinning, trying to see, screaming
for her son. "Samueeeel!"

"EZRA! THERE!" BETH SCREAMED, POINTING AT SAMUEL FLOATING
on the churning surface. Ezra and James were already on the run down
the shoreline to head the boy off.

Maddie and Camille were shouting as loud as they could, "There-there-there!"

Maddie jumped out of the wagon and ran downriver after Ezra. "There, there, there." She leapt in the air and pointed.

Ezra and James flew down the riverbank at full speed, jumping over bushes and roots and outcroppings of rock, keeping their eyes on the boy. Other men followed. Maddie stumbled, fell, got back up.

Beth shrieked from her perch in the wagon. "Ezra! There! Can you see him?" Her voice swallowed in the roar of the raging current.

Samuel was skimming the water, motionless, face down.

Ezra and James, finally ahead of the boy, yanked their boots off and dove headlong into the river, swimming toward the rip current to intercept Samuel.

The boy's head popped up and down. His body floated, spinning in a slipstream behind a large log. Ezra, with long powerful strokes made good headway toward the middle. He was ahead of the boy, ready to grab him. But the current taunted him, pulling Samuel into its swirling embrace and sent him flying past Ezra, downriver.

Camille and Beth went running after Maddie. When they caught her, she was turning in place, grasping wildly as if blind, struck with terror, shaking, calling out, "Samuel, Samuel, Samuel . . . Please, please God, save him."

EZRA AND JAMES FOUND SAMUEL A MILE DOWN, STILL MILES upstream from the mouth of the Loup River where it sweeps into the Platte River.

He had washed up onto the downstream sandbar, his face buried in the sandy bank, feet limp and swaying in the eddies. They pulled the boy up onto the spit. Ezra pumped his chest, opened his mouth and breathed into him. The boy's skin was cold; his eyes stared straight into Ezra. Gone.

Ezra flopped down and leaned against a log. He pulled Samuel to him and rested his cheek on the boy's head.

James stared at the sand. Ezra sat silent, slumped over, exhausted, still panting for breath. His body ached, his blood pounding him in punishment.

Just one more minute, he told himself. *One more minute to rest. So much more to do.*

He got up. He pulled James to his feet, rubbed the boy's face and hands, numb from the icy river water. Then the two gently washed the mud from Samuel's eyebrows and hair. They tidied his clothing and removed the vines and leaves clinging to his neck.

Holding Samuel over their heads, high above the swirling, chest-high water, they carried him from the sandbar across the narrow, slower moving channel to the far shore. Then Ezra carried him in his arms along the shoreline, upriver, toward the waiting families. Ezra's socks had been ground to a pulp by the sand and rocks. His bare feet bled.

His heart sank when he walked around the last bend, out of the brush and into view of the families. Some cringed back as Ezra and James approached. The Reverend and his son, David, walked forward, their arms out. Others turned away, covered their mouths, shook their heads. One woman shrieked, then suppressed her horror as Sarah and Doc burst past her.

Sarah stopped cold when she saw Samuel's legs dangling limp from Ezra's arms. Wheeling, she buried her face in her husband's chest, pounding on him. She began to wail, her horror rising into high-pitched shrieking like a tortured animal. He held her tight, sobbing himself, as she thrashed in fury. Tearing at him. Hitting and scratching viscously, then with diminishing strength she pleaded.

"Why, God? Why didn't you take *me?*"

She pulled back from Doc, screaming. "Let me go! No, God. No, No. Not Samuel, anything but . . . my love, my . . ."

She broke, collapsed in Doc's arms, dead weight. Trembling together, clasping, moaning, the two slowly sank to their knees. They toppled over and curled about each other. Everyone around them was crying. Even the Reverend, even himself.

But Ezra had to go on. Beth was waiting. He had to bring her and the girls across. Before the beastly river rose higher. Before nightfall.

⇒ 16 ⇐

BETH AND THE GIRLS CROSS

Facing the rip current

U nable to stop staring at the Carter wagon, now jostling in
the river and approaching the lair of the snake, Maddie
curled into Beth, and Camille dropped her head onto Beth's
shoulder. She embraced them, trying to calculate when the Carters
would be bitten. As if the snake were predictable.

The wagon lifted and twisted but no spasm. Maybe the snake was
letting them pass through. Just waiting. The wily serpent whispering
to Beth on the wind. *Come on. I'm waiting. Don't fear. I won't bite.*

By the time Ezra and James returned to hitch the oxen, Beth had a
solid grip on Camille and Maddie, who had tried to wiggle past her to
climb out of the wagon. "Stay here!" she demanded. They would rather
go back than drown they told her. She pushed them down onto the
wagon bed. "Sit."

Ezra's face was grim as he walked up. She had intended to reassure
him Samuel's drowning wasn't his fault, but the moment had passed.
"Problem," she said quietly. "They don't want to cross."

He stepped around Beth and glared at the girls. "This is what we
agreed, remember? No turning back." His tone was gruff, firm. "We're
going across in ten minutes. Understand?" It wasn't a question. They
looked straight ahead without comment.

"I know it's cold and you're terrified," he said, his voice growing softer, "but I want you out of those heavy dresses when we cross." Camille's eyes widened. "Wrap them around yourself like capes, so if you go in, you can shed them clean. Boots too. Take them off, tie them together, and tie them down in the wagon. Can you two swim? I should have asked you earlier."

They stared at him.

"Is that a yes?"

"*Ma mère* taught me," said Maddie quietly. "Live'n near the bayous."

"Good. Camille?"

She closed her eyes and nodded.

"After you disrobe—Beth, I want you to take that rope back there and tie the three of you together at the waist." He reached into the wagon and pulled it out. "Like this. Give it some slack, two, three lengths between each of you, and tied, not too tight, around the waist." He stretched both arms wide to show them a single length. "If you go over, the others can pull you back in. If you all end up in the water, the ties will keep you together to help each other. Draw yourself together. Form a raft. OK?"

"Disrobe? I don't think . . ." said Camille.

"No arguments. I want you safe. Not demure." He walked away to get the animals.

Camille and Maddie sat in the wagon bed, stunned, leaning against the boxes, well anchored in the middle, arms and bare feet rubbing against each other.

They're in shock. I've seen it many times, Beth thought. She remembered runaways awaiting their fate with no good options. An old expression slipped into her mind: *Dragons ahead, wolves behind.*

The oxen were hitched, and the wagon began to jostle as the beasts complained with their bodies. They shuddered, bellowed, pawed at the mud, tried to backtrack.

Beth pulled her dress off first. Shivering in light undergarments, the wind cutting right through, she helped Maddie. She shouted at Camille, "Come on. Off!" She tied the rope around Maddie's tiny waist, doubled the knot, gave it some slack and tied it around herself.

Camille shook her head, her face in torment. "I'll be humiliated," she said. "Please . . ." She backed away toward the edge of the wagon.

"For God's sake, Camille. Your dress is wool. Wet, it will take you down like an anchor. Probably what happened to poor Sarah."

The wagon began to roll forward.

Beth leaned into the girl's face. "Snap out of it! Now. Off!"

Camille unfastened and stepped out of her dress, then quickly wrapped it around her shoulders.

Beth tied the rope around Camille's waist, and cinched it. "You'll be safer if you go in the water."

"I'm sorry," said Camille. "I don't know what's come over me. I've never been so afraid."

"Of course, we all are. But we'll make it. Say a prayer."

EZRA BACKED INTO THE RAGING RIVER, TUGGING ONE OF THE LEAD oxen, James the other. Ezra seemed all determination—his face grim, movements swift and sure. *But what's going on with James?* Beth wondered. He appeared to be slapping his chest with one hand as he pulled on the harness with the other.

Ezra shouted at the boy, words Beth couldn't hear above the roar of the river, but she saw James jerk himself free of his agony and begin to work his ox with both hands.

Now in up to his waist, Ezra signaled to Beth to get down low in the wagon and hold on to the girls and make sure the rope was not looped around their necks.

Camille and Maddie screamed when the wagon splashed into the river. Beth pushed the two onto their hands and knees, her grease bucket at the ready. "Find any leak. Seal it!" The three ran their eyes and hands over every inch of the wagon bed and sideboards.

All held fast; the seams, the cracks, even the knotholes that had been plugged with whittled pegs and hammered tight. The wagon swayed in the water, shuddering as the waves slapped the side, as men lifted the wheels from the soft riverbed.

Maddie's lips were already blue. Camille wrapped her arms around her, but Maddie continued to shake, her cotton chemise too thin to ward off the shock of a cold wet wind. Beth draped dresses, shawls, and a small tarp about their shoulders until they settled.

The three sat facing each other, silent in the wind and mist, holding their breath, terrified but glad to be together. Attending to one another with their eyes. Beth tried to rid her mind of Sarah's wagon going over, of Samuel being swept away.

Beth wondered how she had gotten herself into this situation. Only months before she'd had her own world, dangerous as it was, under control. Now she was asked to put her trust in a team of panicked oxen and fallible men who were no match for the mighty river.

"Merciful God be with us," she said into the wind. Maddie and Camille bowed their heads. "Carry us across, dear God. For this, I promise, I won't question you anymore."

The wind blustered across the river, and she imagined God leaning down to whisper in her ear, so softly the girls couldn't hear. "Liar."

The rip current, that river within a river, surged over the heads of the two lead oxen, then slapped each pair in turn as they fought their way into the turbulence. As the wagon entered the domain of the snake, a great wave swelled broadside, first lifting, then twisting, then dropping the wagon. Then it lifted the side again and dropped it, jerking it one way and then another, then again lifted and dropped, and again, faster and faster, until the snake shook the wagon in its teeth like a mad dog. Maddie and Camille were both screaming into the wind, that old ally of the snake that swallowed their voices and fears like a tasty meal.

All three dove for the sideboard and hung on it as it rose in the air before smashing them to the wooden wagon bed. The wagon slowly rose again as they held fast to the upper side, but Maddie's fingers suddenly slipped. "*Ma mère!*" she screamed. She slid and fell hard against the lower sideboard and bounced. Beth caught Maddie's arm on the rebound, and held on until the wagon slapped down hard into the water and righted itself. As the wagon heaved and twisted, Beth pulled Maddie in, then coiled the slack safety lines around the girl's middle and held on with a strength she didn't know she had. *I'm not letting go.*

After a few more minutes of rodeo riding, the bored snake spat them out the other side. *Be gone with ye*, the snake whispered to Beth.

The frenzy easing, Beth shouted for Ezra. She heard men yelling but didn't recognize his voice. Had he been swept away? Her survival instinct told her to hold on and stay low, but she stood to take a quick peek. Left, right. Ah. When she saw him, she allowed herself a soft thought of appreciation for his strength, then flopped down.

"He's there." She smiled.

Beth marveled at the men working under life and death conditions, the courage it took to do this, not just once, but over and over. Once was quite enough for her.

SHE STOOD, NOW ABLE TO HOLD HER BALANCE. PEOPLE WAVED AT her from the rough shoreline. Her heart was still racing, her breath short, arms bruised from gripping the ropes and holding the girls tight. She searched the tattered campsite—scattered wagon, a few fires, exhaustion everywhere, like a worn army—but no sign of poor Sarah and Tom.

Maddie put her hands on the sideboard, about to jump out.

"Stop." Beth yanked her back. "We're tied together, remember." They struggled with the wet knots as the weary oxen pulled the wagon out of the water onto higher ground. Once free of the rope, Beth, Camille, and Maddie tugged their clammy dresses back on.

Ezra was waiting, his mouth drawn tight, his brow furrowed. Camille looked at him and turned away, but he grabbed her upper arm to get her attention. She winced and he let go.

"Sorry, didn't mean to hurt you," he said. "In the future, when I give you an order—for your safety and your sister's—you damned well better follow it. Immediately, without question. Do you hear me?"

She nodded, her eyes filled with pain and confusion. Shocked.

"That dress could have cost you your life. Or Maddie's. Or all three of you. Do you understand?"

"But I did take it off," she said, looking at Maddie and Beth for confirmation, then at the half dozen onlookers. "I'm sorry."

Beth stepped between them. "That's enough, Ezra. She took it off in plenty of time, even if you didn't see it. Now, you said your piece. Let her go. And when you calm down you might apologize."

Beth sent Camille and Maddie off to search for anything burnable— bushes, driftwood, tree limbs. Several families had managed to scrounge enough to get small, sputtering fires started amid the endless drizzle.

As the men unhitched the team, Beth joined in, unstrapping the harnesses, lifting the heavy yokes. She could not stop shivering. Ezra pulled her shawl out of the wagon and wrapped it around her. He continued working feverishly and kept glancing back at the river.

The moment the oxen were released, she took his arm. "Can you stop for a moment? Look me in the eye. Talk to me."

He shrugged, nodded toward the river, and mumbled something about the flood. "People trapped back there."

"You have to go back, I know that. But do you understand, it was not your fault."

"What?"

"Sarah, Samuel. You can't protect everyone. I hope you realize that."

He lifted his head. The pain in his eyes spread over his face, a sorrow she had never seen in him before, at least not since the fire.

"I thought I had warned everyone about heavy clothing," he said. "Samuel's face . . . it's burned into me."

"Where is she? Sarah, Tom?" Beth asked.

He pointed to a solitary wagon pulled to the side of a bluff, canvas draped across two sticks for privacy.

"You're going to make yourself sick over this," she said softly, stroking his hand. "It's not your fault." Ezra looked up at her in pain. There was a vacancy in his eyes as they sat in silence.

The impulse to hold him, to feel the warmth of his body, to comfort him and herself, turned her head light, but she couldn't cross that line. She took a half step back.

"I'm glad you're safe," he said. Then like a spirit he was gone. She saw him wade into the water, yank a reluctant ox that bellowed protest, and begin the return crossing with four other men and a team of unyoked oxen.

AS NIGHT FELL AND THE ENTIRE WAGON TRAIN HAD MIRACULOUSLY made it across, the Captain, Miriam, Reverend and his son David walked from campfire to campfire, speaking to each family about Samuel's death, about their wounds and their fear of going forward. The foursome carried a whiskey bottle with them, even for the children. When they arrived at her campfire, Beth was the only one awake. She took a swig, then another, savoring the burn. Then bid them farewell.

That night Beth couldn't sleep. She paced about wrapped in her shawl, unable to stop shaking, tears rolling down. She wandered into the brush, up over the dunes, not wanting to be seen, or to explain. She finally let go, kneeled in the sand, and cried until she sobbed herself sick. She didn't know why. It wasn't like her to cry so openly, so fully, and she had no right to cry. She had not lost anyone herself. She kept seeing Samuel wave to her, hearing Ezra's voice choked with grief.

SARAH AND DOC STURGIS SLEPT UNDER THEIR WAGON NEXT TO their dead son that night and cradled him as he grew cold as the black sky. The wolves howled, and Sarah woke and pulled her son in tighter. She kept vigil, giving her last boy comfort on the first night of his death.

⇒ 17 ⇐

CARING FOR SARAH

150 miles farther west

Two weeks in, the sky had cleared, the trail drying from mud to firm, lifting spirits. Yet there was an uncomfortable pall of grief that held people in check after Samuel's drowning. No one laughed out loud, no one sported about, cracked jokes, danced. It was a community pulling together tightly, but in a mood that remained cautious, funereal. In particular, the entire train was on watch for Sarah, as if holding its breath, fearful she might do something drastic. No one used the word suicide, but they all feared it. The families took turns day and night caring for her, giving Doc some time to sleep, tend to his patients' ailments.

After dinner, Beth and Miriam started toward Sarah's wagon, which sat on the far perimeter, away from the evening clamor and hustle. Doc and Sarah had asked for as much distance as they could get without disengaging from the security of the train.

Every day that Sarah moved farther away from her boy's grave— her beloved fourth child snugged in the earth below the roaming beasts and howling wind—the more bereaved she became. *She's getting worse, barely eating, losing heart*, they whispered to each other.

Sitting with her friend, drinking tea, Miriam poked the coals at Beth's fire. "I'm so worried about both of them," she said. "Doc and

Sarah want to turn back—I've heard them say as much—but don't dare. And yet have no will to go on. How's Ezra holding up?"

"He's overwhelmed by the stream of nightly visitors with questions and complaints about long days, fatigue, endless mud, dust and wind, hammering sun, rattlesnakes where the women want to urinate. Then there are the family spats they want his advice on. And fears and rumors of what lies ahead, and impatience at the same time. 'Where are the Indians and buffalo?' they ask.

"'In time,' he tells them, but warns each family to be very careful getting in and out of their wagons while they are moving. 'Easy enough when tired to trip and fall under the iron-rimmed wheels. So please drill your children not to scamper on and off unless the wagon is fully stopped. Better yet, tell them to get in and out only from the backend. Lot of people die on these trains, their chests, heads crushed under the wheel. Pass the word to pay attention especially when your mind wanders, numbed by the tedium.'"

"No Beth," said Miriam. "I meant about Samuel, the drowning. How's Ezra dealing with that?"

"Oh, sorry. Wracked with guilt, to tell you the truth. He gets flushed, hot, almost feverish at times trying to undo the drowning. Nightmares. Confusing his dead son with Samuel. Some of the families blame him and take their anger out on him. He doesn't argue with them. But thank God, your wonderful husband has deflected the blame. He tells them, 'As Captain, Samuel's drowning was my fault and mine alone.' Of course, nobody believes that."

"Ezra has a dead son? I didn't realize."

"His wife and son both died in childbirth. Newlyweds. Long time ago. Twenty-five years or so now, I reckon. He's been running from that pain ever since. It finally caught him."

"And you brought him out of his pain," said Miriam.

"I like to think I helped. I was certain I had, but this drowning brought it back."

As Beth and Miriam approached Sarah's fire, several women nodded at them in relief and drifted away, relinquishing watch. As had many others, they paid their respects, offered solace, and dropped off kindling and food and offers of help.

Sarah sat on the ground like melted wax, Beth noticed, sunken, her arms wrapped around her knees, rocking, eyes closed. Behind her, someone had set up a backrest of bedding laid over an old trunk, but she seemed too agitated to lean back fully and relax. At least Doc had been able to pull her out of the wagon and put her beside a comfortable fire, where she could see and listen and receive well-wishers.

Doc perked up, suddenly realizing who was approaching. He stood, brushed his pants, smiled warmly with greetings. He leaned down to Sarah and told her in an overly cheerful voice that her good friends had come. Sarah glanced up, then dropped her eyes. Waves of small, almost imperceptible tremors crept along her face and neck. Not shivers, more like miniature spasms. She looked as if she were waiting to explode, Beth thought.

She sat down on a log beside Sarah and poured some warm soup into a tin cup. She lifted a spoonful, blew on it, and put it gingerly to Sarah's lips. They were pinched and trembling. "You'll like this. Flavor of antelope and rabbit, with beans, a little pork, and sour greens," said Beth.

Her tongue poked out.

"Good. You like? Another sip?"

Sarah slowly pushed Beth's hand away.

Miriam, sitting on the other side, wiped the spittle from the end of Sarah's loose, disheveled hair and tucked the long, dark curls behind her ear. "It's good you are out of the wagon. Tomorrow, we'll walk awhile. Morning, is that best for you? Do you want to talk?"

Sarah shook her head.

"Do you want *me* to talk?" Miriam asked

Sarah nodded.

"OK, good, that's a good sign. I'll tell you about the day. Maddie and Caroline came by to sing to you before breakfast. Like songbirds. Do you remember? Some men left early to hunt for fresh meat, antelope. Today was a hard day's drive. We drove our wagons thirty miles over hot baked ground. Imagine that. After all those days of mud and soft sinking soil. We also saw some Indians . . . Brose prefers to call them the *Ancients*."

While Miriam described the three Pawnee in the distance, down by the trees on the river bank, letting their horses drink, Beth pulled Doc aside. He looked puzzled. "Do you have some of Samuel's old clothing, shirts, pants? Anything not washed and not too muddy. Something with his scent?" She drew the folded pillow case from her pocket.

"Yes, but . . . I put them out of sight to keep from distressing her," he said.

"Show me."

He climbed into the wagon and slid an oak-banded trunk toward the front. He opened it, glancing nervously toward Sarah, as did Beth. From the wagon, Sarah's silhouette in the firelight revealed just how thin she had become.

Miriam had her arm around Sarah, rocking her. Sarah rested her head on Miriam's shoulder while Miriam hummed a tune, barely audible.

"Why would God take him?" Sarah moaned. "Take *all* of them? Why does He want me barren and broken?"

"He doesn't," said Miriam. "He wants you to eat, get stronger." With her free hand, Miriam slowly lifted another spoonful. Sarah chewed a small morsel of meat listlessly.

Doc grabbed a handful of shirts and pants from the trunk and held them out. After smelling them, Beth stuffed some of the most pungent into the pillowcase, then rummaged through the trunk herself, pulling out socks, undergarments, a scarf that smelled of young sweat.

She had never really thought of a toddler having a distinct smell, but of course she hadn't known anything about children before this journey. By now she knew Maddie's and Camille's distinct scents and would, for her own comfort, secretly sniff their necks as they slept beside her in the wagon. It calmed her nerves, settled the day, and stirred something deep within her she didn't understand. She could not imagine Sarah's trauma, losing four boys.

Beth filled the pillowcase to a plump size, with enough leeway to close the end flap. She pulled a needle and thread from her pocket and made some quick stitches to close the flap.

Sarah squinted as Beth handed her the pillow. "The girls made this for you," she said, taking Sarah's hand and running it over the old, soft calico. "Feel it, smell it. I filled it with some of Samuel's clothing, so at night you can keep him close while you sleep. They call it a dream pillow . . ." Beth caught herself.

She was about to explain that this was probably an old folk custom from Louisiana. Jenny had made one for Camille when she was seven, right after her mother died. Camille slept with it for a year until the scent disappeared into her own. Beth wasn't sure how Sarah might react to honoring a custom whose origin was not clear. Passed to Camille from Jenny so its origins could be slave, Choctaw, Creole, or Louisiana bayou. You never knew about these things. Better just to leave that part out.

Sarah traced the faded pattern of roses on the material and ran her fingers over the girls' embroidered vines. Cautiously raising the pillow to her nose, she closed her eyes, sniffed, and rubbed it against her cheek. Finally, she crushed it to her face with both hands, inhaling deeply, whispering his name, crying for him to come out. Beth startled when Sarah finally broke, pitching forward onto the pillow with deep, haunting howls, sobbing and wailing, gulping air. Doc looked terrified. The pillow had unleashed all that buried love and longing, that rage and incomprehension. Her Samuel ripped from her arms by a merciless river current.

She cradled the pillow while an hour passed in quiet memory.

THE FIRE WAS SPUTTERING, DIMMING. DOC NEARLY ASLEEP, ABLE TO let go and doze with the safety of Miriam and Beth in attendance.

Beth walked over to the pile of kindling and firewood, a scattered mess, and loaded her arms—some paper, twigs, chopped branches, a small log, and two dried buffalo chips. On the ground, under some discarded butcher paper was a newspaper opened to an advertisement torn in half. Beth leaned over to read the fragment, then jumped as if she had been burned. Everything fell from her arms.

> $2500 IN GOLD. WANTED, INFORMATION ON THE WHEREABOUTS . . . LOUISIANA, A SLAVE GIRL, AGE NINE . . . COPPER SKIN . . . CAMILLE, FAIR SKIN, BROWN EYES . . .

Kneeling, she glanced around furtively and scraped together the firewood. Dread climbed from Beth's stomach into her throat, constricting it. *Somebody knows!* Her mind raced and conjured a courtroom, her lies unraveling before a hectoring prosecutor and a scowling judge.

Calm, she pinched herself, *calm.* Miriam and Doc were paying no attention. Others in the camp appeared busy. She had to collect her wits. *Think. It can't be a mistake, not lying open this way, can it? But it's torn in half. Why?* Perhaps after hoarding the information in secret, the knower had a change of heart. Or feared being thrown off the train.

She stuffed the scrap deep in her apron pocket, again surveying the camp to see if she was being watched. She walked back, arms loaded, trying to assume a casual posture.

Rebuilding the fire, she couldn't prevent her hands from trembling. She didn't dare look at Miriam or Doc for fear she would give herself away. Would they even care at this point? Nevertheless, she felt exposed, defenseless against accusations to come. Her lies had built one upon another.

Who knows? Her mind searched the entire camp. She hadn't sensed anything out of the ordinary. Personalities and dispositions hadn't changed. No hints, no suspicions. Hostility, yes, but that was different. If it were someone like Maude or Willa, everybody on the wagon train would know by now. *Why the silence? Blackmail? To what end?*

Absently placing one thick branch on top of another, the fire grew until Beth's face burned from the heat. Finally, she leaned back and took a quick look at Sarah and Miriam. They were oblivious to her, still working on the soup. Doc had nodded off, taking the opportunity to sleep. Beth composed herself, stood, and suppressed her erratic breathing.

She joined Sarah and Miriam for ten minutes of small talk, then whispered to Miriam that she had to get back. She kissed Sarah on the cheek and said she didn't want to disturb Tom.

"Everything all right?" asked Miriam, standing. She sensed something was off.

It was awful to lie to her good friend. Beth wanted to confide, the urge was powerful and growing, but she knew better. She couldn't embroil Miriam in their conspiracy. *Don't,* she told herself. *Calm down. Confer with Ezra.*

"Just light-headed. A little nauseous. See you in the morning," she said.

Miriam took her by the arm and walked her out of earshot. "I'll stay, maybe the whole night. I'm worried about suicide."

"Me too. We all are. I'll take tomorrow night if she's no better. We must let Doc get some rest."

Lifting her skirt and trotting through the dust, Beth avoided conversation on the way back to her own fire.

She stopped when passing Camille and Karen, Maddie and Caroline. "You four on your way to see Sarah?" They nodded. "Good, Miriam could use a spell to stretch her legs, close her eyes. She'll be there all night. Sarah's still fragile. Doc's afraid to sleep himself without someone there to watch over her. Let him sleep as long as you can."

"We thought we'd read," said Camille, "some poetry Karen brought and some Bible verses. Maddie and Caroline plan to sing to her again. It brightens her mood."

"I'm sure everyone in camp will be listening. Our two sopranos," said Beth.

"We'll sing her favorite," said Caroline, jumping up and down. "It's called 'Bonny Portmore.' Ballad about all the bonny old oak and ash trees that lined the waters of Portmore. All cut down, Daidí said, for ship building in Belfast. It's so sad and so lyrical it brings Sarah to tears. Good tears. Maddie's already learned how to sing it with a Celtic lilt."

"Wonderful. As a community, we have to pull her through this and if anyone can lift her spirits, it's you two. By the way, Camille, Maddie, she loves her dream pillow. Been hugging it, smelling, reveling in her senses being so close to Samuel.

"Karen, I don't mean to ignore you. How are you and David holding up?"

"Thanks, we're doing better. David is out doing rounds for Doc this evening," she said "Stopping by each fire. Tom was grateful to have his help, to become his medical eyes and ears so he can stay focused on Sarah. And David's sour mood has brightened. He's so pleased to put two years of medical training to use, doing what he loves best. Even his father approves. Which is something."

BETH REACHED THEIR OWN WAGON, SURPRISED TO FIND EZRA stretched out, his head on a bedroll, eyes closed, a piece of stiff prairie grass dangling from his mouth. "You asleep?" she asked quietly.

Eyes still closed, he whispered, "Hiding. Anybody waiting? At least ten people came by to complain about the trail, their children and spouses. And yak yak yak about fatigue, prairie wind and swirling dust devils, howling wolves, skin drying out, rattlesnakes in the grass. 'Where are the rains?' they ask. As if the flooding wasn't enough."

"Ezra, I need to talk."

"Sorry. Now it's me complaining to you. How's Sarah?"

"Thin as a rail, sick with grief . . . but I found this." She pulled out the newspaper scrap, *St. Louis Daily Union*, dated two days after they left St. Louis.

He sat up quickly and they read the torn ad quietly several times. It mentioned Camille and a slave girl, but Maddie's name had been ripped off. *Intentionally?* she wondered.

The bounty had grown by a thousand dollars. "A lot of money," Beth said.

"Somebody must have picked up the newspaper in Kanesville, weeks ago," he said.

She looked at him. "Who do you think knows? And why are they keeping it quiet?"

"Well, we'll take it as it comes," he said. "I'm not so worried. If they intended to act on it, they would have done so by now, don't you think? We're two hundred and fifty, maybe three hundred miles into Indian Territory. I haven't picked up any hints or concerns. No second looks or suspicious eyes. Have you?"

"No, but what if they tell the Captain, he holds a meeting, and they decide the girls and I are here under false pretenses and must . . .?"

"Must what? Calm down. What are they going to do? Throw us off the train? They'd be helpless. They need us. If the girls are banished, then we all leave, and take Brose with us. You think the Captain is going to allow his wagon train to go forward without guides? Or fall into mutiny, because of our stupid lies? No, he'd come to us quietly, sort out the lies. Forgive us, squelch rumors, and carry on. He's an army man, practical. All in this together."

"Easy for you to say. But I don't want to live day in and day out with the contempt of these women because we lied our way onto the train and are now holding them hostage."

"Look, whoever tore that ad up must have come to the same con-clusion we have. Spreading dirt on us gets them nothing and can only jeopardize the survival of their own family. The Captain is more likely to throw them off the train than you and me."

"I think you're right, but I'm going to be forever looking into the eyes of every woman, wondering if she knows. I hate the idea of Miriam finding out I'm a liar."

"Someday you can tell her. She's not a fragile person. Explain our circumstances and she'll understand. Believe me, you're not going to lose her. Admires you; daresay loves you. You know that."

⇒ 18 ⇐

SECRETS IN A BATHING COVE

Beth and Camille

Her feet as guides along the river bottom, Beth put her weight down cautiously on soft sand and rounded stone. Each step into the river grew colder and more shocking. The water slipped past her knees to her thighs, then up to her waist. Balancing on her toes, shivering, she braced herself, then dropped straight down to her neck, her thin chemise billowing around her head. Freezing, glorious breathlessness.

After a moment of paralysis, she relaxed into the intense cold and let it take over completely. Still on her feet, she leaned her head back until the freezing water enveloped all but her nose and mouth. Icy needles bored into her scalp. Her long red hair spread free, swimming on its own in the ripples.

She lifted her legs and floated free on her back, while the slow eddies in this quiet turn of the river picked her up and carried her downstream. Weightless, buoyant, the long rope around her waist slack, she was safe in a new world. One the opposite of dust and sweat, a world without heat, without thudding hooves and creaking wagons. Without pinching leather and parched lips, bursting blisters and burned hands. In this wet world, she might drift a thousand cold, soothing miles and wash up in St. Louis, to awake from a dream she had about Ezra and two strange girls who had been given to her by a good spirit to replace the house she loved and lost. Dying might be like this, cold and wet, trading in one dream for another.

She rotated and was now aware of the rope, first heavy, then taut. Suddenly, it jerked her tight and held her suspended at the end of a long tether, while the river took her grime and sweat and dreams downstream.

Walking awkwardly against the current, first at chest height and light feet, then with surer footing at waist level, Beth made her way back to the small sandy cove surrounded by short cliffs and shrubbery. She splashed Camille as she emerged from the river. Fidgeting with excitement, Camille, shrieked with joy when the spray of cold water hit her.

"Come on. It's safe. We may not find another spot like this," said Beth. They had it all to themselves, thanks to Ezra's discovery.

Camille stood staring at Beth with her mouth open. The wet cotton clung to Beth's body, sculpting her in sheer white like a statue. At this point in the journey, Beth felt no shame at her own immodesty.

"Come on. It's just me," said Beth.

Camille closed her eyes as Beth helped her pull the heavy woolen dress over her head. Then she stood in light linen underwear that hung loosely. She covered herself instinctively while Beth tied the rope around her waist.

Following Beth's path into the river, Camille raised her arms for balance. When she reached waist depth, she took a deep breath and fell flat on her back. At the seizure of cold, she yelled and thrashed, then settled with arms outstretched, staring at the blue sky, floating silently downriver, spinning slightly in the slow current. Adrift in pleasure.

CAMILLE'S MODESTY RETURNED THE MOMENT SHE STEPPED OUT OF the water. She quickly covered herself with her arms and ran awkwardly behind a bush. Beth swatted the dust from Camille's dress, tossed it over the bush, and turned away.

She remembered being as willowy as Camille but wouldn't return to those days if she could. She quite liked the womanly figure she had acquired in the last ten years, and the attention it raised in Ezra when she bent and stretched. Not always, but at certain moments. Just the slightest shift of his eyes, barely perceptible, but she had learned how to catch him unaware, when he had no resistance to her. It made her feel powerful, more than his equal. She had never before allowed herself to enjoy the pleasure of a man's attraction to her. She had never trusted it. But Ezra's stirring came from a place of warmth that made her feel special, desired.

After dressing, they settled quietly onto some large river stones without talking. Wringing out her wet hair, Beth thought about the way Ezra had looked at her last night after the parade of petitioners left. Affection for her or just relief? She chose desire. He never touched her, and she wasn't sure she wanted it, but he might try one of these days, and then what? The area behind her ears tingled in anticipation.

Camille took Beth's arm gently. "Can I ask you a question before we start the laundry?"

Oh, the laundry. Beth had forgotten. "Of course."

"Last night I heard you and Ezra talking about runaway slaves. I know it was a private conversation and I have no right to ask. But I wondered if you were talking about Maddie and me?"

"No, it wasn't you. Something else . . . a way of life now gone."

Camille looked puzzled. "Might I ask?"

Beth wondered just how much she should tell her. The girl still had no idea of Beth's role on the freedom train. The law couldn't get to her out here on the prairie, but she had kept the secret for so long it was difficult to confide in anyone not a part of the Underground Railroad.

"I stole slaves—that's the way the *law* saw it. I hid slaves escaping to freedom—that's the way *I* saw it. I ran a small waystation. Most of the tenants didn't know. A few river pilots served as conductors. And Ezra, of course. He was a partner at times."

Camille's face brightened. "But how? Wasn't it dangerous?"

Beth reminded herself that she had left the scene of the crime. The evidence had burned down. It could not follow her.

"Under the cookhouse, beneath the heavy planks where the stove sat. There was a trap door to get in, hidden below the grain sacks. Terrible place down there. Late one afternoon a slave patrol came through—they knew something—then a second patrol charged into the house with greater vengeance. They searched—tore it apart, actually—the attic, the closets, the coal bin, every crevice. Certain I was hiding someone. But they never found the hole."

"Your cooks must have been part of it."

Beth nodded. "They were. For ten years. Pretending to be my slaves."

"Pretending to be slaves? How strange. What happened to them?"

"Don't know. Camus and Torah, man and wife, ran that very same night the patrols came. Someone had informed. They left a pile of stones on the griddle pointing north, then disappeared. I imagine them living in Canada now."

There was no need to go further, Beth decided. Camille didn't need to know the worst—the lynching of her two guides, conductors, in public, down in front of the courthouse.

She rubbed Camille's hand between her own to change the subject.

"But what about you? You must have had hundreds of slaves on a plantation that big."

Camille flinched. "I grew up with it, not thinking about it, just living day to day. We all did. Father said slavery was necessary, Grandmother said ordained. Aunt Genevieve said it was too late to stop—a necessary evil that kept us from being killed by freed Blacks."

Camille paused, brushed a fly away, then gritted her teeth. "But even as a young girl, I knew slavery was wrong and grew to hate it. Jenny cared for me like a mother, sang to me, eased my fears, told me ancient stories passed down from Africa, and personal stories about slavery. When I was about Maddie's age, I could suddenly feel the anger myself, the helpless anger of men, women and children cowed and whipped for the smallest offense. Families torn apart and sold off. I saw it and felt it. 'Brutality's needed,' Father told me when I complained and cried in his arms. 'You'll understand when you get older. Our life, your life, depends upon this. You'll see.'

"That was the life he wished for me. This from the same man who educated me. Spent hours in his library talking about noble ideas and books. Hired tutors who spoke about liberty and freedom in our new country but demurred about slavery."

Camille ran her finger through the sand. "I think you are very brave, Beth. I could never do what you did. Help slaves run away. Knowing people would kill me for that."

"But you did," said Beth. "You escaped with Maddie."

"That's different. You helped strangers, Maddie's my own sister. I had no choice."

"Of course you had a choice."

"Jenny raised me after mother died," said Camille. Her face brightened. Her voice grew softer. "Then Maddie was born. I was almost nine at the time. I was so delighted. I loved holding her, playing with her fingers, hearing her laugh. I took care of her when Jenny worked in the house. Fed her, read to her, later secretly taught her how to read and write and do numbers. For years, I thought about helping Jenny and Maddie escape, but I couldn't imagine how, and then . . . then, this is the awful part." She paused and the light in Camille's face dimmed. "I realized I wanted them close to me, no matter what. They'd be safer with us. Better off, I told myself. We'd take care of them. But the truth is I was afraid of losing their love. They're the only ones who really knew me. I'd . . ." Camille began to tear up, turning away.

"You'd what? Camille, you can tell me. Look at me. Your secrets are safe with me. You can't shock me."

"I realized I'd hold them against their will if I had to. I wanted them, loved them, and would do anything to keep them with me on the plantation. Even slavery. That's when I knew I was turning evil."

Beth caressed Camille's cheek. "You're only seventeen. You're not evil. You saved Maddie. Just as Jenny asked you to."

"Maddie's not the only reason I ran. We were both about to be sold—in my case, not for money, but for inheritance, rich land and social standing. Same thing, I suppose. Father was willing to let Priscilla sell one of his daughters, Maddie, downriver into brutal field slavery because she brought shame on the family; the other, me, upriver into marital bondage because it expanded our holdings and exalted the family."

Beth took Camille by the shoulders. "Look at me, Camille, listen to me. You're not evil. You broke away from the evil around you. That takes courage. And you'll face a hard road ahead because of it. You'll be tested over and over. But you're strong. Stronger than you realize."

"Selling someone takes such a disgusting twist of mind," said Camille. "Men and women ripped apart, and young children torn from their mothers and sold with no more regard than cattle and horses. I saw the pain, the sheer terror of it, Beth, with my own eyes. Horrible, brutal. And my family still sees it as proper, God-given, even heroic."

"Personally, I know how horrible it is to be sold," said Beth, surprised she suddenly found the urge and willingness to open her past. Perhaps it might help Camille. "It's a feeling of pre-death, when you're about to be permanently trapped, locked in a cage."

Startled, Camille sat back, her eyes ablaze with curiosity. "What do you mean personally?"

"My own father was going to sell me. He sold my older sister, Maureen, two years before I left. Then it was my turn."

"What? I didn't know you had a sister. Dear God, he sold her?"

"Please don't say anything, even to Maddie," said Beth. "Even Ezra doesn't know this. Hannah, the woman who took me in in St. Louis, was the only one I've ever told. And now you, dear. I trust you."

"What happened to Maureen?"

"Soon as her body started developing, Pa got offers. He played them off against each other. Then one day Pa sold her to a man passing through Kentucky with a horse and a mule. Heading west, the man said, needed a wife. Maureen do just fine. Gave Pa lot of money, some gold."

"But your mother? Why didn't she stop him?"

"Poor Ma. She . . ." Beth paused, her face burning. These were her deepest secrets.

"Tell me, please. Did your mother fight for her daughter?"

Beth picked up a stick and struck the sand. "She did. Ma fought Pa someth'n fierce. He was sitting in his chair, and she went at him from behind with an iron skillet. Screamed. 'Not sell'n her!' Hit him good. He came up off the floor stumbling, roaring. Grabbed her and knocked her black and blue on the floor, bleeding, kicked her unconscious. I swung a poker. He blocked it and slammed me against the wall. Then poor Maureen was left to her fate. Terrified, she drank Pa's whiskey fast as she could until she fainted. Limp as a rag doll, the man threw her over his mule and strapped her on. I never saw her again. Never heard a word.

"Dear God, Beth. How awful. How old was Maureen?"

"Fourteen at the time. Still think about her. Still fancy that someone kind came along and rescued her. She'd be about forty now. I have this dream of her living in a comfortable home with two children, a good man who loves her." Beth dropped her head, her voice faded off.

"Beth, what is it?"

"Ma said it would never happen to me, but it did. I was skinny but started to fill. Life was already hard but getting harder for us in the back country. The crops failed. The animals died. Pa was crippled by a bear that tore at his leg. We had no money and Pa was desperate. At fifteen I was raped by a neighbor. Pa went after the man, but the man paid him off and that was that." She paused. *Maybe I'm saying too much,* Beth thought. *Perhaps I should hold back.*

"But you eventually got away, right?"

Beth nodded, "I did. But please, don't say anything to Ezra. He has enough haunting him as it is."

"What do you mean? Don't you love him?"

"Love him? I do, but . . . but no, of course not. Not like that." She stared at Camille, then looked away. What an awful question, asking her for a yes or no, as if it were that simple. No, she'd never give a man that kind of power over her.

"So you *don't* love him? I thought you did."

"I hope not. He's not all together in his mind any more than I am. He was newly married when his wife and son died in childbirth. He ran crazy, south to find his first childhood love, Daisy. Never found her. Then ran west into the wilderness, learned from old Bill to guide, trap, trade, and has never truly stopped running. He came to St. Louis time to time. To see me, his family, help me with the Underground. And with special tasks like installing an upstairs water pump. He thinks he'll be able to settle this time in California, but I have my doubts. I know that much about the man. He's got ghosts chasing him. Don't say anything, please. I shouldn't be telling you his story. So please, no one, not Maddie, not Karen."

"I won't. Promise. But your Pa? You didn't finish . . ."

"It was terrible. One day Ma hands me a big blue cloth with a knot on a shoulder stick, stuffed with clothes, a week of food, and says, 'Go! Run for your life. Right now, and don't never come back. Ever.' She gives me nine dollars she stole from Pa, a pistol, and pushes me to the door. 'No sass,' she says.

"'But I don't know where to go. Where?' Ma slaps me, tells me to stop crying, grow up, shakes me. 'But, but . . .'

"'Listen to me. Your Pa and his buzzards are liquored up down at the still, laughing, talking you up. Joking about break'n you in. But they ain't joke'n. Offering your Pa good money for a time with you. He ain't furious. He ain't saying no. He's laughing in that way of his. Let'm know he's considering. He's trading for you, darl'n. So run, don't stop and don't never come back. You're too good, too smart for his kind. I'll kill'm 'fore they put their filthy hands on you.' Then Ma picks up Pa's shotgun, primes the muzzle with shards of lead and nails, and says, 'Now run.'

"'No, I ain't come'n with ya, darling, she says. 'I'll stay, hold them off. And if your Pa tries to come after you, I'll kill him cold.'"

Beth recited the story as if she were in a dream. She looked over at Camille and saw tears running down her cheeks. "I'm trying not to cry," she said. "But oh God, Beth, so awful for you. How did you ever get away?"

"I ran harder than I have my entire life into the deep woods for hours on end till nightfall. Slept in the bushes. Next day, I ran again, north by the star toward the big river. I was fast as a fox through the forest, across small rivers and straight up wide streams to lose my scent. Finally, crawled into a hole, rubbed myself with plants dogs don't like, and hid for days. After that I ran only at night, sneaked around little bitty towns and sprawling farms. I stole food. Weeks later, I came to the Ohio River. So big, never seen nothing like it. Then stowed away on the steamboats. Mostly, I stayed in the grain bins. Rats would tell me when someone was coming. We all hid together. Then got to St. Louis where I been ever since."

Beth rubbed her arms where the rats had bit her, as if it were yesterday. Her mother's treasured voice was still there in her mind. *You're too good, darling, too smart for his kind.*

"And now here we are in the beautiful cove that Ezra found for us," said Camille. "Just for us so we could talk in private. I'll never forget the secrets you just told me. They feel like a gift, Beth."

"Thank you," said Beth, taking Camille's hand. "Now can you excuse me. I'm feeling flush. I need to splash my face with cold water."

As Beth stood up to leave, she pointed. "By the way, did you notice that wolf up there on the bluff looking at us? He seems alone, curious, not at all dangerous. What do you think? Let's not scare him off."

Beth patted Camille's knee, then walked to the river. She hiked her dress, tucked it in her undergarments and waded into the freezing water to clear her mind. She dipped her hands in and brought the water to her face and freshened her cheeks and forehead, cooled the back of her neck. She dropped some down the front of her dress.

Beth glanced back over her shoulder at Camille, who was pacing the sheltered beach, looking at driftwood, staring up into the trees on the bluff, and watching the afternoon clouds pile on top of one another.

Finally, Beth walked back and sat down on the rock and called Camille over. "Sorry, I got carried away with my stories. I suppose I wanted you to know why I ran, and from what. Our families are so different, but we ran for the same reason—the terror of being sold. It's why I've always felt like a fugitive."

"Do you know what happened to your ma?"

"She told me before I left, 'Don't never come look'n for me, darling. It would be a trap.' I forced myself to disappear. I didn't go back but thought for sure I would one day. Then, I didn't want to find out. She either killed him cold or he killed her. She saved me, that's all I know."

"If I had a mother," said Camille, "I would want her to be like yours, brave, protective. Or like you."

⇒ 19 ⇐

CHOLERA OUTBREAK

Week later, 170 miles farther west

A fter breakfast, the families loaded their wagons, preparing to move into formation for a ten- to twelve-hour trek on a promising day of blue sky and firm ground.

Suddenly Ezra heard a shout, sharp as the crack of a gun, then watched Brose race by on his horse, flashing him a hand signal of distress and a motion to follow. Something was terribly wrong. Ezra's heart clutched and he took off running to catch up. Everyone heard it, saw it, sensed it. Men, women, children dropped what they were carrying, stood and stared at each other.

Brose had left before dawn on a routine scouting mission of the forward trail but was back hours early. He dismounted on the fly next to the Captain's wagon and waited for Ezra. Brose did not often show fear but this morning his face was tortured, his eyes wild.

The three men stepped away from the gathering crowd that was now cautiously inching forward and conferred quietly out of earshot. Every eye in camp watched fearfully.

The only word Ezra remembered was the first one Brose whispered. "Cholera." Heard something about a wagon train breaking apart, trying to scatter, but that singular word blurred everything else in Ezra's mind.

Not a minute later, the Captain turned and walked without hesitation to face the anxious families. He raised his arms to quiet them. "Change of plan. I want you to re-circle your wagons and prepare to spend the day here." He was terse, his voice tight, clearly letting everyone know he was holding back. "We have a problem five, six miles up the trail that Ezra, Brose and I need to investigate. No sense asking questions, because I don't have the answers. I'll tell you when we return."

As the stunned crowd dissipated, the Captain pulled Doc aside and whispered in his ear, telling him to fetch his medical bag and horse. Doc's sudden scurry sent tremors and gossip flying through the camp and urgent questions hurled at the Captain. "Why Doc? Something medical? Dysentery? Typhoid? Scarlet Fever?" But the Captain refused to answer. His reticence seemed unnecessary, Ezra thought. Even cruel.

He was stuffing his saddlebag when Beth pushed in against his shoulder. "Don't shrug me off. What is it?"

He saw no need to torture her with uncertainty. It was going to be hard enough to accept as it was. "Pretty sure it's cholera," Ezra whispered. "Five miles upriver, a train breaking up in panic."

"Dear God. How . . .? Ezra?"

"Don't know yet."

Camille and Maddie wedged between them. Imploring them with their eyes, with anxious twists and turns. Ezra had a sudden urge to put his arm around them and reassure them everything would be all right, but it wouldn't do. He didn't know how dangerous it was, didn't want to lie. He rubbed Maddie's shoulder and squeezed Camille's hand. "Maybe one of you can go sit with Sarah and Johan. Tell her Doc will be all right, we'll take good care of him. Beth, let's not keep these families in agony. Better they know the cause of the alarm. Wait until after we're gone, then please tell the families it *might* be an outbreak of cholera and if so, we'll scout a way around it. Please work with Miriam and the Reverend and perhaps McGrath and his son Tad to keep these people from panicking. To pray for a safe bypass. Tell them they're quite safe right here, where we are."

THE MEN RODE FAST UNTIL THEY CAME UPON THE FIRST GRAVES. Ezra leapt off his horse to examine the ground and read the identities hastily scratched into wooden markers, all ending with the name, *Günter*. Three were left unmarked.

He kicked the loose dirt. "No more than a day or two. These graves are small and shallow, dug in a hurry," he said. He reached down to finger the moisture in the dirt.

"Stay away from those bodies," shouted the Captain.

Ezra pulled back and looked around. "The ones still active must be trying to outrun this," he said.

"Can't outrun it if they're carrying it with them," said Doc.

The thought of people running around contagious, the walking dead, just asking to be shot, sent a chill through Ezra. It was a common folk tale. But the idea didn't square with his own experience. He'd seen it before. Cholera victims don't run. Can't.

Moving slowly up the trail, they rode single file, studying the ground and the scattered debris. There was an eerie silence, as if the animals and bushes were holding their breath. The wind had stopped blowing. The wagon tracks were becoming more erratic, weaving back and forth across the trail, with wagons apparently trying to separate from one another.

Two miles farther up they spotted a lone wagon next to a cold smudge of charcoal, some cooking utensils and clothing scattered around. Small birds picked apart a woolen shawl.

There were no scavengers yet, except for buzzards. One sat on the wagon cover, while two others edged in toward something. Closer, Ezra saw the buzzards leering at two bodies, a man and a woman, lying ten feet apart in dried pools of vomit and diarrhea. She was lying face down, he face up. The stench was overwhelming, even at a distance. The dead couple resembled gray-blue ghosts with sagging skin.

The buzzard on the wagon cover hopped to the ground and took a few probing steps toward the man—going for the eyeballs, Ezra reckoned. *Strange*, he thought, *still intact.*

Ezra and Brose dismounted, pulled bandanas over their nose and mouth, while the others stayed on their horses, also covering their faces.

"Not too close," snapped the Captain.

From behind the dead man a small arm reached up and waved weakly. The buzzard jumped back, hissed, moved side to side, and finally flew back up onto the wagon cover. Ezra stopped in his tracks.

He edged up cautiously until he could see over the dead man. Then to the side. It was a small boy with matted blond hair, no more than five, his face, hair and clothing encrusted in dried vomit. The boy looked up toward Ezra, his eyes unfocused. His head flopped to one side and his body heaved, but he had nothing left inside. He was close to death but still trying to wake his parents, still protecting his father's eyes. Seemed to know instinctively what the buzzards wanted.

"Ezra, you stay back," shouted the Captain. "If that's cholera you don't want to breathe their air. Miasma, isn't that what they call it, Doc? Doc, is this cholera?"

"I've never tended a case, but this has all of the earmarks. The color of the skin, discharge of all fluids," he said, getting down off his horse and pulling a black satchel out of his saddlebag. "I brought some laudanum with bitters, and some cholera medicine, but I have no idea if they'll work. Here, Ezra, I may be able to spoon some into the child."

"Doc, don't you dare touch that boy," said the Captain. "Get away. He's as good as dead. I won't have you bringing cholera seeds back to my train. You too, Ezra! Let's go." The Captain put his hand on the top of his holstered pistol in case Doc or Ezra had any doubts about his intentions.

Probably right, thought Ezra, climbing back on Roan. *Let the boy die naturally. Fucking buzzards.* Ezra pulled out his pistol and shot the buzzard off the top of the wagon. The others flapped their long wings and scattered, but not far. Ezra shot a second.

As the men rode on upriver, Ezra found himself looking back with an uncomfortable queasiness in his stomach. He tried to shake off the grim images flowing through his mind—scavengers closing in, pecking at a dead boy, scooping out his eyes, and then with their sharp beaks daggering his face to bits. Suddenly, he saw an empty skull screaming without sound.

Dear God. Ezra shook his head to clear the macabre thoughts.

Riding past a second deserted wagon, they arrived where the train had finally broken apart. "Total panic, chaos taking control. This is the breaking point, right here," said the Captain. The ground was torn by hooves and sliced by wagon tracks veering erratically, as if it were a battlefield.

Ezra and Brose eased their horses down to the riverbank, where a few wagons had made a desperate dash for the safety of the water in exactly the wrong place. "Five, maybe six wagons," said Brose. "Terrible place to try to ford across to the southern trail. So wide, bad currents. You can see where their wagons cracked open like eggs in this current. Unlikely any of them made it across. Poor souls."

Ezra looked for bodies but saw none, just fragments of wagons and supplies clinging to one of the sandbars in the middle of the river.

Back on the trail, Brose pointed to a possible detour around the outbreak. Off in the distance a bluff to the north, leading away from the river. It led to a long rise bordering and hiding what they suspected was a deep tributary canyon. It could be a long, rough detour. But a detour none the less.

On the way back, they watched the buzzards circling in the distance and stopped to look in on the boy. Had he died? It would be a relief, easier that way, Ezra thought, but to his dismay, the boy was still alive. Damned if he hadn't pulled his chest up onto his father's body and put one small arm across the dead man's eyes. And wiggling his fingers to scare the buzzards. The boy was still taking shallow breaths and able to lift his hand a few inches to keep the birds at bay.

"We could shoot him. That would be the merciful thing to do," said the Captain. "But no, we'll leave him to the mercy of God."

They quickened their pace to a trot as they rode back to the wagon train, talking over ways to drive straight through the breakout or detour around it, and what to do should the party run into more cholera farther up the trail. Brose said he would forward scout up twenty, thirty miles. But Ezra wasn't listening. He lagged behind, brooding, struggling with his conscience.

He spurred Roan to the front of the riders, stopped, and pointed. "That's a strong spirit back there in that boy. I think he could live with half a chance, and I want to give it to him. I *have* to give it to him."

"No!" blurted the Captain. "You stay away."

Doc tried to explain the medical dangers of contact, but Ezra cut him off.

"Just me alone, Captain. I'm immune to cholera. Brose can testify to that. So I'm not afraid to tend the boy, give him a hand out of the grave."

"No. You leave him be. That's an order."

Ezra ignored him. "Doc, what do you do for cholera?"

Doc shrugged. "Some physicians recommend calomel at regular intervals." He hesitated, stroked his chin. "Others recommend transfusions, purgatives, liquid ammonia. There's no shortage of remedies. None of them, in my opinion—"

"You give me whatever you got, but if they don't work, I'll use water. I went through two terrible outbreaks in Native villages. Nearly everyone died. In the last one, Kiowa tribe, this old medicine man said his water remedy—bad-water, good-water—worked better than smoke and rattles and prayers. He saved three members of his tribe. When I asked what he meant, he said, 'When bad water flows out from a lake, good water needs to rush in to keep it balanced, fresh. It's a disease of water, not air,' he told me."

"Nonsense," said the Captain.

"That won't work, I'm quite sure," said Doc. "Doesn't make sense."

Ezra took a drink from his canteen and spit some on the ground. "Well then, Doc, give me what you got."

Doc hesitated and looked at the Captain.

Ezra continued. "Either way, I'll go bury the parents and stay with the boy. If he dies, I'll bury him too, and catch up with you by tomorrow noon."

The Captain's face hardened and his left eye twitched as he fought for control. No one, even Ezra, would defy his order. He slowly pulled out his pistol, but let it dangle in his hand, pointing at the ground.

"You'll not endanger us, Ezra. You'll do what you were contracted to do—guide the train, protect our families—and nothing more."

Ezra bristled. "Don't you ever pull a gun on me, Captain. Ever." He moved his own hand close to the spare pistol tucked in his belt.

"Whoa, stop!" Brose tugged at Ezra's sleeve, pulling his hand away.

"Captain, I'm not leaving that boy to die. I have to live with my conscience."

"You're countermanding a direct order." The Captain lifted his pistol, aimed it at Ezra's heart. "My word is law on this mission."

Ezra's fingers wiggled, tempted to reach. One quick, satisfying lunge for his weapon, even if it meant his own death. It was his pride and that old resentment of authority egging him on. His father used to goad him into explosive behavior that he would then punish. The Captain cocked his pistol, letting Ezra know he'd be foolish to try.

"Stop it! You idiots!" shouted Doc, moving his horse between the two. "Look at me. You. Good. Look at me. You. Good. Now stop this! I've got enough trouble with possible suicide on my hands and don't want another. We need both of you—not one or the other—both, to survive this journey. Use your heads. Your hearts."

"I've made my decision," said Ezra calmly. "I'm not in the army, Captain. I've sworn no oath to you. I make my own law out here."

The Captain glared at Doc, then looked at Ezra and Brose and finally put his pistol back in his holster.

"OK, Ezra, but one condition. You get cholera, you don't return. You stay and die with the boy. You don't bring it back to our families. I want your word on that."

Ezra nodded and put out his hand, but the Captain didn't take it.

"Anyway, you've got my word. Now, I need to get my things and tell Beth what I'm doing. I'll join you in a few days, with or without the boy. I'll wash off all the cholera seeds before I return."

EZRA GALLOPED INTO CAMP AHEAD OF THE OTHERS, WITHOUT looking at the inquisitive faces or responding to any of the people yelling at him for answers. He dismounted quickly and began gathering his things. He braced himself for what he had to tell her.

Beth's eyes opened wide with dread. "Is it? You sure?"

Her composure was gone; she seemed as fear-struck as any in the camp.

"Yes, I'm sure. A few buried, some on the ground, the rest scattered to die. Brose will find you a way around the outbreak, so you'll be safe, but . . ." He paused and Beth looked at him warily. "But there is a boy back there, maybe four years old, fighting for his life. I can help."

"No! Ezra, listen to me." She clutched his arm, his shirt, her voice choking. "It's cholera, for God's sake. You don't know what you are doing."

He could never explain this. She wouldn't believe him. He held her shoulders firmly. "You have to trust me. I've been through cholera outbreaks, two of them, and it doesn't touch me. I don't know why, Beth, but I'm immune. Something is screaming in my head to go back. I couldn't save Aaron, my newborn son. I pleaded with God. I couldn't save Daisy. I couldn't save Samuel. I can't just leave this boy to die."

Beth pushed him arms away, turned her back on him, and shook her head. "You stupid, stupid man." She stomped her foot then wheeled around and slapped him hard across the face. He stood stunned. Then he grabbed her wrist as she tried to slap him again.

So this is it, he thought. *This is what it comes down to.*

She yanked her arm free from his grasp and shouted into his face. "You're leaving us here? *Here?*" Her voice was cold fury. "You said you would protect us, remember? Not some stranger! Us! Look around you. Where are we, for God's sake?" She hit his arm with her fist.

"Stop it!" he shouted.

"Go to hell!" She spat at him and tried to walk away, but he grabbed her from behind, pinning her arms to her body.

He rocked her side to side, slowly, firmly, until her resistance eased. "Shh, Beth, trust me. I know you hate me. I know you're scared. But I'll be back in a few days. I won't get sick and I won't bring it back."

She pulled away from his grasp, and turned to him, her face flushed. He could feel her fighting for arguments.

"Aren't we more important than this boy?"

"Of course, you mean more to me than this boy. You know that. Right now, you mean everything to me. Everything in the world. Do you understand? But you're going to be all right and he isn't."

Ezra gathered clean rags, extra clothing, water, jerky, a small pouch of honey. He also brought out his second Hawkens, several pistols, and ammunition.

Brose arrived with some things of his own and sidestepped around Beth. He handed Ezra some pemmican, whiskey, an extra rifle, and a string of thin shells and feathers.

"Ezra, you keep well. I'm not worried so much about the cholera as the Arapahoe or maybe a Sioux party finding you out there alone. Here's some pemmican—boil it up, give the boy some sup. You hang this charm from a stick at thirty paces to tell the Ancients this is disease territory." He shook the string of thin shells. "They'll listen to this in the wind. Be careful at night. No fire."

Beth stood off to the side, looking dazed. Maddie handed him a small red rock—a protective one, she said. Camille took his hand and pressed it. "Please come back. Please don't leave us alone out here in the wilderness."

Beth had moved toward the shadow of the wagon. Ezra walked over and reached out to say goodbye, but she turned from him and put her face against the canvas. This wasn't like her.

"I'm not abandoning you," he said, his voice low and quiet. I'll be back," he said. "Safe and sound. I promise."

She turned to him, sighed, put her arms around him, and lay her head on his chest. They held each other and he rubbed her back. He pulled her in tighter without thought and turned his rub into a caress. It was the most intimate moment he'd ever had with her.

"I'll pray for you," she said. "And the boy."

EZRA FLEW UP THE TRAIL. EVEN ROAN SEEMED TO SENSE THE urgency and knew exactly where they were headed. As they approached the boy's wagon, Ezra spotted four buzzards in the immediate area, keeping their distance, but walking in circles around the dead, waiting for the spoils. Others circled in the sky.

The small hand fluttered, and Ezra was overwhelmed with joy to see life in the boy. As he rode in, the buzzards took a step back and opened and closed their angular black wings with complaint.

Dismounting, he pulled his rifle out of the sling. A quick shot left one buzzard dead. The others flew thirty yards off and landed, then started lumbering back with their fearsome beaks and black eyes trained on the kill. Roan stomped the ground, pushed his nose toward them, and swished his tail, becoming a formidable beast. The buzzards held back.

Against the stench of infection and death, Ezra tied the bandana around his nose and mouth and went to work. He ripped the cover off the wagon, picked the boy up off the ground and laid him on a quilt in the open wagon. He slid a shovel out from the back end, swung it at the buzzards, then settled down and dug a grave, stopping intermittently to rest, wipe off the sweat, and shuck dirt at the persistent predators. He shot one that came too close and another immediately came out of the sky to take his place.

After laying the boy's parents face-to-face for eternity and rolling them up in the canvas cover, Ezra slid them into the shallow pit and covered them with dirt. With no time for prayers or sentiment, he pushed as Roan pulled the family's wagon directly over the grave. He stuffed everything flammable underneath the wagon for a bonfire—a few smashed crates, clothing, two matching inlaid chests, and some oak side boards he'd ripped free. On top, he poured a bottle of hidden whiskey he found.

Then he lifted the limp boy into his arms and set the undercarriage on fire.

The buzzards stared at Ezra in disbelief and backed away from the leaping, all-consuming flames. They hissed, flapped their wings at him, then lumbered into flight, and once in the air, tore back into the sky.

MIRIAM LIFTED THE CANVAS FLAP, WHERE BETH WAS SITTING ON A box slumped over. "Here, dear, this tea will help settle you. Quite a row, you and Ezra. Brose and I shooed away all the curious ears. Come on, sip it. It will calm you. You know me, just some herbs."

"He left me, Miriam. Perhaps for good. To fend for myself. Left me, the girls, left you, the Captain, Brose, the entire wagon train. Left everyone who depends on him. I can't fathom his indifference, betrayal. He says he can't get cholera. Immune, he says. No one can say that."

"Shh. You're not alone, Beth, and he'll be back. You know that. Soon as the boy dies or recovers. He's not a reckless man. Strong willed, capable, driven at times, but not careless. And not uncaring. There's a reason he went after that boy with such determination and certainty. You probably know why. I don't. I grilled Brose about Ezra's immunity and he said it's real. He's seen it with his own eyes. Ezra worked for days tending the sick in a Kiowa village, helping the medicine man. Very few survived. He's learned to tell which victims have the fortitude and will to live. That boy has it, Brose said. Ezra knew."

"He left me cold, Miriam. Just as he has in the past. Over and over. This time he promised he would be at my side all the way to California."

"You two are such a puzzle," said Miriam. "You fight like an old married couple, but you have the fears of a couple in courtship. Of course, he'll come back."

EZRA LUGGED HIS GEAR AND THE BOY DOWN TO THE RIVER. HE spread his blanket on the sandy flood plain and threw everything on top, then carried the boy into the water. Dropping to his knees, he dunked the boy and started rubbing. He lifted some water in his hand and rubbed his fingers inside of the boy's mouth.

He lifted him and plunged him a second and a third time, trying to remove the crusted excrement. It wouldn't come off. Exasperated, he cut the boy's clothes off with his knife, threw them up on shore and cradled the naked boy in the cold water with one arm while washing his body until the dried matter finally gave way. He rubbed the gray, shriveled skin. The boy shivered.

"That's good. Come on, you can make it. Shiver, shiver back to life."

Climbing out of the river, Ezra wrapped the boy in clean clothing twice his size and laid him on his back on the blanket. The boy gazed but couldn't focus. His eyes wandered aimlessly across the sky. He opened his mouth, but there was no sound.

After making sure the sky was clear of predators and there were no coyotes ready to dash in for a quick meal, Ezra ran up the slope and threw the boy's clothing onto the fire. They flashed into flame. The fire seemed grateful to eat the disease.

He ran back to the river, walked in to where the current was swift enough to carry away any cholera seeds, filled one of his deerskin gloves with water, and walked back to the blanket, the bloated glove extending downward like an udder. With his knife, he poked a hole in one of the glove's fingers to let out a teardrop of water.

Ezra cradled the boy's head in his lap and began dripping the water slowly between his parched blue lips. He squeezed the boy's cheeks and wiggled his face so the drops would roll down his throat. He heard a tiny moan.

The boy coughed sharply and pulled away for a moment, but then rolled his head back into Ezra's palm and opened his mouth for more. The boy knew. Ezra smiled. "Good boy, more," he said as he kneaded the glove.

The boy had taken half a glove of water without vomiting when Ezra laid him on the blanket to sleep in the shade provided by a second blanket propped up with a piece of driftwood.

Ezra sliced a few pieces off a supple willow and walked, as Brose advised, thirty paces from the burning wagon. He pushed the willow poles deep into the ground and tied the delicate amulet to them, then carefully untangled the strings to let the paper-thin shells hang freely enough to catch even the slightest breeze.

The breeze came. Its sound through the shells, faint at first, grew clear as crystal. Carried for a hundred yards, Ezra reckoned, perhaps more. Such a strange protector, he thought, trilling like the songbird of death.

⇒ 20 ⇐

EZRA RETURNS

Five days later with Johan

E zra watched the smoke from the dinner fires rise and waft toward him in the still bright summer sky, surprised at his conflicting emotions—his joy anticipating the reunion and a gnawing uneasiness the train had made so little progress in five days. He expected at least another day to catch up, maybe two, riding slowly, holding the boy swaying in front of him in the saddle. If those were their fires, the wagon train had advanced no more than fifty miles up-river from the cholera zone.

They must have taken the detour, Ezra realized, rather than cover their faces and ride straight through the miasma of disease. And the detour took them over more rugged ground than they expected, perhaps forced them to wind down and up a steep canyon. Perhaps they intended a ten-mile detour that turned into fifty miles. Canyons are like that.

He imagined the anguish the families had gone through, and Beth and the girls struggling without him. His thoughts finally broke open the mental bubble he had been in for five days, trying to steel his mind through sleepless nights without fire, listening for predators and the hooves of tribal ponies.

His stomach knotted. Guilt drained the joy out of his fantasy of reunion. He'd have to face them, all of them. They'd be angry. No use explaining. They'd already heard the excuses from Beth, from Doc, from Brose. The Captain may well have washed his hands of him. Everyone may have already adjusted to his death, pictured him lying unburied beside the gray-blue family, picked by buzzards.

Should he and the boy ride down to the river and wash one more time before they arrived? Their clothes were still damp from the noon-day wash. They had been bathing three, four times a day, as well as every time young Johan had a discharge of bad-water, vomit, or diar-rhea.

That was his name, Johan. He spoke only German. It had taken two days for the boy to realize Ezra was trying to find out his name. He had begged for his *mutter* and *vater* and covered his eyes any time a bird landed on the river bank. *Vaters augen,* he had said, pointing at his own eyes. After coaxing, Johan had finally realized there was another language, and struggled to learn a few words in English that interested him. Bird, horse, water, eyes, sky, tree, chimes, fish, fire, rock, mouth, hands, hair, 'sup' for soup, 'din' for dinner.

Water, endless water. Ezra had fed the thirsty boy until pink replaced the blue-gray, first filling his cheeks, then his arms and chest. So far, he had gone one full day without diarrhea. He could sit in the saddle and keep his head upright, straight, and point and babble in German. But Ezra kept a makeshift diaper on the boy and washed and rewashed it to rid it of the disease seeds whenever he smelled something foul, even when the diaper looked clean. The cholera seeds were so small you couldn't really see them, he realized. He'd let Doc know. He poured canteen water over his hands and the boy's hands every mile or so and kept the boy from putting his hands in his mouth. Ezra would shake his head, wag his finger. "*Nein,* no hand in mouth, understand? Good, *gut.*"

Ezra rode to within sight of the circled wagons, then fired a pistol to let them know he was coming. From Ezra's vantage point, activity in the entire camp seemed to come to a sudden halt. People peered up the trail and covered their eyes to cut the glare. When one child saw the boy sitting in front of Ezra on his horse he yelled, "Alive, they're alive!" and five children echoed the call, let out a whoop, and ran toward

Ezra waving their arms. Mothers screamed, fathers ran, and one man on a horse galloped to head the children off. In front of them, his horse snorting and spinning, the man cracked a small whip and scared the children dumbstruck.

Ezra waved his arms. "Go back. It's not safe," he yelled. "Get back to your families."

Maddie ran past the children, past the horse, shouting her joy at seeing him again. He held up his hands, looking for Beth, but she was nowhere to be seen. "Stop! Maddie, stop. I'm fine. Go back and tell Beth I'm fine, but don't get too near. Not yet. Later I'll hug you."

She stopped in her tracks, looking distrustful, hurt.

"Go on, Maddie, I'm happy to see you, too. Get Doc Sturgis out here," he said. "Tell him the boy is better, but to be safe, everyone should keep their distance for now."

Maddie no sooner turned around than Doc ran past her with others following. Ezra signaled to Brose and the Captain to keep everyone else back.

"Ezra, this is truly astonishing," said Doc. "Look at this boy. What did you do? I hardly recognize him. Was it the calomel?"

"No, it was fresh water and the boy himself. His spirit wanted to live."

"Handsome boy. What's his name?"

"Johan. Speaks German or Dutch. I don't think he should get too close to the wagon train just yet. At least for a few days."

"I agree. But just look at him. Amazing recovery."

"He's been eating. Some soup, pemmican, beginning to chew meat. Tom, he'll need someone to tend him around the clock. Beth and I can't do it. I thought maybe you and Sarah might be willing. I figure you are in the best position to stay at the back of the train until the boy is completely well. Give you and Sarah a chance to meet him in private, without all the others jabbing and poking him with questions. He still doesn't know what happened to his parents. He keeps looking for them; *mutter* and *vater* you'll hear him say. Speaks only a few words of English. Scared of birds after those vultures."

"You buried them?"

"I did. Then burned their wagon on top of their grave to make sure it wasn't disturbed and to kill the cholera seeds."

Doc smiled. "I don't think cholera has seeds the way an apple does, Ezra."

"If so, they're so tiny, Doc, you can't see them. You got to keep washing the boy, washing away the bad water. Bury any vomit or waste down about a foot, fill the boy with good, clean water. Keep his hands away from his mouth. *Nein*, he knows that command. And keep washing yourselves."

Johan reached out his hand toward Doc. "You think Sarah might be willing to take the boy in?" Ezra asked. "I can't do it. Beth, well, I'm not sure she's even speaking to me."

Doc stepped back and shook his head. "I don't know, Ezra. We've lost all four of our boys. She's better, at least eating, but she's still fragile, heartbroken." Doc sighed. "I'll ask. Maybe the diversion . . ."

Doc walked back to his wagon and disappeared inside to confer with Sarah. Ezra waited, sitting damp in the saddle, jostling Johan while the children watched and waved and shouted hello from thirty yards back, their parents holding them by their shirt collars.

FIVE MINUTES LATER, EZRA WATCHED DOC HARNESS A HORSE TO HIS wagon and turn it out of the circle to head his way. As they pulled up, Ezra handed the boy gently to Sarah. She took him tenderly, first in her hands, and then in her arms as if he were a gift, not a dangerously ill child.

Sarah's wide green eyes were all over the boy. She took her bonnet off and shook her dark hair loose, then cradled him, kissed him on the head, stroked his arm. Showed no fear. None. She sang to Johan quietly, caressing his cheek while the boy stared into her eyes.

"Tom, Sarah, you'll need to bathe him several times a day in the river and keep his vomit and diarrhea away from you and your bedding. Bury it. Need to wash yourself after. Here . . ." Ezra pulled out his canteen, poured water on his hands, rubbed them together, and rinsed them off. "Like that. I think he'll be all through it in a couple of days. He's been eating solid food for the last two days, a good sign. And water, give him good water, continuously."

"You're going to make a fine doc someday, Ezra," said Doc.

"Cholera is the only thing I know about. But that may come in handy again," said Ezra. "Now, I need—"

"I know what you need. Beth is back there, beyond that last wagon," said Doc. "She's been through fury and despair. Last night at dinner, I could feel the hope draining out of her, so you have some repair work to do."

EZRA WALKED HIS HORSE TOWARD THE CAMP. HALF THE TRAIN HAD come out to greet him and peer at the boy from a distance, but not Beth. The families waved at him and patted the air as if they meant his shoulder but stood back from direct contact. No one really knew when the disease surfaced, or how it spread, or where it came from, or who it might attack. Made it all the more terrifying. It could kill you in one day.

Ezra smiled and waved and said hello in a quiet voice but didn't stop to chat. He was relieved that they seemed to truly welcome him back, as if his return put things right. They were back on the trail, with the terror of cholera and the laborious detour behind them, and their second guide somehow returning from the dead.

Where was she? He longed to see her. *So strange*, he thought. It used to be years between visits to her without any pain or emotional discomfort, but now he was longing to feel her presence, to stand close enough to catch her scent and study her face, even if he dared not put his hands on her with desire. He pictured her face lit, almost radiant with delight to see him. He knew better, of course, but still his imagination was hungry.

He walked toward his wagon. James looked up at him and smiled. Miriam waved and pointed to the far end of the circle, where someone had just hitched two oxen and climbed into the driver's seat of a wagon.

The wagon rolled out of the way and he saw her standing alone, arms crossed, staring at him.

Unlike his fantasy, there was no sense of delight, no play of light about her face, no sign of welcome or anger or relief. She stood stoic, forcing him to walk over.

Her face was solemn as he gently clasped her shoulders and squeezed affectionately. "It's wonderful to see you," he said. He felt the truth of it was in both of them, but there was no tangible or tactile response. Neither acceptance nor rejection.

He dropped his hands and his smile.

"I'm glad you saved the boy," she said flatly.

"But?"

"But what?" she asked.

"Me. I didn't die. I came back. I'm standing right here in front of you. I thought you might have noticed."

"I thought you died."

"Was the detour bad? Doc said the wagon train encountered some serious problems, but everyone agreed you should be the first to tell me."

"I don't know where to begin, Ezra. You promised me a new life in California. You pledged to make up for my loss of everything—and then just left me in the wilderness, leaving me to think you'd probably die. What was I going to do if you never returned? After a few days, I realized that for the first time in twenty years I couldn't succeed on my own. I needed you, and you probably weren't coming back. I'd have to build a new life, perhaps in the wilderness with three children I barely know, three that I have to keep safe. That's what I've been living with for four days. In my mind, if not my heart, you died."

He took off his hat and ran his fingers through his hair. No sense defending what he did. He had taken a foolish risk. "I'm sorry, Beth. It seems I've been putting you in danger ever since I showed up that day with Maddie and Camille. I can't undo what I did, but I'm back. I'll keep my pledge to you. Put you first."

She looked at him directly for the first time. "See that you do."

"Promise," he said. "Now will you tell me what happened? The wagon train hasn't gotten but fifty miles beyond the cholera site."

"The afternoon you left, the Captain decided to take the detour you and Brose had scouted. That was that, and the gathering broke up. But without you to back him up, some of the families panicked. Four teams bolted and charged into the river to cross to the south side. We had to pull the mutinous wagons out of the raging water. Two oxen drowned. Williamson's wagon went over; they lost everything that was loose but saved their children. The Captain almost shot Williamson, who had led the rebels into the river. Two hours later, under martial law, we set out along the gorge with tribal members of the Ancients stalking us. Pawnees, I think Brose said. They followed us for most of the day and the next.

"I should have—"

"After crossing the natural bridge, we bounced over wicked terrain, trying to get back to the main trail. The axles on two wagons cracked on the rocks, and we were forced to stop for repairs. But we made it back, thirty miles upriver from the cholera. That was yesterday. Yesterday!"

He waited for the toll, but she stopped. "But no one died?" he asked.

She shook her head. "Just you. Most people believed you were dead. I feared so. Everyone consoled me. Especially the girls. Only Miriam disagreed. She took me aside and spoke powerfully. 'Now stop it. He's not dead. You know it. I know it. He's coming for you.' She rekindled my hope."

"Beth, I'm sorry. I assumed Brose and the Captain were sufficient for a few days."

"You think you mean nothing to this train? Sometimes you're inexplicably stupid. Your guilt. You think you can just replace Samuel with some new boy you pick up beside the trail? What happened to you two?"

"It took a while for the boy to recover. I gave him to Sarah, thinking—"

"I saw it. Saw her come alive when she held him. You did what was right, Ezra. I'll give you that. It's just me. You broke my heart."

He lifted his hands to her shoulders, then hesitated. "Would you mind if I put my arms around you?"

She stood staring, lips tight, as if she were considering a great request. He glanced around and noticed a dozen people watching, trying to be discreet.

"All right," she said.

He slowly wrapped himself around her and pulled her in tight, his unshaven cheek resting on her hair. After a few minutes, her body relaxed, and he felt her hand run up his back. She was crying softly into his shoulder. "You're alive," she said.

⇒ 21 ⇐

BUFFALO STAMPEDE

100 miles farther, 670 miles west of the trailhead

The night prairie stirred before the approaching storm. Bursts of wind and flying dust and boiling black clouds cloaked the lightning balls pulsing on top of them. Small animals scurried and burrowed, triggered by the scent of lightning. Other creatures ran for shelter in familiar hollows, holes, and ravines. Birds flew away in great swaths escaping the barreling storm from the west. Antelope bounded and leapt over the vast open land to escape.

A sudden flash and the canvas wagon cover arched over Maddie's head turned bright as day, startling her awake. She sat up, reached. Then with hardly time to scream, the dark snatched her hands and fingers away. She trembled, wiggling her fingers in front of her blind eyes, waiting, holding her breath. Waiting.

The canvas lit up again, this time transparent to the slashes and curling dance devils and plunging forks of lightning that struck the prairie hard. In every direction she watched explosions of light that put an odd stink in the air.

She prayed for her *mère* to reach around her with that soft-skinned, brown-muscled arm that smelled of cane, to pull Maddie in, and squeeze out the night fears as she always had. *What's ma mère doing in that golden place anyway,* she thought. *Why so important she can't come and hold her daughter a spell?*

She swatted away the dust tickling her nose and lay in the dark, snuggling her face into her sister's back. Camille was still snoring. Could there be two golden places, Maddie wondered? The one her *mère* went to when she died and the one at the end of the trail where Ezra was taking them? Maybe they were the same. Maybe her *mère* would be sitting on a pile of gold and smiling and waving when Maddie came jouncing in on her wagon drawn by prancing oxen. Maybe Maddie was already dead, just didn't know it, and on a wagon train of spirits heading to the promised land.

She listened as the thunder started softly, far away. Like someone clearing their throat. Someone who was now coming toward her, but faster and louder. Someone who was growing bigger. Someone now on a horse, galloping atop a river of logs rolling and tumbling across the prairie. And bringing other riders along with him and other animals coughing, snarling, and lifting themselves up in an angry chorus rising high over Maddie. High above her wagon and all the beloveds still asleep.

She cringed as the storm hovered over her like a multi-headed beast ready to bite. It leered at her, laughed at her, then grabbed the entire sky in its horrid mouth and cracked it like a walnut, exploding the night, tossing her hard against the sideboard, screaming.

Beth and Camille bolted upright, their eyes wide, before the dark enveloped them. Maddie threw her arms around Camille and felt her trembling too.

"Calm down," said Beth. "And cover yourself. We're in for quite a storm."

The oxen had started up, bleating, bellowing. They were trapped within the circular corral with wagon tongues lashed to back boards. Maddie heard a few men yelling at the animals—not words, just noises—sharp, commanding, scolding. A few feminine voices, softer and cajoling, resorting to the musical sway some oxen liked.

Maddie lifted the edge of the canvas cover and peered into the circle. Moonlight slipped through the roiling clouds, and she saw the oxen anxiously stirring and circling inside the corral. Men and women jumping out of the way, and horses skittering. The oxen bumped into each other, turned, stopped, complained, and turned again. Trapped and spinning, they were building themselves into a panic, looking for a way to run, she realized.

Thunder vaulted across the sky from west to east like an acrobat, shaking the wagon.

Like some magician with a trick up his sleeve, lightning took off its gloves, spread its hands for everyone to see they were clean, smiled, then pointed all ten fingers down at the prairie and struck it with bolts of white-blue light. The sky came alive like a scream.

Maddie shivered in Camille's arms. Her nose wrinkled at the smell of burnt air. Outside, she heard Ezra's voice, harsh. Now closer, yelling. "The oxen are trying to jump the corral," he shouted. "Get out here! Everybody! Now!"

Beth pulled on a coat. "Get your boots on, Camille, you're coming with me. Maddie, you stay here. Maddie?" Maddie nodded her head in the dark. Beth reached out for Maddie's arm, then squeezed hard. Maddie winced. "Don't leave the wagon. That's an order."

Beth and Camille twisted against each other getting dressed, bumping up against Maddie, who finally scooted out of their way. She didn't want to go with them but didn't want to stay by herself. Maybe Camille would stay.

Before she could ask, their shadows slipped out of the wagon. Beth poked her head back in through the narrow canvas opening. "Get your coat and boots on but stay down low in the wagon. We'll be right outside." Then she was gone.

Wind and hard rain slammed into the wagon and pelted the canvas overhead. Maddie lay curled in the dark, pulling on her coat and boots, wondering what was happening. She felt blind. There was noise everywhere—driving rain, oxen braying, almost screaming, men and women yelling, hooves thudding. Maddie tried to separate the voices, find Camille's, Ezra's, Beth's. Some people were singing hymns to the animals. She recognized Miriam's and Sarah's voices. Had Sarah left little Johan alone in his wagon? Or with another family? Perhaps Maddie should go find him, hold him; they could hide together.

A woman screamed in pain. An angry man shouted, cursed an ox that had knocked him over.

Dust filled the wagon, making her cough and breathing difficult. Maddie tied a bandana around her nose and mouth and began praying.

Then, a new sound. At first it was just a quivering sensation in her side, not so much noise. Then the floor of the wagon began to shudder, and her elbow bounced on the wood. Vibrations were coming up through the wheels, through the wagon bed, and into Maddie's bones, telling her heart to run faster. Her pulse was pounding in her temples. She put her hands over her ears. The metal cups hanging from the stays overhead clanged together. Now sick with fear, her stomach cramped, her throat grew thick and foul. She heaved but nothing came up. *Stay here, stay here*, her mind shouted over and over. *Don't run.* But it was all she could do not to jump out, run to her sister, find Beth, hold Ezra around the waist, anybody. But she might get trampled out there under those terrified oxen.

Veins of lightning as delicate as tree roots stretched a hundred miles across the prairie and etched the wagon cover over Maddie's head. They glowed like spiderwebs in moonlight, then dissolved into the night. Then they came again, faster, closer, more forceful. Now with great white daggers slashing the black sky. Lighting up the wagon cover jiggling over Maddie's head.

Maddie's teeth ached. Her head bounced. The boxes and barrels danced about on the wooden floor. She climbed on one to hold it down.

Something else was out there. Something on the other side of the corral, and it was moving. She lifted the edge of the canvas to peer out at the black prairie. Wind and rain lashed her face. She put it down, but she could hear the prairie thundering and huffing, and could smell sweet grass, dirt, and the tang of dust and mold.

She lifted the cover again, squinting into the black rain and flying dust.

Frayed lightning lit the sky. Aghast, her mouth opened wide but no sound came out. In front of her raced a river of buffalo, as tightly bound together as black minnows in a silver stream, their great wooly heads down, their necks arched, their feet a blur of speed and dust. The light went out.

Maddie dove down onto the floor of the wagon screaming and wrapped her arms around her head to hold it steady, covering her ears. Her wagon was a fragile egg, about to be spilled into the dirt and ground under the hooves of the buffalo.

"Ezra, help me! Camille! Beth!"

Suddenly, Beth's voice shouted at her from the front of the wagon. "Maddie, you stay in here! Cover yourself!"

"I'm scared," she yelled back, but there was no reply.

Fortunately, the rain stopped abruptly.

BETH AND CAMILLE DODGED AROUND THE POWERFUL HIPS OF THE panicked oxen, sometimes getting clipped and tossed against the wheels and into the dirt. They worked their way to their assigned posts on the perimeter, and both began swinging their torches inward to scare the oxen away from the openings, to keep them from jumping the wagon tongues and running with the herd. Tens of thousands of wild buffalo, maybe hundreds of thousands, maybe even a million flowed around the wagon train on both sides, like a mighty river parting around a small white island.

Sweating, breathing hard, Beth was tired from holding her torch. She rested her arm and watched the rhythm of the other women and older children wielding torches at every opening between the wagons. They had created a ring of dancing fire to keep the terrified oxen in. To keep the mad buffalo out.

The men worked in teams close to the oxen. They cornered the panicked beasts and tried to grab them, rope their necks, and wrestle them to a standstill long enough to hobble their legs. Men were kicked and shrieked. Beth watched some rolling away in pain.

Now she heard the ring of iron stakes being driven into the ground to tether the animals.

Beth glanced quickly over her shoulder at the chaos on the prairie to see if she could locate Ezra. Hard to see but he was out there in the dark, right in front of her, out there with Brose facing the stampede, diverting the buffalo. He had told her the buffalo could see the white of the wagons and would go around, even when stampeding, but she had sensed hesitancy in his voice. Why else would he and Brose be out there, right out there in front of her, at the juncture where the herd split with dozens of rifles and pistols? She saw a muzzle flash in the dark. Then another. Another.

Beth yelled over to Camille, who was standing at the next opening with her feet planted, swooshing her torch left to right and right to left in the face of a belligerent ox determined to run with the wooly ones. The flaming torch and the head of the ox danced side to side as Camille screamed silently at the ox. Her voice was swallowed in the melee.

With no ox pressing her position, Beth turned for a moment to look at the buffalo coming at them like a tidal swell, then splitting only a few hundred feet in front of her eyes. Ezra and Brose stood at the juncture, firing an arsenal of guns. With older boys running freshly primed weapons out to them.

Their massive heads down, the charging buffalo seemed incapable of turning their muscled bulk, but at the last instant, just before they ran over Ezra and Brose, they sheared off, half flowing in one stream to the left, half to the right. Beth stared in awe as their improbably thin, nimble legs leaned so far over in the sharp turn that their black jaw-beards swept the ground.

THE STAMPEDE WENT ON FOR MORE THAN AN HOUR, MAYBE TWO, Beth could no longer tell. Her arms ached, she coughed dust. Was there no end to this herd? She was growing numb to the madness, the endless river of black buffalo, the flying prairie dirt bouncing off her back, the deafening vibration and noise. She was on her third torch but now too tired to hold it up. She laid it on a rock for a moment of rest and shook the weariness from her arm. She glanced over at Camille who was still going strong. A young woman with relentless energy and determination. No doubt thinking of Maddie alone in the dark madness.

The corral was growing quieter. Most of the oxen had been hobbled and were beginning to settle, giving up their compulsion to run. But still, the buffalo came. Flooding out of the darkness. Still, James, Tad, and two other boys ran freshly primed weapons out to Ezra and Brose. And still, they fired. Fired hot, finger-stinging rifles.

Beth picked up her torch. Was she imagining what she hoped was the end? In the darkness she couldn't tell. But the vibration in her feet had changed. The noise of thundering hooves diminishing. *Dear God, it's ending.* And yet sharper sounds had been added—feverish yelps in the night. Growling. Sounds of guttural ferocity. Then a familiar howl, and then another. Coming directly at her.

When the sky lit up again, she turned toward the prairie and saw Ezra, Brose, James, and Tad running at her at full speed. The buffalo were still parting, but finally, she could see an end to the herd. Thinner, more spread out, but the last few hundred still veering off to the right and left, following the deepening ruts.

Beth screamed for Ezra. Behind the buffalo stragglers and in full chase, were wolves. Gangs of howling wolves. Not just a pack or two, but what appeared to be dozens of packs. To her horror, Beth saw one massive ferocious mob, working together, spreading out, their jaws wide. Primed for a night of feverish blood lust.

She pushed her torch out in front of her, waving it fast, signaling to Ezra and Brose. "Here! Over here!" she screamed. *Dear God,* she wondered, *are wolves smart enough to take a short cut straight through the camp to cut off the circling buffalo?*

Just to her side, Ezra, Brose, James, and Tad skidded to a stop, spun around, and knelt, aiming their rifles. The first wolves had turned right and left, following the scent of the buffalo. But two of them, mouths open, teeth barred and jaws foaming, bolted directly at them. Leaping in great bounds directly at the circle of wagons and the fragile families.

The men fired. The two wolves dropped. Others cried in pain and scooted into the dark.

Again they fired, spreading the packs. But the wolves continued to race around both sides of the circled wagons. Making the most horrific high-pitched howling sounds. As if singing to each other in the joy of a blood-thirsty hunt.

CAMILLE COULD STAND IT NO LONGER, LISTENING TO THE RIOTOUS wolves and the screams of the children inside the wagons. She took off, abandoning her station, waving her torch to clear the way, shouting, "Maddie!" She passed one terrified child who had jumped out of her wagon and was weaving among the hobbled oxen, looking for her mother. Camille grabbed the girl by the back of her dress with one hand and handed her up into someone's outstretched arms. She could not see who. Could not stop.

Reaching the front of their wagon, she raised her torch and yelled for Maddie. She couldn't very well climb in with the torch, she realized, but wouldn't be able to see into the wagon without it. She hesitated. "Maddie! Where are you? Yell to me."

Instead, she heard a deep-throated growl, a warning. Then saw the teeth and yellow eyes coming at her from underneath their wagon. She jumped back and lowered the torch. The wolf pulled back a few feet, shying from the flame. He was glancing left and right but favored one hind leg. He lifted it off the ground, then put it back down gingerly and winced in pain. He lunged and snapped at the torch.

"Maddie, hide!"

The wolf made a quick lunge for Camille's leg but she thrust the torch in front of him. Poked at him with fire. He stopped, backed up, then crept forward cautiously toward her. His head down, eyes up, limping, but his body lowered for lunging. Snarling. She backed up slowly, trying to pull him away from Maddie. She wasn't sure whether the screams she heard were her own.

She jabbed again and swung the torch in front of the wolf's face. The wolf followed the light. Then, with amazing agility, he spun around and leapt up onto the wagon tongue. Or tried. His hind feet were scrambling, clawing to hold onto the wood, whimpering in pain. But he pulled himself up with great strength onto the tongue, then the wagon seat. He peered through the dark slit at Maddie.

Camille charged and thrust the torch like a sword into the wolf's face. "Maddie, get out the back! Maddie!" She grazed the wolf's muzzle as he reared, and her body slammed against the wagon tongue. She bounced off, reeling backwards. She struggled to keep her balance, but dropped the torch.

The wolf, seeing his opening, leapt off the wagon seat for her face and throat. Its fangs were still bared when it slammed into her chest, knocked her off her feet, and landed on top of her. Screaming, Camille struggled to get free, out from under. Waiting to feel his jaws break her neck. She squirmed along the ground in panic, pushing at the wolf, feeling his dead weight on her chest. Looking everywhere for help. Unaware the wolf was dead.

She saw Brose walking toward her. Everything else in the world had come to a stop, all sound, all movement. Just Brose. She might have been shouting or whimpering, screaming, she couldn't tell.

His rifle was still smoking. She hadn't heard the shot and could barely hear his voice as he pushed the wolf off her with his foot and pulled her to her feet.

"Can you hear me?" He shook her gently. "It's over." He nodded down at the wolf. She scurried behind him. "Don't worry, shot him mid-air, dead before he slammed into you. I'll get rid of him. You got some scratches, claw marks, bruises. But don't see teeth marks. Do you feel any bites?"

She looked at him in a daze. Still in shock. "Go find Maddie. Calm her," she heard him say as if underwater. "Wolves are gone. Then off to Doc with Maddie to clean your wounds and hers."

She wrapped her arms around herself and watched Brose grab the wolf by the scruff of his neck and drag him outside the circle of wagons, out into the dark. Out into the rain of dust falling softly like snow. Out where the mad buffalo had torn through the night. Out into oblivion.

Her senses returning, she scrambled into the wagon. "Maddie? You're safe. Can't see you. Where are you?" She heard a box move, saw a shadow coming for her. Maddie threw her arms around her, shaking in terror. Camille held her and rocked her until they both broke into tears, clinging to each other. Never had they been so afraid.

Maddie felt so small and fragile, weeping in her arms. *Two more seconds and the wolf would have had her—or myself.*

Camille felt the claw marks on her arms and touched her throat, fingering where the wolf might have bitten her. How were they ever to survive out here? A piece of canvas and a wooden box with wheels was all that had separated Maddie from the madness of the night.

This place, this immense and powerful place. Alive with lightning. Crazed with dark movement. Thundering buffalo, marauding wolves. Now that it was over, it seemed even more frightening. Ezra said the trail got worse from here, but what could be worse? Camille could not imagine.

Yet there was an odd feeling stirring in her. Her sense of smell sharper. Her body shivering with life. She had met the wild in all its raw majesty and ruthlessness. It left her feeling thrilled.

Out here, Camille was small, insignificant. The world immense. She was in awe, hungry for life.

⇒ 22 ⇐

MORNING BUFFALO HUNT

Maddie and Ezra bonding

A ribbon of sunshine flowed up Maddie's shoulder onto her neck. She savored the warmth, stretched like a cat, and opened her eyes. Then rolled on her back, listening to the infinite, exquisite silence. It was gone, all of it. No storm, no birds, no screaming oxen, no stampeding buffalo, no snarling wolves. The few voices outside her morning cocoon were subdued, as if trying not to disturb those still asleep.

She pulled away from the maze of arms and legs and stared at her sister. Camille's dress was torn at the top and on the side, her hair and face were streaked with mud, and a purple bruise ran up her arm past the wolf claw marks that Doc dressed before her merciful sleep. Tempted to touch her, Maddie held back and watched her mouth twitch. Then whimper when she rolled on her side. There were more bruises along the back of Camille's neck, and a long scratch mark along her collarbone. Beth's left cheek was deep blue, almost black, running up just under one eye.

Maddie slid down the length of the wagon and peeked out. The air smelled of crushed grass and sweet mud. The ground in the corral had been ripped apart, and debris was scattered everywhere—splintered wood, scattered iron and chains, bits of clothing, burnt stubs of torches.

One wagon was tilted sideways, a wheel broken; others looked strangely skewed. But where were the oxen? The corral was open. Had they escaped?

She jumped out, looked around. The cloudless sky was everywhere. In front of her and behind her and everywhere above and surrounding her, swallowing the earth. Blue as a band uniform.

Aha. There they are. Her eye caught the beasts together in the distance, the beloved oxen grazing in one of the few green spots within sight. The swath of prairie torn by the buffalo stretched to the horizon.

A sharp whistle caught her ear. She lifted her head to spot Ezra and Brose riding down from the bluff. She could see their buckskins dulled with dried mud from the stampede, but their faces washed clean, their cheeks shining in the morning sun. They lifted their hats to her, and she raced fast as a gopher into the prairie to greet them.

Ezra reached down and pulled her up fast with one hand into the saddle. His hair was wet—from a far-off streambed, he said. She ran her hand through and smelled the streambed, salted with sweat.

They dismounted short of the wagon circle. Then he walked her back to her wagon, squeezing the back of her neck, as if gently guiding her forward. "Rough night. Brose told me about the wolf. How's Camille?"

"Bruised. Clawed. Sleeping. But Brose saved her. What happened to the wolves?"

"They had their feast, maybe a dozen packs all together, and left. But the buffalo—a herd the size of St. Louis—are grazing up there about five miles north." He pointed. "We'll go hunting right after—"

"No." She pushed his hand away.

"No what?"

"They're too big and mad. I don't want to ever get close to them ever again."

He smiled at her, with that quirk she liked, one side of his mouth a tuck higher than the other side. A mischief-smile, her *mère* would have called it.

"You make'n fun of me?" she asked.

"I thought you wanted to see them?"

"Not anymore."

WHILE BETH AND THE OTHERS WERE EATING BREAKFAST, EZRA climbed into the wagon and shortly emerged with a large bundle wrapped in brown merchant paper. He put it on the ground and untied the heavy cord. Maddie had seen the bundle before, buried in the bottom of his trunk, but he had said it was off limits and she had forgotten about it. Everyone rose to see what was inside.

"I've been saving these for the mountains, but now's a better time. Maddie, I hope these fit." He tossed her two doeskins. She caught them and paused, waiting for explanation. He handed a pair to James.

"Camille, this was the best I could find in a hurry." He lifted up a soft doeskin shirt by the shoulders, fringed along the sleeves and across the chest. He handed it to her and held up the pants.

Camille smiled, turned the shirt around. "It's pretty. Where'd you . . .? Why?"

He tossed the pants to her. "Bought them in Kanesville that last day."

"These are boys' clothes," said Maddie, wrinkling her nose in disdain.

"You'll be a lot more comfortable hunting in these."

"I'm not—"

"Beth, I have some for you too."

"Oh, lucky me." She shook her head, laughing, as much in disbelief as rejection.

"I know, I know. Just wear them under your dress. They'll protect your legs from the dust and insects. Comfortable doeskin. You won't be sorry."

Maddie fingered the shirt he gave her. It clung softly to her hand. It was pretty and tempting. Fringed just so, with tiny green beads. She might put it on over her dress. But pants?

"Well, go on," said Ezra. "Get your skins on. We got to get moving." He shooed Maddie toward the wagon.

"I'm not going," she said, as she eagerly climbed into the wagon to change.

MADDIE TWIRLED IN HER SKINS, THEN REACHED UP FOR EZRA'S hand. He clasped her by the forearm and swung her up in one easy move, as if she weighed nothing, setting her in front of him on the saddle. He put one arm around her waist.

"You'll be safe up here, but hold the pommel. Your horse can follow us. We'll need him to help carry the meat."

"You tricked me into going by giving me these skins."

She tried to turn around to see his face, to see if he looked smug like he'd won, but Ezra just held her tight, facing straight ahead. She could feel his chest laughing.

Brose and James mounted their horses and raced off. Ezra and Maddie followed slowly up and over the first long swell, only to see Brose and James disappear over the next rise.

They rode leisurely, in silence, up one long undulation and down another.

She was alone on the prairie with nothing in front of her except Roan's head, the grass, the birds, the slow rolling landscape. She saw flashes of life moving through the tall grass, glimpses of a tiny foot or a tail, but nothing complete. An antelope in the distance. After last night, she relished the silence, being held snug. No voices or shouts, no rumbling storm, no pounding hooves, no howling. Just the touch of wind on her face and the rustle of the grass, the screech of a surprised bird, and being alone with the rhythm and sway of the saddle.

"I'm glad you came," Ezra said.

His voice jarred her from her thoughts. Maddie leaned back against Ezra and put her hand on top of his. She took a deep breath and let go of some of her tension. She'd never had a father hold her, not that she remembered. Maybe this was what it felt like. She wasn't mad any more. She was glad he tricked her. She wanted to ask him questions, mostly about herself, whether he liked her and wanted to keep her the way he would Daisy if she were around, but was afraid of his answers. Afraid to break the spell.

"Will they make me a slave again in California?" She turned around. He was squinting in the sun.

"Why'd you ask that?"

"Just want to know."

"You'll ride in as a free girl, and Camille's job will be to keep you free until you're old enough. Protect you the way she did from the wolf. But you'll have to fight your whole life for freedom. Your *mère* knew that. Every animal out here knows that. That snake there, these birds. They want their freedom. We'll find you a good family. You want to be with your own people, don't you?"

"I want to be with Camille. But no one will take us both, not as Black and white sisters." She held back, afraid to ask what she really wanted to ask. *How about you? Will you take us?*

He didn't respond; just clicked his tongue, telling Roan to speed it up. Maybe he would want her by the time they got to California, she thought. Maybe he'd need a daughter out there.

"Did you ever want a daughter?" she asked.

"Not for a single second. Why'd you ask?"

She could feel his chest chuckling. She knew better than to say anything.

They rode on in silence. She wasn't sorry she asked, just embarrassed. *He probably doesn't like children. Probably hates girls. Maybe boys too. He told me once that he was much too mean to have children, but I don't think so.*

"I had a son once." His voice was soft, sad. He reached forward and patted Roan on the neck, then sat back. "Aaron. He lived for an hour. Had his whole life in one hour. I felt like I should have been able to save him. He died in my arms. One hour."

Maddie held her breath, imagining living just one hour. At least she'd be held.

"Will you tell me about Daisy? Is that why you love me, because I look like her?"

"Who said I love you?"

"*Ma mère* did in my dream. The pelly bird did. The wind did."

"They'd surely know," he said. "Now you tell me about your people first. Then I'll tell you about Daisy. Where'd you come from?"

She asked him what he meant, but he ignored her, said something about perhaps another day. Then clicked his tongue as Roan labored up a steep slope. "Get ready."

As they crested the hill, Maddie sat straight up and gripped Ezra's hand and bounced and whooped, staring at a black carpet of buffalo covering the land in all directions, up one rise and down and up another rise, and another, as far as the eye could see. The great herd grazed as one, eating the entire prairie. She felt dizzy, as if she might fall off the horse. Ezra held her tight.

"Hold on. We'll get closer."

The herd was immense, bigger than any living, breathing thing she could imagine. She hadn't known the night before there were so many, or that they could be peaceful.

"I don't want you to forget this," he said.

He pointed to a companion ridge on the far left, from which Brose and James were working their way down toward the herd. Her eye went to the far right, where nearly a mile away, three of the Ancient people were circling a bull with their ponies.

"Look, Ezra."

"Sioux. They're spinning that bull. See how the bull turns as they ride around him in a circle. They're confusing him so he can't set his feet to charge while they shoot him full of arrows."

They rode down the long slope toward the herd and a rendezvous with Brose and James.

Maddie's joy vanished as they got closer. Her stomach knotted, her arms trembled as she stared at their sad eyes, short horns, and massive heads, big and wooly. Bulls wearing their thick black humps like a thick winter shawl over their shoulders. One bull lifted his head and looked directly at Maddie indifferently, chewing. She shuddered. If that buffalo intended murder, he was a clever one, she thought, pretending to eat. He put his face back into the grass and walked forward. She wondered what it would be like to wander around on top of your dinner that way. A dinner table as far as the eye could see, covered with good green food.

Don't have to go buy anything, hunt anything, gather anything. Just face in the grass.

Approaching the herd obliquely, Ezra pointed to a half dozen bulls moving away from the rest, their heads down, grazing. He dismounted, swung Maddie from the saddle, and led her, slightly stooped over, up on his toes. She emulated him, stooped and tender toed, until they reached elevated ground, within easy range.

Brose and James joined them at the top, where they talked quietly, almost a whisper, picking out the best. They pointed at one.

Chills ran up Maddie's spine. That bull might start running at her. The entire herd might look straight at her, get mad, and charge. Ezra told her not to be frightened—last night they were crazed by the lightning. But . . . but, if they shot this one, she thought, the other bulls might want revenge.

Ezra knelt with his Hawkens, a rifle powerful enough to take down a charging grizzly, and signaled to Maddie to come over. He patted the ground next to him. She shook her head. He waved more emphatically.

"I don't want them to get mad at me," she said.

"Shh. Keep your voice down. Come here. Just lean in here and help me do the sighting. I'll take the recoil, you pull the trigger. Easy like." Ezra waved her in closer until they were side by side. He moved his head so she could sight along the barrel.

Brose waved, pointed again.

Ezra acknowledged the choice.

"We're going to take that one, Maddie. Now, we can't shoot the head. Rifle balls just bounce off that mat. We'll start our aim at the forelegs and then lift our aim to the lower torso and fire into the unprotected heart and lungs." He steadied the rifle, raised it just a hair.

When you're ready, I'm going to count. Fire on three. Just squeeze. Don't jerk the trigger." He re-centered aim, then let Maddie take over. "That's it. Hold it right there." He lifted three fingers in the air to count off visually to Brose and James. Her heart was racing. He steadied the rifle.

"Three," he said.

The barrel kicked upward, Ezra's shoulder took the blow, and Maddie's ear began to ring. Brose and James must have fired at the same time. She hadn't heard them but saw the smoke from their rifles. Their buffalo made half a turn toward the herd, wobbled, and fell on its side. Its back legs kicked twice, then stopped.

Maddie put her hands over her mouth. She had killed a buffalo. She held her breath, waiting for his friends and relatives to come after her. But they didn't. They moved away slowly. James was jumping up and down, Brose hooting, while Maddie stood in awe, voiceless, her heart pounding, sweating under her skins. She felt faint. Ezra steadied her, patted her back and said proud things.

Several rifles cracked from the far ridge—other hunters from the wagon train. She watched the herd try to move away, pushing into each other. But they were tired from last night's stampede. After a few hundred feet, they stopped again and continued to graze.

Maddie followed five steps behind as Ezra, Brose, and James walked their horses down to the slain buffalo. Ezra waved his arms overhead to move some stragglers that were sniffing the ground near the kill.

Brose brought out the knives for butchering. Working on different sides, Ezra, Brose and James began to remove the thick coat—wonderful blanket, Ezra said to her—while Maddie walked around the animal, studying his massive shoulders and head. She felt the buffalo's cold nose and tiny, sleek ears, then ran her fingernail over the rings along his horn, counting his age like Ezra told her. Twelve. She grabbed a fist full of the tough matted hair surrounding his head and squeezed. It was springy.

At the other end of the buffalo, she found his small hindquarters strangely out of proportion to the massive head and shoulders. The tail was sleek as a cat's but tufted on the end. It reminded her of the dusting brush her *mère* had used on the chandeliers in the *grande maison*.

Maddie stepped away after the hide was removed. She was uncomfortable, her stomach queasy, staring at the body of the buffalo disrobed. Sleek, red, naked flesh, with its wooly head still intact but eyes dull as quartz. The men worked fast, carving out the choice pieces, they said. They used names for the cuts Maddie didn't understand and bantered, almost joyfully, while she waited for the vengeful buffalo friends to turn on her. *She's the one that pulled the trigger.*

Brose removed the tongue and held it out to Maddie. She stared at it in disbelief. Horror. It still seemed alive, as if it might lick her if she leaned forward.

"Take a bite."

She shook her head. He showed her how, blood streaming from his mouth. She refused. Ezra came over and took a bite, invited James, and told Maddie it was her duty as a hunter to honor the buffalo she killed. A sign of victory and an act of reverence and humility. Thanking the Great Spirit.

Reluctantly, she closed her eyes, held the tongue gently in her hands, and took a bite. It was tender and almost sweet, not as nasty as she had imagined. When she opened her eyes, James handed her a canteen, and all around her were smiles. She felt proud and embarrassed by the attention. Looked to see if the other buffalo were watching. *Now she's eating his tongue*, they might whisper.

THEY DRAPED THE MEAT AND ROBE ACROSS FOUR HORSES AND BEGAN the long trek back to camp. Maddie walked next to Ezra, enjoying his protective shadow against the sun, replaying all that had transpired.

She relaxed when Ezra cupped the back of her neck and squeezed. It was his way of asking for her attention, showing his affection.

"Anybody in camp ever call you a runaway, a fugitive?"

"No. Jackson and Clifford call me slave girl. Some women still call me names when no one is looking, but not runaway. When Caroline and I sing to them after dinner, they sit and relax, applaud, ask for more. Then sing along, pat our shoulders. Why'd you ask?"

"Some inkling. Let me know if they do." He paused. "Now, what do you know about your family? Your roots?"

"You promised to tell me about Daisy. What did you like best about her?"

He gave her a half-hearted smile as if he would tell her, but not just yet. His all-in-good-time look. "Where'd the Indian in you come from?"

"*Mon grandpère.* They killed him."

"Who did?"

"Some slavers. Found them in the swamp lands. They stole *ma mère* after they killed him, when she was four or five. Then sold her and *ma grandmère*, Neakita."

"Both grandparents Indian then. What tribe?"

"No, Neakita was Black like me. An escaped slave. An escape artist, they said."

"Who said? What do you mean?"

"That's the story. She was Black, escaping and caught, over and over downriver. Then she be escaping into the big swamp. For years. Happy years. She married a Choctaw man and had a baby. *Ma mère* is their baby. The slavers sold them both."

"Apart?"

"*Ma mère* was so mad at *ma grandmère* her whole life. 'Neakita escaping this and slipping that,' *ma mère* would say, 'but with no mind to come and free her own baby.' She'd spit in her hand whenever she say that."

"Your *grandmère* must have had a slave name . . . before . . .?"

"Neakita is only name I know."

"Pretty name. Mean anything?"

"*Ma mère* say it come from a Choctaw song about a white flower. 'Wherever a mother's tears fall, Neakita will grow,' the song says."

"Did she die? What happened to her?"

"*Ma mère* asked her whole life about *grandmère*. A slave man came to the plantation one day, said he knew about Neakita, and if *ma mère* give him a ham bone, he'd tell her."

"And?"

"Told her she escaped again from a swamp-boat captain. Then became a free cook on a trading ship from New Orleans. Gone off to the Pacific, wherever that is. She never come back to free her baby. That's why I hate her too." Maddie spit in her hand.

They walked on in silence. He seemed caught up in his thoughts.

"What do you want to know about Daisy?" he asked.

She glanced up, eyes sparkling. "Everything."

"She was smart, funny, playful, fast. She looked like you, same gait and quick step. Same expressive face, same gestures. And she laughed like you too. We laughed all the time. She was your age, your size, and just as feisty last time I saw her."

Maddie moved closer. "I'm feisty? I like that. What else?"

"We did our chores together every morning. Until we were nine, we were allowed to play in the afternoons, climb trees, wander creek beds. She was the best part of my life. I loved her. I thought we'd be together forever. We said we would."

"She was your slave?"

"Not mine. My father's. He sold her one day." Ezra snapped his fingers hard. "Just like that."

"Why? Because you—?"

"She stole something, hid it in the barn. They caught her."

"Stole what?"

"A pair of silver spurs—Mexican, beautiful—my father's favorite, hanging on the wall in his office."

"Why didn't he just whip her? That's what they did to me when I stole. Twelve switches for food. Twenty for the hairbrush. He didn't have to sell her just for Mexican spurs."

"He had a nasty temper, Maddie. Terrible. An auctioneer came to the house, and dragged her away. Father made me watch. He held his hand over my mouth, the other around my throat. She was screaming my name."

"You look like you're about to cry," said Maddie. "Why was your pa so cruel?"

"I can still hear that scream, see the terror in her face, as if it were yesterday.

"I found out years later—Thomas, my brother, told me—that it wasn't really the spurs that did it. It was because I was stupid enough at age nine to tell my mother one afternoon that I loved Daisy and wanted to grow up and marry her and free her. I thought Mother would understand. 'Cause she loved Daisy too. But that was the end."

"I like it that you loved her so much," said Maddie. "And now love Beth. And love me. And love the wind and the prairie and the buffalo. I'm going to like this day with you forever."

⇒ 23 ⇐

ALKALI POISON

One week later, 100 miles farther west

The wheels sank deeper into the pulverized rock, sending powder as soft as talcum skyward, billowing up into a plume of dust several stories high that ran the full length of the train. The brown talc enveloped the wagon train as might a tunnel of dust. Walking beside the lead oxen, James felt his panic pushing up from his lungs, starving for clean air, into his brain. To relax he closed his eyes and flew home like a bird into the green forests of western Michigan. Sitting on top of a towering pine he felt the fresh clean wind rising off the sheen of Lake Michigan. Air clear enough to calm his panicked heart.

For all those trapped inside the tunnel, the dust and grit filled their ears and noses and clung to the wet spot on the bandanas where their mouths gasped for air. The unprotected oxen wheezed and choked and plowed ahead.

James could hear Camille and Maddie yell encouragement from outside the tunnel of dust. But he couldn't see them or respond through his mask. *Lucky they're not in here*, he thought. *They'd be miserable. Glad they're far enough away to breathe, with enough wind to holler to me.* It shouldn't matter to hear their voices, their cheer, but it did. It kept him pushing forward. He was doing it for them.

He knew one hundred feet to the upwind side of the tunnel, where the air was fairly clear, women and children were walking in clusters of five and ten, watching their steps through the rocks and scattered scrub. Those in the lead used sticks to poke for hidden rattlers, who were cautious enough to give the women and children fair warning. By now, the children had attuned their ears to the *chitchitchit* of the fearsome snake from twenty feet away.

Inside the tunnel, James's bandana and kerchief were layered across his face, completely covered in dust. His hat snugged down over his ears and tied down with rawhide strap under his chin. The crude, wooden framed, bottle-glass goggles that Ezra made for him saved his eyes but were rubbing his cheeks and forehead raw. The dirty glass created a world of dust-brown shapes that moved about like ghosts—dust-brown wagons, dust-brown oxen, dust-brown people.

Every morning, James watched in envy as Ezra and Brose rode off into clear skies to scout the flanks and forward trail. Lucky guides, always ahead of the dust. For his part, James was plain tired of this job. Tired of the dust. Tired of the oxen. Tired of comforting them, tired of talking to them, tired of commiserating with their fate, and tired of cracking the whip when they dawdled.

A putrid smell twitched his nose and began growing, seeping through the enveloping cloud. James lifted his head when he heard women and children yelling, some shrieking from the downwind side of the train. The wagons slowed, then the train stopped completely. Something dead, vile out there. James did not want to see the bodies of ill-fated travelers, but his curiosity about the smell, worse than anything previously encountered, drew him toward the crying children. He braked the wheels, left his wagon and wheezing team, and walked through the cloud toward the voices.

He stopped where the dust thinned enough to see. He pulled up his googles, held his nose, then walked through the gathering crowd, who were shouting and reeling in horror. He gagged on first sight. Three dead oxen—bloated, splitting apart, covered with maggots. The creatures lay in contorted positions, their mouths twisted and covered in dried blood and clotted foam, eyes plucked. Thirty yards farther off the trail another ox had died with his head plunged into a pool of alkali water, his rear legs and haunches sticking straight up out of the hole, rigid as dry timber. Positioned as if the ox dove off a high board and was fossilized in place as he hit the water. *Dear God. Poor beasts.*

"Mules know better, but oxen don't," Ezra had told him. "So keep'm away from the poison water, whatever you do. Concentrated alkali eats their stomachs. Horrible death."

The train had planned to stop close by for midday meal but continued on for another hour, until the foul smell faded.

"Johan, yell to James, over there in the dust cloud," said Maddie. The boy was walking between her and Caroline, each holding one of his tiny hands. "James, we're holding him up to keep you company," Maddie shouted. Every ten steps or so, James knew they'd lift and swing him. Johan laughed and trilled in a mishmash of English and German.

James imagined the boy twisting his neck to see if Sarah, Camille, Miriam, and Beth walking behind him were paying attention. "*Sehen* Mama, Johan flizz like *vogel*," James heard, as he imagined them raising Johan to soar like a bird in the air. Amazing how quickly Johan has come around to health with all those people doting on him.

An hour later, as the smell finally dissipated, the train slowed to a crawl, then moved the wagons into a tight circular corral, lashing each wagon tongue to the back of the adjoining wagon to pen in and water and feed the half-crazed, wheezing animals.

As soon as the wheels stopped rolling, the wind grabbed the great shroud of dust covering their heads, tossed it up into a whirlwind, and spirited it away. The landscape reappeared. Removing his googles, James stood blinking in awe at the immensity and clarity of blue sky, at the hundred-mile views. And marveled at the sharp contrast of snow-capped mountains, poised like proud distant sentries on the western edge of the high desert. There was not a tree or blade of grass in sight. Scrawny dried bushes and some tumbleweed. If you squinted, a parched living garden where flowers slept, waiting for rain to awaken their bloom, and small creatures hid in shaded retreats and dashed for food.

James untied one of the wagon tongues, unhitched his team, and drove his six dust-choked oxen into the corral. The animals balked; they could smell the poison water out on the plain. Their nostrils flared, their heads turned in search, but with James's prodding and whip cracks, they moved in a morose single file. James gave his final ox a smack on the rear and turned away to unload water from the wagon.

The moment he turned his back, the last two oxen spun around and bolted out of the corral into the open land to find the beguiling water. The black, wet pupil of another alkali pool, even out of sight, drew them like an alluring eye.

James dropped the water barrel and ran after his two oxen in a panic before he remembered he had forgotten to close the opening. *Dear God!* He wheeled around and saw oxen from his and other teams breaking out.

"No! No!" he screamed and started back, then stopped. He watched the entire camp leap into action, re-lash the tongue, and take off on a run. A few on horseback tore out to cut off the lead animals. James stood with his hands on his head, turning in circles, his mind flooding with shame and indecision. Then he turned and ran as fast as he could after his own two.

JAMES FOUND THEM HALF A MILE AWAY CIRCLING THE POOL SHAPED like an eye, cautiously stepping through the white chalked ring surrounding the black pupil of poison water. Taking the whip from his belt, he cracked the air. They ignored him, put their heads down, and walked to the center, where they dipped their tongues into the five-foot wide black well to drink.

Fear finally concentrated his mind. Somehow, James had to save his oxen from a miserable, agonizing death. With precision, he stung their ears with his fast whip and drew blood. They backed away. But not for long. He struck again. They dodged the whip and waited. Unfortunately, they were learning. He raised his hand and started running around the chalk circle after them, but the two oxen walked sideways, eyeing him, staying opposite. Between the sharp lashes, they knew they had a moment and dashed in for a quick drink.

Panic rising, James now furiously lashed their backs and tried to sting their nostrils and ears. They watched, moved their heads side to side to avoid the whip and bellowed. Finally, both oxen accepted the punishing lash, jumped ahead of the whip, turned their backside to James, and plunged their muzzles deep into the poison.

James hadn't seen them ride up and dismount, but Beth, Camille, and Maddie out of nowhere charged into the chalk ring, yelling at the oxen, pushing the hulking beasts from the sides and from the rear. Then pulling their tails.

"Watch out," James screamed as one ox shifted his weight to kick. The kick was wild, just missing Maddie.

"Get away from the whip."

Camille stepped back as the lash bit into the animal's haunch, drawing blood. The ox jumped and lifted his face from the water to look around for his tormentor. James saw his opportunity and cracked the whip just above the ox's sensitive tongue. He bellowed and pulled back ten feet, bucking and kicking furiously. The instant he settled he started for the pool again, while Maddie and Beth raced in and grabbed his tail. The beast dragged them forward, the heels of their boots dug in, they nevertheless skidded like a sled across the salt. The ox plunged his head back into the hole.

CAMILLE COULD READ THE TERROR IN JAMES'S EYES. THESE OXEN were going to die, just like the ones beside the trail that morning. "James, what did you do? How could you be so careless?" Camille shouted.

She stopped scolding and looked around for something, anything to hit the ox. There was nothing but salt and dirt and a few small rocks. "James, do something!" she pleaded. He looked so helpless, nearly crying as he swung the whip with fury, again and again but to no avail.

"Stop!" she yelled at James to allay the whip. Then she charged in and screamed in the animal's ear, "No! No!" The ox turned angrily, bellowed in her face, and pushed her with his muzzle. She stumbled back but before she fell, Maddie pulled her to safety.

A RIFLE CRACKED RIGHT BEHIND THEM. CAMILLE AND MADDIE jumped aside and crouched down. "Get away," yelled Ezra. He, Brose, Robert McGrath, and Beth fired an arsenal of guns over the heads of the startled animals. The oxen spun around as if ready to run. But at the first pause in the gunfire, the beasts turned back and buried their muzzles deep in the pool.

Beth, Brose, and McGrath continued to fire while Ezra pulled a large satchel from his horse and flung it to the ground. Pawing through it, he pulled out some hickory staffs, a half dozen canteens, and chunks of raw meat.

One ox backed up, began weaving erratically, and then as if struck by lightning, bucked and began to spasm. The second reared back from the pool, crying out in pain. Trying to run, the two wobbled on their feet, bellowing to each other for help. One ox sank slowly onto his front knees, and then toppled over, kicking his legs and moaning, his eyes wide with terror. The alkali was eating his stomach. The second stumbled about as if drunk, then leapt straight up, crow hopping, twisting his body. He landed with a wobble, stumbled until he tripped over his own feet and fell on his side. His legs and hooves were flailing, running through the air.

"Watch those legs," Brose yelled. "They're loco. In pain."

"Get ready!" Ezra shouted. "I'm going to need all of you." He was on his knees, cutting meat furiously. He'd learned from earlier trains that meat, pork in particular, could save a beast's stomach. Didn't know why, just that it worked.

He grabbed Beth's arm and pulled her to the ground. "Here!" He shoved a fist-sized piece of raw bacon and a hickory stave into her hands. "Do what I do!" He jammed his own stave deep into another ball of meat and tied it on with rawhide. She quickly followed his lead.

He was amazed at the steadiness and sureness of Beth's hands. Camille's were shaking. She clenched them together. "What should I do?" she asked.

Both beasts began to writhe in the dust, crying in agony.

"We've got to get this pork down their throats. Beth, you work with Brose and Robert. They'll hold that one down for you. Follow my lead." He turned his eyes toward the second ox. "James! Camille! You're with me. Maddie, stay back." He looked at Camille and thrust his bacon-clad stave at her. She flinched and pulled back.

"Take it!" Ezra yelled, shoving it into her hand. "When I say go, Camille, you push it down his throat as far as you can. James, I'll hold his neck steady while you pry his mouth open."

Ezra climbed on top of the animal and wrapped his arms around the enormous neck near the head. He clasped his hands, pinning the weakened animal to the ground, then twisted the ox's head upward so the mouth pointed up.

James gripped the top and bottom of the ox's mouth, his hands slipping on the foaming saliva. Bracing his foot on the bottom jawbone, he slowly pried the mouth open.

"Now, Camille!" Ezra yelled. "Shove it down! Quick!"

Camille froze. Maddie shoved her hard in the back and she stumbled forward and sank to her knees. She saw the beast's frantic eyes and red maw, drooling a bloody slime. The ox made a horrible noise and crimson spit sprayed across her face, dripping down her cheek and over her clenched lips. She spit it out, but a putrid fog from its mouth enveloped her.

"Now! Quickly. Now damnit!" yelled Ezra.

Camille closed her eyes and pushed the meat gingerly into the creature's gullet. It wouldn't go. The ox was gagging on the meat and his own tongue, making strangling noises, trying to shake his head held rigid in Ezra's arms. More slime splattered her. She tasted it seeping between her lips. She wobbled with nausea. Then tried to wiggle the meat past his windpipe.

"Stop acting like a goddamned princess and jam it down!" screamed Ezra.

Camille vomited into the ox's mouth. Then, humiliated, she lifted her head, cried out in unison with the ox, and plunged the stick with all her might. The meat slid past the windpipe and down the esophagus. The ox jerked and kicked, tried to roll. It started to gag again.

"Push it down! Farther!"

She held the stave firmly and pushed. A soapy foam filled the ox's mouth and rolled out. The smell was foul, overpowering.

Camille backed away.

"Good, Camille. Now get another one in there!" Ezra demanded.

"I can't."

"You can. You're strong."

She pulled the stave out, strings of foaming meat still clinging to the end. She dropped a second piece of loose bacon in the ox's mouth, and then with the stave in both hands, plunged the bacon down into his stomach with one quick motion. She pulled the stave out and staggered backwards. She was dripping, trembling. Humiliated, disgusted, relieved. She fell to her knees.

"You did well," said Ezra. He said it kindly, like he meant it, she thought. Like he hadn't just screamed at her.

The ox moaned but began to settle, breathing more slowly and steadily. The panic washed from the beast's eyes.

Ezra stood up. "James, take my horse and get them some fresh water and hay from the wagon. We'll try to ease them back on their feet."

"Will they live?" asked James.

"Go!" Ezra yelled, gritting his teeth.

Camille caught Ezra's eye. She started to speak but he pointed at the ox.

"Come on, you and Maddie, help me get this animal back on his feet," he said. "Better if he moves around. Which one is he?"

"This is Bo Peep, the wheel ox," said Maddie. "I'm glad we saved her."

"It's a him," he said.

"Not to me."

Beth walked over and squeezed Camille's shoulder. "You did great. Just precisely when we needed you. I was sure these two were going to die. Now they have a chance."

"I didn't think I could do it."

"But you did it. Exactly when we needed it. That's what counts."

"He called me a goddamned princess."

Beth put her arm around her. "I know," she said gently. "He pulled up your fury to break you out of your fear. To get you to do what you had to do. You found the courage and did it well. You should be proud. You can talk to Ezra when he's calmed down."

"He's furious at James," said Camille.

"Can you blame him?"

LATER THAT EVENING, EZRA WALKED OVER TO JOIN THE FAMILY FOR early supper. They were sitting on makeshift benches in a loose circle, Maddie and Camille on one bench, James on another, Beth on a third with space for him. They had started without him.

No reason for them to wait, he realized. He had been busy for hours rounding up the oxen, conferring with Brose, and trying to calm the Captain and a dozen others so angry that they wanted to flog James. Ezra flat out refused.

"No, he's my responsibility. I'll deal with him in my own way," he said. "And I will take it quite personally if any one of you touches him."

Ezra had avoided James and Camille all afternoon. He had been stewing on what he might say and how. What tone, what words. Like it or not, he had become the father of this newfound family. In two months, or was it three, it had become more than casual pretense. He was raising children for the first time in his life, prepared or not. They were emotional, unpredictable, nothing like the hardened men that had been his traveling companions for a generation.

Camille and Maddie stopped chatting, went silent as Ezra walked in. They stared at him without a word. James scooted his bench back a bit and looked down at his feet, fidgeting. Beth, with a faint smile, handed him a full plate as he sat down next to her.

It was desert food, expedient and cold—tough buffalo meat and the greasy cakes cooked before they left the river. Grim fare, but he was ravenous. He took a big bite and wished he hadn't. The meat was hard to chew.

James's eyes darted up to meet Ezra's, and the boy flinched as if he expected Ezra to snap his head off. Ezra's own father certainly would have.

Ezra remembered the pain of his father's rants and tirades, belittling Ezra and his brother for every mistake. Either to make them stronger or crush their spirit, it was never clear until the day he sold Daisy. A quick, brazen, cruel act, forcing Ezra to watch as Daisy was shackled and dragged off for auction screaming for Ezra to save her. Now, left with nothing of paternal guidance to draw upon, Ezra wasn't sure how to proceed, but was determined to do better than his father. He felt he owed it to Beth and the girls, James, and his own lost son to rise to the occasion.

He put down his fork. "We were lucky today." His voice was more scolding than he wanted it to be.

"Careful, Ezra," said Beth, touching his arm. "It's been a hard day for all."

"Would it be better if I talked to James by himself?"

"No, this affects all of us," she said.

James hung his head. "I'm sorry I slipped up." He slumped forward, his voice weak and raspy.

"Sit up. Look at me."

James jerked his head and straightened his back.

"You were damn careless today." Tough words but his tone was now controlled, even. "The train could have lost a half dozen oxen, and we came very close with two of our own. I know you understand the consequences of losing two."

James was squirming, murmuring yes.

"It puts the full burden on the other four oxen. It dooms them. If not in the mountains were heading into, then in the punishing desert. We have only a few spares for the entire train. And it's going to get rougher."

Ezra pointed at Camille and Maddie. "Look at them, James. Go on, take a good hard look. Make sure you understand what's at stake. Their lives."

James looked at Camille, who gave him a faint smile of support. Then at Maddie.

"They depend on us. And we depend on them. And all of us depend on the oxen, who depend on you to lead them. That's how life works on the trail."

James shuffled his feet and ran his hand through his hair. "I know, I'll be more careful . . . honest." He stared at Ezra. "Honest, I promise."

Ezra looked at him skeptically. "You're doing a man's job, but you're not yet a man. You're thirteen. The oxen don't know that. They listen to you."

"I—"

"They don't know that your mind wanders off. That you're bored, restless, angry, cooped up. Your mind goes elsewhere, and you put them in danger."

James gripped his pants at the knees, twisting them into knots.

"After dinner I want you to go bed them down comfortably, give them extra water, then stay with them until they calm down, fall asleep. They trust you. They love you. That's the thing about you. These animals trust you to lead them. I remember being your age, what it's like, but not carrying as much responsibility over life and death as you do right now." Ezra's voice softened. "You're a fine drover, James. Very skillful, more than most men. You made a mistake today. Learn from it. But don't let it crush you."

"I understand," said James, sitting up straighter, staring at Ezra with tears in his eyes.

Ezra saw the misery begin to drain from the boy, his pride return; a sign that he had reached James, taught him without the ferocity and cruelty of his own father. Maybe he, Ezra, was learning too.

He paused, turned to Camille. She braced herself. "Camille, you did well today." His voice became deeper and kinder. "I'm proud of you for helping save that ox. Sorry I yelled, shocked you. It was a nasty jibe. I used it to jar you into action. Truth is I don't see you as a princess. Never did. I see you as a young woman of uncommon grace and courage, learning how to live in a new world. Forgive me."

MADDIE FOUND JAMES BEDDING DOWN HIS ANIMALS, SAT DOWN close to him, and took his hand and with her other stroked the neck of the dozing ox in front of her. "Ezra was hard on you," she said.

"Yeah, well . . . deserved it. I could hear you and Caroline singing over there. Singing to her family's oxen, I suppose. Glad you found a friend."

"Have you found a friend yet?" she asked.

James shook his head. "I don't like these boys much. They're like a wolf pack, picking on all the small children when they think they're out of sight. They're different during the day, when we're all business, working hard on the trail. They treat their oxen well, care for their wagons, care for their families. It's just at night when they pack, looking for weak kids to bully. I hate them for that. They stay out of my way now. Fear me for protecting you. They don't like me much."

"Well, I like you. Camille loves you. Same with Beth and Ezra, and Caroline and me and Powder Bell, the oxen with the black ear. And so do the prairie dogs, and snakes, and soaring eagles, and antelope. Everybody except maybe the buffalo. They're mean when frightened."

Maddie changed the subject. "You going to be glad to find your brother in California?" she asked. "Sometimes I hope you don't, so you have to stay with Camille and me. We're going to be a family in California, and we'll need a brother. You know how I know? That pelly bird been following us told me in a dream. She's *ma mère* who went to heaven to become a pelly bird to guide us to freedom. She loves you too and calls you brother James. So, you see, you have no choice. If you find your brother, he can join us. We could use two brothers if he's as nice as you."

"Hadn't thought of that," he said. "I hope I can find him. I'm scared I can't. He doesn't know I'm coming. He may be angry. May not like me anymore."

"Of course he will. He'll be so proud of you, coming all this way just to find him."

⇒ 24 ⇐

BEAR RIVER

An oasis, 1000 miles west of trailhead

T he girls were asleep in the back but Beth sat up front on the wagon seat next to James as the train creaked along a well-worn trail in moonlight, under the dark trees, beside the marshland, looking for a place to camp along the Bear River. They passed isolated campfires down near the inviting water, skirted around a small Shoshone village celebrating with dance and drums, and finally settled on a quiet meadow with shade trees and easy entry to the river. They circled the wagons, watered and bedded the oxen, and fell instantly asleep.

All save Beth. As she slid into slumber, she remembered Ezra and Brose telling the families during these last grueling weeks of dust and drudgery, grinding rock and parched land, to hold on for the Bear. An oasis to lift your spirits, they promised. We'll have three days to rest, bathe, feast. So hold on. Beth had, but barely.

At dawn, Beth and the girls raced for the water. By agreement, all the women were in the river first, stepping naked into the cold water at sunrise with mist coming off the surface. They shivered into deeper water and sank to their necks amid the clamor of ducks, the scampering of sandpipers, and the overhead flutter of the elegant herons and egrets. They shared the river with animals drinking from the river bank downstream—deer, elk, mountain lions, rattlesnakes, wolves, marmots, bears, and smaller dart-in-and-out kind of creatures.

Beth helped Camille and Maddie wash their long hair. They in turn helped her untangle and wash her matted locks. As if her emotions had been sealed tight by filth and fatigue, the sparkling water, the beauty of the trees, and the tenderness of morning air released her first smatterings of joy. *Three whole days*, she repeated in her mind as she drifted on her back in the slow eddies, thinking of Ezra. Restoration of the body, soul, spirit, that's what he promised her. She'd take him up on that.

SHE FOUND EZRA AT NOON, PACING AROUND LOST IN THOUGHT. Cheerful, colorful, and talkative at breakfast, he had grown suddenly gray and sullen. While everyone else was off fishing, dozing, foraging, swimming, he circled the camp aimlessly, avoiding her.

She pursued him with a growing sense of dread. "What's wrong?"

"I was going to show it to you but . . . well, affects—"

He handed her a piece of parchment. "It's a letter from Thomas. The stranger who brought it is Creighton. Been riding nonstop for over a month to catch up with our train.

She sat, opened it, and smoothed the letter, mottled with sweat and rain, against her thigh.

Dear Ezra,

June 1, 1849. I write in haste. As you know, I have my spies, my sources in the pro-slaver community. I have just learned that Camille's father hired Jenkins to pursue you at any cost. Three men, including Jenkins himself, are already en route to San Francisco by sea. And a separate group of four—some say five—fast riders left on horseback more than a week ago to track you down. This Antoine Bonaire—

Camille and Maddie's father—has contracted to reward Jenkins with twenty-five slaves shipped to California once the girls are back in his hands. 25! Do you grasp the power of this bounty? Your life, Beth's life and Homer's may be in danger. I ask you to reconsider. I know how stubborn you can be, but please consider surrendering these girls so that you can survive.

My courier, Creighton McConnell, knows nothing of the contents of this letter. That is up to you. He remains in my employ and has agreed to continue on with you to California. Should you need an extra gun, he can be a ferocious fighter. You can trust him completely.

Love, Thomas

"Give them up?!" Beth jumped up, then covered her mouth to prevent shrieking, Nobody paid the slightest attention. "Did he really ask us to hand them over? Like we don't care for them. No wonder you look half sick. I'm sure Martha didn't know about his request."

"I couldn't scream, '*Go to hell*,' any louder in my head if I tried," said Ezra. "Been shouting at Thomas, fighting him in my mind for the last hour. He can kiss my ass."

"He must be afraid for his son, Homer," she said.

"If they hurt Homer, they'll never get their twenty-five slaves. I'm sure Jenkins is smart enough to realize that," he said.

"Well they're not getting my girls. I'll fight . . ." She turned in circles, hands on her head, heart racing. "Listen to me. I've never had children. Never wanted children. But these two feel like my own. And not just mine. Ours, Ezra. I'll kill to protect them if I have to—"

"Might come to that, if these men catch up to us," he said. "I don't think we should tell Camille and Maddie. It would terrify them."

"Agree. Terrifies me. If Creighton is to be a protector you should be straight with him. Let him know what's in the letter, the situation we're in. Then swear him to secrecy."

"Come, I'll introduce you to Creighton."

MADDIE AND CAROLINE, CAMILLE, AND KAREN WERE WALKING THE riverbank with Johan, swinging him in the air, singing to him. They taught him the names of the animals, the birds, trees, flowers, and berries. He particularly loved the brown bears, egrets, and the flocks of jealous quacking ducks patrolling the river. The boy cringed and covered his eyes whenever the shadow of a large eagle or hawk glided past, imagining vultures. Maddie pulled his hands away to show him that her eyes, his eyes, and everyone's eyes were safe. "Maddie, tell him, *Augen sicher,*" said Karen. "*Sicher* means safe. *Nicht sicher*, not safe. Good words for you to know as he learns."

From behind, "Will you take a walk with me?" Tad's deep, soft voice came out of nowhere. Camille turned and shocked him by saying yes without hesitation, then a second time by taking his hand. Maddie and Caroline giggled. Karen smiled, shook her head in disbelief, and stepped away with the youngsters in tow.

After ten minutes of quiet strolling, Camille stopped. "Tad, I've been walking ten, twelve hours every day for months. I'm tired of walking. If you don't mind, let's go sit by the river, put our feet in, let them soak." She led Tad a few hundred yards upriver to a grassy meadow covered in flowers and patted down a spot to dangle their legs in cool water. They sat and she moved just far enough away to separate their bodies.

"I've been difficult, I know. Avoiding you. I'm sorry. It's not you. It's me. I cannot become emotionally entangled. Karen may have already told you why."

"She has but give me a chance. I hope to change your mind."

"You can't. I need to find someplace in the world where Maddie and I can live openly as sisters. Can you name one?"

He shrugged. "Not any place I know."

"Ezra says California is up for grabs, but it could well become a slave state. Or it could go the way of Oregon, excluding blacks. Canada is always a possibility, but so far away. You see what I'm up against? I need to raise Maddie on my own until she is eighteen. That's nine years from now. Come find me then; I'll be twenty-six. And you'll be . . ."

"Thirty-one. Maddie's not a problem for me," he said.

"Not now, possibly, but your family would never allow it."

"You don't know anything about my family."

"Your parents are on this train. I've barely spoken to them. But by their eyes, they're still wary of me and Maddie. Where are you from? No matter, it's the same everywhere. You'd find yourself isolated from your kinfolk, neighborhood, friends, workers, even your church."

"Pittsburgh. A number of free blacks there, but few, if any, openly mixed-race families. At least I haven't met any. I imagine they'd have to keep it to themselves, a family secret." Tad shifted his weight to get a little closer. "My dad's in the foundry business. A foreman. Wants to get enough gold to go back and open his own cast-iron supply business. And wants me to take it over. He's stubborn and determined but that's not for me." He scrunched his face up. "I want to get out of the smoke and grime, the gray skies, the stench of smelters and cupolas, and well . . . I have some dreams too."

"Like what?"

"Marry someone like you. Travel the world. Settle, maybe raise horses in California with big open sky, and miles of fertile land, mountains close by. Or . . . if that doesn't work—and this will sound childish—join a circus, become an acrobat. I'm quite good."

Camille smiled.

"I was trained by my uncle, who owns a couple of stables, so I worked with him to learn about horses. Told me he had been in a traveling circus for years as an acrobat, before he met my Aunt Beatrix, and she put her foot down. 'You want me, enough of that nonsense on high wires,' she told him and that was that. He wanted her.

"He showed me some floor acrobatics and I begged him to teach me and he finally relented. For three years in secret—my parents still don't know—in a backroom in his stables, using thick horse padding and straw to break my falls, swinging from bars and pipes. Even a secret trapeze in the big barn high above the corn crib. Not a soft fall but at least you don't break your back."

Camille laughed. "You've got a big imagination. I like that. But aren't you a bit large to be an acrobat? Don't you have to be nimble?"

"You don't believe me? Watch—"

She stopped him with her raised hand. "No, please, Tad, just stay seated," she said. "I want to be with you right now, not watch you perform."

He was smiling. "You've never said that before. That you want to be with me."

"Sometimes I do. In moments like this. But I don't want you to get the wrong impression. This is not courtship. At most, it's friendship."

"To be near you, talk with you like this, it's all I want."

"But when we get to California, Tad, I want you to forget about me. Go find a nice girl who wants to raise horses and children with you."

"I can't possibly forget about you. I dream about you."

HOURS AFTER DINNER, FOOD PACKED AWAY, THE ENTIRE TRAIN settled around the big fire for sunset. Beth watched in awe as the sun began to drop below the mountains and the dimming Western sky slowly swelled like a red-breasted bird. One that spread long red, tapered wings out along the horizon, then suddenly rose higher and higher until the entirety of western sky and land were reborn red.

In those moments, shadows on the ground lengthened into long black streamers. Giddy children ran after them, casting their own long black shadows that chased the shadows.

As the sunset faded and the darkening night exhaled its first puff of crisp air, women disappeared to bed their children. When they returned with their shawls and foot blankets, they had another shot of whiskey and snuggled into their menfolk as the earth cooled and the fire crackled.

Ezra lingered with the others beside the roaring campfire, stretched out, chatting and drinking whiskey and coffee, lulled by the rush of the river. But he grew increasingly uneasy as the laughter subsided and the couples began lounging more intimately.

Beth had herself moved in closer, her breast sliding against his arm, her face close enough to kiss should he lift her chin, her hand on his thigh. Aroused by her scent and touch, her physical warmth, his heart quickened. When she looked up, whispered something about *tonight*, he lifted her chin and kissed her slowly, playfully. Then shifting his body around, he was able to hold and caress her face with both hands. Then pressed his lips to hers in a dance that she returned with passion. He felt her shiver. He wanted to feel her skin. In his mind he began undoing the top of her dress and sliding his hands in.

Suddenly, as if waking from a dream, he sat back. His arousal unnerved him. She had been flirtatious all evening with him, no other word for it. And the surge of passion it stirred in him was real. That kiss powerful. But was she simply acting for the crowd to put their suspicions to rest? Flirtation had been pleasant enough in the beginning, and he had played along, enjoying a touch here and a touch there. But then the fullness of her body had pressed against him. And the unexpected warmth and intensity of her kiss overwhelmed him like a prairie storm. Was it real or pretense? Where were they? He couldn't stand the confusion.

He stood and dusted off his pants. "I hate to leave," he said, looking straight at Beth, ignoring everyone else, "but I have to get up early." It wasn't exactly a lie but close. Truth was he didn't trust his own urges. He had dodged around physical touch and intimacy with her for years, but it suddenly felt unleashed, uncontrollable.

Beth turned away, looking embarrassed. On his feet, he leaned down and kissed her quickly, then walked away as all conversation immediately around them stopped. He didn't look back. Nor did he invite her to join him in his tent.

Miriam slid over. "Don't fret, Beth. He wants you alone. I saw his face. He's not rejecting you, dear, he's luring you. His desire is brimming like a boiling pot, like a bull in heat. Here are the herbs I mentioned to keep you safe. They don't need hot water, anything liquid will do."

Beth smiled, embraced her. Poured a pinch of Miriam's herbs in a cup of water and stirred with her finger. She sipped it.

FOR SOLITUDE, EZRA HAD PITCHED HIS TENT WELL BEYOND THE perimeter of wagons. It was the first night in the Bear Valley, and he knew couples would be up late drinking, laughing, dancing, cavorting.

He unlaced the tent and stepped through the flap into the square-cornered canvas pyramid. It was invitingly spacious, wide-pegged, and at its peak, a head taller than Ezra. But a mess, things just tossed into the tent that morning as he unpacked. He'd tidy up, clean his weapons, and wait for her. Or go to sleep.

Twenty minutes later, Ezra heard feet coming toward his tent, quick and light, those of a woman or a child. Beth put her head through the tent flap. "May I come in?" Her face looked flushed, nervous, and her eyes jumped when she saw him. He had taken off his shirt and was sitting barefoot on a large black buffalo robe, cleaning a pistol.

He signaled to come in. She stepped through and closed the flap. "No, leave it open," he said. "It's been closed all day. A bit stale in here." He studied her eyes. There was no flirtation. Flustered, he thought. Her breathing seemed fast and shallow. He'd have to put her at ease. With a smile and a tug of his head, he patted the furry robe next to him.

She took a few steps into the center, looking around. Surprised at the height, she touched the top of the tent. Strange, she thought, in months of travel she had never been inside.

She glanced about his home, clutter pushed to the edges—a brown bearskin rumpled in one corner, a folded gray blanket, a red Hudson Bay with three stripes for high quality, assorted articles of clothing, rifles and pistols, ammunition, tins of food and tobacco.

"Not much to look at," he said. "Do you want to sit?"

She nodded but remained standing with her personal bag over her shoulder.

"Well?" he asked. "Are you feeling hesitant?"

"We have to spend the night together," she said. "I told the girls."

"Have to or want to?"

"Both." Still standing, she removed her bonnet, brushed her hair back and laughed. "Some of the women—well, most of them, it seems— notice we rarely touch and don't sleep together. They're watching us. If we don't at least make an effort, here of all places, we feed their suspicions. Miriam warned me earlier. She told the women the reason I always sleep in the wagon with the girls is because I'm afraid of getting pregnant. That bought us some time."

She sat down. "We both felt it out there next to the fire—the passion, I mean. And they saw our kiss. You're quite good at it, Ezra. Sent a shiver down my spine. Never been kissed like that in my whole life."

She put the bag down and folded her hands in front of her. "We need to spend the night at least pretending we're lovers."

"Why pretend? We're alone."

Ezra stared at the contours of her face, her body, aroused again with her so close.

Beth was fidgeting, sitting cross-legged. Even blushing, he thought.

Trying to calm her, he leaned across the large, black robe, reached into the corner, and pulled out a small bearskin. He refolded it and put it next to her as a pillow. She leaned on it, facing him, staring at him.

"Thanks." She sat up, took off the green silk pelerine that draped her shoulders. "Martha said to save this and the dress for a special occasion. Tonight seemed so special, I thought . . ." She folded the cape carefully and put it in her bag, then leaned sideways on her elbow, half reclining against the pillow. Her dress was a soft, maroon cotton, with flecks of green. No sign of fussiness to it, he noticed, just a well-sculpted bodice; no flounces, no petticoats taking up air, and no constraining corset. The pleats and seams created an enticing V-shape running from her shoulders to her waist, directing his eyes up and down her body. She was lovely.

An evening breeze kicked up dust outside. Ezra walked over and closed the flap, then lit a candle and placed it in a small carriage lantern a few feet beyond their heads. "There, now I can see you better."

He circled around and knelt beside her feet and tugged at her boots. "Do you mind? May as well get you comfortable, too," She looked surprised, he thought, but said nothing. He slid the boots off, then the freshly washed but well-worn socks, and massaged her toes. Then each instep, holding her ankle in one hand, her foot in the other. He'd not expected her feet to feel so tender, so intimate. He stroked the texture of her skin, then massaged the depth of her instep, the curves of her heel and ankle. She shuddered, closed her eyes, accepted his strong, gentle hands. After her reverie, she slowly extracted her foot from his hands. He pulled the Hudson Bay over her legs.

Lying down next to her, he stretched to the back of the tent, retrieving a leather-covered whisky flask. He uncorked it and took a drink, then offered it to her. She waved it away. Setting the flask behind himself, he made a pillow of the gray blanket to recline on, facing her, near enough to inhale her breath.

Ezra moved the lantern still closer. "There," he said, smiling. In the warm glow, she gave him one of her looks: serene, mysterious, alluring. Her nervousness had faded. She seemed at home.

"You're so beautiful."

She smiled faintly. "You've never said that before. Exactly that. Do you mean it?"

"I do. Always thought so, from the first moment, but hesitated to say it. But truth Beth, I love to look at you, feel your presence, watch you move."

She reached over, sliding across his chest, for the whiskey flask, as if inviting him to feel her. He caught her scent and closed his eyes, savoring the soft flow of her body over his. She uncorked the flask and took a small sip. "Whew, pretty raw stuff."

He took one as well. It was so strange, he thought, after all these years, to love a woman again. He found it an unsettling blend of eagerness and caution. One area of life he could no longer fully control.

"When we get to California, would you mind if I was around you quite a bit?" His question was oddly phrased, he realized, but she got the drift.

Her brow knit. "I'd welcome it, of course. But quite a bit? Do you mean all the time? Permanently? I don't know if I trust you enough." She laughed. "Are you offering?"

Was he? He hadn't realized he was so close to asking. It might just drive her away. "No," he said. "I'm not offering."

"Thank you." She ran her hand over his. "You know I don't want to be married. Never have. If I did, you'd be my first choice. My only choice in this lifetime."

"Then what is it? What are you afraid of?"

She stared at him, perplexed. "You don't know after all this time? I thought I was clear. I'm afraid any man I marry will steal me. Strip the *me* out of me. Take away my life. My independence. Everything I've built. Everything I am. It's not personal to you. Not you, Ezra. You're the most trustworthy man I know, but I don't trust any man that way. To give myself over."

At least it wasn't personal. "Good reason not to," he said, smirking. "You and I are about equal up in our disregard for marriage. I wouldn't be very good at it. I was once, but not anymore."

She reached for the whiskey.

He stroked her hair and kissed her, then slid his lips to the hollow of her neck, listening to a sound, a release deep in her throat, almost a purr. He pulled back to catch his breath.

He rolled on his side, leaning on his pillow, his face close to hers. "You're impossibly beautiful. I dream of you, watch you when you're not aware"

"Oh, I'm aware. I watch you too, you know." Unable to silence the question in her mind, she started, then stopped. Then pushed forward. "Ezra? Do you love me?"

He didn't answer.

She took his hand and they lay there quietly. It bothered her that he had stopped kissing her, didn't answer her question directly. What did that mean? Her mind and body were stirring with desire, something she'd always known was there but had kept deeply buried.

"Do you want to?" she asked.

"That's not a fair question. Do you?"

"I want to know if *you* do," she insisted.

He turned toward her, ran his fingers deep into her thick hair and her head. Kissed her neck. He could see blood pulsing in her throat.

"I don't want you to feel I was dishonoring you," he said. "I don't want you to walk out of this tent feeling ashamed, diminished."

"Oh, stop it, Ezra. Dishonor? You can't dishonor me. I'm a grown woman. I decide for myself what's honorable."

She sat up and undid the top of her dress, loosened the stays. "I don't want to make full love tonight, Ezra. Maybe tomorrow night or the night after. Right now, I want to feel your hands on my body. I want to know what it's like. She took his hand and guided it inside the top of her dress and held it while he caressed her. His touch sent shivers down her legs.

His heart quickened as he felt her nakedness for the first time. Her skin so tender, the breast so giving when he squeezed, felt it flowing in his hand.

"Understand," she said. "I've never had a good experience with sex or passion. Ever. I've been raped, groped, and briefly had one very bad lover who turned into a brute. But in terms of love, real intimacy, honest lovemaking, I'm thirty-eight and still have no idea."

"Shh. I know that. Everything about you right now, Beth, excites me." He was savoring her skin, her fragrance, softness, and those little low sounds of pleasure. Her open-mouth breathing.

"Tomorrow night, when I'm fully exposed, I want you to kiss me all over the way you've kissed my neck and lips tonight. Your mouth on me, hungry, passionate. Yet able to pull back, if I ask. All right?"

"Of course. Slow and easy. I want you comfortable, unafraid, curious. Fully open. I want us to discover together what brings you pleasure."

She shifted her position so he could keep his hand moving straight down to her stomach. Then suddenly froze. "I'm afraid my dress will rip if you go further. Better, let me take it off. I was going to take it off anyway to sleep."

He slid his hand out slowly. She stood, unfastened the constraining hooks, and tugged the dress over her head. She was draped all in white cotton undergarments. A loose comfortable pantalette from her waist to her ankles, and a long loose chemise from her neck to her knees that would double as her night dress. She carefully folded the prized maroon dress and tucked it in her bag.

"I love that dress on you," he said.

She lay back down, took his hands and placed them up under the chemise. "Now you can touch me freely but not yet below the waist. Maybe tomorrow. I want to begin our new freedoms with each other slowly."

"You're in charge," he said. He ran his hands up along her neck and shoulders, and his fingers through her hair, and caressed her face and ears. Then slowly massaged her breasts, shoulders, and stomach as far down as the boundary line. All to comfort her.

For him, the freedom to explore her was heart-stirring. The blood was pounding in his head, his legs twitched with eagerness. Yet he knew somewhere in her mind she was testing him, testing his control. Whether she could trust him completely with their passion. And stop him at a moment's notice

"Believe it or not, going slow, becoming aroused at your pace makes the fever in me build. Even your small moans when I touch you kindle the fire in me. We'll go slow as you want."

"Thank you for caring so much, Ezra."

"To answer your earlier direct question, Beth. Yes, I do love you. I think I always have. Knew it almost immediately. But I fought it, as you know, feared it.

She kissed him. His eyes were locked on hers, looking for panic, fear. He didn't see it. "I'm sorry you were hurt . . ."

"Don't be," she said. "And please don't dwell there, Ezra. Stay with me, right now, right here. Real love, Ezra, that's what I've always wanted. Being loved, cherished. I did not think it was possible."

Ezra patted the pillow blanket. She lay down on her side, rested her head next to him. He stretched out beside her. His face close to hers.

"I treasure being this close to you, Ezra. This honest. Your body, voice, smell, touch, even your breathing comforts me. I want to sleep with your arms around me." He pulled her in tight.

"In all the years I've known you we've never done this," she said. "Never even tried. Your arms around me while I fall asleep."

"You're precious," he said. "I knew you were the day I met you." He kissed her and blew out the candle.

FIFTEEN MINUTES LATER, SHE STIRRED, PROPPED HERSELF UP ON her elbow. "Ezra, are you awake?

"Can't sleep a wink."

"I can't either. My heart is beating too fast, my legs squirming for you," she said. "I don't want to wait for tomorrow."

"Me neither."

"Thank God," she said.

⇒25⇐

FORT HALL

Oregon Territory, 1100 miles west

F ort Hall was not the frontier stockade of tall sharpened posts Beth had imagined, but rather a high-walled adobe fortress surrounded by a half dozen circled wagon trains. To the sides of the fort, closer to the trees, Native habitation—tall, conical, deer-skinned teepees of the Shoshone and Bannock tribes, with trellised drying racks covered in furs with outstretched legs, paws, tails. Indeed, as Ezra told her earlier, Fort Hall was simply a trading post, not a military fort.

As they approached, Maddie broke away from Ezra's hand in excitement and raced ahead toward the great double doors of the Fort, then stopped cold, turned and raced back, looking fearful.

"What's wrong? What is it?" She gripped Ezra's arm, whimpered, and dug in her nails. Then pointed. Thirty-forty yards ahead, standing by the entrance was a welcoming party of sorts—four coarse men in mismatched furs and frayed, graying beards, passing a whiskey jug. They stared in silence past Ezra and Maddie to the women right behind them—Beth and Miriam, Camille and Sarah—who stopped talking. Johan jumped up into Sarah's arms.

Not knowing the reception they'd receive, Ezra turned and shouted to the group. "We'll wait right here for the other families to catch up and go in together." He looked at Beth and tugged his hat. She and the other women responded by easing their bonnets forward to put their faces in shadow. Each of them was carrying a pistol in her pocket or shoulder bag, not knowing what waited inside. Ezra himself was making a display of arms—two extra pistols jammed into his belt, a rifle, boot pistol, and large knife. He brought James over and asked him to walk to the side of the women closest to the rough men at the gate, cradling his rifle.

Another ten families soon gathered. Bringing up the rear were the Captain and Doc Sturgis, both lightly but visibly armed. Ezra heard them talking loudly about the medical supplies Doc hoped to buy.

Ezra nudged Maddie lightly to start moving. "Come on. You're OK. Trust me, Pablo. We'll lead the way." Pablo was Maddie's code name for use in the Fort. At his insistence, she was in her buckskin pants and shirt, her hair pinned up, wearing one of his old flop hats stuffed to keep it from falling over her eyes. A precaution. At first glance she would pass for a boy. A mixture of White, Black and Choctaw, she could also pass for Mexican descent. Easier that way, less dangerous, he told her. By law, Black folks were no longer allowed to enter Oregon Territory, and were subject to capture, even though there was no one here to enforce the law. Law at Fort Hall was whatever Grant, the owner, said it was, and he cared for little except theft and murder.

Maddie pressed against Ezra's hip and pointed with her eyes. On the far side of the gate, two captured Black men were sitting against the wall of the fort. "Easy," he said. His own blood was rising, his hair tingling. He patted her shoulder. "Steady, Pablo."

"Si, Papá."

The captured men were slumped forward, hoods over their heads, hands tied behind their backs, with their blistering ankles shackled in sun-hot irons. They had no boots. Squatting beside them was a man with a rifle, presumably a guard but half asleep, head down, face shaded with a wide-brimmed hat.

"Their feet are bloody," whispered Maddie, with good sense not to point.

Just beyond the captives, Ezra noticed a tall, thin man wearing a dark hat with a reddish fur band. He stood in a shadow. His face was weathered, lean, scowling. He stared at Maddie, as if studying her. In the man's eyes, Ezra saw the glint of an abductor. The rifle dangling from Ezra's hand rotated toward the man, a slaver he presumed, then as they passed, he raised the muzzle a few inches. The man ignored the warning and stared at the women, drawing heavily on a long thin cigar.

"Keep your eyes straight ahead, Pablo," said Ezra. "Inside, you and your sister be careful of that man, the one with the red band. I don't trust him."

THROUGH THE DOORS, BETH SAW A LARGE PLAZA THAT OPENED wide. She was surprised. The activity was not so much frightening as bustling, commercial, lively, with a wide assortment of people, Merchants, grizzled mountain men, trappers, travelers, and teamsters. Dozens of Native men, some in shirts and some bare-chested, others of mixed race in white men's clothing, and clusters of Native women out shopping with broods of bright-eyed children balancing baskets of edibles on shoulder poles. And everywhere eagerly crowding in were hundreds of would-be gold miners, most young men sporting fresh beards, all feverishly buying supplies for that last, long hard push to California. They had no experience, Ezra knew, just odd maps, rumors and hearsay.

The wagon party stood as one just inside the gate for a moment to get their bearings. There were three main channels of commerce, wide market lanes to the left and right and an open, crowded but less organized center.

"Shop carefully," Ezra said. "Remember, there will be no more towns or similar market settlements between here and California, that's seven hundred hard miles. Get provisions for your family that can last."

Before they walked off, Ezra waved his hands overhead. "Your attention, please. The Captain and I will be meeting with Grant, the owner-proprietor of the Fort, to discuss supplies and get good prices for things you don't see, while the rest of you shop for food. Creighton and Brose will join you shortly. They left earlier to select and tag fresh oxen in the pens near the fort. Now, for safety please stay together in groups and don't let your children wander off."

He turned to Beth. "The Captain and I should be no more than an hour or so. If you need us, we'll be right up there in that corner office." He pointed to the second story running along the back wall of the fort, built Mexican-style, with a porch overhang and a railing. "Come get me if you need me. Just barge in."

Beth glared at him. "Forget something?" She pointed.

"Oh, yes, of course. Thanks." He waved. "James, come here, son. I want you in charge of protecting your sisters. Watch Camille and Maddie—call her Pablo—like a hawk. Keep your wits about you. Remember there are five of our men within quick shout if you need help. McGrath and his son Tad close by. See them? Reverend and son David right over there, along with Burns. Brose and Creighton are just now entering the fort. Got it?" James nodded. Beth smiled.

They'll be safe in numbers, he reasoned.

AS HE WALKED OFF, BETH CONFERRED WITH OTHERS WHO HAD NOT wandered off about where to start. Along the right side of the fort, merchants were selling fresh meat—deer, elk, buffalo—cutting and stitching leather, and hammering iron. They agreed the left side looked more inviting, lined with tents, stalls, lean-tos, and tall wagons piled high with goods. It had the rich frenzy of urban life that Beth loved. Almost a circus atmosphere. Merchants yelling over one another, stepping in front of their stalls to hawk a profusion of goods. Beth could see blankets, flour, fresh greens, roots, vegetables, purgatives, harnesses. Farther up the lane, some Natives were parading some small, muscular horses in a circle of onlookers.

"Vegetables!" Miriam shrieked. She took Beth by the hand as the group rushed forward and started rummaging through boxes of fresh greens and piles of turnips, onions, and beets. Even potatoes, squash, peppers. They haggled over the price of cabbages and moved to the next vendor.

Maddie and James were drawn toward a pitchman selling gold-finding sticks not ten yards away in the open center. "Stay close," Beth shouted. Camille looked about, dropped onions into her basket and hurried after them, taking Maddie's hand. "Pablo, don't wander off like that."

The man waved a supple willow stick over the ground, weaving it back and forth, searching like a snake's tongue. When it got near the secretly buried gold nugget, the stick twitched with a life of its own and struck the dirt. He dug it out and held it up, to cheers.

The man with the black hat and red band bought one and held it out to Maddie who instinctively backed up. Camille yanked her away firmly and rejoined Beth. "Be careful of that man, Maddie. He's too interested in you. Could be dangerous. Understand?" Maddie nodded and they moved back into the swarm around the fresh produce.

EZRA LED THE CAPTAIN TO THE BACK OF THE FORT, THEN UP THE rickety stairs, charred on one side, to the second story landing. He peered into the open door to Grant's office, a place Ezra knew well, and knocked. The large room was empty—dark, with only one small window and a candle on the hand-hewn desk. He called out, "Hello, Richard. It's Ezra."

Grant's wife, an Iroquois woman, never seemingly fond of Ezra, came through the side door from their apartment into the office. Tall, dark, with graying hair pulled away from a strong face. She pointed to the chairs in front of Grant's desk and looked askance at Ezra.

Five minutes later, a portly man with a barrel grin entered the room. Grant gave Ezra a firm handshake. He and Ezra and Brose went back a long way, but Grant was mercurial. Not just the chief trader for the Northwest Hudson Bay Company, but the man who effectively owned the fort. For friends, he could get the best of everything, from fresh oxen and food to spare parts. But first, deference had to be paid. The Captain's presence was a much-needed symbol of authority.

"Charles," said Ezra, "let me introduce Captain Richard Grant, commandant of the fort. And Richard, this is Captain Charles Winthrop, leader of our train. He and Zach Taylor fought together in Mexico."

They gripped hands and stared at each other. This was Grant's domain, his kingdom. He wasn't really a military officer but liked the trappings and respect of military authority.

"Sit!" said Grant.

"Brose—"

"Aye, he was here early this morning with your short list," said Grant, rolling his "*errs*" with a rotund Scottish burr. "Oxen, you want? Well, *theerre*'s a tough one."

He walked behind his desk, sat down, and leaned back with the air of a potentate. "So give me your full order."

The Captain leaned across the desk and handed him two pages of itemized supplies.

Grant read it fast, then put on his spectacles and studied it. After a few minutes, he lifted his head. "We've got everything, and I can give you a good price—at least for these times—but oxen?"

Ezra knew the man to be a cagey dealer. They were taking no chances. "Brose scouted your corrals this morning," he told Grant, "so I know what you have."

"He did, did he?" Turning his head to the spittoon, he finished his thought. "Man's a liar as surely as his name is *not* Ambrose Two Eagles."

"He said you had some good stock on hand. Twelve fresh, maybe more."

"You see that crowd out there," said Grant. "Nothing like it since the Oregon Fever in '44 and '45. You remember, Ezra, you was in the middle of it. But these ain't Oregon homesteaders. This gold is bringing out every greedy ferret from Tennessee and Missouri. I can hardly keep supplies on hand. And animals—mules, oxen especially—are impossible to keep. You want six fresh? How fresh?"

"Eight, full strength. We want to swap out three of ours—healthy, just overworked, need a month of rest. And pay gold for six. That's nine for eight."

"Mules I got. Extra wagons I got."

"Mules can't handle the Big Push."

"They can if . . . well, hell, you know that, Ezra, but them other greenhorns out there don't."

Ezra switched the subject. "I saw some slaves out there in chains. And a man who looks like a slaver, black hat, red fur trim. Know him? Is he buying slaves for California?"

"That's Turpin. Buying? Ha. Stealing more like it. I thought you knew him. He came in here two weeks ago, maybe longer. Asking about you of all people."

"Asking what?"

"Asking if I know'd ya. Seen ya. He's part of a bandit family. Got a camp north of here a few miles. Him and three grown sons, one cousin. Now rounding up Black men and stray Indian women that wander by. Since the exclusion laws, blacks trying to get out of Oregon head right into their hands. Free or slave, they don't care. All bring a big price. But bad for my business here."

The Captain put his hand flat on the desk and slid it toward Grant. "Do I understand correctly—this Turpin family is rounding up blacks for shipment to California?"

"Sorry business, but he ain't alone. Slave masters passing through tell me they intend to do to gold what they did for cotton. Plantations. They promise these poor Black men if they behave, don't run, and work hard digging gold for them for a year, they can buy their freedom. But they're cheats. I don't think—"

"How much is that?" asked the Captain.

"Ezra knows more about this than I do. But, say a man pulls an average twenty dollars a day from the river, that's seven thousand a year to start. Get yourself ten slaves and you raise a lifetime fortune in one year. Tempting, got to admit." Grant licked his finger and made a mark in the air, tossed back a shot of whiskey, and poured another to the top. "A real slaver's paradise, this newly captured California. That's—"

The Captain slammed the desk with his fist. "Over my dead body! Southern slavers will not prevail in California!" Grant's whiskey spilled onto his lap.

Grant stood angrily, brushing his pants, and called for his wife to come clean it up. She hurried in with a rag, another decanter, and some hard biscuits.

The Captain leaned toward Ezra and whispered, but with his passion rising, loud enough for Grant to hear. "If it comes to war, and it might, Zach Taylor is on our side. I know the man. A slaveholder himself but wants no extension into these new lands. I have his word. That's why I'm going to California. Would appreciate your help when we get there, Ezra."

Finally, Ezra understood the Captain. It wasn't gold or land driving him west. He was an ardent abolitionist but had kept it under wraps. Maybe Beth already knew; she was so close to Miriam.

CAMILLE HAD FINALLY STARTED TO RELAX AND ENJOY THE CARNIVAL atmosphere. It was such a welcome change after months of open, empty land. She had longed for a real city, a town, but this would have to do. At least there was an abundance of food, even fresh milk, meat, butter, and bread. Games, gambling, and swarms of young men with curious, eager eyes that sought her out as they passed. Even with faces hidden behind fresh beards, their attention reminded her of Louisiana.

A pitchman stood in front of a large tent, his foot resting on a leg bone the size of a tall man. Above the tent, a charcoal-scrawled sign: "*Dragon Bones. Biggest Bones on Earth. Ten cents.*"

The pitchman, seeing them approach, tipped his head back, and spread his arms in theatrical welcome. "Step right in. Dragons large enough to make an elephant look the size of a dog. And I got the jaw-bone, snout and skull inside to prove it. Ten cents. Dazzle you."

"Real dragons?" asked Maddie.

"You bet. Living in the Snake River Valley, just over yonder." He pointed west. "They especially like wagons heading to California. At night, they stick their long snouts into the canvas and eat the trave-lers—especially little girls—less'n these travelers wear a special bag of herbs around their neck. Bags cost a dollar. Got a few left."

"It's a lie," said Beth, pointing at the bone. "Carved by locals. Let's pass."

Doc ran his hand along the femur, dug in his nail, leaned down for close inspection. "No, this is real bone. I'd personally like to go in." He turned to the pitchman. "Forty cents. For all seven of us."

"Fifty."

Doc ignored him and turned, speaking to Camille and Maddie. "They're ancient reptiles. Not dragons, as we think of dragons. And the new scientific name is *dinosaur*. I've read some of the papers of Sir Richard Owen . . . most interesting."

"All right. Forty-five," said the pitchman. "But you go in two at a time. Don't want them knocked over."

Doc and Sarah went first, then Miriam and Beth. Beth emerged still trying to convince Miriam and Doc that they were fakes.

Camille, Maddie, and James took their turn. Once inside, flap closed, Maddie froze and Camille felt a surge of terror race through her own blood staring at a skull the height of her head and longer than her outstretched arms. It was propped on two small stumps. They walked around the skull, touching it here and there, tracing the inside of the huge nostrils and eye sockets with their fingers. A piece of giant jaw-bone lay on the ground, still holding a few rapacious teeth.

James wiggled one tooth the size of his hand and put his palm on the point. He invited Maddie over. She ran her finger down the serrations on one side of the tooth.

A flap at the back of the tent opened up, and a man they hadn't seen before waved them forward. "The rest are in here. Even bigger bones," he said. Camille glanced at the front of the tent, then ducked her head under the flap in the back. Maddie followed, James in the rear. Camille remembered Ezra telling her about the monster bones he saw riding through the open northlands. He'd come across them suddenly, pieces of massive bone protruding like tree trunks from washes and ravines or cemented into outcroppings of rock.

WITH THE WHISKY CLEANED UP, GRANT SAT DOWN AND SLAPPED HIS palm hard on the desk. "Well then, let's talk oxen! I'll give you five."

"Ten," said Ezra, standing up. "And two new wagons." He thumped a heavy bag of gold dust on the desk. "That's enough for six. Rest on credit."

"Credit? Wait, you fox. You said eight, with three of yours in swap and payment for six in gold."

"Terms changed," said Ezra.

"Horseshit. Nine it is! With three swaps and gold for six. Plus two good wagons. Deal?"

"Deal." Ezra smiled at the Captain.

Grant walked to the office door and whistled. He handed a breathless young man the list of supplies—rope, hickory spokes, canvas, repair tools, wheel rims, planks, sardines, choice cuts of buffalo meat. "Everything on here. And yes, eight oxen, and fresh ones," he commanded. "Do right by my friends."

At that moment, Beth burst through the door past Grant in panic, screaming. "Ezra, Help! Camille and Maddie have disappeared! Been taken! James was clubbed, he's hurt."

Ezra and the Captain grabbed their weapons and bolted for the door, but Grant raced forward and beat them to the stairway. "Listen, damnit! Is one white? Little one Black?"

They stopped. Grant glanced around to make sure no one was listening and motioned them back into his office. Beth hustled back inside as well, breathing heavily, tears running down her cheeks.

"I forgot. Turpin was ask'n about two girls might be traveling with you. Older white one, younger small, Black, he said. That's what I remember. If it's his slavers what stole'm, I know where he took them. I can help. I hate the bastard." He walked to his desk and spread out a piece of paper, started drawing.

Ezra's heart was pounding, watching Grant draw a crude map of the slavers' camp. Ezra's rage and fear made it hard to listen. The Captain, ever the cool military man, studied the map, listened carefully to Grant's description.

"I'll get you more accurate, detailed map, this afternoon," said Grant. "After I send out my Bannock, my best spy. He misses nothing, remembers everything, moves like a ghost. If your girls are there, he'll find them. Now, you didn't hear any of this from me. Agreed?" He looked at them with a worried expression.

"Agreed."

"Turpin we already talked about. There are five total and a sixth maybe, but he's never been seen. Their camp is in a good defensive position, two miles north. The only way to take them is by surprise." He drew a second map—trail, outcroppings, forest, boulders, tents, and wagons. "They have a hidden sentry in a tree, don't know where. One you'll never see or find. I'll have him taken out."

"Who'll kill him?" Beth asked.

"Better you don't know. It'll be done quietly. No gunshot. And he'll send you a signal when finished. Probably an arrow hitting a tree above your head. He'll know exactly where you are. Sometime after midnight, depends on the moon. So be in place."

⇒ 26 ⇐

THE RESCUE

Raid on the slavers' camp

That night, shortly after 1:00 am, the rescue team crouched under a tall pine on the edge of the slaver stronghold, with hands, faces, necks streaked with green juices and dirt. The sky was with them, Ezra thought, the moon but a sliver hidden by clouds.

Shzz. Thock. A long swift arrow, still vibrating in the tree ten feet above their heads brought them to their feet. Their signal from the Bannock meaning the sentry was dead. That left five. They silently cheered with raised fists, then conferred without words, checked their gear.

Then fanned out, moving as silent as the shadows among the boulders, outcroppings, and pockets of pine toward their designated targets.

Ezra crawled the last ten yards around a boulder to the front of the tent, pistol in one hand, knife in the other. It was partially open, the flap obscured by a pine bough with a trip wire tied to the man's ankle. The foot twitched, as if he were running in a dream, his breathing heavy, raspy. Ezra sheathed his knife; no precious seconds were needed to cut the canvas. He figured in a single lightning move he could dive over the trip wire straight into the tent and land fully on his target, Turpin, the leader and patriarch of the family gang.

He waited to let the others get into final positions. Squeezing his fist, he imagined Turpin's lean, muscled neck in his grasp. "Be careful, the man is old but not frail," Grant had told him. Turpin was surprisingly strong and agile for a sixty-year-old, with the instincts of a killer. "Capture him quickly," Grant advised, "and his sons and that cousin might surrender."

Ezra closed his eyes to let his mind search the darkness for Camille and Maddie. They were out there, within shouting distance. He could feel them in the night air. His head turned slowly right to left and stopped. *There.* His heart jumped. *We're coming.*

Another minute. When the Captain's signal came—a chittering sound—the five would attack as one. Each man would have two seconds to surprise, seize and, if necessary, kill his slaver.

Brose was in place. He had said he wanted Turpin, but settled for Elam, the eldest son, who slept with a twelve-inch knife and could twist himself around you like a serpent, according to the Bannock spy, then jab for your kidneys. "I'll take him. I know the move," Brose said.

Ezra looked around for the others. The light was dim but he caught sight of the Captain's face moving toward Quin, reputed to be the most ruthless and reckless of the lot. Creighton would take Ferris, the second son and quickest draw, who slept with a pistol next to his head. McGrath, a bull of a man himself, was now on his belly crawling toward Shep, the strongest but slowest.

Grant's Bannock spy had drawn them a detailed map, showing exactly who slept where and the best approach to the various tents. The captives were all in the rear of the site, Black men chained to the wagon wheels and Native women bound and gagged inside the wagons. Quin, he warned them, might not be in his tent. While the others invariably returned to their tents after drinking and cavorting, Quin often fell asleep with the women. But by this hour, all would be asleep, their faith placed in their sentry high in the trees—the one now with an arrow through his heart.

Sound of a rifle being cocked, and Ezra froze. *Had someone awakened?* He held his breath, listening. Moments passed, but he heard only silence and wind, a small scampering animal. It must have been one of their own young men, he realized. Forty paces to the rear, hidden in the boulders, were McGrath's son, Tad, and the Reverend's son, David. They were positioned as second tier, sharpshooters to take down any slaver who escaped.

A badger growl, the Captain's prep signal, meaning everyone was in place. The attack was imminent. Ezra braced himself, quivering. Then the nervousness, fear, and anger flowed out of his body. He was suddenly calm, almost serene, a state of mind he had learned in the wilderness. Silence.

Chitter.

Ezra lunged like a wolf over the trip wire straight into the tent, landing hard on the old man, knocking the wind out of him. He felt the seizure of the body in panic, wild swing of the man's arms groping the ground, searching for a weapon, anything. Turpin tried to regain his breath to yell, but Ezra cracked his skull with his pistol. He went limp, groaning. Ezra rolled him over, stuffed a rag in his mouth, and tied his arms behind his back. Then, hobbled the man's legs with a rawhide tether so he could not run.

All around him, Ezra heard the sounds of struggle, grunts and shouts, scuffles of men fighting in the dirt. A single scream, a pistol shot, then another.

A panicked voice and the sound of running boots not fully laced. "Pa!"

A rifle cracked. "Missed him," a young voice said. "There. Hiding at ten o'clock." Another shot.

Ezra yanked the old man out of the tent, propped him up like a shield and put a pistol to his head. He cocked it. "Come out! I've got Turpin. Your Pa's about to die."

No answer. He saw that Brose had Elam on his knees, arms bound. Both men were bloody. Brose held his side, waved away Ezra's look. Creighton had the red-bearded Ferris flat on the ground, unconscious or dead. McGrath was standing over Shep, who was bent over in pain, wincing through a gag.

But the Captain and his target, Quin, were nowhere to be seen.

"Captain?" Ezra yelled. There was no answer. "Quin," Ezra shouted as loud as he could, "I'm gonna shoot your Pa, less'n you come out." He shook the old man by the neck. "Tell him to surrender."

"Fuck ya."

Suddenly, flashes in the night, a rapid exchange of gunfire behind the boulders where Tad and David were stationed.

"Got him," the Captain said, paused . . . then shouted. "David, get Doc up here. Fast! Run! Tad's been hit!" They had positioned Doc a few hundred yards to the rear, on his horse, ready for emergencies.

The Captain carried Tad into the open, laid him on the ground, and cut open his shirt. The boy was groaning, squirming, bleeding from a bad stomach wound. Blood was spurting.

The Captain stuffed Tad's shirt in the wound and pressed down hard, while McGrath cradled his son's head, his voice choking. "Dear God, please! Hold on, son. You'll make it. My beloved boy, look at me. Look at me!" Tad's eyes wandered.

Turpin squirmed and kicked. "Where's my boy? Quin?" he gasped through the stranglehold Ezra had on his throat.

"He's dead," the Captain said.

The old man lurched backwards. Ezra threw him into the dirt and went to help Doc.

Tad was now gasping, choking, blood streaming from his mouth. Doc pulled the shirt out of the wound and probed to cut off the flow of blood. He pinched something with his fingers and asked Ezra to hand him his sutures. He tried to sew with one hand, holding the vessel, artery, organ, whatever it was under the pool of blood with his other hand.

Tad stared at his father, moved his mouth, tried to talk. He gurgled blood. His eyes opened wide, then stopped. His mouth went slack. McGrath shook the boy, moaning, caressing his face. His head dropped onto his boy's. His eldest, his namesake.

Doc stepped away, covered in blood, shaking his head.

Ezra pointed to Brose. "Help him." Doc forced Brose to the ground and pulled up his shirt. It was a clean, shallow knife wound, he said, just above the hip with no major damage, no artery, no tendon. He poured whiskey on it, sewed it up, and wrapped it. "Don't bounce on it. Keep that bandage clean."

A FEW MINUTES LATER, EZRA AND BROSE PROCEEDED SEPARATELY and cautiously toward the wagons, in case the intelligence was wrong and there was still another slaver hiding. Ezra saw two Black men chained to wagon wheels, and another tied to a tree nearby, looking terrified, squirming to hide.

In contrast, one chained to a wheel stared boldly at Ezra. He tossed his head to the right. "The new ones you want be back there. Now don't forget about us."

"Any more slavers back here?"

"If you got five, you got'm all. Name's Angus. Unchain us and we go quietly. We just want a chance to run." He rattled the neck chain. "Keys in that second wagon."

While Brose went to the second wagon, Ezra peered into the first at two native women bound and gagged. Crow, he guessed by the beadwork. He climbed in, cut the ropes and yelled for Brose to come talk with them. But as soon as the ropes came off, they scooted to the far end of the wagon. They looked at Ezra fearfully, then jumped out and ran for the woods.

Brose found two more Native women in the second wagon, and the keys. He cut them loose and went to free the Black men. "They can help us wreck this camp," he said to Ezra.

The third and fourth wagons were filled with supplies.

By the last wagon, Ezra's heart was racing with fear, eyes stinging with sweat. *What if they're not in there?* His hand was shaking as he opened the canvas. In the dim light, among scattered supplies, he saw Maddie and Camille lying on their sides, bound hand and foot, with hoods over their heads. Probably gagged.

"It's Ezra. We're here to take you home."

They squirmed and yelled through their gags as he climbed in. They clearly didn't recognize his voice, tight and strained as it was. Ezra took a breath to settle himself and to speak more calmly. "Me, Ezra. It's over," he said. "You're going to be OK. Beth is waiting." Ezra, smiling for the first time, watched their bodies relax. He yanked the hoods off and stared at their terrified eyes, bruised faces, brimming with tears. They blanched at his painted face.

"It's me. Now, easy, Maddie, don't move while I cut your gag. There." He rubbed the sore red marks around Maddie's mouth while she tried to talk. "Shh, shh, take your time." She couldn't get her voice back. Raw from screaming, he guessed.

"Camille, stop squirming." He cut and removed her gag, which had been aggressively shoved into her mouth. She coughed and gulped for air, trying to scream. "Easy now, get your breath."

As soon as he cut the rawhide around Maddie's wrist and feet, she jumped into his arms, sobbing.

"Wait, Maddie, let me free Camille. I need both hands." She sat back. He cut Camille's ropes. "There. Now . . . now. Let me check." He examined Maddie's neck and face while she hung onto him. "Are you hurt? Either of you? Where?"

Bruises, abrasions, he decided, but no broken bones or puncture wounds.

Camille leaned her face against Maddie's back, still struggling to get her breath. "We heard shots," she said.

"We killed one of the slavers." Ezra hesitated. "Captured the others."

"Who came with you? Brose? Captain?"

"And Creighton, McGrath and his . . . and David."

How was he going to tell her? Tad had been interested in her from the moment he first saw her. He wanted to come on this mission. Wanted to prove himself to her. And now this.

"What's wrong?" Camille asked. "Why are you looking that way? Your eyes darting?"

"I'm sorry, I don't know how . . . Camille, I'm sorry . . . Tad was killed."

She broke. A wounded scream that cut right through him. She covered her face and turned away, moaning in anguish. Ezra put a blanket around her shoulders and held her, rocking her. She didn't resist. His heart was pounding. Tears were pushing into his own eyes. He had been consumed all day by the fear that he had lost the two of them. Now this. Her pain. And McGrath's pain. It was awful. He could see McGrath's anguished face in his mind, contorted in horror. Her face was buried in his shoulder.

"Let's go find the others. Let them know you're safe."

"God, forgive me," said Camille, her voice quavering. "I never meant to hurt him. This is all my fault."

"No, Camille, you did nothing wrong. He came to rescue you. He fought for you. Courageously. He'd be so happy we found you safe."

ONE BY ONE, THEY FREED THE BLACK MEN AND REPLACED THEM with the four remaining slavers. They tied their hands and feet, then chained them to the wheels using the same iron collars and ankle clamps. The slavers were silent, fearful, averting their eyes, afraid to draw attention—all except Turpin—as four freed Black men and six angry men in camouflage milled around them in semi-darkness, spitting on them, cursing them. All now brandishing weapons, poking at them, and after Tad's death, talked openly about vengeance, killing them.

Turpin jostled his chains and shouted at Ezra. "Fuck you. Jenkins never gives up. Me neither. Me and my boys be coming after you."

"Doubtful," said Ezra calmly. "Grant says there are two hungry wolf packs hanging around here. And I'm making sure they come for you first. Then your boys." He stuffed a rag in Turpin's mouth, lifted his shirt, and with his knife swiped a long, shallow gash across the man's middle. Not into the organs, just deep enough to bleed slowly, soak his shirt. "Want you to draw them." Then he put a bag over Turpin's head.

"Wolves. You won't see them. You'll hear padded feet, a guttural growl, sniffing. Feel their breath on you. Hear their snarling hunger. The touch of their muzzles on your stomach. Licking the blood. Then feel them eating you from the inside out."

The Captain and Brose carefully checked the bindings. Then they gagged and hooded the rest to ensure their silence and increase their disorientation. The slave camp was two miles from the fort. Their strong defensive position, Ezra knew, would be their downfall. It might be a week before anyone came looking, if anybody cared.

Angus, the one who seemed to be the natural leader of the freed men, agreed to the Captain's plan. The freemen would take everything of value from the slavers—their horses, weapons, valuables, boots, gloves, food—and flee to Canada. It was closer than California and safer. Heading back to the Oregon coast where they had started was asking for enslavement.

"God speed," said Ezra, as he shook Angus's hand.

EZRA AND BROSE WRAPPED TAD'S BODY IN CANVAS AND LAID HIM over Doc's horse for the long walk back to camp. McGrath continued to stumble over rocks and roots until Ezra held him up. He had McGrath put his massive arm around his shoulders for support. Brose took the other arm. The girls walked with Doc and David, talking about their ordeal and Tad's death. David held Camille up as she stumbled forward.

The families would be up around the campfire, waiting anxiously for their return. The train was now packed, fully provisioned thanks to Grant, and ready to leave at first light if not before.

4:00AM. BETH CLIMBED OUT OF THE WAGON AFTER CALMING THE girls, listening to their agony and terror, and finally getting them to sleep. She saw a half dozen campfires lighting the circled wagons. The Reverend and a small crowd gathered around the grieving McGraths.

Most children were initially asleep, or so it seemed, with so little chatter in the air, then their reverie suddenly broke open with joy for the rescued girls and cries in the night for the dreaded news about Tad. No one could go back to sleep.

Ezra was folding his tent when Beth touched his shoulder from behind. "They're exhausted, finally down, sleeping. You should get some sleep yourself, at least an hour or two."

"Maybe," he said. "How are they? How are you? I'm still shaking with rage and relief."

"Me too. I need to go back and lay down next to them in case they wake up. They weren't raped, I found out that much, thank God," she said. "Bruised. Turpin told his men that Jenkins had laid down the law—no harm, no rape, or the bounty is forfeit."

"Sooner we get away from this place, the better," said Ezra. "McGrath doesn't want to bury his son anywhere near the fort. I told him there was a serene, secluded place about thirty miles ahead that he might like—water, trees, beautiful formations—where we can hold a proper funeral. His wife, Deidre, seems to like the idea. Poor family is sick with grief."

Ezra lifted his head and put up his hand for silence. They listened to wolves howling in the distance. Not just one, but a pack. The families stopped as one, lifted their heads, then broke into cheers.

"Brose is up there keeping guard, just to make sure no one rides up to find those slavers alive," Ezra said. "After we get a good start on the trail he'll catch up. He has a way with wolves. He's probably leading them to the feast."

"I'm sorry, I need to get back to the girls.

"What's wrong?" he said.

"Yesterday, after entering the fort you left us unguarded, while you went off to negotiate. And we walked right into the slavers' trap. One that, had you been there, wouldn't have closed."

"I put James in charge of the girls' protection," Ezra said, embarrassed.

"He's thirteen, walked in innocent and was clubbed out of sight. I'm just saying, if you had been there as our protector, not off negotiating for wheel spokes . . ."

"You're blaming me? I feel as awful as you do."

"If you'd stayed with us, you would have smelled the trap."

"Yeah, I might well have. But those men were determined. We would have had that shootout one place or another."

"I thought we agreed after you disappeared to save Johan, you wouldn't be so headstrong. Now I need to go back to comfort the girls. In the future don't be so careless with their lives."

She walked away in a huff, then turned. "Oh, I almost forgot. I overheard Maude Simpson whisper to her husband after the girls returned. 'I guess that means the reward is still open.' Maude and Oliver. Must be the ones with the ad."

⇒ 27 ⇐

HUMBOLDT RIVER

Lifeline through the Nevada lands

Maddie picked a half-buried book from the sand, wiped off the dust, and fingered the red leather cover that was curling and cracking from the desert sun. The inside was still soft and inviting, interleaved with notes, poems, beautiful quill-work, drawings, and personal letters. She'd keep it, even though it was falling apart, the pages pulling away from the spine. Even though Beth would almost certainly say no.

Her eye caught on a letter carefully penned on blue paper, inscribed to "My Beloved Marjorie." She'd read it tonight, she thought. Snuggled against Camille's shoulder by the fire, where the two of them would imagine Marjorie and the man who wrote the note and make up their story. Maybe that was his grave up on the ridge in the distance. One of the small crosses standing against the blue desert sky, like tiny people with their arms outstretched, inviting her to come visit.

Every day, there were more of these hasty graves and tossed treasures. The desert, she came to realize, was a place of death and wonder.

She glanced over at Camille, who was wandering through the large field of cast-offs, picking up things people had thrown overboard to lighten their wagons as they became desperate. Camille held up a dish, then another one out of a crate.

The red book had been lying next to a silver tea tray half-buried in the sand with a bullet hole in the center. Maddie stared at it. *Who would shoot a tray?* Her sister might. Camille was out shooting everything after dinner, practicing with Ezra. Hating slavers, shooting Tad's killers.

Maddie shouted to Camille to come look, but truth was she yelled to her sister every few minutes to feel closer. Ever since Fort Hall, Maddie lived in terror that a slave patrol would come riding hard through the desert, snatching up Black girls. "Can't happen," said Beth, and Ezra promised it wouldn't, and Maddie wanted to believe them, but still . . . in her dreams, they came. Slavers thundering on huge horses, shouting, leering, and grabbing, and she could not run away fast enough. They'd snatch her off the ground screaming and kicking and she'd wake up, shaking. Night after night. Camille would tuck her blanket, kiss her, soothe her. Beth would murmur softly and pat her to sleep. Beth said she would stay in the wagon and sleep with the two of them, as long as they had the night fears. And seeing Turpin's leering face in their dreams. "Don't rape them," they heard Turpin warn his men when they opened the flap and peered in. "Jenkins's orders," Turpin yelled. "If you do, obliged to shoot ya."

Still holding the book, Maddie, forgetting Ezra's warning about touching metal exposed to the desert sun, reached down for the glittering, blister-hot tray with the bullet hole. Instant searing pain so sharp she yanked her arm away, yowling and flung the red book up into the desert wind. Dumbfounded, still dancing about, she watched the pages, poems, and notes fly upward like freed birds. Racing after the drawings, she got a few as they swooped across the desert floor, but watched the blue note bend and twist, rising on wings higher and higher over the desert. On its way to Marjorie.

"Are you all right? Are you hurt?" Camille shouted above the wind. Then, smiling, held up what appeared to be a porcelain ball, perhaps a large teacup or a creamer.

Maddie poured some canteen water on her sensitive finger tips and continued exploring. She kicked a small feather bed covered with dust and dozens of tiny bush birds pulling apart the cover. They flew off with bits of cotton tatters and disappeared into the thick willows that lined the slough on the other side of the trail. The smell of the slough—she'd never get used to it—made her sick. Even at this distance she could not escape the stench, the rot and slime carried on the wind. Soon, their fun time would be over, and she and Camille would be walking straight into that vile swamp to fetch water.

This precious time to wander among forbidden treasures was their reward. Ezra was proud of them for bearing up, and Beth gave them an hour every afternoon to rummage through the windblown discards scattered along the Humboldt River. Now that they were hundreds of miles into the desert, the pickings were richer, just as Ezra said they would be. Things more personal, more cherished. The last possessions dying people tossed overboard.

Maddie lifted odds and ends from the dust with the toe of her boot, trying to find something interesting without burning herself.

Her face brightened when she saw an ornate trunk half-buried in a depression behind a full sage, as if someone had tried to hide it. She walked around it, yelling to Camille.

Grabbing the leather handle, she pulled it from its shallow grave and tugged it up to more level ground. Using a tuft of cotton from the mattress she dusted off the top and sides, then buffed the trunk to bring out the sheen. It gleamed with a finish of cream and blue embossed metal, banded with finely crafted oak. With a rock, she smashed the small, engraved lock, then knelt down beside the trunk, careful not to touch the hot metal, and slowly opened the lid.

The interior was lined with satin that gave off a faint scent of rose. She unbuckled the tooled leather straps and peeled back the linen dust cover to reveal a meticulously folded green silk dress. Maddie wiped her hands on her buckskins, lifted it out carefully and stood, letting it fall to its full length.

She shouted. "Over here! Dresses!" Camille looked up and waved, as if she'd be there soon. The woman who owned the trunk must have been petite, probably a few inches taller than Maddie and as tiny-waisted. Maddie imagined her with raven black hair and porcelain skin, then changed the skin color to rose-brown like her own, and replaced the woman's eyes with her own, along with her own smile, cheekbones, neck. She pretended flirting in a full-length mirror.

Maddie folded the green dress in half and laid it across the open lid. The next was blue and just underneath, the edge of something maroon. She wiped her hands again on her buckskins, then carefully folded back layers of dresses and petticoats and bustles to look at the hair accessories, fans, a small hand mirror, a bottle of perfume, and a pair of soft night slippers embroidered with blue beads the size of salt grains. Maddie tucked the slippers inside her buckskin blouse. She knew she wasn't supposed to bring anything back to the wagon, but these were small and light, and perhaps Beth wouldn't notice.

The deeper she went into the trunk, the more it released its intoxicating aroma of perfume and powder. Maddie lifted up the clothing, put her face down deep in the trunk and pulled the dresses on top of her head. She took a deep breath, and then another, and closed her eyes.

The scent carried her into a fragrant parlor, filled with flowers and fountains and perfumed air, where her *mère* sat combing the tangles from her hair. She sponged away the dust on Maddie's face and let Maddie cry on her lap and tell her about the slavers that came after her every night in her dreams. "Shh," her *mère* said. "I'm here. Those men are gone, *chère*."

"I'm coming to find you, *ma mère*. Wait for me."

"Shh. You tend to your sister now."

Maddie heard Camille's voice, muffled. "I'm walking up behind you. Don't be scared. It's me."

She felt Camille's touch on her shoulder, and she slowly pulled her head from the trunk, blinking in the burning sunlight and the vile smell wafting from the slough. She wanted to crawl back down inside the trunk and stay there awhile.

"Isn't this beautiful," said Camille, handing Maddie a cream pitcher, nearly spherical, glazed with small red roses. It felt pleasantly rounded in Maddie's palm, fragile and nearly weightless. She ran the porcelain against her cheek and held it up to the light. It was as translucent as a thin shell and grew warm in her hand as the pitcher filled with sunlight. *Maybe on a cold night*, Maddie thought, *Camille could pour the sunshine on her feet.*

"It's the only unbroken piece in the entire crate," said Camille. "I love it. It reminds me of the *grande maison*. It makes me want to go home for breakfast, with soft boiled eggs and hot tea and Father's face."

"Don't say that!" Maddie pushed the creamer back at Camille. If anything could be worse than following the Humboldt River week after week into the bleak, broken desert, it would be returning to the slave quarters without her *mère*, facing their wicked father. She wished Camille had never told her he was her father. That hurt so bad.

"Don't look at me like that," Camille said. She ran her rough, blistered hand over Maddie's cheek. "I was just longing out loud. Just yearning for a break from the heat and this smell. You understand?"

"Can we keep the trunk?" Maddie asked. It just flew out her mouth. She knew better, but she had to say the magical words. Camille looked at her gently, smiled, then reached over Maddie's shoulder and pulled the blue dress from the trunk. She let it fall full length, held it against her waist. Then dropped it back inside.

"Not messy like that!" Maddie snapped. She pulled the blue dress out and folded it carefully, laid it in its proper place in the trunk, and then put the green one on top just as she had found it.

Camille apologized, then with Maddie's permission, tucked the frail pitcher into the folds of the dresses. She stepped back to let Maddie close the lid. Together, they pushed the trunk back into the depression behind the sage. Maddie threw holy dust on top to conceal it.

They stared at it silently as if they were burying a fine lady.

"I'll come back for her," said Maddie. "After we get to California."

Hand in hand they left for the Humboldt River across the trail and into the slough.

THE HUMBOLDT RIVER MADE NO SENSE IN THE NATURAL SCHEME OF things, Ezra told them. Rivers gather and grow wider and fuller as they flow towards the sea. But the Humboldt grows thinner, evaporating as it meanders three hundred and fifty miles into the desert bowl. "Never gets to the sea. It grows weaker and weaker and finally dies in a sinkhole," Ezra told them. "That's why the old guides call it the 'Humbug River.' We'll be at the Humboldt Sink in a week."

Camille watched Ezra walk toward them with his confident stride, carrying the awful oak sieve bucket with holes near the bottom.

He handed it to her and she took it at arm's length, repulsed by the smell.

"Are you all right?" He didn't wait for an answer, but instead took Camille by the hand and Maddie by the arm and pulled them in close. "Listen to me, you two. I want you to be especially careful out there today. It's thicker than yesterday, worse than anything we've seen. The mud has real sucking power. And it's filled with decaying oxen. You can walk on their backs to get across, or use what boards are left. But don't be careless. Don't hesitate for a second to pull on that safety line around your waist if you start to sink. James can free you up. Pull you out. Understand? Don't hesitate for a single second thinking you beat the mud."

He squeezed their wrists, as he did every day, to show them the force of the mud in that location. Today, the pressure was frightening. Camille rubbed her wrist when he was done. She was growing fonder of him. He was around more these days, more attentive, helping them adjust as conditions got harsher. Teaching her how to shoot. He said the worst was yet to come and he needed them to fight. "Needed," that's the word he used. She liked that he needed her. Wanted her. He was beginning to treat her, even love her, like a daughter. She needed that.

Their job this afternoon, like every afternoon, was to pack the bucket with fresh grass and weeds, work their way to the Humbug water, push the bucket down into the slime, let the water filter its way up through the grass, and draw it off into leather bags.

Ezra had taught them this technique weeks earlier, just as the Humboldt began to turn bad. "This damned river," he explained, "curls back on itself like a coiled snake, then cuts a new channel forward and leaves the coils to rot, to become water-logged sloughs. You two are the lightest in the family, so your job will be to walk the boards across the marsh-mud to fetch water. Can you do that?"

They had stood silent, hoping he would give them a different chore. But he didn't.

"Good," he said, as if they had agreed, then showed them how to filter the water. Not that it did any good. Day after day, the salts grew more concentrated, the slime thicker, the taste more foul. And just when Camille thought it couldn't get worse, it did. "You'll never get used to it," he said. "Just filter the worst of it. Drink it. Maddie, you hear me? Don't fight it. It will keep you alive. You may think you don't need it but you do."

Beth took Ezra aside as the girls left. "Ezra, I don't like this. Aren't there other sources of water less dangerous? Isn't there a better, safer trail? You're putting our girls in peril again and acting so casual about it. Maybe James could go for water and the girls manage the rescue line. Are you going to be close enough to help these girls if they begin to sink and scream? . . . I swear, Ezra, if anything happens to our girls out here, I'll never forgive you."

"They mean as much to me as they do to you," he said. "I am being careful. They're strong enough and agile enough to do this job. I've watched them and coached them day after day. It's hard, awful work, sure, but they are strong enough to do it. And, Beth, they're good at it. They need to feel useful, to share the burden. Can you stop hating me for Fort Hall? No, there's no other source of water out here. And no, there's no other route as direct as this one, and there is no other trail that has a stinking life-saving river running beside it."

WITH MADDIE TWO STEPS BEHIND, CAMILLE WALKED TO THE WALL of willow at the edge of the slough, blinking, gagging on the hot smell. Birds flew as she parted the bushes and peered in.

"Maddie, come on, be strong. Think about . . . well, killing slavers or rapists."

"No. Stop saying that."

Maybe this is God's punishment for Tad's death, Camille thought, as they worked their way through the willows, to the clumps of tall grass that blanketed the mire. Camille could feel the mud sucking at her feet, then curling over the top of her boots. The surface mud was hot from the sun, cooler underneath. She took Maddie's hand and waded through, just fast enough to keep from sinking. She gave two sharp tugs on the rope to tell James they were all right. He tugged back.

She climbed up on a line of boards placed there by earlier trains, then stepped onto the back of the first dead ox. She gave Maddie a hand up, and both stood frozen, appalled at the sight. Dozens of dead oxen, standing up, their swollen corpses half in and half out of the muck. Ezra said to use them like steppingstones. She hadn't any idea what he was talking about.

"Blessed Jesus, help me," said Maddie. "Do we have to?"

"Yes."

Thank you, Tad, for saving us, Camille thought, as they made their way forward, precariously balancing from one ox to the next. The air off the mud was putrid, hot, sweet. Flies swarmed where the oxen had split open at the mud level. Insects buzzed around their faces. Camille looked back every few steps to make sure Maddie was behind her. She followed dutifully, with an expression of disgust and fear.

"Help!"

Camille heard a slap and turned to see Maddie sprawled on the back of an ox. Her face pressed against the animal's crusted hide in the middle of a swarm of flies.

"Easy. Easy. Stop crying," said Camille, more harshly than she intended. She pulled Maddie to her feet, wobbling, and brushed the flies away from her face.

"You're going too fast," said Maddie. Then suddenly lurched and vomited, while Camille steadied her. She used her bandana to wipe Maddie's face.

"Shh, easy. Sorry. I won't rush. Now keep your balance. If you get dizzy, let me know, we'll sit down. You OK to move?" Maddie nodded. "Good. Hold on to me. Just a little farther." Maddie clutched the back of Camille's buckskin shirt. It was harder to balance with Maddie tugging, but Camille would bear up. Slow and steady. Thank God for these oxen lending their backs.

They jumped off the last ox onto some weathered planks resting on more solid ground, then followed the boards through the last thicket.

Finally, they stood face to face with a river that didn't move.

No, it was moving, just more slowly than yesterday. Still thick and milky-green but inching forward. Tendrils of algae clung to the shore, tangled together like fishermen's nets.

Camille kicked free a clear spot.

She pushed the bucket down into the thick soup and watched the filtered water slowly percolate to the top, a bubbling swill cooking in the desert sun. Maddie eased the water skin sideways and let it fill with the filtered water. They filled two, each a bit heavy and cumbersome.

It took the strength of both to pull the oak bucket from the sucking mud. Camille dug out the putrid, slime-saturated clumps of grass and threw them into the froth. She smelled her gloves. It took her mind back to the breath of that poisoned ox at the alkali pool. She rinsed them in the river broth and wiped them on her pants.

Leaving the bucket for the next run, each carried a leather sack of water back across the boards, across the puffy white stepping stones, through the mud marsh, to the wagon. They poured the water into a barrel, gathered more filter grass, tucked in their shirts, and returned for more water.

They made five round trips in the withering sun without stopping, getting faster with each run, then stopped for ten minutes, sat to catch their breath.

On their feet again before their muscles cramped, they mustered the energy to make another five runs before they collapsed and crawled into the late afternoon shade under the wagon.

Everything hurt and everything around them smelled of the vile mud, even the wagon wheels. Camille stared at the caked mud on the wheels as her eyes grew sleepy, thinking of James rolling the wagon through the edge of the slough to wet the wheels every day. "Wood needs to drink just as much as you do," he said, "to keep the rims tight."

Beth pushed a ladle of stinking water under the wagon. "Here, before you sleep. You need it."

Camille dreamt of relief from the sun, of the night desert cooling quickly, then dropping toward freezing when her body began shivering, and she'd roll over in her blankets and take the dream of her mother with her. She was seven. It was her birthday party, and she was wearing a hat with a blue feather when she blew out the candles. The world turned radiant when her mother kissed her upturned face.

That was the last birthday she ever saw her mother.

≫ 28 ≪

CROSSING THE GRAVEYARD

Desperate crossing, 1600 miles from trailhead

The thin green lifeline the train had been following for hundreds of miles through the desert and barren mountains finally ended in a great green smudge, the Humboldt Sink, where the river's slime cooked away in a desert bowl.

Just over the lip of that bowl, over the brown ridge to the west, they'd enter into what the old timers—the trappers and pioneers—called the Graveyard, where people and animals went mad and died in the sand.

Resting beside the Sink, Beth found it hard to breathe the afternoon air. Even as she rolled on her side in the shade from a piece of canvas Camille and Maddie had propped up over some low willows at the edge of the marsh. Her arms ached from carrying water. The girls were now off cutting grass for the animals, while James was force-feeding the oxen in preparation for tomorrow's journey into the Graveyard. The beasts lay on their sides next to the wagon, panting. Beth's eyes fluttered shut in the wretched heat.

"Beth? Where are you?"

She stirred awake and looked for Ezra's voice, mumbling to herself. "Over here, how many places are there to go around here?"

He suddenly loomed and handed her a leather water bag. "Have James fill this and hide it in the wagon. I want you to save it for emergency. For the very last day. We'll be pooling the water, but we'll run out. Every family will be doing the same."

She tried to read his eyes. They were comforting and full of purpose; a man in love with his job, as well as her and now with their alliance as family.

"I've been having these awful dreams," she said.

"Me too." He cut her off. "You'll have to keep Maddie and Camille watered. They'll be slowly dying out here but won't know it. You hear me?"

"I understand. Just get us through. I'll do my part. Just don't abandon us."

"Stop it. I'm with you the whole way. You know that. So don't doubt me. I know you're weary and frightened but listen up and focus. We're leaving tonight, not tomorrow." She gasped. "A shock, I know. I wanted to tell you before the Captain announces it at dinner. Please don't pass the word. Let him announce it."

"Tonight?" She shuddered. As long as it was tomorrow, it wasn't real. But today, well, tonight . . . *Dear God.*

"We'll travel at night when the desert is cool, and rest during the heat of the day. Conserve our strength and water that way."

THE WAGON TRAIN LEFT HURRIEDLY AFTER DINNER. AS THE SUN and the temperature dropped, the sudden flush of cool desert air lightened the families' step and mood. *Forty miles in four days, how bad could it be?* they chimed. *After four million steps, up and down mountainsides and across prairies, through crashing storms and thundering stampedes, what's a little desert?* They joked and sang, even whistled in the cool breeze as they entered the Graveyard.

At the top of the rise, Beth looked back at the Humboldt Sink, the only green spot in a vast sea of brown and gray. The last remnant of the river that had kept them alive. Walking away was like leaving a nasty relative, she thought. One you hated but who had fed you, kept you alive, and then after dinner showed you the door, spit on you, and said, 'Now git.'

The next river forty-fifty miles away, the Carson, Ezra assured her, would be entirely different. Fresh, loving, clean water, cold as ice, flowing down from the mountain rooftop of California.

AN HOUR BEFORE DARK, EZRA TOOK MADDIE'S HAND AND WALKED her away from the train to talk about staying alive, drinking as she was told, nothing more, nothing less. She knew this, had heard it repeatedly. Why was he telling her again? He was scaring her. He picked up rocks and handed them to her, explaining their stripes and color, some fractured from heat with sharp edges, others rounded as if tumbled about in water for eons, he said. His voice, she thought, sounded as if he were somewhere else.

He pointed to the high brown bluff to the south that extended for miles, as if she should care. He held her hand. That's where her thoughts flew, not to the high brown bluff, but to his warm hand, squeezing hers to the rhythm of his words.

"See that line up there . . . Just below the ridge . . . The white one . . . Does it look like a chalk line?"

He wanted her to nod, so she did.

"That's the kind of mark lake water leaves on a shoreline." He stretched his arms wide and turned in a circle. "This was once all under water, as far as you can see in every direction, and as high as that chalk mark. I'm sure of it. A massive lake, just imagine that, Maddie." He squeezed her hand again. "I wanted you to see it so you can tell your grandchildren. I don't know why, or how, a lake this big could come and go."

"Noah's flood?" she asked.

He laughed. "Maybe, just maybe. Promise me now that you will stay alive. For your sister. For Beth and myself. For yourself and all your wonderful life ahead. You must drink the water we give you. It will keep you alive. No cheating. Promise?"

He stared into her eyes until she nodded.

THE FAMILIES BRACED THEMSELVES AS THEY MOVED INTO nightfall. The land grew cold and the stars took over the sky. Huffing, the oxen kept their heads down and moved in slow rhythm through the dust while the travelers lifted their heads toward the heavens, trying to find a whiff of clean air and watching the stars appear in patches through the fog of dust kicked up by hooves and wagon wheels.

To the side of the trail in the starry dark, Camille pointed out the shadows of abandoned wagons, and Maddie waved at a simple wooden cross over a grave mound. They gagged on the scent of rotting carcasses. Before their fears could take over, Beth tried to calm them, "That smell? Likely mules or oxen, not people." The three stopped talking as their ears picked up a coyote miles off. Its lonely howl echoing through the empty hills.

At dawn, the train stopped to water, rest the oxen, take stock of their supplies, and let the young children out of the wagons to clear their lungs. The wind took the dust cloud away. Camille and Maddie dropped a blanket on the cold desert floor beneath the wagon and fell instantly asleep.

Beth, shuddering in the chill, covered them up, still amazed at what they could now endure. She drank a cup of the slime from the barrel and handed another cup to James, who no longer saw any point in dusting himself off.

Standing up straight and stretching her back, she looked at the muted landscape of gray, buff, and rust. It was an eerie, unfocused land, with no river to lead the eye, no mountain worth a second glance, just a trail through the chalky emptiness. *As if the world is hiding itself,* she thought.

Mercifully, the smell of carcasses was gone, and Beth walked away from the wagons into what looked like a field of snow. Reaching down, she picked up a handful of crusted white salt and threw it up to the winds, where it whisked away into the slanting morning light.

Everything screamed for water. Only one day out and her thirst had become an ever-present thought. She dreamed of the Carson River and imagined wading into that shimmering mirage of ocean now directly in front of her, rising from the earth, waving the air just above the horizon to tantalize her. *Come on in, the water's fine*, the mirage beckoned.

Back at the wagon, she climbed underneath next to the girls and dusty James and slept fitfully. By mid-afternoon, she was lying on her back in the shade of the wagon with her eyes wide open, her mouth agape, parched, gasping for air. She could feel the heat radiating off the sand, now creeping under the wagon.

Turning on her side, she began to squint at the desert, to see it for what it really was, a place that asked you to die. A place that waited for the water-borne creatures to fall on their faces and burst like balloons and desiccate, releasing their fluids to a land that would fight you to the death for a drop of your water.

Maddie startled awake in the blazing afternoon. Her tongue was so thick, she mispronounced words. "My *muth* is sticking *togesher*," she slurred. "I'm *aflaid* of *ma muth*."

"Easy, easy." Beth pulled her over and gave her an extra cup. "Don't worry, I have more. Drink, sweetie." Beth lay back down, praying for the cool night air to come back and relieve her. Ezra came by and tucked another leather bag of water under Beth's head. She took a sip and passed it to Maddie and Camille.

Food was of little interest. They wanted more water, but at Beth's insistence they chewed some dried meat and grease-filled cakes, made with the last of the precious flour from Fort Hall.

Miriam poked her head under the wagon. Beth tried to talk but she was afraid to let the moisture out of her mouth. "Shh," Miriam said with heavy lips, and handed Beth a secreted cup of water for herself and the girls. "I'll bring you more. You stay well." Blessed Miriam.

Ezra woke Beth from her dreams to give her and the girls a sip. Water was carefully measured out for the oxen, the children, and less for the men and women. Every vessel, barrel, leather sack, and canister had been put to use, but it was diminishing fast. Beth watched Camille pretend to drink hers, then hand it quickly to Maddie.

The Captain told everyone to sleep, to reduce physical movement during the torturous afternoon. They would leave as soon as the desert began to cool, the temperature dropping below one hundred degrees, a few hours before dark.

BY THE THIRD DAY, EVERYONE ON THE TRAIN TALKED WITH parched mouths about waterfalls, about the sound of rain falling on crops, about rivers and rushing streams they remembered, of pumps on the farm, of fountains in the cities, of canals and ditches, of lakes and ponds, of swimming and splashing, tossing water aside as if it were nothing. They handed their water dreams to each other likes small cups and drank the words. They shared memories, then held their noses and took their meager cup of Humboldt stench, salty but heaven-sent.

That evening the Captain pulled everyone together to talk about the march. "We're halfway across and the water is more than half gone. Ease up, and those of you who have been sneaking extra, stop it. We've got to keep the children and oxen alive."

Beth knew the rules. Maddie got more water than Camille and James, who were considered adults. *They're not adults*, she thought, *not really.* They were her children, for God's sake, at least in all manner that Beth cared about. She would find a way to sneak them some extra water like every other mother on the train. She had to stop Camille from giving hers to Maddie. She had to remain agile and alert to keep them all alive. She knew they'd gather strength from her.

Beth had never thought about dying of thirst before. Now, as her tongue swelled, her headaches mounted, and the moisture in her mouth no longer seemed to come, premonitions of death crept into her mind. She began to think about how wonderful saliva was. Every little bit was exquisite. Everybody said to save your urine for the animals, but she had none.

The Captain said they would leave within the hour, stop briefly twice in the night for water, and arrive at the edge of the great desert dunes by morning. That would be the last big push—miles of sand where you couldn't get solid footing. It would be dangerous to try the hot, loose sand in the afternoon sun after they arrived at the dunes. They would have to cut rations in half again, and all water supplies would be moved to a single wagon, under armed guard.

"All of you have squirreled away some extra water for your children," the Captain continued. "I won't try to recover it, but please keep it for the very end, the last few miles, the last hours through the dunes late tomorrow."

He paused, looked around, grimacing. "We are going to leave another of our wagons right here and save the water for the strongest oxen. We'll kill six of the weakest—yes, six—fill the empty bags and barrels with their blood for the oxen to drink. We'll butcher two, and you can suck the meat for blood. Now, I don't want any fighting or complaint. You can't afford the exertion."

Camille pulled Maddie, who stood there stunned, whimpering, into her arms. She, like the younger children, began to cry for their oxen. They had grown to love these beasts, had given them pet names and often comforted them during the stops—Bluebell and Pumpkin Pie, Sugar Moth and Billy Boy. The children were told to be brave.

THE WAGON TRAIN ARRIVED AT THE DUNES EARLIER THAN expected, just before dawn. Ezra sat with the Captain, Brose, Doc, and the Reverend over breakfast—some of the butchered meat and a quarter ration of water. They had to decide whether to let the families sleep through the day and walk the dunes at night, or to begin immediately without sleep and push through the withering day-time heat.

"It'll take all day to go the five miles," said the Captain. "No let up, no rest."

"I don't think we can survive the midday heat," said Doc. "The temperature of this sand could reach one hundred thirty, perhaps higher.

They'll blister their hands as soon as they touch the metal wheel rims or the harness rings, or even brass buttons. Better to wait for nightfall."

Ezra shook his head. "Brose and I scouted three miles ahead and I can tell you without a moon, it'll be too hard to differentiate the trail at night, too easy to veer off, get the wagons mired in the sand. It would take a double team to pull them out, and our oxen no longer have the strength. We should take our chances during the day."

"Dear God," said Doc. "When people fall, we'll need to get them off the scorching sand immediately." Ezra's eyes widened at the thought of faces blistering in the sand.

The Captain finally agreed, and the families passed the word—daytime, leaving immediately. Last day. They urged each other to hold on for just one more day by putting one finger in the air when they looked at each other so they didn't have to speak. *Brace yourself, guard your children*, they said in garbled tongue. Sometimes just in sign language. *Pick up anyone who falls.*

AT DAWN, THE BUCKETS OF BLOOD WERE FED TO THE OXEN, AND they marched into the dunes. They stopped at noon to rest and several of the oxen refused to get up, even when lashed. With some water they might revive, but the water was needed for the horses, the children, and finally the adults.

They abandoned three more oxen, and without much protest, threw most of their personal belongings overboard and pushed on. Several of the older children fainted in the sand and were moved into the wagons, next to the toddlers, until they could revive and walk again.

Camille had stumbled and fallen twice. Then yanked to her feet by Beth. She was weaving like a drunk when Ezra put her up on his horse and put Maddie on his back and began walking, leading Roan. Maddie said she could no longer feel her tongue. Camille leaned forward in the saddle and fell asleep until the sun burned her neck and cooked her back. She squirmed and sat up. Ezra took her down and put Maddie in the saddle for fifteen minutes of rest. Camille took his arm for support. Roan was panting and growing wobbly, trying to hold his balance in the hot sand.

Beth and Miriam walked next to Ezra and the girls, dune after dune. They couldn't talk and had nothing to say. Beth had never felt such pain. Her body cramped and seized up and screamed out for her to give it water. Her muscles ached. She could feel her mouth hanging open. The hot air seared the inside of her cheeks. She tried to lick the inside of her mouth but her tongue refused. There was no saliva.

Beth fought the pounding headache and the desire to retreat into her misery. Kept reminding herself she was a mother for the duration and had to prioritize her children's survival. Poor Maddie was nearly delirious in the sun. Camille used her own strength to hold Maddie up, to keep her feet moving, without complaint. Beth came up on the other side of Maddie and gave her an arm. Trying to say to Camille, "Let me take her," the only thing that came out was, "Aaagh . . ." Camille tried to smile but her mouth simply gaped. Beth could see the girl was determined to live and keep her sister moving. Such fortitude. Where did it come from?

They stopped for water and drank the last. The afternoon sun was in full fury and the sand burned their feet right through their boots when they stopped walking. They climbed in the wagons, but everything was too hot to sit on. The Captain, Ezra, and Brose conferred. Less than two miles to go, but the sand was getting deeper. The wagon train needed to go around the last set of dunes, but this could add another mile or two. Half the oxen had dropped in their yokes.

The Captain walked around and looked in the wagons at the young children who sat and stared in a stupor. They no longer had tears to shed and could not cry out in pain. Beth watched as he conferred again with Ezra, Brose, and Doc. She had never noticed before how old and weary the men looked as their bodies dried out. They stooped. She knew they had not had a drink all day.

We can't die out here, her mind screamed. *Not this close. Damn it, Ezra. Please God, not this close. A few miles to good water.* She drummed it—*good water, good water*—into her head. She had seen bodies, scores of them, from other trains beside the trail, blistering in the sun like bright red meat. This was not going to be her fate. She would not let Camille and

Maddie die here. But James? Where? She suddenly looked about in alarm. Glanced right, left, despite the pain. Ah, there he was, hanging onto the harness of the lead ox to keep his balance in the furnace of hot sand.

Eyes down, putting one foot in front of the other, Beth suddenly heard brakes, wheels locking, oxen jostling in their yokes, and looked up to find the train completely stopped. The Captain was telling every-one—somehow, he still had enough voice—to unhitch their teams and leave the wagons where they were.

What? No. Why? was the unspoken chorus of parched mouths. Puzzled people too weak to fight an order.

"Right here!" he shouted. "I mean it! Leave them! Put the children onto the backs of the oxen. Strap them on. We're going to make a run for the river. Straight up and over the big dune, instead of around it."

Everyone looked stupefied, staring up at a dune the size of a large hill that rose and kept torturously rising.

Ezra moved from wagon to wagon. "No time to lose. Unharness. Bundle your children up. Tie them onto the cattle, so they don't fall off. We'll come back for the wagons after we recover."

Beth thought about leaving her meager possessions behind in an open wagon for someone, anyone, to come along and steal. How absurd, she realized. Anything you stole would simply bog you down. There could be ten pounds of gold in her wagon and no one would dare take it. She patted Hannah's brooch in her pocket. At least she had that. *Hold on, Hannah, stay with us,* she whispered in her mind.

They moved forward in a disheveled mass of families and cattle, with young children strapped on top, older children in tow, and worked their way up the long, seemingly endless rise of sliding sand.

Every step uphill was agony. *If only the dunes were to go down,* she screamed in her head. *On the other side maybe there's water. What if there's not?* She motioned to the girls. Hold on, hold on. Then put her hand to her mouth and tipped it as if drinking. Water, yes. Hold on for the wonderful, wise, loving water. *Please dune, end. Go down, I beg you.*

BETH STOOD AT THE TOP OF THE RISE, STARING AT THE DREAM before her. A thin green line off in the distance. The tops of tiny trees running along an unseen river. The few families that could talk sent the word down the line, "Carson River. One mile."

She watched Ezra on his horse trot ahead of the crowd with a dozen empty leather water sacks draped over Roan's back. Brose was right beside him with the same. Where on earth did they find the strength?

Turning to Camille, Maddie, and Miriam, she pointed and tried to say, "We're going to make it. Thank you, God." But what came out of her mouth was, "*Taahh . . . gahh.*" They returned her garble with slurred parched sounds and nods and weak smiles through cracked lips. Their eyes sparkled with relief, hope.

She was appalled at how black their tongues were, so swollen with thirst they couldn't close their mouths. The wind blew dust into their faces, into their mouths, into their eyes, but it was wonderful. There were trees out there and water out there, the best of waters, waters defying the desert with one thin wet line. End of the wicked desert. *I'll never go back for that wagon,* she vowed. She saw Ezra and Brose, now out beyond the loose sand, riding hard on firmer ground toward the river.

Waiting for deliverance and inching forward, no one could speak or shout. Fearing they might die in the last mile. The heat seemed to make a buzzing sound off the sand as Beth watched the men come riding back with bulging sacks of water. The horses slowed as they reached the looser sand.

The crowd, the begging families and cattle, stumbled toward them, their legs moving in slow motion. Grabbing at the water bags, they gulped and passed them to their children, who drank with shaking arms and drawn faces. Oxen smelled the water and bellowed for their share, but it was gone too fast. Each person had a pint, two or three for the children near delirium. Some had collapsed, lying in the baking sand. They were quickly lifted up and shaded by bodies and shirts.

The oxen grew restless and dangerous, twisting and turning to locate the smell of fresh river water on the breeze. The children were removed from their backs before the crazed beasts struck out on their own, running, stumbling, wobbling toward the river. Ezra threw

Maddie over his shoulder and put Camille up on Roan. "Come on, James," he yelled. "Don't give up."

Beth felt James's firm hand on her arm, pulling her forward. She smiled as best she could as she in turn grabbed Miriam's hand and took her in tow. The three tugged each other forward. "No slacking," Beth tried to say, although it came out *"Na slahg."* Enough to make her laugh if she could wiggle her throat.

The oxen ran and trotted with renewed energy the last half-mile over the hard-packed desert ground and plunged into the river. The families tried to run, but even on firmer ground their legs would not hold up. They staggered and fell, got up or were pulled up, and walked hunched over, with sunken faces and wide, hopeful eyes. They stretched their hands toward the deliverance.

Finding new strength, Beth began to run with the girls in tow. She had never seen anything so beautiful as the tall, swaying cottonwoods and the green shade and flowing water. Panting, dry mouth open, she charged through the trees and fell flat into the river to gulp. It was pure, clean. She coughed and drank more, enveloped in the chill of mountain water. It tasted of ice. Her whole body tingled. Her mouth ached in the welcome embrace of melting ice.

Right behind, Ezra lifted Camille and Maddie and carried them, one under each arm, into the river. Then held them by the collar so they wouldn't drown. They drank desperately. The dust dissolved from their bonnets, their sunburned faces, their stiff hair, and they smiled with swollen tongues that filled their mouth.

Ezra let go and they rolled on their backs, drank some more, rolled over and finally stood up, spitting water at each other from their blistered mouths. With weakened arms, they threw water into the air. Plunging their heads back in, they drank until the ice-cold water numbed their faces and bodies.

Beth watched them crawl up onto the bank, exhausted, with Ezra right behind. He then ran after some of the oxen that were floating away in the current, with little regard for where they might land.

Beth and the girls came together, crawling on hands and knees in the cool, green grass beneath the broad cottonwood trees. They embraced each other. Maddie began to shake, crying and trembling, without tears or words. James walked up, pulled open the girl's embrace, and sank into their arms. He patted their backs. "I thought you'd die," he said, his words slurred, thick, contorted. He sobbed and dropped his head down, lifted it, and then sobbed again, until he caught himself. "Thank God for you," he said. He kissed Maddie on the cheek with his sun-parched lips, then Camille, then Beth. He stood and wiped the tears and walked away toward the oxen, then began running after one floating down the river. Beth had never seen him so moved, so embarrassed, so completely a boy.

She heard the wailing begin as families tried to resurrect their unconscious and delirious loved ones. Somebody had died, she heard the words, and maybe more than one. Soon enough, she thought. Right now, she couldn't bear to find out who. She glanced about for those she loved and saw Miriam and Sarah and Johan stirring in the grass. Doc, David, and the Reverend were ministering to the fallen ones. There, waving at her, thank God, was Caroline, and over there, Karen. They had all survived. She lay back and relaxed, took another cup of water.

Twenty minutes later, Ezra walked up briskly and scooped up Maddie and Camille, danced them around, both at the same time, kissing their heads. "You were so strong. I'm so proud of you." He laid them gently on the ground.

Before he could get away, Beth grabbed him around the waist from behind, and pressed her face into his wet shirt. He turned and held her face in his hands, brushed the wet hair away from her eyes, kissed her cheeks and forehead, then her eyes and ears, lips and neck. "I love you," he said. "For everything you are."

THAT NIGHT THE REVEREND THANKED THE LORD FOR SPARING their lives and prayed that Arabella, who was in a coma, and Carl, delirious from heatstroke, would fully recover. Then he turned his attention to Oliver Simpson; his wife, Maude and their daughter, Ruth, had both died in the final stretch. Oliver was nowhere to be seen. Probably walked off into the tangle of trees, Beth thought. Poor man.

She detested him, his unctuous manner, his slurs at the girls, but this was a tragedy he didn't deserve.

"The funerals will be tomorrow. I know you are battered, but please extend the love of God to Oliver. May the Lord watch over him and keep him."

SUNUP THE SECOND DAY, THE MEN AND OLDER BOYS DROVE THE oxen back to the wagons. The dread of the beasts as they entered the desert was palpable, Ezra thought, but once they spotted the wagons, the animals seemed to trot toward them, as if relieved that their wheeled companions were still alive.

They picked up the debris scattered beside the skewed wagons and tossed it in. Ezra found a diary next to Oliver's wagon. It was Maude's. He fanned it and watched as the missing half of the bounty ad fluttered to the ground. He clenched his fist, his mind burning with fury. He fought to calm himself. *She's dead. Oliver has no one to turn to, to scheme with.* He glanced around to see if anyone was looking, then stuffed the ad and the diary into his pocket.

The oxen were easily yoked and began to pull with new vigor back toward the river.

LATER THAT DAY, MIRIAM STRETCHED OUT FLAT IN THE GRASS next to Beth. "Where's Ezra? How's your tongue? Mine is still swollen."

"He and Brose left to look at the trail we're going to climb into the Sierras in a few days. Up a gorge they said. Back tonight." Beth blinked away tears as she said it; she wanted him here to share this precious moment. They had made it together, survived, brought the girls through. She wanted an hour to rest in his arms, feel his hands in her hair. Maybe tonight.

"They're off scouting the forward trail, already?" said Miriam, shaking her head. "Before the funeral? Before we've begun to recover?

Man never stops. Your girls were so strong, Beth. Their determination through that awful heat and sand astonishes me. I just love your family."

"Me too."

Beth knew she had little more than a week, perhaps two, before the truth came out about their sham marriage. She worried that Ezra might suddenly feel honor-bound to tell the party even if she didn't. Everyone, she feared, would then turn on them, but Miriam was the one Beth cared about the most.

If she could somehow hold on to Miriam's trust, she might be able to tolerate being shunned by the others. Of course, the girls' lie was the real problem. For their safety, the bounty on their heads would have to remain a secret. The families, she realized, still had no idea why the girls had been kidnapped at Fort Hall.

Miriam poked her. "You look worried, Beth. What are you thinking about? Where your family is going to end up in California? I hope we land close by. You're such a treasure."

Beth took a deep breath. She stared at the intense blue sky, afraid to meet Miriam's eyes.

Miriam rolled on her side. Her eyes sparkled. "I have a secret, Beth. I was so worried crossing the desert that something would happen, but I'm fine . . . I'm pregnant."

Beth shot up. "What? How . . .?"

"Same way as you, dear. Isn't that your secret, as well?"

⇒ 29 ⇐

Scouting the
Eastern Escarpment

Sierra Mountains

E zra and Brose rested against a boulder, while Roan tested the cliff edge with his hoof. Solid. He leaned his long neck down to drink from a tiny pool on a slab of wet granite.

Not a hundred feet below Roan's head, the river cascaded and thundered in ferocious descent down the Carson Gorge, falling and dashing itself against the massive boulders grown round and bald from endless assault. Mist rose from the frigid, raging waters. It was the same Carson River that down below flowed gently past the wagon train before it meandered into the desert to die in the Carson Sink. Same river that saved their lives staggering out of the graveyard.

"Another mile or so to the top," said Brose, drinking from his canteen.

"Noon already," said Ezra. He took a bite of venison and pointed. "We need to do something about this dangerous curve right here. Let's roll some of these bigger rocks to the edge to guide the animals and keep the wheels from drifting too close."

"*Bueno.* Right after lunch." Brose pulled some more jerky from his bag. "You still pretending you can settle with Beth and those girls of yours? You don't have a settling bone in your body."

"Maybe my bones are getting soft. Mind your own problems."

"Better figure it out. Only a week, ten days at most, to the gold camp at Big Bar."

"I have a promise to keep," said Ezra. "First thing, soon as we arrive, I promised to build her a boarding house, at least a crude one to house some of the miners. I'm thinking six to eight rooms in a line, four miners to a room, and an outdoor kitchen and dining area, right along that high-water shelf above the diggings. You know the one I mean, where the Mokelumne River opens out into the big bar? Very central. Those miners will pay anything for two good meals and a bed, maybe half their daily diggings. After she's rich, we'll see if she wants to continue our sham marriage."

"Sham? From what I saw, you two stopped shamming your marriage at the Bear River. Then went nonstop like grizzlies in heat until we hit Fort Hall. Been fighting off and on ever since. With a little time here and there for love. I know about these things."

They ate in silence. Air a bit thinner up here, Ezra noticed, making him aware not only of the elevation but his age. *Twenty years ago, I could have run up this gorge without stopping*, he thought . . . Or maybe not. These days, he realized, he was always lying to himself about what he could do, what he used to do.

He studied the tortured trail above and below them. It was the last major obstacle to the gold fields. The desert was the worst, but this, the eastern escarpment of the Sierras, was a close second. It rose from the desert floor like a three-thousand-foot-high medieval wall keeping out the rabble, hiding the bounty of California from eastern invaders.

Only a few trails pierced the wall, and all were rugged gorges, cut like a knife over thousands of years by hard-driving rivers. Ezra tried to imagine Beth's face staring up at the rock-strewn gorge and this trail, difficult for a horse, tortuous for a wagon. No use trying to hide it. She would press him immediately, expecting a full, unvarnished description. She had become astute at reading his evasions. She seemed to know his mind even before it came out of his mouth.

She'd demand the truth. He'd probably dodge, and they'd fight. It felt surprisingly good to fight with her, he thought. Not physically, but as equals, up close face to face, sweating and shouting. An outlet for their passion in these hard times and hard places. She was hard to love and impossible not to love, just like the land itself.

"We both know the truth here," said Brose.

"About Beth?"

"No, we'll get to that later. Wagons. Pay attention. We'll have to get all sixteen to the top of this gorge—all six miles of it—in a single daylight, before we can rest. We don't want to spend the night in here. Gives me the *sombríos* just thinking about these people being washed away in the dark." Brose pointed to the upland—to the jagged ledges and sheer canyon walls, pines growing out of crevices, boulders balanced in precarious positions.

Flash flooding was rare this late in August, Ezra knew, but Brose was right about not spending the night in here. And flooding wasn't his main concern. In the dark, some child or animal could easily take a false step and go over the edge. They would have to drive hard all the way to the top of the gorge in one day. To the place called Hope Valley, the first plateau in this eastern climb. Well named, he thought.

Finishing lunch, they moved a half mile higher, then stopped. They had been clearing the trail of rocks and debris all morning, but nothing quite like the massive, waist-high boulder blocking the trail in front of them.

They first used iron crowbars to lever it out of its pocket. It budged forward a few inches, then fell back. Next, they axed down a long, lean pine, wedged it under the boulder and over a stone fulcrum a few feet away, then shimmied up the 25-foot tree trunk to hang their full weight from the far end. Both hanging off it, the pine bent like a bow. The two of them began bouncing, jumping high off the ground, springing up with the pine, then pulling down hard. Finally, they jostled the boulder loose and it rolled to the edge, where it paused, as if deciding whether to jump. Then slowly went over. They raced up, breathing hard, and stared with satisfied grins and aching arms as the boulder careened through the chasm below, finally crashing and breaking apart, swallowed by the river.

Ezra's back ached when he sat down to catch his breath. His head pounded in the thin air. "We're not so young anymore," he said.

Brose shook his head. "You especially. Me, I got another twenty years out here, but you, *amigo*, are put'n on the gray. Better find another line of work." He spit and smiled at Ezra. "You hang onto that family when we get to the gold camp. Give you my advice, if you want it."

"You're going to give it to me anyway." Ezra pulled a piece of a cold, smoky trout from his kitbag.

"It doesn't have to end," said Brose.

Ezra eyed him suspiciously. "Meaning what?"

"We know wagon trains always, always, always bust apart after they arrive, flying in all directions. *En trozos, amigo.* But it doesn't have to be that way. I been watching this *poco de amor*, this little flicker of love that lives inside you grow. Even if you can't see it, I can. I know about these things."

"You know about these things?" Ezra laughed, pushed his fingers through his sweaty hair.

"*Si, Consuela, mi bonita, en Monterey.*"

"Oh, horseshit. She's probably married to a one-eyed mule driver with broken teeth by now. She's not waiting for you."

It was hard to imagine life without Beth at this point, but like every wagon train he and Brose had ever guided, Ezra knew it would come apart. It was the natural order of things. Every vow, every covenant, every good intention made on the trail would disappear as soon as the wheels stopped rolling. All those close feelings steeled with collective purpose, forged from exertion and dependency, from fondness and kinship and survival, would dissolve the moment they walked into the camps and became infected by gold fever or land fever or business fever or just plain, wild freedom. *What the hell does Brose know?*

"They seem pretty fond of you," said Brose, "and they've changed you. I've never seen you like this. Ever. This affection you feel for them. This *poco de amor*. And I've known you for a long—"

"Stop interfering," Ezra snapped. "Camille and Maddie will have a place with Beth, at least to start, and James will go off to find his brother. So they're taken care of."

Brose laughed. "And Beth?" He threw a rock into the gorge. "She wants your fake family to go on and become real, and your fake marriage, too. That's love. I know about these things."

For months, Ezra had been trying to imagine where he might end up. A businessman in San Francisco sending supplies up to the gold camps? Traveling merchant? A landowner down in the foothills? Back on the trail? A loner drifting like a windblown seed that never wants to take root? Wherever he saw himself in his dreams, however, Beth was always there with Camille and Maddie; the three of them together, waving for him to come join them. *"You love us, don't you know that? Come care for us."*

"That's the hell of it. It could all be a mirage," Ezra mumbled. For him, as with Abigail and Daisy before her, love was always coupled with sudden, horrid loss. *When I want it with my whole heart, it disappears. Snatched away in front of my eyes.*

Brose's face twitched. "What did you say?"

"Don't ask is what I said."

THEY THREW THEIR SCRAPS ASIDE AND CLIMBED THE LAST BIT OF the gorge, moving debris off the trail. A few other trains had passed this way and had done some of the clearing, but there were still impassable spots. Roots, boulders, and high ledges to skirt around. Tree tangles and stumps, places where the trail narrowed with only enough room for a horse or an ox to squeeze through.

Places where the wagons would have to be hauled up on a makeshift ramp or more likely taken apart and lifted piece by piece and then reassembled. "How many ledges will need disassembly?" Ezra asked. Two?"

"I counted three," said Brose. "I figure we'll lose an hour at each one."

"Yeah, and that's if we go like clockwork, and the parts don't get mixed up," said Ezra. "OK, let's head back down and tell the families what we're facing. They'll need to rest a few more days to regain their strength and courage. And practice taking their wagons apart and putting them back together fast. Over and over. Which part in what order. A jigsaw puzzle.

"When everybody's ready and not before," he continued. "We'll stage the wagons at the bottom of the gorge for the night, so we can begin climbing in the easy part, even before first light."

"Give us a full fifteen, maybe sixteen hours before dark," said Brose. "Should work."

"Better work." Ezra picked his way down the trail, Brose behind him.

"You should hold on to that woman," Brose yelled. "She's good for you. You need a warm woman, just like I do. And children to love. And a new life. You're too old for this shit."

Brose should talk. Ezra turned around in the saddle and yelled back above the sound of the water. "What about your *bonita?* You going to marry her? Is she still here in California?"

"*Consuela? Quien sabe?* Who knows. *Me hace feliz.*"

She makes him happy. Ezra scoffed. "What difference does that make?" he yelled over his shoulder, chuckling. Then shook his head. Two old mountain men about to change their lives, just for a little happiness. *Un poco de felicidad.*

Ezra rode on, letting Roan pick his way carefully down the steep trail. He thought about Beth, about his growing love for her and for Camille and Maddie. Then his thoughts abruptly turned to the dangers they'd face when Jenkins's second gang arrived in California, coming for the girls. Ruthless bastards. His entire body tightened at the thought. His fists clenched on the reins, heart began to race, stomach knotted. He'd protect them. He'd find a way. He had to.

He stopped gnashing his teeth and brought his mind back to the task at hand. "Brose, first thing . . ." He turned to look over his shoulder. "Let's take the time to train these families how to take their wagons apart and reassemble them. Fast. By feel as much as sight."

"*Si, amigo.* And keep their wagon wheels wet for days before we leave to tighten the spokes and the felleos. Be hell to pay if those iron rims start coming off half way up the gorge."

"*Acordado. Sería desastroso,*" said Ezra. "Each morning, we'll have them roll their wagons into the river to drink."

30

CLIMBING THE
CARSON GORGE

Ladder to California, 1800 miles from the trailhead

No one slept that night. After moving the wagons into the staging area, they stared at the sky-burst of desert stars. Tossing in the dark in their bedrolls and peering up at the shrouded mountain range looming over them, taunting them, daring them.

They were hardened, rested, and prepared, but this granite monstrosity was something almost biblical, sacred, unspoiled, frightening. They lay awake, then ate breakfast and left in the dark, moving fast into the lower, flatter regions of the climb.

By early sunrise, Beth could see where the mountain was torn, sliced down the middle leaving the shadowed maw of the Carson Gorge. As the light lifted, the jagged, rocky ascent slowly revealed itself from top to bottom. Fear raced from her trembling legs up her spine to her scalp as her eye followed the trail, as best she could make out, as it began to climb and to narrow. And in the upper distance the same trail began to twist back on itself in tight loops amidst the lingering shadows like a serpent climbing a broken garden wall.

Her mind pushed back against the impossible. *We'll never make it,* she thought, *not all the way, certainly not up there for God's sake.* Her legs trembled, she felt momentarily flint-headed, wobbly. She closed her eyes to regain balance, calm herself. *Easy, easy,* she told herself. Just as Ezra told her for the last two thousand miles, every time she stared at the impossible and asked how, he'd say, "One step at a time, Beth. One breath at a time." Oddly, it made her smile, remembering the obvious.

Dark coffee, the stark morning sun, and the first real obstacle focused her mind. The wagons were maneuvering between two boulders the size of small cabins, the wheel hubs scraping the granite, the axles near breaking. While the oxen leaned into their task, the men lifted one side just enough to pop the wagons through one at a time.

"Shouldn't you take the wheels off on this side?" Beth asked, leaning down beside the wheelwright supervising the maneuver.

He turned his head and glared at her. "Nah. Just need a scootch. They'll hold. Stay back."

How do you know, she wanted to ask, but of course that was his business. She moved up to the front where she might be of more use.

A mile up the trail, where the grade grew steeper, Beth looked up at a cracked precipice of rock, where boulders the size of wagons were lodged precariously in open crevices. Water had somehow carried those massive pieces of stone partway down, then left them dangling. Even though her stomach grew queasy, she couldn't stop looking at them. They might sit like that for a thousand years, then the slightest thing might release them—a bird, a scampering squirrel, a gentle wind.

And then which wagon would they crush? She wiped the fine river spray from her eyes, praying it would not be her own—not Maddie nor Camille nor Ezra nor James nor Miriam nor Sarah, Johan, Doc, Charles . . . on and on. "Take anyone, dear God, but not them." She squirmed, the guilt rising from her stomach to her throat. She was now asking God to take someone else's life instead of the ones she loved. She bowed her head in shame. "God, please don't listen to me. Amen." She wondered if God was used to confusion.

Why do I always do this? She had done it her whole life, pray for someone else's demise to spare her own. God must be wondering about her. She looked up again at the suspended boulders. No use trying to direct their course, she realized. If one of those monsters came rolling down, it would scatter them all of like tenpins.

Another mile up the gorge, the Captain began yelling up and down the train, "Unyoke the oxen when you get up here."

They were blocked, this time by a twenty-foot wall, too high for a ramp. They were forced to lead the animals one by one up a narrow path around the wall, while the families carried the contents of their wagons to higher ground, arm load by arm load.

Camille worked below with the men disassembling the wagons— the wheels, the bed, and the undercarriage—while Beth and Maddie moved up the trail and sat near the children in the shade of a large overhang. Maddie kept squirming, pressing to be allowed to work with Camille.

"No, you can't help down there. Wait until the parts come up. Then help."

Separate teams of oxen hauled up individual pieces, while groups of men and women, including Beth and Maddie, reassembled the wagons at the top. The families had practiced for two days before the ascent and, importantly, had colorfully marked the pieces of their own wagon for quick, sure identification. They had learned the peculiarities and fitting of each piece—whittling edges that stuck, greasing tight fits, getting faster and faster with each teardown and reassembly, learning exactly where to hammer and how hard.

It was surprising and pleasing to see how feverishly Camille could work the rope lines alongside James down below. Every bit his equal, Beth thought. The girl had grown strong in two thousand miles of physical hardship. With heavy gloves and a jacket to protect her arms, Camille gritted her teeth and lifted as roped pieces started up and bumped and snagged their way up the small cliff to more open ground. Atop, Maddie passed tools back and forth and carried water. Sometimes she'd hold a wheel steady, keep it from wobbling, while the wheelwright and his helper firmed it onto the axle.

Time was the enemy. It had taken a full hour to move the wagon train forward a hundred yards. Ezra looked to the sky repeatedly, as did others emulating him, worried about their race with the sun. It was now overhead, shrinking the cool shadows that protected the children from the heat.

The altitude, the chimney effect of the canyon, and the fog of evaporation off the river kept the air circulating in the gorge, mercifully bleeding off the heat radiating from the stone canyon walls.

They took a quick break around noon. Ezra dropped his hat and gloves and plopped down to stretch out next to Beth with a broad smile, his chest heaving. She waited for his complaints but heard none. He began guzzling water and pouring it over his head. Even in the cautious, fearful mood she was in, he could still brighten her heart by seeking her out. She ran her fingers through his wet hair, wiped his sweaty face, and kissed him.

"Love you," he said and held her eyes long enough to let its import take hold.

Her face softened, the tension in her body let go. "Love you too. Come on now. You need to eat, not just chug water." She pulled apart some cold fried fish and handed him pieces between gulps of water. "Slow down, you'll choke." She took out her knife and cut some smoked duck into smaller chunks.

"Where are we?" she asked him.

"More than halfway. We're getting better at this. That practice with the wagons is saving us hours. Every wagon is a little different, but these families have learned their quirks and fixed the snags."

"Now, tell me the truth," she said. "Will we make it out of this gorge by nightfall?"

He looked up the sun, then rolled over to look up the canyon. "Can't see the top yet, but it will be close."

"Before you run off, Ezra, please have a word with Maddie. She's not listening to me. She can be a little brazen, scampering up and down this trail, jumping up on rocks with a sheer drop."

"She's got great balance, but you're right. She doesn't understand that wet granite can be treacherous. Feet can go right out from under you. Happens so fast you're right on your back, sliding. I'll talk with her right after lunch."

She raised her eyebrows. "Promise," he said.

Ten minutes later, the Captain hollered. "On your feet. Time to march. We're racing the sun." Beth could hear the growing tension in his voice. She shoved the rest of the meat at Ezra, which he stuffed into his pocket and left.

Maddie was now far ahead, helping Sarah and Johan and the other young mothers and children. As a group, they were making their way carefully up the trail, out ahead of the train to protect them in case of backslides and rocks kicked loose by the animals. At the rear it was like walking on a river of pebbles.

Beth watched as Ezra grabbed Maddie's arm from behind and held it while he talked with her, gesturing at the wet sheen on the granite. Maddie squirmed to get away, but he held her tight until she stopped fighting, settled, and nodded. He kissed her cheek.

Beth had spent little time in her life around young children. They had been easy to ignore in her world, simply inconveniences. Now, she marveled at the awareness required to keep them safe, at the balancing act of these women who had to be continuously attentive to gruff men and careless, playful children. They had attuned themselves to sense danger before it happened. She watched in awe as the younger children were moved by quick, sure hands, guided by instinct from one rock to the other before it could give way and tumble down deep into the canyon. Beth knew she didn't have the experience, even after all these months. She still struggled each day searching for the right harmony of spirit and mental balance to guide her in this extraordinarily complex world of families. She hated it; she loved it.

Not more than fifty feet ahead, James was struggling with one of the unhitched oxen. It was one of three given an hour's reprieve from hauling the wagons. The ox was clearly agitated to be in the rear of the trio and tried desperately to push ahead of the other two. First to the left and then to the right, it tried to pass. But the one in front cut it off repeatedly.

The determined ox tried to scramble around those in front by jumping up on a low slab of granite to the right of the path. James grabbed the harness, tugging, then yanked hard at the belligerent beast just as it stepped on a wet spot on the granite slab. Its feet went right out from under it. It landed with a slap on its side and started sliding, slowly, its feet flailing, pulling James forward onto the face of the granite sheen. Two men grabbed James's ankles; his wrist was caught in the harness. He lurched hard, side to side, and shrieked when his hand finally twisted free from the harness. The men held onto to his ankles as the ox, thrashing and bellowing, slowly slid down the long, wet granite face. It went over the edge, fell eighty feet onto a boulder below, and bounced with a sickening thud. Then it disappeared into the cascade of water.

James lay on the ground, holding his arm, trying to muffle screams that simply leaked out of his throat in high-pitched agony—the cry of a wounded coyote—that echoed off the canyon walls. Beth ran for him, pushing people out of the way, her mind fixed on the terror of losing him. Each of his screams sliced into her. She was aware of men and women shouting for Doc, but James was hers to care for; she had to get to him.

"Don't touch him," Doc yelled to her, as he made his way down the trail. "Stay back!"

James had been pulled onto a blanket and was now thrashing on his side, his dislocated shoulder twisting his arm at a terrible angle. Beth hovered over him, her hands lightly holding his contorted face, when Doc arrived. He moved Beth out of the way and leaned down.

"I got you, son. Can you hear me? Hold still while I put your shoulder back in place." He propped James onto his good side, gently folded the twisted arm at the elbow, then lifted the arm by the elbow and slowly rotated it until Beth heard a loud snap. James's face melted with relief and he blinked into the sunlight as if he had just awakened. Beth sat on the ground beside him and cradled his head in her lap. *So close,* she thought. *Thank you, God, for sparing my brave boy."*

Doc ripped some cloth to make a sling as he talked to Beth. "Good thing the arm rotated out, or he would have been dragged over. Why his hand was wedged in there . . .?" He shook his head. "Well, I don't know what he was trying to do. Save the poor ox, I suppose."

He finished the knot around James's neck. "You'll be all right in a few days, but I'm tying your arm down. Make sure it stays snug at your side. No more heavy lifting for you, son, not today, not tomorrow. You'll have to make your way up the mountain with the children and the other injured."

James shook his head. "No, I'll be OK. I can work." He looked at Beth, pleading with his eyes to avoid the humiliation of leaving the battlefield, of walking with the children.

"No, James. You do as you're told. You're going to need that arm." She ran her hand over his cheek. "Now go help Maddie." She pointed far up the trail at Todd Johnson, on a makeshift crutch, who an hour earlier had his leg pinned between a wagon and a boulder; the bone was broken but not shattered. Beth disliked the man and his sons for having bullied Maddie. "Go take care of her. You know what I mean." James looked up at Maddie and Todd Johnson. James's face was pinched, but now with a mission, he seemed more alert and less humiliated.

By late afternoon they had reached the final wall, where they spent nearly two hours removing everything once again from the wagons, carrying the bundles up the path, then taking the wagons apart one by one, each piece secured to double lines to be lifted up and over the face.

The sun dropped behind the mountain, leaving a glow above the crest but diminishing the light at their feet. Long shadows distorted the canyon around them, blurring the steps in front of them.

Beth could feel the anxiety growing all around her, tempers snapping, fear riding just under the surface as the families fought to maintain emotional control while trying to speed up. They were exhausted, their eyes playing tricks on them as the shadows deepened. It wasn't clear they'd make it out before dark. The air had thinned and without the sun, the gorge was cooling rapidly, feeding their fear.

This was a dangerous time, when attention wavered, and missteps were likely. Beth working with Ezra, moved up and down the strung-out train rapidly, encouraging everyone to watch their footing. Gathering the children close, even tying some with rope to their parents. Helping the stragglers work around obstacles. "We're going to make it. Watch your feet. Avoid wet sheens."

Camille had taken control as drover, leading their team of oxen up the trail. Beth was astonished at her skill in maneuvering around boulders, her ability to calm the animals, talking to them as if she had done this for a thousand miles, as if she had miraculously assimilated James's deft touch with the animals.

"Stay calm, be careful, watch your step," said Beth, patting each man and woman on the shoulder or back, reminding them that the end of the journey was near. But this was also the most dangerous part.

"One more hour," Ezra shouted up and down the line cheerfully. "We'll make it before dark." Beth didn't believe him, nobody believed him. But the promise of one last hour kept morale up, so she repeated it.

Beth remembered how full of spirit they had been at dawn, nearly rapturous, taking their first steps onto the Sierras, climbing the ladder to California.

Now there was no joy in the beauty of the sunset coming upon them fast. Only exhaustion and fear.

⇒ 31 ⇐

HOPE VALLEY

Reaching the rooftop of California, August, 1849

I
t was past dark by the time the families emerged from the staircase canyon and staggered like a battered army into Hope Valley—a long, generous, grassy meadow high in the Sierras, which in the starlight appeared to have no edges.

Instead of circling the wagons as soon as they reached level ground, the families kept going in silence, slowly branching out as they went, dispersing without a word of discussion or complaint. They were simply tired of one another, tired of being confined by granite walls and torrents of water, by flaring tempers, and endlessly having to assist, lift, and lend a hand, a back, a shoulder. They wanted nothing so much as solace and rest, a bit of privacy and retreat from another long and terrifying day.

Ezra led his bedraggled family to a soft spot near the river, in the shadow of some trees, rich with the smell of deep grass and mountain flowers.

Staring at her reflection in the water, Beth found it remarkable that the river in front of her eyes, meandering like a lazy country stream, sparkling in the starlight, was the same one she had climbed beside all day. A river that five, six hundred yards downstream from where she stood flung itself over the lip of the meadow to tear its way savagely down the Carson Gorge.

Beth lifted her eyes and stared at the dark profiles of higher peaks to the west and prayed the trail ahead would go between them or around them. She was too tired to ask Ezra. Today was enough for now.

Camille and Maddie unhitched the team, speaking to the weary animals, patting them, thanking them. Then Camille and James led the oxen to the river to drink and into the rich grass to eat and bed, while Ezra and Maddie went to gather wood for the fire.

With a moment alone, Beth stretched out on her back in the grass, breathing deeply, staring at the wash of stars that covered the black sky. She had made it, actually made it, to the rooftop of California. She spread her arms, exalting in conquest. This journey of four million steps. In her weary feet, she could feel every one of them. Over rock and blistering sand. Through mud and marsh.

How could Ezra do this, over and over, she wondered? This trail? This exertion? It was a horrendous job, riding a horse back and forth across the continent for no good reason other than to turn around and go back again. Could she love a man compelled to migrate like an animal? And if he gave up everything for her, would she have to do the same for him? She didn't know. How could she give up who she was? Well, she couldn't and wouldn't, so he better not ask. But he hadn't. She loved him all the more for that, for accepting her; her untamed independence.

But best, he now reveled in her passion and told her in quieter moments she was thoughtful, kind, and lovely. *Lovely, he finds me lovely.* She rolled the sound of that over in her mind. She had never thought of herself as lovely. Beautiful upon occasion. Striking at times. But lovely felt somehow richer, not so visual, filled with love. Maybe it wasn't the word. Maybe it was the man feeling it.

Sprawled on the ground, she realized how much her entire body ached. She massaged her sore shoulder and neck and gingerly touched the rope burn across her forearm. Perhaps Doc or Miriam might have some salve left, or willow tea to ease the fatigue. After she got the fire started, she would wander over and ask them. That is, if she could find them and if she could stay awake that long.

BETH WAS STIRRING A STEW OF DUCK AND TROUT, LACED WITH SOME shriveled onions found beside the river down below, when Miriam appeared out of the night, carrying a wicker basket.

"Found you, not easy way over here. I brought you some tasty greens from the other side of the meadow, and a special treat." She turned her eyes toward Camille and Maddie, fifty feet away, leaning against the wagon. "Those girls look ready to drop. Why are they still on their feet?"

"They'll collapse after they've had dinner. Not too tired to eat, they say."

"They're a pair," said Miriam. "I've never seen them work so hard as they did in the gorge today."

"How'd you and your baby fare on the climb? I worried about you."

"Fine. She—pretty sure it's a she—is a hearty one. She did better than me. I've partially recovered but truth tell I was bone tired and thought I'd collapse that last hour. Brought you some things." Miriam reached into the basket and scooped out the greens, and underneath at the bottom a small, flat jar with a lid. She dropped the greens into the pot. "Stir them in, they'll bring out the flavor. Smells like duck."

Miriam stepped closer, lifted the mysterious jar up close to Beth's face and took off the lid. Beth sniffed and pulled back. It was watery and dark. "Dear, this is a special tea I made to take away the soreness and exhaustion and refresh you. Enough for you to enjoy the night. Beautiful place, is it not? Go on, taste it, I've got to get back . . . No, not for everyone, just for you. I brought some balm for James's shoulder."

Beth sipped the tea, finding it strange that Miriam would not offer it to anyone else. The girls were equally worn from the day's battle, and James was in pain, but Miriam said better they should simply go to sleep. "Just for you," she said.

The tea was pleasant enough, warm and soothing, with the musky smell of a forest floor and the taste of pine and chalk and . . . something else. She drank quite a bit. It went down smoothly. "What's in this?

What am I tasting?"

Miriam rattled off a few things. "Willow bark, St. John's wort, ginseng, saffron, laudanum, and some other things for soothing."

After finishing the tea and some quick gossip about the Johnsons, Miriam took her jar and basket and disappeared into the night. Beth rubbed her sore arms and leg, called the girls over to finish the cooking and to set the dinner on the tamped down grass near the fire. James came over and she sat him down for dinner, pulled back the bandaging and rubbed Miriam's balm on his tender shoulder. He winced, then settled, smiled. Beth waited for her own aches and pains to fade as they ate a quiet dinner. Just eating, no talking, by silent agreement. Took too much energy. No one was up for rehashing the epic of the gorge. Not tonight.

Camille and Maddie were asleep by the time dinner was over. They had simply put down their plates, stretched out in the grass beside the crackling fire, and fallen fast asleep. James ate their leftovers, then crawled, knees and one hand, underneath the wagon and wrapped himself in a blanket. He was asleep in seconds. Beth pulled an extra blanket on top of him, while Ezra carried Maddie to the wagon and returned for Camille.

Camille stirred and looked around as he carried her. "I can't take another step."

"No, it's over. I'm so proud of you. Now go back to sleep." Her eyes closed. He slid her limp body into the wagon next to Maddie.

As Ezra walked away, Beth patted the girls, pulled the blankets up snug. Looking at Camille sleeping like a rumpled dream, she thought about how someone looking at her frail frame would never suspect her strength. Suddenly overwhelmed with emotion, she whispered, "I adopt thee." Then gently placed her hand on Maddie's head. Maddie stirred and turned as Beth whispered, "I adopt thee." She'd tell Ezra when the time came. But she imagined he already knew.

BETH AND EZRA STRETCHED OUT ON THE BUFFALO ROBE NEAR THE
fire, but she squirmed, unable to get comfortable. The mountain air was
chilly but the heat and light from the fire were uncomfortable. She stood
and picked up her bag.

"Let's move the robe down there." She pointed to a large out-
cropping of rock fifty yards away, close to the water.

She shooed Ezra off the heavy robe and dragged it toward the spot,
as he walked back to the wagon to fetch a few things. He didn't say
what.

There was a soft grassy area behind the massive rock, next to the
river, that offered Beth an unobstructed view of the stars and the kind
of privacy one only dreamed about on a wagon train. Glancing back at
the meadow, she saw no wagons or campfires in the vicinity. They were
completely alone. She knelt down and smoothed out the folds in the
thick black wool and patted it firmly into the grass.

She sat on the robe waiting for Ezra, holding her knees to her chest
and rocking, now feeling woozy and alert at the same time. Her aches
had thankfully disappeared, followed by a warm, quickening sensation.
Miriam said the tea would refresh her. But it was now growing beyond
that. *What was in that tea? Is "bright" a feeling?* There was a hint of
snakeroot in that tea, but something else a bit sweeter . . . No matter.
Beth now felt as if she had awakened fresh from a summer storm.

Compelled to get out of her clammy, filthy clothes, she scooted
down on the robe and pulled off her boots and soggy socks and peeled
off her buckskin pants. Stood and took off the buckskin shirt, her over-
dress, and the sweaty cotton layers underneath. Disrobed, naked, the
chill air raised goosebumps up her legs, torso, arms and neck. She
wrapped her arms around herself and tiptoed to the edge of the river.
Looked about. No sign of Ezra. The water was cold on her hot, sweaty
feet and ankles. She went cautiously in as far as her knees. Found the
bottom firm with sand and stone, and the current so languid she need
not worry about being swept downstream.

She waded in further, savoring the biting chill, then scooped the
water up with her hands and rubbed it quickly along her arms and
across her chest and shoulders. The cold shocked her, sent tremors
down her body. She splashed her sweaty neck and face, then brought up

handfuls face first, tasting the salt from her dissolving sweat. Finally, waist deep, she dropped fully under the water and splashed around, trying to free herself of the dirt and grime and the agonies of climbing the gorge.

Coming up with her head just above the surface, hair dripping, her mind went totally silent, awed by the stars that enveloped her, and their sparkling reflection off the soft flowing water. She held her breath, her heart slowed. Stars overhead, stars in front of her and to either side of her, even underneath her as she stared at their reflection in the sparkling water. She turned in wonder. She breathed in the smell of meadow grass and wild jasmine before dropping her head below the surface again.

She shook her hair under the water and ran her fingers through the caked dust and sweat until it loosened its hold. Finally, her tresses began to flow freely. Out of breath, she jumped up, glistening, gasping, looking for Ezra.

There he was, as if she knew it before she surfaced. Standing on the bank, his eyes on her. She watched him toss a pile of blankets and things onto the ground and begin removing his clothing. Eyes still on her as he disrobed. First his work jacket and shirt, then he bent and pulled off his boots and pants.

Suddenly, there he was, all of him—upright, slim, tall and compact, naked in starlight. He put something like a stone on a string around his neck and waded into the water. He dove under and disappeared into the silent river. She waited, nervously. After a minute or two, far upstream from her, he jumped fully into the air for a loud gasp of breath. He smiled, dove under again, this time in her direction. She knew he was coming for her. Her body tingled and she held her breath, but she saw no telltale ripples or bubbles on the surface.

She felt his hand grasp her leg and then he slid his body straight up hers and held her, one hand stroking her arm, shoulder, and neck, the other tugging on the small of her back. Pulling her into him. He was shockingly warm and soothing where their skin touched, in contrast to the cold water and chilly air on her backside.

He swung a small deerskin pouch hanging on a string of rawhide around his neck. It was covered with tiny holes and foamed slightly.

"Soap."

"Where in the world?" She squeezed the bag and felt the slippery surface over the smooth doeskin.

"Everybody in the camp is asleep, except for Miriam. I went to our wagon for blankets, fresh clothes, whiskey and things, and she appears out of the dark and hands me this bag of soap like it was a treasure. 'For Beth,' she says, smiling as if she knows something, then walks away. Did you two talk about this?"

Beth just smiled. She let him soap her everywhere in front, sweetly, cautiously. He ran soapy fingers through her hair. Then she turned around away from him as he worked on her backside and up into her hair. It would be his turn soon, but she wanted to savor the flow of his hands gliding over her skin, over her shoulder blades and down her back, over the swell of her hips and down her thighs. Then reaching around, up her front, soothing her with flowing hands.

She spun around. "Your turn," she said. She scrubbed him up one side and down the other with urgent fast hands, then went back over his body with light caressing hands in slow, gentle soaping pleasure. She felt him release, then a soft moan. She dug her hands and nails into his thick hair, stuck together like the bristles of an old paint brush. She soaped, rinsed, then soaped his hair again. "Ready?" she asked. Together, they dropped below the surface to rinse off.

They stood and held each other silently, their foreheads pressed together.

"Come on," he said, taking her hand, pulling toward the shore. She realized as they climbed out that they had drifted downstream a bit. In the distance, she could hear the water diving headlong down the Carson Gorge. If you are water destined to die in a sinkhole in the desert, she thought, that would be a good way to go, in one last tumultuous roar, screaming, "*I am falling free and water wild.*"

They raced for the blankets and pulled two around themselves and stood wrapped, rubbing each other.

"I love it here," she said.

"Place reminds me of that old story the Ancients teach their children," he said. 'If you find yourself lost in the forest, stop. Stop and listen to the forest. Stop and look at the trees. Look at everything around you.

You may not know the forest, but the forest knows you.'"

He dropped to his knees on the robe, tugging her hand. She pushed him down on his back and, half kneeling, swayed over him, touching his cheek with her fingers. She caressed his face.

He rolled her on her back, massaged her neck and scalp under her thick hair, gently releasing the tension. She tipped her head back and let him soothe her.

"Everything in me is coming back to life," she said. "I thought I'd lost you in the desert."

"You could never lose me. Not anymore."

"We made it all the way to California, Ezra, and we did it together. I love you for that. I don't know what's going to happen after this but working side by side with you gives me a new sense of you and us. Of hope. How many days until we land?"

"A week through the mountains, nothing like today. Then a few days down into the foothills, more gentle land, and we'll be in Big Bar, a prime gold camp. Rich—"

"Shh, enough explanation. Just listen," she said.

He stretched out on his back beside her, lacing his fingers through hers, staring at the stars silently. She really didn't want him to say anything more.

He leaned over, kissed her lips as her eyes stayed open, lingering on the stars. "Are you warm enough?" he asked, pulling the edge of the blankets and robe around them both.

"I am. Quite."

Beth settled against his side, her eyes roaming the universe of stars. More than she ever imagined. She was happy, perhaps for the first time in her life, she thought. Overflowing with joy. Life could be no better than this. From here she could easily walk into the Carson River, lie on her back, and float under the stars and over the waterfall, holding on to this moment for eternity. Something inside her had ended, that's all she knew, and something inside her was stirring, beginning.

The Saga Continues...

When Ezra stares at the gold camp in front of him in August 1849, after two thousand miles on the trail, he sees the reality of California in a new light. A land of transients, no more permanent than his wagon train. A shambles of tents and shanties, people tearing up the river bed, taking what they want and moving on. No loyalty to place, no roots, home or community. A makeshift world, as ephemeral as stage props.

He can see the pain in Beth's eyes. How can they rebuild their lives in this mess? She wants a home, a business of her own, a safe place for their girls where Black and white sisters can live openly. A community that has meaning, not just a grab-and-run society. Settled folks with links and ties and responsibilities. A place where bad men will not steal her children. He wants to give it to her.

After constructing a crude but highly lucrative boarding house right on the banks of the Mokelumne River—a gold mine in its own right, perfect for miners desperate for a bed and two good meals a day—Ezra sets his sights on a bigger dream. He will build an elegant hotel and home in San Francisco for Beth and the girls. And to finance it, he proposes a new undertaking with his shrewd city-dwelling nephew, Homer. Installing a gambling parlor in the brand new McCorry Hotel will bring in enough revenue to pay off all their debts . . . unless Beth puts her foot down first.

As tensions mount, the hotel with its many secrets—chamber, tunnel, collapsible fire escape—will also serve as a staging area and fortress from which to battle the slavers determined to reap the ever-increasing bounty on the girls' heads. With Christmas just around the corner, their wagon train companions join Ezra and Beth to work out plans for the inevitable battle . . . never suspecting that a fire is about to sweep through San Francisco, adding further chaos and destruction.

LOOK FOR THE EXCITING SEQUEL: *THE MCCORRY HOTEL*

Further Reading

Below are a few excellent reference books I drew from that I would recommend for those interested in the California Gold Rush. I found all rich in factual material and personal accounts.

JOHN BAILY, *THE LOST GERMAN SLAVE GIRL* (NEW YORK: ATLANTIC MONTHLY PRESS, 2003). Baily offers a story that reads like a novel but provides great insight into the fascinating laws and customs surrounding slavery in Louisiana in the 1840s. A compelling story of a young slave girl with no memory of her past thought to be a lost relative by those from a German village sold into indentured servitude in New Orleans. They kidnap her and legally fight to keep her. How dare you enslave a white German girl and claim her to be Black? Case is bitterly fought all the way to the Louisiana Supreme Court. Wins her freedom but not that of her children.

J.S. HOLLIDAY, *THE WORLD RUSHED IN: THE CALIFORNIA GOLD RUSH EXPERIENCE* (NEW YORK: SIMON AND SHUSTER, 1981). A masterful, comprehensive piece of work by one on the great scholars of the Gold Rush era. Chock full of stories, letters, maps and first-person accounts. A must have for those who want to dig into this era of history.

MERRILL J. MATTES, *THE GREAT PLATTE RIVER ROAD* (LINCOLN, NE: NEBRASKA HISTORICAL SOCIETY, 1969). An amazing compendium of information about the great corridor of western expansion that follows the Platte River through Nebraska and beyond. Mattes spent two decades of his life haunting libraries, following old trails and consulting over 700 original journals. You'll find lots of first-hand accounts of the prairies as the early trackers and traders and explorers found them. Hard to imagine the size of the buffalo herds that once called the Platte River home.

Keith Heyer Meldahl, *Hard Road West* (Chicago: University of Chicago Press, 2007). A tour de force of the 2,000-mile overland journey on the California Trail. Meldahl expertly weaves the personal stories of travelers with their marvel at the landscape, but then as a geology professor takes us along the trail with compelling lectures and insights to help us understand the ancient geology that shaped the west and continues to shape the west. Want to understand the land you're passing through, get this book. Photos and maps galore. The California Mother Lode area (where Route 49 runs today), for example, was once the edge of the continent looking out over the Pacific, but then the Farallon Plate came sliding in creating a slow-motion collision that fractured the edge. As Meldahl says, "The collision zone will become the Mother Lode, for quartz veins follow fractures and gold follows quartz." So there you have it, gold seekers.

Acknowledgements

My family

First, I'd like to extend my appreciation to my family who stuck with me over the years. Jane, my wife, was kind enough to listen, read, comment, discuss drafts, and engage in discussions about plotting, and most importantly, insist the characters were interesting and believable. An avid reader, she pushed novels at me that helped to open my eyes, my mind, my heart. I'll be forever grateful. She always been with me in spirit and love and has suffered through the ups and downs of someone learning to write fiction the hard way. By that I mean foolishly, pig headedly, blindly, thinking writing was a solitary act. How wrong I was.

I got help and inspiration from my two wonderful daughters, both very creative personalities. Kat, my eldest, is one of the most creative people I know. She's an excellent writer and fantastic story teller, as well as a compassionate and supportive person.

Julia, my youngest, is one of the most adventurous people I know, and it's her spirit and love of new places that infuse my storyline and shape my characters in ways she is not aware of. Julia was my partner on many inspiring outdoor adventures.

My writing groups

I'd like to thank my original writing group, Antoinette May, Lucy Sanna, and Kevin Arnold, who were looking for a fourth at the time they launched the Gold Rush Writers Conference (GRWC) in Mokelumne Hill, CA. It was fortuitous. I had just started writing a novel about the Gold Rush, went to the conference and was invited to audition for the group. That's where things started for me. It's a wonderful thing to be critiqued on the spot by accomplished writers reading and listening to your work. One thing became clear: writing is rewriting, sometimes over and over, and suggestions large and small can stay with you and become important in ways you did not immediately grasp.

Writing groups grow, morph, and reassemble as lives and situations change. I'd like to thank the next assemblage I was part of, which included not only Lucy and Antoinette, but also Sally Henry, Genevieve Beltran, and Bob Yeager, exposing me to a wider variety of wonderful styles and creative approaches. They took my work to task and helped me improve the structure, flow, characterization, and dialogue. I'm forever grateful for their generous contributions, camaraderie and support. Lucy in particular has been a constant source of support through the years.

Rob Swigart, a very accomplished writer, who has an affinity for drawing writers together, created the next group, whose weekly meetings ranged from three to eight writers reading and marking up manuscripts. For me, it was a time of absorbing new approaches to narration and digging for emotional depth. I want to particularly acknowledge Lucy and Antoinette who continued on as strong participants. Mercedes Cerna brought loving insight through her stories and characters, and her psychological intuition. Sally Henry brought music to her long, languid prose. Sandy Towle shared his wisdom and insight with the group and brought life and fire with his action scenarios. Evaleen Jones contributed her dramatic insights and joyful outlook. Rob raised the level of intellectual mystery and brought the fusion of science fiction and archaeology to new heights.

For the past five years, I've been blessed to work with a smaller group of talented writers, including Rob, Sherrill Jaffe, and Jane Swigart. We don't pass out manuscripts these days, we simply read aloud a new or revised chapter and ask for feedback. This cuts out the compulsion to line edit while trying to absorb the story. Sherrill brings a level of clarity and concision to her highly personal and polished stories which have a way of weaving forward and backward for emphasis. Jane's evocative winding tale of family life on a Wyoming ranch just after WWII brings a forgotten past of horses, cattle, and breathtaking mountain ranges into the light of today.

WONDERFUL EDITORS

I would also like to acknowledge the talents of Victoria Merkle who through both developmental and copyediting helped make this novel more coherent. She insisted on bringing the community of the wagon train to life, making sure secondary characters brought out the emotional depth of the primary characters, and made sure they didn't just pop up but had an arc. I'd also like to thank Kate Winter, editor and story consultant, for her many talents in helping make *Rush* a more readable novel.

OLD FRIENDS

I'd like to give a shout out to two old friends, John Fennel from high school days, and Mike Hobbs from college days, for their enduring interest and encouragement over the years. They kept my spirit up.

About the Author

BRENT G. BARKER is a science writer, editor, and amateur historian living in California. This is his first novel.

Brent spent countless hours researching the historical under-pinnings of *Rush to Freedom* and its sequel. He was interviewed on the History Channel for an episode entitled "Ten Things You Don't Know About the Californian Gold Rush."

In addition to historical fiction, Brent has penned a science fiction/fantasy novel about a new energy system for bio-climate clearing, and has published over 100 articles in the fields of energy and energy research.

Brent has enjoyed a career combining his passions for research and analysis with the joys of imagination and writing. He has worked for several research institutions in complementary capacities as analyst, economist, futurist, writer, editor, and professional communications manager.

www.ingramcontent.com/pod-product-compliance
Lightning Source LLC
Chambersburg PA
CBHW070308040726
47501CB00018B/390